A
Long
Shadow

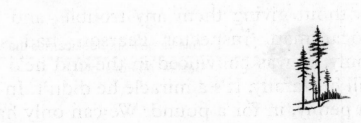

**Also by Charles Todd
in Large Print:**

A Test of Wills
A Cold Treachery

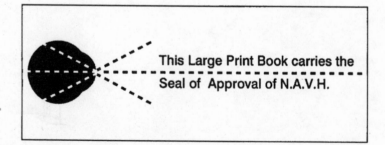

This Large Print Book carries the
Seal of Approval of N.A.V.H.

A Long Shadow

CHARLES TODD

Thorndike Press • Waterville, Maine

Published in 2006 by arrangement with William Morrow, an imprint of HarperCollins Publishers.

Thorndike Press® Large Print Reviewers' Choice.

The tree indicium is a trademark of Thorndike Press.

The text of this Large Print edition is unabridged.
Other aspects of the book may vary from the original edition.

Set in 16 pt. Plantin.

Printed in the United States on permanent paper.

Library of Congress Cataloging-in-Publication Data

Todd, Charles.
    A long shadow / by Charles Todd.
      p. cm.
    "An Inspector Ian Rutledge mystery."
    "Thorndike Press Large print reviewers' choice."
    ISBN 0-7862-8537-0 (lg. print : hc : alk. paper)
      1. Rutledge, Ian (Fictitious character) — Fiction.
  2. Police — Great Britain — Fiction.   3. Large type books.
I. Title.
PS3570.O37L66 2005b
  813'.54—dc22
                                      2006000826

For Ruth and Jon Jordan

Extraordinary mystery fans,
extraordinary people.

This one's for you.

As the Founder/CEO of NAVH, the only national health agency solely devoted to those who, although not totally blind, have an eye disease which could lead to serious visual impairment, I am pleased to recognize Thorndike Press* as one of the leading publishers in the large print field.

Founded in 1954 in San Francisco to prepare large print textbooks for partially seeing children, NAVH became the pioneer and standard setting agency in the preparation of large type.

Today, those publishers who meet our standards carry the prestigious "Seal of Approval" indicating high quality large print. We are delighted that Thorndike Press is one of the publishers whose titles meet these standards. We are also pleased to recognize the significant contribution Thorndike Press is making in this important and growing field.

Lorraine H. Marchi, L.H.D.
Founder/CEO
NAVH

* Thorndike Press encompasses the following imprints: Thorndike, Wheeler, Walker and Large Print Press.

I

Dudlington, 1919

Constable Hensley walked quietly through Frith's Wood, looking left and right for some sign that others had been here before him. But the wet, matted leaves showed him nothing, and the cold sun, slanting through bare trees, was more primitive than comforting. It would be dark soon enough. The light never lasted this time of year, unlike the gloriously bright evenings of summer, when it seemed to linger as if unaware of dusk creeping toward it.

And one particular summer evening . . .

He came to the end of the wood and turned to retrace his steps to the small clearing where he'd left his bicycle.

Halfway there, he could have sworn he heard someone moving behind him, a soft step barely audible. But his ears were attuned to the lightest sound.

Wheeling about, he scanned the trees around him, but there was no one to be seen through the tangle of undergrowth and trunks. *No one living . . .*

Imagination, he told himself. Nerves, a small voice in his head countered, and he shivered in spite of himself.

After a moment he went hurrying on, not looking back again until he'd retrieved his bicycle and mounted it. Then he scanned Frith's Wood a final time, wondering how a place so small could appear to be so gloomy and somehow threatening, even in winter.

The Saxons, so it was said, had beheaded men here once, long ago. Taking no prisoners, unwilling to be hindered by captives, they'd come only for booty, and nothing else. Not slaves, not land or farms, just gold or silver or whatever else could be bartered at home. A greedy people, he thought, giving his bicycle a little push to start it forward. Greedy and bloody, by all accounts. But nearly fifteen hundred years later, the name of the wood hadn't changed. And no one cared to set foot there after dark.

He was glad to be out of it.

Yet he could still feel someone watching him, someone on the edge of the wood, someone without substance or reality. Dead men, most likely. Or their ghosts.

One ghost.

He didn't look again until he'd reached the main road. Out of the fields, away from the wood, he felt safer. Now he could pedal back the way he'd come, make the turning at The Oaks, and sweep down into Dudlington. Anyone seeing him would think he'd been at the pub, or sent for from Letherington. He'd been clever, covering his tracks. It made sense to plan ahead and not go rushing about. If he had to go there.

Of course a really clever man, he told himself, would stay away altogether.

The way behind him was still empty.

2

London, New Year's Eve, 1919

Frances was saying as their cab dropped them in Marlborough Square, "Maryanne will be so happy to see you. It will do her good!"

"Yes, well, don't expect me to play bridge," Rutledge answered her, half in jest, half in earnest. He had worked for the past hour to convince her that he was in good spirits. She had always been too quick to read shadows on his face. "You haven't forgot the last time, have you? At the Moores'? I was partnered by that awful woman, what was her name? Stillwell? She dissected every hand ad nauseam. Put me off bridge for the better part of a year!"

In the square behind them he heard the gate creak as someone came out of the garden and walked briskly away. The policeman in him noted the fact as the footfalls stopped, another gate down the street opened and shut, and there was silence once more.

"You don't bring in the new year playing bridge, silly! Besides, you ought to know Maryanne doesn't care for card games," his sister informed him, walking up the steps to the door of Number 18. She glanced up at him, thinking how handsome he was in his evening dress, his dark hair and dark eyes a sharp contrast with the gleaming white shirtfront. Too bad she couldn't persuade him to wear it more often . . . he'd become reclusive since the war. Was Jean's shadow still hanging over him? She didn't want to believe it was France. Or shell shock lingering . . . He refused to talk about himself, however hard she probed. And Dr. Fleming was as tight-lipped as her brother. "Maryanne said something about an entertainment — probably a new soprano . . ." Mischief danced in her eyes as she waited for his reaction.

"Good God! That was at the Porters', just before the war. She was Austrian and made the chandeliers quake."

"Now that's an outright lie, Ian! She was Italian!" Frances's laughter was silvery in the cold air, her breath a frosty puff. "She insisted you take her in to supper and then spent the rest of the evening trying to persuade you to visit her in Venice!" She lifted the knocker and then added, "Jean was in a terrible huff. She was left with that colonel, the one with —"

The door opened, and Maryanne Browning enveloped Frances in a warm embrace. "Hallo, my dear, I'm so glad you could come! And Ian — you've been a stranger far too long. Give your coats to Iris, here, and join us in the drawing room!"

She swept them with her, made introductions, settled them with drinks, and sat down herself to resume a conversation about Canada, which their arrival had interrupted.

Rutledge knew most of the people there. Simon, Maryanne's brother, vicar at a country church in Sussex. Dr. Philip Gavin, a Harley Street surgeon, and his wife, who had been friends with Maryanne for years. A younger couple, the man missing an arm from the war, were the Talbots, George and Sally. Rutledge had met them at one of his sister's parties. Across from him sat a naval officer, Commander Farnum, and his wife, Becky, who lived just down the road from Frances. The last guest was a dark-haired woman of infinite poise, whose eyes were turned on him as if she could read his thoughts. The intensity of her gaze made him uncomfortable. Her name was Mrs. Channing, and she was new to him.

Maryanne's husband, Peter Browning, had died in the influenza epidemic of 1918. A civil servant in the war ministry, he had appeared well at seven in the morning as he kissed his wife good-bye. At three o'clock, he dropped dead at his desk, overwhelmed by swift, massive infection. A silver frame on the mantel held his photograph: a thin-faced man with kind eyes. Rutledge had liked him immensely.

The evening passed with pleasant conversation, and Rutledge found himself relaxing, the voice in his head silent for now, the company interesting enough to draw his attention away from his own thoughts. They had been bleak enough, lines from the letters lying on his desk still echoing in his mind. He was glad to escape them, if only for an hour or so.

Mrs. Channing, sitting across the room from him, made no effort to charm her fellow guests, and yet she seemed to become the heart of the party, her voice never dominating but often bringing laughter with a well-timed comment.

He found himself wondering what her age was — closer to his than Frances's, he decided. Or perhaps younger than both of them, it was hard to tell, because she seldom spoke of herself or of her late husband, as if too private a person to thrust her experiences on strangers. There were no benchmarks . . .

An attractive woman, most certainly, with what Frances would call good cheekbones, her dark hair touched with gold under the soft spill of light from the sconce behind her, her extraordinary poise intriguing, her laugh pleasing.

Rutledge's deep dread of watching his soul stripped naked in public — the abiding fear of someone discovering the guilt he carried with him, the horrors of shell shock, the voice of a dead man he heard as clearly as his own — faded. The policeman in him was lulled as well, and any misgivings he'd felt when introduced to her had vanished.

All the same, he was glad to be seated down the table from Mrs. Channing, his hostess on his right and Mrs. Talbot on his left.

Dinner was nearly up to prewar standards. It began with a consommé à la Celestine, followed by a roast loin of mutton with a port wine sauce, baked onions, potatoes à la duchesse, and spinach, with anchovy éclairs or an apricot gâteau to end.

14

Maryanne explained that her cook was a French refugee and a miracle worker, a widow who had charmed the butcher and the greengrocer into slavish devotion.

It was not until they were settled comfortably again in the drawing room, the tea tray removed, and the hands of the great clock in the hall touching 11:25, that Maryanne surprised everyone with the news that Meredith Channing could raise spirits.

"And I've asked her to conduct a séance to bring in the new year — and the new decade," she ended, excitement bringing a flush to her face. "She's to discover if all of us will be wealthy and happy in ten years' time."

The women laughed, Maryanne's enthusiasm contagious. But Farnum and Talbot exchanged glances and stirred uneasily, while Simon started to say something to his sister, and then held his tongue. And in the back of his mind, his dread lurching into life again, Rutledge heard Hamish exclaim, *"No — !"*

The single word seemed to fill Rutledge's head and ricochet around the room. But no one turned to stare at him, no one else could hear it. He stepped back, shaken.

15

As if she'd sensed the apprehension among her male guests, Maryanne went on, "It's all in fun, of course. We did this on Boxing Day at the Montgomerys'. John raised Napoleon, of all people. The most outrageous things happened, and we laughed ourselves silly —"

The other men made polite if half-hearted noises and moved reluctantly toward the table, leaving Rutledge stranded in the middle of the room.

Mrs. Channing came to her hostess's aid, her eyes on Rutledge's face. "I fear we have one too many, Maryanne. I did say numbers mattered. Perhaps Mr. Rutledge would be content to watch, rather than take part?"

Maryanne glanced at him in disappointment. "Oh, Ian, that would be no fun for you at all. I'll sit out, instead. I don't want to give away any of the tricks and I might, at the table."

"No, Mrs. Channing is right," he said, his heart thudding in his chest at the thought of confronting his own ghosts in public. It was all he could do to keep a rising panic out of his face. "I'm a policeman, after all, hardly susceptible to raising the dead, although Dr. Gavin and I might find the talent useful."

He had managed to make light of it, and they laughed, although he felt anything but amusement. *There were too many dead on his soul — it would do no good to raise them, if he couldn't offer them life again.* And if by accident Mrs. Channing summoned Hamish —

It was unthinkable.

Panic was closer, the spacious room shrinking uncomfortably, until all he could see was Mrs. Channing's face, as if in a halo of brightness, her expression compassionate.

Beside him Frances placed a steadying hand on his arm. She was saying, "Ian's had a very trying day. He's likely to raise the most boring spirits you can imagine. But I've always admired Sir Francis Drake, and I wouldn't mind asking him if he actually did bowl while waiting for the Armada!" It was the first name that had come to her. She moved to the table and smiled up at Dr. Gavin. "Unless you'd prefer someone in the field of science?"

"No, no, Drake will please me too," he answered, holding her chair.

With a last apologetic glance at Rutledge, Maryanne gathered her other guests. Then she added over her shoulder, "If you change your mind, Ian —"

17

"I'll tell you," he answered, relief bottled up in fear of what was still to come. It was a farce, this séance craze, but it was sweeping England just now, and more than a few men of good repute had been gullible enough to comment publicly on the possibilities of reaching behind the veil of death.

They dimmed the lamps with shawls, made up their table, and Mrs. Channing took her place at the head of it, asking everyone to clear their minds and join hands in silence.

The ticking of the hall clock could be heard clearly, and to one side of the group, Rutledge found himself gripping the arm of his chair. He uncurled his fingers and in defense tried to crowd his mind rather than empty it.

After a moment her voice filled the room, low, melodious, almost mesmerizing. In spite of his fierce resistance, he could feel the peace that seemed to wrap him, and the security that it seemed to offer. But there was an undercurrent of tension in the voice as well, as if, he thought, she was aware of him sitting to one side, observing, outside the ring. Disapproving.

The skeleton at the feast. He shivered at the thought.

"We are gathered here, at the turn of the

year, to call upon those wandering in the night, those with knowledge, those willing to come to our table and reach across the darkness that divides the living from the dead, and take my hand in friendship . . ."

He tried to think of an excuse to leave altogether, one that wouldn't embarrass Frances, or cause comment. Instead he was pinned to the chair, his mind frozen, unable to function, and he could hear Hamish calling this the Devil's business, urging him over and over again to go. *Now!*

But there was no escape.

Mrs. Farnum exclaimed anxiously, "I felt the table lift!"

"And so you should, as the spirits surround us, taking their places beside us, looking over our shoulders. There's a little dog among them, a King Charles spaniel —"

Sally Talbot drew in a breath. "It couldn't be Jelly, could it? Oh, please, tell me it's mine."

Her husband said quickly, "Now, Sally —"

"Oh, but it would be lovely to know he's well and happy on the other side — you don't know how I've missed him."

Mrs. Channing's voice rose above hers. "— and behind him is the King himself. We welcome you, Your Majesty, and we ask you to tell us the name of the little dog

19

that has so graciously announced your presence —"

The door behind them opened, and Iris whispered into the dimness, "Inspector? The Yard is on the telephone."

He got to his feet with such haste he nearly knocked over the small table beside him. Gritting his teeth, he made his way as quietly as he could out of the room

It was Sergeant Gibson on the line, wishing to confirm a detail in a case that had just been closed during the afternoon. Taking the upright chair in the stuffy little closet where the phone had been installed, Rutledge gave the sergeant the date he was after, and put up the receiver. For a moment he sat there, so relieved to be out of range of that compelling voice in the drawing room that he could feel himself taking the first deep breath.

It was as if he'd been granted a reprieve — and he intended to make the most of it.

Stepping out into the hall, he turned to the housemaid and asked, "Will you summon a cab for Miss Rutledge, when she's ready to leave? And tell her that I've been sent for by the Yard?"

"Indeed, sir, I will."

Iris helped him into his coat, and he left, relishing the winter air, cold and cleansing, feeling as if he'd been miraculously spared an unspeakable ordeal. Overhead the stars seemed extraordinarily bright above the streetlamps, and the noisy evening traffic on the road beyond the square had dwindled into an occasional motorcar passing.

Bless Gibson! he thought, and Hamish echoed the sentiment, a dark growl that seemed to rumble in the space behind him.

On the steps, he turned to look up at the drawing room windows. Frances would give him hell for deserting her, but the Farnums would be glad to see her safely home. There would be no need of the cab.

He tried to tell himself that Mrs. Channing possessed no strange or exotic powers. But he could still feel her eyes on him, and recall the way she had made certain he was not in the circle. He went cold at the thought that she had somehow known his secrets, that she had seen into his mind and found the shadow of Hamish. And refused to make that knowledge public.

But that was ridiculous.

Walking home would clear his head of such nonsense.

Flipping up his coat collar against the night air, he went down the pair of stone steps to the pavement.

His shoe struck something that rolled, making a tinkling noise across the walk and into the gutter.

His first reaction was surprise. It was a sound he knew.

Moving to the curb, he bent down to search intently.

Light spilling from the windows behind him picked out a metal cylinder a little distance away. He retrieved it and recognized it even as his fingers reached for it. A .303 cartridge casing from a Maxim machine gun, its shape cool and familiar in his hand. There had been thousands of them on the battlefield, as common as the mud underfoot.

But what was it doing here, on a quiet street in London?

He stood up quickly, his gaze sweeping the fenced garden in the square, then scanning the street in both directions.

There was no one in sight.

Hamish said, "It's no' here by chance."

A sense of unease made Rutledge turn to look up at the housefront. He could see the drawing room, the curtains drawn, only a faint glow behind them from lamps shaded by shawls. The quiet, spellbinding voice of the woman conducting the séance seemed to echo in his head.

The cartridge casing hadn't been there when he arrived at the Brownings'. It would have been dislodged then, as he or Frances mounted the steps. And no one else had arrived after they were admitted to the house.

Turning the casing in his gloved fingers, he could tell that it wasn't smooth. The lines were irregular, as if something had been cut into the metal surface. Loops and swirls, not initials.

Soldiers by the hundreds had done this sort of thing in the long watches of the night or the deadly boredom of waiting for the next attack. In hospitals and convalescent homes, passing the time as they healed, men had been encouraged to make such things as boutonnieres, vases, cigarette lighters, and even canes out of empty cases of every size. Even copper driving bands from artillery shells and lumps of shrapnel had been turned into souvenirs. An exercise in patience.

In the light from the nearest streetlamp, Rutledge tried to judge what the design was. It was useless, he couldn't see anything but the glinting surface where the metal had been polished.

Not that the design mattered. He was more interested in how such a thing came to be here, in front of the house where he'd been a guest.

Hamish was saying, "It doesna' signify. It fell from the pocket of someone passing by."

"I heard it fall. So would whoever was carrying it. Why not look for it?"

"It wasna' of great value."

"Who could have known that I'd leave early . . ." It could as well have been Dr. Gavin, he told himself. Called to a deathbed. Or Mrs. Channing, séance over, leaving Maryanne's guests to talk behind her back about the evening's entertainment.

Neither of them had been in the trenches.

"I wouldna' make sae much of it."

"It's out of place."

"Aye. That doesna' make it sinister."

Yet in a way it did. It was as if in an unexpected fashion the war had reached out to touch him again.

"Yon woman has unsettled you."

Perhaps that was all it was. But the casing in his fingers was real. He hadn't imagined it. *Where had it come from?*

Hamish was silent, offering no answers.

After a moment, Rutledge slipped the casing into his pocket. Then he turned away from the Browning house and began the long walk home.

Rather than settling his mind, the walk had given Rutledge too much time to dwell on other matters. The letters on his desk. One of them from his godfather, David Trevor. And that reminder of Scotland, of what had happened there months before, had stirred Hamish into grumbling activity.

David had written in haste . . .

Young Ian has measles and I've left him to Morag and Fiona. I'm banished to my club in Edinburgh, and thoroughly miserable at missing his first Christmas with us. Much as we've looked forward to your visit, the doctor advises no excitement. I've promised the lad a pony if he stays in his darkened room without fuss. That's all I'm allowed to do. You might search out a saddle, and have it shipped north for Boxing Day, if you like . . .

It had been a visit intended to mend fences.

Rutledge had last seen his godfather in September, just before Fiona and the child had come to stay with Trevor. He'd found it hard to face the young woman Hamish might have married, the woman whose name he'd spoken as he died. Harder still to greet her as a friend, when Rutledge knew himself to be responsible for Hamish MacLeod's death. It was a shadow that lay heavily between them, even though he'd never confessed the truth to her.

Yet he'd told himself, as he had left behind the snowy fells of Westmorland barely three weeks ago, that perhaps the time had come to return to Scotland to face the tangle he'd made of his life and find a little peace. It had seemed possible then. A fair-haired woman in a wheelchair had made anything seem possible. Even confessing his nightmares to those who cared about him. Clearing his conscience so that he could feel something again besides despair.

But his good intentions had been swept away by another letter that had arrived hard on the heels of the first. It had stripped away hope. Now he was glad not to travel north. Glad to be spared what would have been a futile errand. He'd convinced himself that love would make a difference. He'd have ended up making a great fool of himself instead.

But such protests rang hollow in his ears, and all the while Hamish called him a coward.

Even after Rutledge had retired, the soft

Scots voice kept them awake, taunting and accusing by turns, raking up memories, driving him like a spur.

He lay there, counting the hours as the clock struck each in turn, his thoughts shifting from one unsettling image to the next. A narrow track of road twisting through the heavy drifts. A child's face. A woman standing in the cold snow light of an open door, her hands on either side of the frame and the room behind her dark as the grave. The sound of a weapon being fired, so loud in the confines of the kitchen that it seemed to ring in his head even now.

Shifting again, he tried to find a more comfortable position — a drowsiness that might lead to sleep.

Instead he remembered Mrs. Channing's expression as she greeted him only hours earlier — that fleeting pity, a sense of understanding in her face, as if she'd read his thoughts.

Or had known him somewhere before.

France?

He stared at the barely visible walls of his bedroom.

Why had she reminded him so strongly of the war and the trenches? Or was it only that bloody shell casing he'd never taken out of his coat pocket?

By the time he'd drifted into uneasy sleep, he began to dream of the war, as he so often did, jerking awake as the whistle blew to send his men over the top — he could smell the trenches, he could smell the cordite, the sour sweat of fear that bathed his men even in the cold air. He could feel the rough wood of the ladder, the terror of anticipation, waiting for the soft *thunk!* as a bullet hit its target and someone at his elbow went down. He could hear the yelling, the deafening sound of steady machine-gun fire as they walked out into the barren hell of No Man's Land, moving quickly toward the unseen enemy —

And then he was truly awake, the noise and smells and drenching anguish of counting his dead fading into the darkness of the familiar room.

His gaze fell on the second letter lying on his desk by the windows, the paper faintly white in the ambient light. He knew the words by heart, now.

"Don't come back to Westmorland —"

The desolation he'd felt when he first opened the single sheet swept him again.

How do you learn to live again, he thought, where there is no hope, no warmth, no laughter?

He lay there, trying not to think or dream or remember, until first light.

Meredith Channing was also awake until dawn, her mind unwilling or unable to settle into peace.

So that was Ian Rutledge, she thought, that tall, handsome, haunted man.

Not at all what she'd expected. Maryanne Browning had said, discussing her guests each in turn, "He was in France for four years, and doesn't often attend parties now. Such a shame! He and Peter were better at charades than any of us, and it was always great fun. But his sister has promised to persuade him."

"Was he severely wounded?" she had asked.

"He was in hospital for several months, I'm not sure why. Frances never said. But nothing serious, apparently. He's returned to the Yard. Of course the woman he was to marry broke off their engagement as soon as he came home, and wed someone else. That must have been a crushing blow. We were all so heartbroken for him, but I never liked Jean, myself. I thought he could do much better!" And then the first of her guests had arrived, and Mrs.

Browning had gone to greet them.

Mrs. Channing saw no reason to tell her hostess that she'd seen Ian Rutledge before, once, but only at a distance. She hadn't needed to include him in that silly business at the table to know his secrets.

War, she thought, is such devastation for the living — for the dead — and for those who are not sure any longer where they fit in.

But that brought her little comfort. There were some things that one couldn't explain away.

Grace Letteridge lay awake as well. The woman who cleaned for her on Tuesdays had told her she had seen Constable Hensley coming out of Frith's Wood.

"I was taking the Christmas bells to the attic for the rector. The window was all dusty, and I took out my rag to clean away the worst of it. And I could just see him, hurrying away on that bicycle of his, for all the world like a hunted man. I can't for the life of me understand why he goes there. You'd think he'd stay away, like everyone else." She shook her head, considering the constable's foolishness. "But then he's not one of us, is he?" she added. "Else he'd *know*."

A guilty conscience, Grace thought now. It makes people do foolish things. Betray themselves, even.

She turned on her side, not wanting to think about Hensley — or Emma.

Emma was dead, and yet she might as well be alive. What was it the Romans believed? That a spirit wandered if the body wasn't given decent burial? Emma's wandered. Grace was certain of it, and it gave her no peace.

Someone knew the secret of what had happened to Emma Mason. And Grace was convinced it was Hensley.

Why else had he failed to find Emma's murderer?

3

Rutledge stood on the cliffs above Beachy Head Light. Below him the gray waters of the Atlantic moved in angry swirls, clawing at the land. All around him the grass seemed to sway and dance, whispering in the echoes of the wind like disturbed voices.

He had come here after a difficult twenty-four hours forcing a would-be murderer to give himself up and release the hostages he had taken in a small cottage outside the village of Belton. The man, tired and unshaven, unrepentant and silent, offered no explanation for stabbing his wife. He went with the constables without giving them any trouble, and the local man, Inspector Pearson, had said only, "I was convinced in the end he'd kill all his family. It's a miracle he didn't. In for a penny, in for a pound. We can only hang him once."

"He had nowhere to go," Rutledge

pointed out. "And whatever anger was driving him, it had finally burned away." He could still see the eyes of the man's mother-in-law, staring at him in undisguised relief, something in her face that was old, as if twenty-four hours had aged her. Her daughter, trembling with exhaustion and pain, allowed the doctor to wrap her in a blanket and take her away in his carriage to his surgery. Blood had soaked through her dress, and her hands were clenched on the blanket's folds as if to hide the sight. Her mother had followed in a second carriage with an elderly aunt, a thin, pale woman who appeared to be in shock. Even the ex-soldier standing near the horses mirrored her numbness, his face turned away.

As soon as the affair had been dealt with and he was free to go back to London, Rutledge had driven instead toward the sea, leaving his motorcar and then walking down to the cliffs. Beyond lay France. It was said, during the war, that the big guns could be heard here along England's coast. But they were mercifully silent now. Had been for a year and two months.

Looking back over that year, he could recognize his own long struggle to survive. The strain, the tension, the constant badgering of Hamish in the back of his mind had taken their toll. Jean's defection . . . The still unsettled business with his godfather in Scotland. And now the letter from Westmorland.

Had he really fallen in love, there in the north? Or had he been beguiled by those easy domestic moments in the kitchen, when life had seemed so simple and comfortable? A lonely man could have mistaken such brief respites for feelings that weren't there — on either side.

He couldn't be sure anymore. Even though he'd gone over and over his own emotions.

Elizabeth Fraser's letter had ended:

It is better for me to live as I am, where I am, than to imagine I could fit into any other world. I have a history in London. It would do no good to pretend I haven't. And I don't want to reawaken the memories there. They would be too painful. Don't come back to Westmorland, Ian. I beg of you. I am safer alone . . .

He was too tired to try to work it out. As long as Hamish was there, in the shadows of his mind, he'd be mad to love anyone. It was reckless even to consider the possibility. He had nearly got Elizabeth killed, after all. He shuddered. What would he have done then? Mourned her as his lost love? From guilt?

He could hear Hamish's derisive laughter.

A small stone, dislodged by his shoe, ran down to the cliff's edge and tumbled over, out into space. He watched it spin out, then disappear into the sea far below.

It would be easy to step over the face of the cliff after that stone and end the struggle, end the uncertainty, silence the voice, crush out the ghostly faces of men he had led and failed. It was tempting. It was in some ways the answer he had postponed in the hope that somehow he would heal.

"It's no' so simple," Hamish said. "Leaping o'er the edge willna' change the past. And it canna' change what you are. Ye'll be dead and so will I. Ye'll ha' killed me twice. That too will be on your soul."

The voice was clearly Scots on the wind, coming from nowhere, and it was steel. After a moment, without answering, Rutledge turned back the way he'd come, to where the motorcar was waiting.

He had already turned the crank, heard

the engine ticking over, and was climbing in, when something on the driver's seat caught his eye.

It was another shell case. In fact, a pair of them, linked together in a short length of a machine gun's ammunition belt — collected and thrust there, because the casings were normally ejected from the weapon as it fired. He picked up the pair and stared at them. The same size and caliber of the one he'd found in London. And this time he was in no doubt — they'd been left where he alone would find them.

There was a pattern around the metal perimeter of one casing, and he turned it around to examine it in the pale light of the winter afternoon.

An odd pattern, a delicate staircase of poppies that curled around the brass surface, but where there should have been blooms, there were tiny skulls with hollow eyes staring up at him.

Death's heads.

Hamish said, "A warning."

The same thought had crossed his own mind. "But why on only one of them?" Rutledge asked, curious, still examining the workmanship.

"May be he thinks ye ken why, well enough." After a moment he added,

36

"There was a private soldier in one of the companies doon the line. I didna' know him well, ye ken, but his sergeant found one of his carvings with a death's head on it, and the next time o'er the top, the sergeant died of a bullet in his back."

Rutledge had never reexamined the single casing he'd found outside Maryanne Browning's house. He'd been far more interested in why it was on her doorstep than in what was cut into its surface. As far as he knew it was still in his dress coat pocket.

He looked around the headland, tasting the salt on his lips as the wind turned and blew off the sea. There was no one else out here. No one at all.

Yet the cartridge casings hadn't been in the seat when he left the motorcar to walk out to the cliff's edge. That was a certainty.

If anyone had followed him here from the village — where was he now? Lying flat somewhere in the scrubby grass or long since gone on his bicycle, making a silent retreat?

Turning slowly in a circle, Rutledge scanned the landscape once more, as far as he could see.

The emptiness around him seemed filled with something malevolent.

He couldn't shake off the sense of being watched. But there was not even a gull in the sky overheard.

There hadn't been anyone in the square in London either.

After a moment or two, Rutledge tossed the casings onto the passenger seat and put the car in gear. All the way to London, he reminded himself that while someone might have known he was going to the Brownings' party — Sergeant Gibson had tracked him down, after all — no one could have guessed that he would drive out to this god-forsaken headland late on a cold and windy January afternoon. He himself hadn't expected to come here. It had happened on the spur of the moment, a whim dictated by a need for silence and peace. Someone would have to be a mind reader . . .

He was nearly certain that there was no reason for anyone to follow him from the village where the hostages had been taken. It was far more likely that someone had tracked him from London.

But why?

4

Reaching his flat, Rutledge couldn't stop himself from looking down at the front steps. There was nothing there. He walked inside, went up to his rooms, and turned on the lamp before going in search of the other cartridge case, the one from New Year's Eve. It was still in the pocket of his dress coat, and he examined it in the lamp's bright glow.

Poppies. Rows of them gracefully circling the casing, the petals of each bloom very beautifully etched into the brass alloy. But between the leaves and stems he could just barely see something hiding in the greenery. Was that an eye peering out? Or had the engraver's hand slipped? Hard to say. He'd have thought nothing of it, if he hadn't seen the latest example. Now the deliberately vague socket took on a more sinister air.

"By the same hand," Hamish pointed out, and indeed the skill of workmanship proved that.

The question was, Rutledge thought uneasily, what would have happened if he hadn't left the Browning house early that last night of the old year? Would the casing have been retrieved until another opportunity presented itself? Or left to be swept up along with the leaves and debris in the gutter, a malicious impulse that hadn't been successful? What had he set in motion by finding it? Worse still, what did this harrying have to do with his years in the trenches?

He remembered Mrs. Channing, the only guest he hadn't met before that night. Could she have guessed that he wouldn't stay for the séance if he could find a polite reason for walking out on Maryanne's party? Then how had she managed to step outside and leave that casing where he would find it? While he was drinking his port with the other men?

He hadn't served with anyone named Channing.

He searched his memory for the faces he'd seen in Belton, people quickly gathering out of morbid curiosity to learn how a man's murderous rampage ended. She hadn't been there, he'd have recognized her. Who else, then? Who of half a hundred people might it have been? Someone at the back of the crowd, surely, half hidden, wanting to see without being seen.

"Or none of them," Hamish retorted.

As for Beachy Head, it was open, without much in the way of cover.

I'm too good a policeman to have missed him! he told himself. *If he followed me, I'd have seen him.*

It had taken nerve to step out in the open, reach the motorcar, toss in the casings, and vanish again. *I could have turned at any moment, and caught him.*

"You had ither things on your mind."

"I wasn't there that long!"

"Longer than ye ken."

Rutledge shook his head.

"He was in the trenches," Hamish went on. "Else, where did he come by *these?*"

Rutledge flinched, half expecting Hamish to lean forward to touch the cartridge casings. He scooped them up quickly and put them in the drawer of his desk, turning the key. "Why machine-gun cartridges?" he asked aloud, "or poppies?"

Hamish answered him. "That last night — before the firing squad. It was a machine gunner we were sent to take out. And in the spring, poppies bloom in Flanders. They're red, the color of blood."

A few days later, Rutledge was on his way to Hertford to give evidence at the trial of a man he'd apprehended some months be-

41

fore. He had stopped briefly for an early lunch at a pub in a village that lay some distance behind now, and he was trying to make up his time. With luck, he'd be in the county town in another half an hour, well before he was due to meet the KC.

The road had narrowed for a mile or more, shrinking now into a stretch that was barely wide enough for one vehicle, let alone two. To one side a winter-bare hedgerow ran up a slope and down again, giving him a feeling of being shut in between it and the flickering shadows cast by a copse on his right.

It was claustrophobic, reminding him of a magic-lantern show gone mad — light and dark, light and dark, the trees flitting by like irregular fence palings and without substance.

As he geared down for the bend ahead, Hamish said, "You'll have us both in the ditch —"

He never finished the warning.

A shot echoed, sending half a dozen crows flying up out of the trees, crying raucously in alarm just as the windscreen in front of Rutledge shattered, glass spraying like bright bits of water into his face. And he could feel the wind of the bullet passing his ear before thudding somewhere in the rear seat behind him.

Fighting to control the motorcar as it veered across the road and straight for the clumped roots and dried wildflowers at the foot of the hedgerow, Rutledge was swept by horror.

The shot had missed him — but it couldn't have missed Hamish, directly behind him.

The bonnet came perilously close to burying itself into the earth beneath the hedgerow before he had cut the motor and the vehicle rocked to a halt.

His face was wet with blood, but he was barely aware of it. What filled his mind was the silence in the seat behind him.

I dare not turn and look.

If he's badly hurt — what am I to do? I can't touch him — !

As the initial shock receded, he reminded himself that Hamish was already dead, buried in one of the muddy cemeteries in France.

The relief that swept him was followed by a cold, intense anger.

He was out of the motorcar, the door swinging wide behind him, racing toward a break in the hedgerow some twenty feet away.

The shot had come from a revolver, he was certain of it. He knew the range, and his ears had unconsciously registered the direction of the sound, even though he hadn't seen the muzzle flash. And the only thought in his mind now was putting hands on the man who had fired it.

"Ye canna' leave the motor here!" Hamish shouted behind him. "Yon bend —"

But Rutledge was scrambling up the stones, weeds, and packed earth at the foot of the hedgerow, ignoring the stubby twigs and branches that plucked at his clothes and scraped his hands. He found the thinning patch where one of the knot of trees had died out, pushed his way through it with a final effort, and plunged into the rolling pasture beyond.

He wasn't sure what he'd expected to see there. But except for a grazing horse at the far end, the pasture was empty.

His years in the trenches had taught him to pinpoint snipers in their lairs, and the skill came back to him with accustomed ease. He strode along the hedgerow, searching for crushed blades of grass, scuffed earth — any signs that pointed to where someone stretched out on the ground or crouched by the thick tangle of tree limbs and dead wildflower stalks, waiting to fire.

Underfoot the grass was a dull yellow and damp, quickly soaking into his leather shoes as he broke into a trot, following the line of the hedge. He knew the angle of fire. Less than fifty feet away from where he'd climbed the hedgerow, he found what he was looking for — a muddied patch and above it a single twig snapped in two. He squatted there on the ground, looking back toward the lane, and he could see there was a perfect field of fire from this spot toward where his motorcar had been passing as the windscreen shattered.

Not an accident, then. But what? He couldn't believe that boys had been trying out their father's war souvenir. The shot had barely missed his head. The question was, had it missed on purpose, or because the shooter wasn't skilled enough to hit his target?

Then as he straightened, he saw, shoved into a thicker part of the hedge not more than a foot away, three shell casings, in a length of belt.

His anger had drained out of him, and he turned quickly to scan the pasture again, suddenly aware of how vulnerable he was, if the man with the revolver took another shot. No one there. Nothing to prove anyone had been there.

It was as if it had all been a figment of his imagination. The horse was grazing peacefully, and the crows had settled again into the trees across the road. And yet there was the shattered windscreen, and here was evidence of someone lying in wait, taking aim — pulling the trigger. Not an accidental firing but a careful ambush.

And the shell casings left behind as a taunt.

I could have killed you. But I didn't. This time.

He spent nearly half an hour quartering the pasture for tracks, searching for any sign of how the shooter had come here, or left. At length, unsatisfied, he went back to lift the casings out of the hedge, and look at them more closely.

Behind him Hamish said, "Three."

Soldiers in the trenches were a superstitious lot. It was said German snipers waited for a man to light a cigarette, then pass the match to the men beside him. And as the third cigarette flared, the sniper had made his kill. Three.

Like the other casings, these were .303s, from a Maxim machine gun. It had been the most widely used weapon in the war, half of Europe copying its design for their armies. And the machine gun had been the most deadly weapon of the war, sweeping the stark, shell-pocked, wire-strung terrain called No Man's Land with a hail of bullets that could bring a man down and pass on in a matter of seconds to kill everyone beside him long before any of them reached the first line of enemy trenches. It had, Rutledge thought, caused more casualties than any other weapon. The gunner and his crew could hold off a hundred men, and there was no way to stop him.

Rutledge stood there studying the cartridge casings. Like the others he'd found before, these were clearly meant for him to examine.

Even in the gray afternoon light he could see the skull carefully set in the cup of a poppy blossom, nestled where the stamens should have been. The blossom was beautifully formed, the petals open and lovingly shaped, the death's head staring up at him with blackened eye sockets cut deep enough into the metal to give them a ghoulish realism.

Without thinking he touched his gloved finger to the dark sockets and then saw there was a smudge on the leather.

Rutledge could have sworn that it was blood. But whether his own, from the cuts on his face, or from something on the carving, he couldn't have said.

He found a man in Hertford who could

47

replace the shattered windscreen, but there was nothing to be done about his own face, except to ask the doctor recommended by the garage owner's wife to pluck the deeper bits of glass out of his skin.

"I'd report this to Inspector Smith," Dr. Eustace told him. "We can't have silly fools running about the countryside with loaded firearms! This sliver could have blinded you, if it'd struck your eye instead of your eyebrow!" He held up a splinter of glass, bloody on the tip.

"It was an accident," Rutledge answered him, trying to infuse conviction into his voice. His face was stinging like hell. He wasn't about to discuss the shell casings with anyone, let alone a provincial inspector who would begin to ask questions he couldn't answer himself. But all the while Hamish was telling him that the shot had been a near thing. For both of them.

"And ye must ask why he didna kill you, when you were in his sights."

"On a public road?" he retorted silently as Dr. Eustace went on with his digging. "I'd rather know why he followed me to Beachy Head just to leave a warning. Why not shoot me on the cliff and simply roll my body off the edge and into the sea? I was an excellent target, standing there

48

against the sky. It would have been the easiest way to be rid of me without a trace."

"Aye, but I canna' believe he wanted it to be sae easy." And after a moment, Hamish added, "He likes playing wi' you."

"He'd have had to be ahead of me," Rutledge responded grimly as the doctor probed for the last shard of glass and then handed him a mirror. "But how did he get clear so fast?"

"You'll have to put this powder on the wounds," Dr. Eustace was saying, reaching for a small packet on the table behind him, "else they're likely to fester. You won't look very pretty in the witness-box, in spite of my handiwork. But at least the worst of the damage is cleaned."

Rutledge stared at himself in the mirror. Tiny red wounds spotted his face, giving him the appearance of a man with measles.

"It doesn't matter," he answered the doctor. "The cuts will heal soon enough."

But he could remember the sound of shattering glass and the familiar whistle of the bullet rushing past his ear. Hamish was right: it had been damnably close! He had felt the wind of its passing. Either the shooter was a very good marksman, or he'd come closer than he'd intended.

It was rather like being stalked by

someone who didn't exist. But the bruised grass by the hedgerow told Rutledge it wasn't a shadow following him.

He remembered too the uneasiness he'd felt at Beachy Head. He'd felt it again in that pasture, a tall target there by the hedgerow, a target even a poor marksman couldn't have missed.

He didn't like being vulnerable.

He didn't like a nameless, faceless pursuer at his heels, invisible because he couldn't be identified.

"Aye, he could be anywhere," Hamish told him. "Even in yon courtroom, staring down at you from the gallery."

It was a thought Rutledge carried with him into the witness-box.

But if this stalking had been an attempt to change Rutledge's testimony, it had failed.

He saw the prisoner in the dock convicted and walked out of the courtroom with grim satisfaction, even as he scanned the faces around him: five or six women, twice as many men, three ex-soldiers still wearing their army-issue greatcoats, one of them on crutches, and a baker's boy in his white apron, his face speckled with flour.

There was no one among them he recognized.

But did one of them know him?

50

5

Constable Hensley was not a glutton for punishment, but he was not a man of self-discipline either. When the note came, he stared at it for a moment and then crumpled it in his fist.

There was no salutation or signature. Just the words *"I saw you there in the wood."*

He'd have sworn that he'd taken every precaution. Who had been out in the fields, or for God's sake, along the road that afternoon? Why had they been spying on him? What did they know? Did they have any idea how often he'd gone to the wood? That he was unable to stop himself from searching it over and over again, looking for any sign that the ground had been disturbed?

Where had he — or she — been, this watcher?

How many times had he been watched?

He remembered that strong sense of someone else in the wood. The sound of a footfall somewhere behind him. Now that

51

he considered the possibility, he was sure that he hadn't imagined it after all. Frith's Wood was always intimidating, with that ominous feeling of something there that was not natural. Not even human.

But this time it must have been a human agency. And he had been so locked in his own fancies, he'd mistaken it for ghosts. He swore.

"If I'd had my wits about me, I'd have had him!"

For the rest of the day he went about his duties with only half his mind on what he was doing or saying. All he could think about was what had taken someone else to the wood. Was it only to watch him? Or had this person been up to no good and interrupted by Hensley's unexpected arrival?

Then why send the message? Why give himself — or herself — away by admitting to being there?

That was a question that muddied his thinking to the point that he began to imagine nuances in conversations or sly glances caught out of the corner of his eye. Even the rector, for God's sake, had pounced on him, wanting to know if he'd heard any news of twins born to a second cousin in Letherington, where he'd claimed to be. He'd wormed out of that one by saying he'd forgotten to ask. Then he'd wondered who had put the old fool up to it.

For more than a week, Hensley resisted the gnawing mystery of the note shoved under his front door. In the middle of Friday night, he'd come wide awake, remembering that he'd left the wood first. What had happened there after he was gone?

Which appeared to him to explain the note — it had been sent to frighten him into staying away. *I saw you . . .*

A man with a guilty conscience would take that as a warning and not risk going back.

Hensley, on the other hand, was eaten up by worry. What had the writer found? And why, after all this time, had he been poking around there? What was worse, once he'd got the wood to himself, what had he done?

The constable took every precaution. He rode out of Dudlington, traveled three miles north of the village, and left his bicycle well hidden behind the stone wall that ran along the road, shutting in the stock that in good weather grazed in Long Meadow. Then he walked another mile before turning back to the wood.

He'd been a right fool the last time to leave his bicycle where anyone on the main road could have glimpsed it. He was sure that that was what had betrayed him.

The wood lay on the north side of Dudlington, beyond Church Lane, in a fold of the land where the Dower Fields ended. This time Hensley kept the trees between himself and the village, using it as a shield. Approaching it now, he wondered what it was about this one dark place in a landscape of open fields that seemed so evil.

Why hadn't the Harkness family, who'd owned this land for generations, cut it down centuries ago and set the land to the plow? He'd have had it done in a fortnight, in their shoes.

He'd been hardened in London; he'd seen death in many forms. He was a policeman, for God's sake, hardly likely to be moved by nonsense about old bones. And this was just a stand of trees, the undergrowth just a tangle of briars and vines and fallen boughs.

But then countrymen were a superstitious lot. It was their stories that had set Frith's Wood apart from the beginning. Passed down from father to son, over centuries. *"Don't go in there — the dead walk there. Restless, because they'd had no time to pray before they were cut down. Shun the wood, if you know what's best for you."*

In spite of his bravado, the closer he got to the trees, the harder his heart seemed to pound. Still, the note had been real enough. Ghosts didn't put pen to paper.

But what if he was walking into a clever trap?

He stopped at the edge of the wood.

In for a penny, in for a pound, he told himself, bracingly. And he stepped into the shelter of the trees, grateful for the respite from the cold wind that had pursued him across the bare fields.

He walked slowly, studying the ground as he always did, poking at briars and the dried stalks of shrubs to see if the matted tangle beneath had been disturbed.

He was only some thirty feet into the trees when the hairs on the back of his neck seemed to stand stiffly against his collar.

Stupid sod! he scolded himself. *There's nothing here but your own wild fancy. The sooner you do what you came here to do, the sooner you'll be away again.*

He walked on, catching himself on the verge of whistling. He was nearly through the wood now, and he'd found nothing suspicious — no one had been digging here or shifting rotted logs — nothing that could explain what had brought someone else here.

Had this been a wild-goose chase? Then what had that damned note been about?

There was a sound behind him, and he whirled, not sure what he was going to see.

Nothing.

Another five yards. Ten . . . Fifteen.

God, he'd looked back four times already! It was the wind, rubbing dry branches together. Flicking the dry heads of dead wildflowers against one another. He should have thought about the wind.

Another twenty feet. Not much farther, now. But he'd have to go back the way he'd come, back through the whole damned wood.

This time the sound was nearer. He turned quickly, listening for the shuffle of feet in the dead, wet leaves.

Instead he heard a bird in flight, feathers riffling through the air.

Something struck him in the back, a blow like a fist, piercing his body, tearing into him like a hot poker jammed hard into his ribs. His breath went out in a frosty gust and had trouble sucking in again.

Even as he realized what it was — even as he knew for a certainty that it was a human agency and not a phantom that was intent on destroying him — he could feel his knees buckle and a terrifying sense of doom sweeping through him.

He'd been shot by an arrow. His fingers could just reach it, the shaft round and smooth. And he'd be found here, in Frith's Wood, with all the village knowing he couldn't stay away.

He mustn't die here!

But he knew he was going to. It was his punishment.

He sank to his knees and then fell forward, blacking out before the pain touched him.

6

Inspector Smith, dining with Rutledge at The Three Feathers in Hertford after the court had adjourned, said, "While you were waiting for the verdict, we caught your assassin." His voice was smug, as if he enjoyed showing this man from London that provincial policemen were every bit as good as those at the Yard.

Rutledge, looking up quickly from cutting his cheese, said, "Who is it? Anyone I know?"

"Hardly an acquaintance — a local boy. He came forward of his own accord, I'd no more than got my question out before he was telling me he'd done it."

"Did he tell you why?"

"Just that he thought it was a good day to go out shooting."

"Why did you question him in the first place? Has he shot at people before this?" And where, Rutledge added to himself, had a boy found those cartridge casings, to hang them so conveniently at the scene?

Smith, not liking the direction

Rutledge's questions were taking, frowned. "We went to him because he's generally roaming about the countryside in fair weather. He's particularly fond of the Massingham grounds — they include the pasture you described. Mrs. Massingham is kind to Tommy, and he sometimes takes advantage of that to go hunting."

"With a revolver?" Rutledge asked, eyebrows raised.

Smith shook his head. "Slingshot. He couldn't tell me where he'd got the weapon. Not very bright, is Tommy Crowell. Never a troublemaker before this, you understand, but there's a first time for everything, and he's old enough to get into mischief you'd forgive a younger boy. My guess is, he found the weapon somewhere — in a house or barn — and simply helped himself to it, without a thought of asking permission. He's always had a weak grasp of private ownership. Not thievery so much as just 'borrowing for a bit,' as he'd put it."

"There can't be that many loaded revolvers lying about in Hertford!" Rutledge persisted. "Does your Mrs. Massingham have one?"

Smith was on the defensive now. "Her husband was a cavalry officer. He kept his weapons locked away. To my knowledge, she hasn't touched them since he was killed in the Boer War. She said as much."

"Which means," Hamish responded in the back of Rutledge's mind, "that she wouldna' know if one was missing."

And Smith, in awe of the Massinghams, most certainly wouldn't have questioned her word.

"I'd like to see this Tommy Crowell for myself." Rutledge folded his serviette and nodded to the woman who had served their meal. She turned to bring him the reckoning. "Where does he live? Or have you taken him into custody?"

"Now?" Smith asked, gulping the last of his tea. "There's no need —"

"But there is," Rutledge told him, already scanning the charges. "I'm leaving for London early tomorrow. No, don't bother, I've taken care of it."

Smith almost ran at his heels on their way to the door. "The boy can't pay for the damages to your windscreen," he said, huffing with the effort. "I've already spoken with his mother. There's no money —"

"I'm not interested in money," Rutledge answered as he reached his motorcar in the yard behind The Three Feathers. "Where is he now? Have you charged him?"

"I wasn't intending — I was going to

hold him overnight to put the fear of God into him, in the hope he'd show me where he tossed that revolver. But his mother begged me —"

"Then take me to where they live!"

Smith cranked the motorcar for Rutledge and then climbed into the passenger's seat. "A mile from the Massingham estate, there's a lane that turns down to the east. Follow that another mile or so, and I'll tell you where to stop."

Rutledge drove out of Hertford, back the way he'd come, and found the lane with no difficulty. It was rutted, and the motorcar bounced unpleasantly for some distance before the row of cottages came into view, smoke from their chimneys wreathing the roofs in the cold night air.

Smith indicated the third house on the left, and Rutledge came to a halt. "Let me speak to the mother. You'll terrify her, Scotland Yard invading her sitting room."

He got out and knocked at the door. A worn woman of perhaps forty answered, and then stared in alarm over his shoulder at the tall man behind Smith, dressed in a London-made coat and hat. "You're not going back on your word?" she began accusingly. "I promised I'd keep him to home."

"There's nothing to worry you, Mrs. Crowell. I'd just like to speak with Tommy for a bit. This is Mr. Rutledge. It was his car that was damaged, but he hasn't come about repayment."

They stepped under the low lintel and into a small, cluttered room. It was apparent that Mrs. Crowell took in laundry. There were baskets of neatly folded clothes and bed linens set in every available space, and the odors of hot irons and strong soap permeated the house.

Apprehensive, her eyes on Rutledge, she called Tommy from his room under the eaves. He came clattering down the steps, a big, rawboned child of about sixteen, his face changing from open curiosity to frowning uncertainty as he saw his mother's guests.

Stopping short, he looked from his mother to Inspector Smith, his expression shifting with every thought that passed through his head.

Before Smith could speak, Rutledge stepped forward and held out his hand. "Hallo, Tommy. My name's Rutledge. I'm from London. You're quite a good shot, you know. Hit the windscreen dead center!"

Tommy Crowell burst into shy smiles at

the praise as he shook Rutledge's hand. "Thank you, sir. I've had a good deal of practice."

"Ever thought about the Army?" Men hardly more than a year or so older than Tommy had served under him, as Hamish was reminding him.

Mrs. Crowell began to protest, but Rutledge sent her a warning glance.

"The Army?" Tommy hesitated. "Ma wouldn't allow it."

"What do you prefer, when you're hunting? Shotgun? Revolver?"

A wariness crossed the boy's face. Rutledge noted it, and added, "I'm a better shot with a revolver myself." And as the words came out of his mouth, he saw himself standing over the body of Corporal Hamish MacLeod, and drawing his service revolver to deliver the coup de grâce, looking down into the pain-ridden eyes begging for release. The cottage room suddenly seemed small, airless, sending an instant of panic through him.

"Fiona . . ." Rutledge could hear the name as clearly as he had that night on the Somme, as the improvised firing squad stood there watching.

A hand touched his arm, and Rutledge nearly leapt out of his skin.

It was Smith, and for an instant he couldn't remember where he was, or why.

"I'm sorry?" he said, swallowing hard. He'd missed the boy's answer.

Tommy said, repeating his answer nervously, "I've never fired a real weapon." He turned to his mother, and she nodded. "I'm better at this." He reached on a shelf by the mantel and took down a slingshot. It was strong and well made. And someone had carved and stained it to look like horn. He held it out with a mixture of pride and anxiety. "You won't take it, will you? Ma won't let me use it anymore, but I like to look at it."

Rutledge examined it, turning it in his hands, asking, "And you shot out my windscreen with this?"

Tommy nodded. "I must have done. It's what I was shooting."

But Rutledge had dug a bullet out of the frame of his motorcar where it had buried itself after narrowly missing him. "Then where's the revolver?"

He shook his head in confusion. "I don't know, sir, truly I don't. I must have lost it!"

Smith started to speak, but Rutledge was there before him. "Did you lose it in the pasture? Where the horse was grazing? Were you lying by the hedgerow, and dropped it after firing at my car? Where the road bends," Rutledge added, as Tommy seemed unable to grasp the exact location.

"That's the Upper Pasture, where the road bends." The boy's face changed. "Inspector Smith didn't say it was the Upper Pasture — I — he said where the horses are, and that's the home paddock. I don't go to the Upper Pasture, not anymore." The vehemence in his voice was unmistakable, and his face had paled, making him look even younger than his years.

"Why? Because of what you'd done there?"

"No, sir, no — I don't like the dead soldier there. I'm afraid of him."

Rutledge had quartered every foot of that ground, and there had been no dead soldier. Nor even the makings of a grave.

But it was clear that Tommy had seen someone there. Or something.

In spite of Rutledge's efforts, he got no other information from the Crowell boy. Whatever had caused his terror had emptied his mind of details, and he shook his head over and over again, saying, "I don't — I don't know."

In the end, Rutledge handed back the

slingshot and said, "That's a nice piece of workmanship, and I think your mother ought to allow you to have it again." With Smith at his heels, blustering, Rutledge went out to the motorcar and cranked it himself. The night had turned cold, with frost, surely, by morning. Pulling on his gloves, he got behind the wheel.

Smith was still protesting.

Rutledge said, "I don't believe he ever touched a revolver. Whatever you ask him, he agrees with. 'Where is the revolver?' 'I don't know where it is, sir.' That's the literal truth — he doesn't. Because he never had it. You've asked him a direct question and he gives you the best answer he knows how. But whatever — whoever — was in that Upper Pasture must have done the firing."

"A dead soldier? That I knew nothing about? You didn't buy that cock-and-bull tale, did you?"

But then, Hamish was saying, Smith knew nothing about the .303 casings.

"Not even a suicide?"

Smith answered, "Look, if the boy is lying about the revolver, he's lying about the dead man as well. It's a matter of self-preservation. He doesn't remember what he did with the weapon, and so he gives you a corpse instead. You're a policeman, and corpses are what you deal with. Even Tommy Crowell understands that."

"He doesn't lie. Simple people seldom do. He told you he didn't know where the revolver is, and he doesn't. If he saw a dead man in that pasture, he described him in terms he could understand."

He recalled Tommy's exact description. *"He was dead, buried. I saw him and I didn't like it. And I ran."*

"Buried, as in a churchyard?"

"No, not in a churchyard. There were no flowers, and no tombstone. Still, he was lying there, buried."

"I can hardly scour Hertfordshire for a dead soldier! It's a waste of my time and the time of my men."

"No. Whoever was in that pasture couldn't have been a local man."

"You can't be sure of that."

Rutledge glanced at him, saw the angry face etched by the motorcar's headlamps, and answered him carefully. "It's your patch. You know it best. If you find out anything, you know where to reach me in London."

"If it's not a local man," Smith said, pursuing the issue doggedly, "it was no accidental shooting, was it? He knew where he was aiming." When Rutledge said nothing, he fell silent, thinking it through. Where the rutted lane met the main road and the motorcar's tires fought for a grip in the icy mud as Rutledge turned, Smith went on. "You have an enemy out there, then. I'd not care to be in your shoes." He turned his head to look behind Rutledge, as if searching out Hamish. "I'll thank you to take your troubles out of Hertfordshire as soon as you can. We don't need them."

7

Bowles was pacing his office by the time Rutledge had received his summons and knocked at the door.

"Where the hell have you been?" the Chief Superintendent demanded angrily. "I sent for you a good half hour ago! And what's happened to your face?"

"I've just got in from Hertford, sir —"

"I don't give a dance in hell where you've come from. You're leaving for Northamptonshire straightaway. There's trouble in a place called Dudlington in the north of the county. A constable has been shot with a bow and arrow, for God's sake!"

"A bow —" Rutledge began, surprised, but Bowles cut him off.

"He'll live, no thanks to the bastard who did it, leaving him in the weather to die of his wound. It was intentional, this shooting, we're certain of that. And I want whoever it is brought to justice now. Do you understand me? Hensley's one of my men, or was, when I was an inspector in

Westminster. He went north over my objections, and look where it's landed him."

Bowles's face was red and blotched with fury. He shoved a file of papers at Rutledge.

"Well, don't stand there, man! I want you to interview Hensley tonight, if those fool doctors will let you, and get to the bottom of this business. They've got him in hospital in Northampton, and the local man says he's just out of surgery."

It was useless to plead fatigue or other pressing business. Bowles was not a man who cared about anything but getting his own way. And blustering anger was a well-tested method of keeping his subordinates from arguing with him.

Rutledge took the file and left.

Down the passage he ran into Sergeant Gibson in conversation with the man sweeping the floor.

Gibson turned away to speak to Rutledge and said dourly, "If you want the truth of the matter, Hensley left under a cloud. I never did know the ins and outs of it. A personal matter. He managed to keep it from Old Bowels' ears, I'm told. The Chief Superintendent thought he was the perfect copper. Threw him up to us any number of times."

Rutledge said dryly, "Then there'll be no end of suspects for this attempt at murder."

Gibson caught himself before he grinned. Instead he retorted, "How the mighty are sometimes brought low." And with that he was off down the passage, leaving Rutledge standing there.

Dudlington was a tiny village of stone-built houses topped with gray slate roofs and a single, slender-towered church, huddled together in the midst of open fields, as if for warmth or comfort. The rich brown of plowed acres and the yellow green of winter pasture lay like a blanket around them, but the houses turned their backs to the land, as if ignoring it, and the barns were a low afterthought, tucked here and there, as if no one had known what to do with them. It lay north of the county town, but Rutledge's first call was in Northampton.

He found his way to the hospital there, only to be turned away because Hensley was still recovering from his surgery.

Rutledge spent what was left of the night in a hotel recommended by an orderly and returned early in the morning.

Over the objections of Matron, he

stepped into the ward to see if Hensley was awake.

The constable was in the men's surgical ward, halfway down the row and on the left, watching through half-closed lids as a nursing sister bathed his neighbor in the next bed. There were some six or seven other patients in the long room, two of them snoring heavily, and the others lying quietly, as if in too much pain to move.

Hensley looked up as Rutledge stopped by his bed. "You a doctor, then?" he asked hoarsely. "I was told they were giving me something for the pain."

He was pale, his barrel chest swathed in bandages, his thinning dark hair combed and parted, as if he'd already been tidied by the plump sister who now turned to Rutledge.

"It's not visiting hours for another forty minutes," she told him crisply. "I'll have to ask you to leave!"

"I'm here on police business, Sister," Rutledge said, bringing a chair from another bedside to place it next to Hensley's.

She tried to stare him down and failed. "You won't tire my patient, then. Or I must ask Matron to throw you out."

"No, I won't tire him." Rutledge sat down, dropping his hat on the foot of the bed. "How are you feeling?" he asked Hensley. It was a rhetorical question, asked as a courtesy.

"Bloody awful," Hensley complained in a strained voice. The roughly handsome features were drawn, giving them a sharper edge. He made an effort to collect himself. "I'm told the doctors here saved my life. I can't say. I don't remember much about what happened. Who are you? Not a local man . . ."

"The name's Rutledge. I've come from London to look into this business."

"Was it Old Bowels who sent you?" Hensley asked, showing more interest. "He always did look after his own." Not waiting for Rutledge to answer, he shifted uncomfortably. "It's these damned bandages — they stick and pull at the stitches, and there's no help for it. Bad enough what they did to remove the point of the arrow. Aches like the very devil! Between that and the catgut, I've not had a minute's peace since I came out of the ether and found myself in this bed." He shot a black look in the direction of the sister, but she ignored him.

"You say you remember very little of what's happened. Do you remember where you were when the arrow struck you?"

Even as Rutledge spoke, his mind conjured up an image of the windscreen shattering, and he pushed it back into the shadows.

Hensley looked away. "I'm told they found me at the southern edge of Frith's Wood. I can't say if that's true or not. If it was, I didn't get there under my own power."

"Would this wood normally be a part of your regular rounds? Close enough, for example, for you to see or hear something that attracted your attention? Even if now you can't remember going that far?"

Hensley answered him with more intensity than the question merited. "The last thing I remember was riding my bicycle along the road to Letherington, well to the east of the wood! How could I see or hear anything from there? I draw a blank on the rest of it. They tell me I came to my senses as they were lifting the stretcher into Mr. Staley's wagon. If I did, I couldn't tell you what was said to me."

"Do you have any idea who might have shot you? Would someone practice archery in the wood, or hunt rabbits there?"

"Not in Frith's Wood, they wouldn't. People avoid it." He stirred again, trying to find a little comfort. "At any rate, the trees are too close for true archery or much of anything else."

"Is there anyone in Dudlington who bears you a grudge?"

Something flitted across Hensley's face, a shadow of guilt, Rutledge thought.

"I don't have any notion what happened, much less why," he answered just as a patient three beds away began to cough heavily. The sister hurried to his side, and Hensley watched her prop the man higher on his pillows. "No one goes to that wood. Not if they've got any sense. Least of all me. I can't think why anyone might drag me there. Unless it was to hide what he'd done."

"He's no' a light man to be hauled about," Hamish said, stirring, his voice no more than a thread in Rutledge's mind. "No' in the middle of the day, when people are about."

"What's wrong with this wood?" Rutledge asked. "Why do people avoid it?"

"It's haunted by the dead. So it's said."

"What dead?"

Hensley shut his eyes, as if keeping them open was an effort. "It's not a police matter. Saxon dead, a long time ago. The story is there was a massacre, raiders herding everyone from the village into the

75

wood and slaughtering them. You haven't been there, you don't know what it's like. Strange. That's all I can say."

"Who found you?" Rutledge asked.

"I don't know. I asked Dr. Middleton that, and he said I wasn't to talk." He shifted again. "They did tell me I lay there bleeding for more than two hours. I was that cold, they thought I was already dead. That was afterward, on the journey down to Northampton. I can recall a little of that."

"Anyone on your patch who uses a bow?"

He moved his hand slightly, indicating he didn't know. "Sister," he called as the nurse eased the coughing patient and started down the ward with her basin of bathwater. "Is it time yet?"

"I'll tell you when it's time," she said. "Mr. Rutledge, I believe you've asked enough questions."

Hensley turned his head restlessly. "Bloody woman," he said under his breath. "I'm the one here in the bed, not her. How does she know how I feel?"

"How often do you go to Letherington? Could someone have expected to find you on the road there at a particular time of day?"

"I go to Letherington when I need to meet with Inspector Cain. Or report to him. There's no pattern to it." He hesitated. "I thought I heard crows above the fields, making a bloody racket. I stopped my bicycle and stood there, looking around. That's the last I remember."

Distracting Rutledge, Hamish reminded him, "Ye ken, the crows flew up fra' the trees by the road at the sound of yon shot. No' at the sound of the motorcar."

That's true, Rutledge agreed silently. They weren't disturbed until the revolver was fired. Whoever it was had lain quietly in wait for some time. Long enough for them to settle. He brought his mind back from Hertfordshire to Constable Hensley's attacker. What agitated them in this case? Not an arrow being loosed.

The man in the bed was saying, "At a guess, I never got to Letherington. But you'll have to ask Inspector Cain about that. I remember setting out, I remember the crows." He shook his head, as if bewildered. "It wearies me, this business of not knowing."

"If you can bring back any more details, ask Matron to call Chief Inspector Kelmore or one of his people here in Northampton, and he'll get word to me."

Rutledge retrieved his hat. "Do you have a station in Dudlington?"

Hensley's voice was weaker, and he closed his eyes against the dim lamplight. "We don't run to station houses. I use my parlor as my office. You'll find whatever you need there. Make yourself at home. I won't be back for a bit, if these bloody butchers have their say."

Rutledge stood for moment beside the bed, looking down at the wounded man. He appeared to be in no hurry to find his attacker. And that in itself was odd. No anger, no fierce need to help speed the inquiry along.

But then Hensley's eyelids opened, and he said, as if realizing his own mistake, "I'll worry about it when I'm better. I can't now. You can see that. Tell Inspector Kelmore I'm not fit enough for questions yet."

Matron was coming with a little tray of medicines and a cup of water. Hensley saw her, and his face cleared. "Thank God!"

Matron nodded to Rutledge as she reached the bed. "You promised me only five minutes."

"Yes, I was just going. Tell me, do you know what became of the arrow that was taken from Hensley's back?"

"You must ask the surgical sister about that."

But the surgical sister, when Rutledge had run her to earth, said, "They'd removed the shaft before he was brought here. You must ask Dr. Middleton what became of it. As for the tip, it was an ordinary metal one. Chief Inspector Kelmore took it, but I doubt it did him much good. We had rather butchered it, extracting it from the rib. Constable Hensley was very lucky. His injury might have been far worse. If the arrow had got past the ribs, he'd be a dead man."

Rutledge went in search of Chief Inspector Kelmore and found him in his office, a stuffy little room reeking of pipe smoke. Kelmore was a graying man in his late forties, with yellowed teeth and ears too large for his head.

The Chief Inspector shook hands with Rutledge and said, "I was just leaving. The wife's ill, and I'm taking the rest of the day off. They've sent you here about Hensley, have they? Lucky he wasn't killed, according to the surgeon." He began to dig through the contents of his desk drawer, then reached instead for a box sitting on the floor. "Here's what's left of the arrow. I expect that's what you came for." He passed the broken shaft with its mangled metal tip to Rutledge. "Nothing unusual about it, except where it was found, in a constable's back."

Rutledge studied the wooden shaft, then the tip. "I should think it would have depended on the distance the arrow flew as to how deep it might have gone."

"Yes, that was my view as well. Hence the luck I spoke of. I daresay whoever loosed this arrow is afraid to come forward and admit to his carelessness." He held out his hand for the tip.

"And that's what you put it down to? Carelessness?" Rutledge asked, returning it.

"What else should I read into it? As you'll see for yourself, Dudlington is hardly a hotbed of murderers. I can't think why someone would have wished Hensley ill. Seems to be a decent enough chap, had no complaints against him. Nor has Inspector Cain, who oversees Dudlington, along with two other hamlets, Fairfield and Letherington. Letherington, to the north of Dudlington, is the largest of the three. Fairfield is a little more to the east." He pointed to a county map on the wall.

"I'll call on Cain tomorrow. Was there

any indication in that wood — what's it called? Frith's Wood — how Hensley had been carried or dragged there?"

"I don't think they looked. Does he claim he wasn't in the wood when he was shot? That's odd."

"He says he remembers riding his bicycle on the main road, and the next thing he knew he was on his way to hospital. He doesn't know how he got to the wood. Or when he was shot."

"They do say that sudden and severe injury can shock the mind, and events just before it happened are lost. His memory might return as he heals. I'm not sure why the Yard was brought into this business before we'd had a chance to look into it ourselves. But there you are. No offense intended."

"None taken. I expect London was concerned because Hensley came from there. And it was possible that someone he'd helped convict had a long memory."

"That's always possible, of course. Yes, I can see where it might have caused concern." Kelmore stored the arrow away again and rose to his feet. "I'll speak to Hensley myself tomorrow. I must go. The doctor is coming to my wife, again, and I must be there. If there's anything you need, let me know. If you can't find me, leave your message with Sergeant Thompson. He'll see that I get it."

He was ushering Rutledge out of the tiny office and into the drab corridor. "How are you getting to Dudlington? It's isolated, you know. No bus service."

"I have my own motorcar."

"What luck! You can drive me home. It's on your way out of town."

8

It was nearly dusk when Rutledge came to the turning for Dudlington, and if he hadn't been on the lookout for it, he'd have missed it.

An inn, standing alone on a rise, was all that could be seen in a wide landscape of fields running from his left down the slope of the land toward a little stream only visible because of the straggling line of trees that followed it. In the distance he could just see a low line of roofs that indicated barns.

He passed the inn as he turned, and made a note of it. Then he was in the village some hundred yards beyond.

Holly Street was narrow, with houses on either side set directly on the road. Farther on, Whitby Lane turned off to his left, and when he followed that, he saw that Church Street, coming in on his right, led to the churchyard, with the slender steeple of the church rising over the roofs surrounding it.

No one was about, except a dog trotting down the lane toward his dinner. And there was no sign to indicate where Constable Hensley lived. Rutledge turned the motorcar near the churchyard and went back the way he'd come, toward the inn.

The Oaks stood on higher ground than the village, a large inn for its location, with a pedimented front door that spoke of better days.

He opened the door and found himself in a spacious lobby that had once been the entry to the house. A handsome stair climbed to a landing and turned out of sight.

There was a bell on a table by the door, and he rang it.

After a moment a woman came out of the back, tidying her hair, as if she had just taken off an apron.

"Good afternoon, sir, are you stopping for dinner? We don't serve for another two hours."

"I'm looking for a room."

She was skeptical. "I don't know that we have one available. I'll just ask Mr. Keating."

She left him there in the hall, and soon a balding man of about forty-five came out to speak to him.

"You're looking for a room, is that it, sir? For the night?"

The inn appeared to be empty, except

for the man and the woman.

"For several days. Inspector Rutledge, from London." He was curt, tired of delay.

"Ah. You're looking for Constable Hensley's house, I take it. Second on the right, Whitby Lane. Not hard to find — follow the main road into the village and you can't miss it."

"I've no intention of staying the night at Hensley's house. I'm looking for a room here."

Keating was silent for a moment. Then he said, "We've got a room or two. I keep them for travelers. This is a rather isolated part of the world, as you must have noticed, and we're accustomed to people late on the road, looking to stop the night. But I'm afraid we're booked up, just now."

The words were firm, brooking no argument. But where were the motorcars or carriages by the door to support Keating's claim?

Rutledge was about to point that out when he recalled what an elderly sergeant had told him years before: "I remember the day when a policeman under the roof frightened away custom. I'd be offered poor service and a cramped little room at the back, beneath the eaves, in the hope I'd go away sooner."

He didn't think Keating was prepared to offer him even that. The innkeeper stood there, inflexibility in every line, although the pleasant expression on his face stayed securely in place. Short of calling the man a liar, there was nothing more to be said.

Rutledge turned on his heel and left.

He found Hensley's small house squeezed between a bakery and a green-grocer's. The door was unlocked, and he let himself in, feeling the chill from no fire over the last several days. The cold seemed to hang in the air, and the darkness in the tiny entry compounded it.

Retrieving his torch from the motorcar, he walked back inside searching for a lamp. The bloom of light dispelled the sense of emptiness, but it wasn't until he'd got a fire going well in the parlor that served as an office that he took off his hat and coat and set them aside.

The parlor was a square room, windows only on the front, and it was occupied by a desk sitting across from the hearth, papers scattered over its surface. Rutledge paused to look at them and found nothing of interest. Notices from Northampton, a letter inquiring for a Mr. Sandridge in the town, and a logbook that had been kept meticulously until the day Hensley was shot.

In the back was a sitting room, a kitchen with an empty larder, and upstairs a bedroom with sheets on the bed that were damp and wrinkled.

"It willna' do," Hamish told Rutledge. "It's no' a place to be comfortable."

Rutledge took out his pocket watch and looked at it. The Oaks would be serving dinner in another forty-five minutes, and the thought of a warm meal and a bed pulled at him. Keating be damned.

There was a voice from the hall at the foot of the stairs. "Halloooo!"

He went to the top of the steps and called down, "Inspector Rutledge here. What do you need?"

"Well, I told myself it couldn't be Bart Hensley." She moved into the light of his torch as he pointed it down the stairs in her direction. "What are you doing here? He hasn't died, has he?"

"No." He could see her now, a tall, slender woman wearing a knitted hat and a gray coat with a black collar. "I've come to investigate what happened to him."

"Well, then, dinner is at eight. I usually prepare it for him. An arrangement we've had since he came here in 1915. You might as well take your meals at my house too. There's not much choice in Dudlington.

I'm your neighbor next but one, on the other side of the bakery. Oh, and you can leave your motorcar just by the side of the house. It's out of the way there." And she was gone, shutting the door firmly behind her.

Rutledge presented himself at the house on the far side of the bakery, exactly at eight. The door was opened, and the woman invited him in. "My name is Barbara Melford. I'm a widow, I live alone, and I am paid for each meal. The dining room is this way."

Her house was larger than the constable's, with good furnishings and a fire in the dining room where the table was set for one.

"You don't take your meals with Hensley?" Rutledge asked.

"I am paid to feed him, not to keep him company. As I've already said, I'm a widow. And I'm not looking to marry again, least of all, not to Constable Hensley."

He could see her clearly now in the lamplight: a woman in her thirties, smartly dressed — for his benefit and not Constable Hensley's — trying to cover her apprehensiveness with a chilly demeanor.

Hamish, taking a dislike to her, said, "Why did she invite you to dine?"

For information?

Rutledge took the chair at the head of the table and pulled his serviette out of a china ring with blue violets painted in a garish pattern.

"We've had no news about Constable Hensley's condition. Was his surgery successful?" Barbara Melford asked as she brought in the soup, creamed carrots with leeks.

"Apparently, although he was in a good deal of pain when I spoke to him," Rutledge answered, choosing his words with care. "Nothing was said about when he might be released."

"I can't imagine being driven that far with an arrow in my back!" she commented, returning to the kitchen while he sat in the dining room in lonely splendor. It was a pretty room with drapes of a floral brocade and an English carpet under a table that could seat eight. Rutledge found himself wondering if Mrs. Melford had ever entertained here, when her husband was alive.

He was tired, and it was a very tense meal, as his hostess brought each course in silence and disappeared again, but he could feel her eyes on him through the crack in the door leading to the kitchen.

Once he tried to question her about what had happened, but she answered brusquely, "I can't see the wood from my windows, thank God! You must ask someone who can."

There was a flan for dessert, better than many he'd had, but he didn't linger over his tea. As soon as the first cup was empty, he folded his serviette, and calling to Barbara Melford to thank her, he started for the door to the hall.

She came to speak to him then, following him as far as the front door to point out a silver tray on the small table at the foot of the stairs. "You'll find your account waiting here every morning. I serve breakfast at eight sharp."

"I'll be here."

He stepped out into the cold night air, feeling it strongly after the heat of the dining room. Hensley's house was still chilly, the fire struggling to do more than heat the parlor. He searched for the linen cupboard and at length discovered clean sheets and pillow slips as well as two or three fairly new blankets.

Making up the bed, he considered his conversation with Hensley, wrapped in pain still, but alert enough to answer questions guardedly. Why, since he'd been found in that wood, would the constable refuse to admit he'd gone there? For one thing, moving a large man with an arrow in his back would have been difficult, and dragging him would leave marks. That would have to be looked into, tomorrow.

"And where is the bicycle he was riding?" Hamish asked.

"I'll find out tomorrow. There should be someone who can tell me. The doctor, for one."

"At a guess, yon widow doesna' care o'ermuch for the constable. She must be desperate for money, to put up wi' him."

"Or she finds him willing to talk more than he should about village business. A man can be flattered into boasting."

It was late when Rutledge finally got to bed. The house seemed unfamiliar and unwelcoming. And he hadn't found a key for the door. Yet Hensley had used the parlor for his office.

"Which means," Hamish answered the thought, "that there are no secrets to be found here."

Rutledge was up well before eight, dressed, and already searching through the meager files in a box in the parlor. It appeared that Dudlington had no experience with crime as such. The constable had registered every complaint with meticulous care. A lost dog found and returned to its owner. A quarrel over a ram's stud rights. Pilferage at the greengrocer's, traced to a small boy with a taste for fruit. A domestic matter, where a wife had accused her husband of spending more time than was necessary — in her view — repairing a chimney flue at Mrs. Melford's house.

He set the files back into their box and stood, looking around the room. There were no photographs here — or in the bedroom for that matter. And little else of a personal nature. But he'd discovered a letter in a desk drawer, a commendation from the then Chief Inspector Bowles for Hensley's services in apprehending a murderer in the City.

Then why was Hensley in this outpost of empire, serving his time chasing after lost dogs and calming irate wives?

It was apparent that Hensley had kept the commendation letter with some pride . . .

Rutledge glanced at the wall clock and saw that he had three minutes to get himself to the Melford house for breakfast.

The meal was as well cooked as last

night's dinner, the eggs done exactly to his taste, but he asked as the toast was brought in, "I tried to find a room at The Oaks. They all but turned me away. Do you know why?"

"Mr. Keating has always been a private sort. He doesn't seem to care for guests staying there, not beyond one night. Mostly he serves meals to travelers, and of course the pub is popular with the men here in Dudlington."

"Who was the woman? An employee? Or his wife?"

She laughed, breaking the stern set of her face. "She may wish she was his wife, but Frank Keating is a misogynist. The woman is Hillary Timmons. She lives near the church. There aren't many opportunities for employment here."

"Which is why you feed Constable Hensley for a price."

"Indeed. I'll just fetch the warm milk for your tea."

Dr. Middleton was an elderly man, his face lined but cheerful. He welcomed Rutledge with a nod and took him back to his surgery, which was no more than a room at the rear of his house.

"Did you see Hensley? How is he faring?"

"Well enough. In pain."

"I should think he was. That arrow was in deep."

"How long have you been the doctor here?"

"Seven years last month. I retired from practice and came here to die. But I haven't had time to get around to that." He sat behind the table in a corner that served as his desk and gestured to a chair on the other side. "My wife died, and I lost interest in living. She was born in Dudlington and is buried in the churchyard. I feel closer to her here."

"Where had you lived before?"

"Naseby. It's not a very challenging practice, but I'm the only doctor within twenty miles. Babies and burns and bumps, that's mostly the extent of my duties."

"Dudlington is a quiet village. There was hardly a soul on the streets when I came in last night."

"That's an illusion. For one thing, there's the weather this time of year. The wind howling across those wide fields doesn't invite you to stop on the street and pass the time of day for a quarter of an hour. And the men are mostly stockmen, up at dawn and home after the livestock has been fed and bedded for the night.

Many of them come home for their midday meal, which means their wives spend a good part of their day in their kitchens. They do their marketing in the morning, and this time of year, it's dark by the time the children come in from Letherington, where they're schooled now. We had a schoolmaster before the war, but he enlisted as soon as Belgium was invaded. He hasn't been replaced."

"Did Constable Hensley have trouble keeping the peace? His records are sparse, and it's hard to judge if that's because the village is relatively quiet, or because he was behind in his paperwork."

"We've had our share of trouble, I won't deny that. On the other hand, people often don't bother to lock their doors. Human beings are human beings, which translates into the fact that you don't know what they're capable of until they're pressed. Still, we seldom have the sort of crimes you'd find in London. Arson, rape, breaking and entering, theft of property. It doesn't mean that we're better than Londoners, just that we know one another very well, and the man who steals my horse can hardly ride it down Church Street without half the householders recognizing it on the spot." He smiled. "But don't be fooled.

Everyone knows your business as soon as you set foot in Dudlington. Gossip is our pastime, and you'll do no better than Constable Hensley at ferreting it out." The smile broadened. "I shan't be surprised to see a flurry of patients this afternoon with all manner of minor complaints. Every one of them expecting me to tell them what I made of this man from London."

"Then what does gossip have to say about someone nearly killing Hensley with a bow and arrow?"

The smile vanished. "Ah. That I haven't been privy to. I wish I were."

"Then tell me about Frith's Wood, where Hensley was found."

"It's not a place people frequent." Middleton sighed. "Case in point. No one has ever cut firewood there, they don't wander there on a quiet summer's evening, and they will walk out of their way to avoid having to pass in its shadow. My late wife told me she'd never played there as a child, which tells you something. There's an old legend about a massacre there in the dim dark past, and such superstitions tend to strengthen with time. Consequently, the wood is avoided."

"Have you ever walked in the wood yourself?"

"Never. Except for once about three years ago. Not because I'm superstitious, but it would upset people. Why meddle?"

"Tell me about finding Hensley."

"It was nearly teatime. I was sitting in my chair in the parlor, napping, when Ted Baylor came to my door. His dog heard something in the direction of the wood and began barking. Baylor wasn't inclined to investigate, but after he'd seen to his livestock, he decided he'd better discover what the dog was on about, before it got dark. When Baylor let him out of the yard, the dog made straight for the wood, disappeared into it, and barked again. Baylor was of two minds about what to do, but he finally went in after the dog, and there was Hensley lying on the ground, cold as a fish. Ted thought he was dead, and told me as much. But it was shock and the cold air, and I managed to bring him around once I got him here and warmed again."

"And you broke the shaft of the arrow?"

"There wasn't any choice in the matter. I couldn't very well leave it sticking out of his back. I asked Ted Baylor and Bob Johnson to hold it steady while I cut it with my knife. I thought the tip would come out without doing more harm, but it was lodged in the rib, and I don't have the facilities here for major surgery."

"Do you still have the shaft?"

Middleton pointed to a basket on a table under the window. "It's in there. Nothing distinctive about it. Just an arrow fletched with blue and yellow feathers."

Rutledge crossed the room to examine it. Middleton was right, the shaft was wood, and not homemade. The feathers appeared to be a little bedraggled, but from age or use, he couldn't say. Their condition hadn't stopped the arrow from flying true — or again, perhaps it had, if the bowman had intended a killing shot.

Hamish said, "It's no' possible to tell if this was a woman or a man. Or how far fra' the target the archer was standing. If yon arrow was aimed at the constable's back, the archer didna' care whether his victim lived or died."

"He lay there in the wood for several hours. No one came back to finish what the arrow had begun," Rutledge agreed, unaware that he was answering Hamish aloud.

Middleton said, "It's not likely someone went to the wood to practice at the butts. For one thing the trees are too close together, and for another, it's just not done. Not here in Dudlington, at any rate. Unless you were an outsider and didn't know the history of the place. Of course, if you were looking to murder Hensley, I suppose that was a prime place to do it. Superstition or no superstition. But that makes no sense. You could slip into his house and cut his throat while he slept, if that's what you were after, and not take a chance on being seen walking into Frith's Wood. Or risk finding out that the tales of haunting are true."

"What became of Hensley's bicycle? He claims he was riding it on the main road, before he was attacked."

"I don't suppose anyone thought to look for it. I for one believed he'd been on foot. There was no sign of it near his body, I can tell you that."

"Did Hensley offer any explanation about why he'd ventured into the wood in the first place?"

"He didn't have to. I could imagine the reason for myself. We've always wondered if Emma Mason was buried there. And I think he's spent the last three years searching for her grave."

9

"Who is Emma Mason?" Rutledge asked. There had been no file for a missing woman, or a murder, in Hensley's parlor.

"She was a local girl. Seventeen at the time she vanished. We searched the countryside for miles around. No one had seen her leave, and no one knew what had become of her. Her grandmother was distraught — she would have led the search parties herself, if she'd been up to it."

"Foul play, then?"

"We couldn't think of anyone who might have harmed her. And we couldn't come up with a sound reason why she should leave. Abruptly, without a stitch of clothing missing or even a toothbrush with her."

"Then why suspect she was buried in the wood?"

"It was the only place," Middleton answered with sadness, "that someone could have disposed of a body without being seen by half the village looking out its back windows. A logical place, so to speak. But we covered every inch of the wood, and there was nothing to indicate that the ground had been disturbed. I doubt if anyone could have dug a grave there, anyway, with so many roots. Still — the search had to be made, if we were going to be thorough."

Following the directions Middleton had given him, Rutledge left his motorcar at the church and walked across the fields from there. He had gone no more than a few hundred yards when he realized how open the land was under a bowl of gray winter sky. The grass was brown, there were no trees except along the stream, and all the way to the horizon, nothing broke the emptiness.

He felt suddenly vulnerable.

If someone had followed him to Kent and to Hertford — why not here?

The grass crunched under his feet, and the wind had a bite to it. He could see the wood now. Bare branches stood out darkly against the slate color of the clouds, like fingers reaching upward. It was a larger wood than he'd expected, and denser. Impossible to see beyond the trees to the next field, the trunks and undergrowth weaving a thicket.

Behind him he could see the week's wash

blowing on lines in the backs of houses, the slate roofs dark under the gray clouds overhead, and the tall, thin spire of the church soaring into the sky like a lonely sentinel.

A dog barked from a house on the far side of the church, near a small barn. Ted Baylor's dog?

By the time he had reached the wood, Rutledge was aware that Hamish was tense and lurking in the back of his mind.

He stepped into the line of trees, sensing the eyes of villagers watching from behind their lace curtains. He had a feeling that if a Saxon warrior met him at the edge of the wood and lopped off his head with a long blade, no one would be surprised.

Hamish said, "It's no' a very good idea to tempt the dead."

"No. Not while walking over them."

Walking was difficult, dead or no. Fallen boughs and rotted trunks were traps for unwary feet under the mat of wet leaves. He stumbled once and caught himself with a hand on the nearest tree. There was a small area where the leaves had been churned by a multitude of feet. Hensley, then, and his saviors.

Looking around, Rutledge wondered how anyone had managed to get the badly wounded constable out of the wood, tight as tolerances were. Somehow they had got it done.

He examined the ground for some distance on either side of the site where he presumed Hensley had been found. But there were not enough signs to indicate whether the man had been dragged to the scene or fell there. It would surely have been as difficult getting him here as it had been to extricate him. Rutledge realized he needed a good deal more light to be certain. But on the whole, as Hamish was saying, it appeared that Hensley had been in the wood and on his feet when he was shot. Whether he had intentionally lied about that or honestly couldn't remember any of the events before the arrow struck him, it was hard to say.

Some distance away, in the soft earth by the bole of a tree, Rutledge found a deep indentation that indicated someone had been standing here. But whether it was the man with the bow and arrow, or Hensley himself, it was impossible to tell.

With Hensley down, Hamish was reminding him, there had been no one to do an investigation of the ground in his place. The doctor had been busy with his patient, and his helpers had been in a hurry to get out of the wood as quickly as possible. If they'd searched at all, it was cursorily.

Rutledge moved on, studying the earth underfoot intently before taking each step. But the clues were small and hard to see. A stalk bent here, a leaf dislodged there, a twig broken where someone had brushed by it. There was no way to know who had disturbed any of them, Hensley or his attacker.

The odd thing was, he hadn't started a rabbit or seen a bird flitting from tree to tree, twittering with curiosity. The wood was empty and quiet.

And that was ominous in itself . . .

How difficult would it be to dig down into the composted soil, to make a grave? Would that have been Hensley's fate if he'd died straightaway?

Even a killer might have qualms about burying a man still alive.

Rutledge shuddered at the thought.

It could probably be done, this digging. But it would have left scars on the ground for all the world to see. That is, if the world bothered to come and look here.

Rutledge made his way deeper into the trees, taking his time. The farther he went, the dimmer the light, as if it had been sucked away from the heart of the wood.

What's more, it was hard to see behind or ahead, and that alone would make a man feel —

He stopped short, listening.

But there was no one moving behind him, though he would have sworn he heard footsteps there.

Who would be bold enough to walk into Frith's Wood after him?

Hamish said, "I canna' say I like it in here. We'd best be gone."

But Rutledge continued straight ahead, hoping to come out of the wood on the far side.

Instead he had gone in a half circle and wound up where he'd come in.

I've got a better sense of direction than that, he told himself. Yet it would have been easy enough to get off track as he avoided thickets and trunks grown too close together.

He stopped to listen again, but the footfalls he'd believed he had heard were silent. In a way, that was more chilling than knowing they were still behind him.

It would take ten men and the better part of a day to cover all the wood as carefully as he'd done in his own circle, and he wasn't sure he could find ten men in Dudlington who would be willing.

Frith's Wood was an excellent place for an ambush.

On his way back to Hensley's house, Rutledge saw a stooped man puttering in the small garden of what must be the rectory, set as it was almost in the precincts of the church. He turned that direction and came to lean on the low wall that separated the churchyard from the rectory grounds as he called out, "Inspector Rutledge, Scotland Yard. May I come in and speak with you?"

The man looked up and waved. "Come around to the gate — just there."

Rutledge did as he was told and found his way around the side of the house to where the man waited, leaning on his pitchfork.

"I'm Frederick Towson, rector of St. Luke's," he said, taking off one of his gardening gloves to offer his hand. "Or has someone already told you as much?"

"No. I've only just met a handful of people here."

"I saw you walking toward the wood. Looking for clues, are you? Come in, and we'll have some tea to warm our bones." Towson smiled. "Yours may not be as old as mine, but this cold isn't particular."

Rutledge followed him into the tall, narrow stone house, surely far too big for one man to manage on his own. There must be a woman who came in to clean. He made a mental note to find out who it was.

"I try to do a little work in the gardens each day, to keep my hand in, but the truth is, my thumbs are brown, not green. If anything grows at all, it's through the kindness of my neighbors. They come to offer advice, and I listen." He opened the kitchen door and pulled off his muddy boots before stepping inside. Rutledge stopped long enough to use the iron scraper, shaped like a sleeping cat crouched by the door.

The kitchen was a warm, cozy room painted a pleasing shade of blue. The furnishings were old but well polished, and there were blue-and-white-patterned curtains at the windows, matching the cloth on the table.

"Sit down. I'll just put on the kettle."

Rutledge tried to judge the man's age, and decided he was perhaps sixty, although his hands were knotted and crippled by rheumatism. Those knuckles, he thought, must give Towson a good deal of pain at night.

But the rector was quick and economical in his movements, and he had the wood-burning cookstove fired up in no time. From a cupboard he took out bread and butter, setting them before Rutledge with a pot of jam.

"I'm fond of a little something with my tea," he explained, reaching for the bowl of sugar and then disappearing into the pantry to find milk.

The tea was steeping when he finally settled down across from Rutledge and sighed. "I've heard no news of Hensley. Is he recovering — or dead?"

"Recovering. But in a good deal of pain. You can see the wood from your upper windows, surely. Did you notice him walking that way three days ago? Was there anyone with him? Apparently he can't remember where he was just before he was shot. I'm trying to fill in the gaps."

"I can see Frith's Wood only from the attic windows, I'm afraid — because of the church cutting into the view. And I was in my study, working on my sermon. You'd think I knew how to write one by now, but it comes hard. I expect I've said everything I have it in me to say." He smiled wryly. "No, the first I knew of the incident, one of my neighbors came to tell me. By that time, Hensley was on his way to Northampton. Even Middleton, good as he is, couldn't handle a wound of that nature." He nodded as Rutledge got up to fill their cups. "Thank you, Inspector. Ah, this is what I need, inner warmth."

"You and Dr. Middleton are of an age," Rutledge said. "What is Dudlington to do when you are gone?"

"I expect someone will fill our shoes. Nature doesn't much care for a vacuum, you know."

"Tell me about Hensley. Has he been a good man to have here in Dudlington? Is he likely to grow old here as you've done?"

"I expect he might, or so I'd have said last week. I can't think how someone came to shoot him with an *arrow*. Very uncivilized thing to do."

Rutledge hid his smile. "Did most of the people get along well with him? He comes from London, after all, and knew very little about living in a village this size. He might have had difficulty understanding the differences. That could have made enemies for him."

Towson was busy buttering slices of bread. "We don't have all that much crime here. I daresay he kept out of everyone's way, most of the time. He told me once he was rather glad of the respite."

"Tell me about Emma Mason."

The knife stopped in midair. Towson stared at Rutledge. "You move quickly, young man. How did you come to hear that name?"

"It doesn't matter. What does matter, though, is the lack of a file in Hensley's records documenting her disappearance. A case of that magnitude? He must have interviewed people, traced her movements. There should have been something put to paper."

"I expect Inspector Cain, in Letherington, kept all that. Emma was — still is, for all I know — a young girl on the brink of womanhood. Charming and intelligent and well liked. You can see for yourself how small Dudlington is, and of course everyone knew Emma and had watched her grow up."

"Do her parents still live here?"

"Her father fell ill and died of a tumor in his bowels when she was a child. Her mother brought her home to Mary Ellison — Emma's grandmother — and left her there to grow up. Then she went away and never came back again, as far as I've been told. Mary was devoted to the child, and I don't think she's been quite the same since

Emma disappeared."

"Why would Emma go away without telling anyone?"

"That's the mystery. Emma was — it didn't make sense that she'd do such a heartless thing. There wasn't a cruel bone in her."

"And nothing had been troubling her before her disappearance? A young man? Her schooling? Living with her grandmother?"

"If it did, none of us knew it. She seemed — sunny, never down." He finished his slice of bread and began to butter another. "I will say one thing about Emma. Men — er — noticed her. She was quite lovely, dark hair, dark eyes, slender and shapely. I myself could see that she was an attractive child. It may be that someone else saw her a little differently — as perhaps more mature than she was. Perhaps she didn't know how to cope with that kind of attention. A village like ours seldom breeds such beauty, you know. It could have been a temptation to some. Still, that's not an excuse to run away."

"And what about the wives of the men who noticed her? Were they jealous?"

"I expect they were. Emma wasn't a flirt, mind you. But she would smile at you, and your heart would skip a beat. Even mine, at my age. A lonely man might read into that more than was meant. And tell himself that she fancied him. If you see what I mean?"

Hamish said, "He's no' sae unworldly as he appears. And a lonely man could be yon constable."

"Yes," Rutledge answered slowly. "Did Hensley show an inordinate interest in her?" It might explain the missing file. He would hardly keep evidence pointing to himself.

"He spoke to her in passing, everyone did. But whether it went beyond a few words exchanged, it's hard to say. The rectory is not in the heart of the village, you see. And I'm not as stable on a bicycle as I once was."

"Where does Emma's grandmother live?"

"On Whitby Lane, across from the bakery. She's a little hard of hearing. You'll have to remember that."

Across from the bakery would put the Ellison house nearly opposite Hensley's. He would have seen Emma coming and going every day.

As he rose to leave, Rutledge said, "Do you know of anyone here who owned — or used — a bow and arrow?"

"The only person who ever showed an

interest in the bow was Emma. And that was when she was twelve."

Rutledge stopped briefly at Mrs. Ellison's house, but she didn't answer his knock. A little hard of hearing, he remembered, and crossed the street to Hensley's, looking up as a smattering of sunlight broke through the clouds and touched the pink brick of the buildings with a warm rose light. He nodded to a young woman carrying bread out of the bakery. She ducked her head, as if she hadn't seen his greeting.

Opening the door, he walked into the hall of his temporary home and climbed the stairs to Hensley's bedroom. He'd seen a pair of battered field glasses on a shelf between the windows and he intended to borrow them.

He found them where he'd remembered seeing them, next to the window. But as he reached for them, he discovered that this bedroom window in Hensley's house stared directly into another window just across the lane. A window in the house where Mrs. Ellison lived.

He held the glasses to his eyes and was surprised at how clearly he could see into the room opposite.

Was that Emma's room? And had Hensley been using the glasses to watch her at night?

"Why else were they sae handy?" Hamish asked.

It was an unpleasant thought.

He shoved the glasses into his coat pocket and was turning to go down to the motorcar when he saw it.

A cartridge casing, standing upright in the middle of his bed. This time without any carving defacing the smooth surface.

Whoever was stalking him had tracked him to Dudlington.

10

It was not a surprise. In many ways, he'd expected it. But Rutledge stood there looking at the small casing, not touching it. What disturbed him most was the fact that once more he had been so easy to find. Surely no one could guess that he would be staying at the wounded constable's house — unless of course it had been a logical step after discovering that Rutledge didn't have a room at The Oaks. After that, the motorcar left at the side of the house would have betrayed his presence.

Had anyone seen this invisible stalker walking into the constable's house? After all, it was near the baker's shop and the greengrocer's, where people did their marketing.

Rutledge went back to the window fronting the street. Looking in one direction, he could see two women coming out of the greengrocer's, talking animatedly to each other, and in the other, young children walking hand in hand, a nanny behind them, her starched apron hidden by her heavy coat.

And then two men in muddy Wellingtons came around the corner, heading briskly up the street toward the inn. Or the fields. It was hard to tell. Three houses away, a woman brought out a broom to sweep the walk in front of her door.

It wasn't that Dudlington was empty — it was that whereas a larger village or town might have forty or fifty people on the streets at any given moment, this tiny pocket in the middle of nowhere seldom saw more than ten abroad at a time. But the doctor had said gossip was the mainstay of life here. And a stranger would have drawn faces to the window, peering from behind the curtains to see where he was going and what his business might be.

Hamish said, "It'ud tak' an army to interview all o' them."

Rutledge examined the cartridge casing. Was it intentionally plain? Or had whoever was stalking him run out of carved casings?

"It doesna' matter," Hamish pointed out. "There's other business here."

But beyond the shelter of the village streets, the land was flat and sere and rolling. No protection. A perfect field of fire.

Rutledge shivered. It was like No Man's

Land, where the only trees were blackened, disfigured apparitions in a barren, bloody world.

He started to put the casing in his pocket, out of sight. And then thought better of it.

Would whoever had set it out for him to find come back later to see if it had delivered its message?

It was an interesting point and worth considering.

Finally, with care, Rutledge set the cartridge casing exactly where he'd found it, and then went down the street to take his luncheon at Mrs. Melford's.

She had set out sandwiches and a pudding for Rutledge. If she was in the house, he couldn't hear her moving about.

He ate quickly, and then left. Driving up to The Oaks, where the main road ran beyond Dudlington, he found the proprietor in the bar serving several men in corduroys and heavy boots.

They looked around as Rutledge stepped through the door, then went back to their beer, ignoring him.

Rutledge nodded to the proprietor and sat down at a table near the window. When Keating came over to ask what he would have, he shook his head. "Later, perhaps."

Conversation, which had stopped short at his entrance, resumed stiffly, as if the subject had been changed in midsentence.

It was another twenty minutes before the men took their leave and went out the door. The proprietor, collecting the empty glasses, said, "You have a chilling effect on custom."

"Indeed." Rutledge watched the men walk across the road to the fields and stride over them toward the stream. "Do you know Constable Hensley well?"

"To speak to. He's not a regular, you might say. I don't know that anyone would call him a friend." Keating set about washing up.

"Has anyone asked for him in the last — say, two days?"

"Asked for him? Everyone wants to know how he's faring."

"Someone who doesn't live in Dudlington."

"We see our share of strangers in The Oaks. It's the road yonder that brings us most of our custom. You know that. What is it you're asking me in your roundabout policeman's fashion?"

Rutledge smiled. "You know very well. Have you given directions to Hensley's house to anyone stopping here? Or discussed the constable's condition with anyone passing through?"

"Someone's knocking at your door, unwelcomed?"

It was so near the mark that Rutledge considered him. "It's not wise to obstruct a policeman in the course of his inquiries. What do you have against the law? Or is it Hensley that you dislike?"

"I don't know that I care for either, to tell the truth." He set the first glass on a mat to dry.

"Did you know Emma Mason?"

Keating stared at him, caught off guard by the sudden change in direction the conversation had taken. "Everyone knew her," he said finally, his voice flat.

"What do you think became of her? Is she dead? Or did she run away?"

"I have no opinion on the subject."

"Everyone else has."

"I own The Oaks. I don't have much to do with the people in Dudlington. They come here if they choose, or not. If they want to sit at my bar and drink, then I bring them their pints and leave them to it."

"Did Emma Mason ever come here?"

"What would she be doing here, at a licensed house?" he countered, without answering the question directly.

"You aren't a native. You've lived elsewhere. She might have found that attractive."

"Here, now, I don't meddle with schoolgirls!"

"I didn't suggest you'd meddled with her. Only that she might have wanted more than Dudlington could offer. That she might have liked the idea of seeing motorcars or carriages on their way to more exciting destinations. It might have put the thought into her head that here was an escape. Did she look her age?"

"I don't know how she looked. If you want to know, ask in the village, not here." He was angry, far angrier than the question merited.

"She has to be somewhere," Rutledge answered mildly. "She's either alive or dead. She's either buried in Dudlington or she's gone away with one of the men who stopped here for a drink or directions or a dinner. They wouldn't come to the village, there's nothing in it for them. She had only to walk up the main street and climb the hill to reach The Oaks, and even if she didn't set foot in the door, she could see the motorcars and the men —"

"You can get out of my pub!" Keating shouted. "Now! Or copper or not, I'll take pleasure in throwing you out!"

Rutledge got to his feet, moving without haste. "I haven't come here to cast doubt on the girl's virtue. Her disappearance isn't even my case. But the name keeps cropping up in connection with Frith's Wood. And Constable Hensley was nearly killed in that same wood. You can see why I'm — curious."

Keating slammed his fist down on the bar, rattling the glasses and bottles on it. "Emma Mason was a child. A decent child, with more beauty than it was safe to possess. If I thought Hensley had touched her, I'd do more than send an arrow into his back, I'd have wrung his neck! You'd have had your case of murder then, right enough!"

And with that, he disappeared through the door behind the bar, slamming it after him.

The wind had come up, and with it a cold, spitting rain. Rutledge walked to the motorcar and took up the crank. The leather seats were cold as the grave, he thought, climbing in. And the heater offered such little warmth that it might as well not exist.

He turned into the main road, heading north. This was the way Hensley would have traveled to Letherington. The road ran straight and narrow between the low stone walls that followed it to the right, and the open vistas of Dudlington's pastures and fields to the left. As the land climbed with it, it began to bend to the right, away to the east. On a sunny summer's day, when the cattle and sheep and horses filled the meadows, and light glinted on the winding stream that bisected the fields beyond the village, it would have been a pretty scene. Old England, and worth fighting for.

He crested the hill and paused to look back. There was the village, the inn already out of sight, the church spire standing tall, and Frith's Wood visible as bare treetops, seemingly nothing out of the ordinary at this distance.

He set the brake and got out of the car, walking to the stone wall and climbing it. Taking out Hensley's field glasses, he surveyed the ground, slowly turning in a full circle.

Then he studied the wall itself, on the pasture side away from the road, scanning the dark crannies at its base.

Nothing.

He was about to put the glasses back into his pocket when he saw crows in a field farther along.

Hensley had mentioned crows rising.

He scrambled down and went back to the car.

Half a mile on, the bend of the road took him away from Dudlington, and even standing in the motorcar, he could see only the tip of the spire. Characteristic of Northampton, it rose above the church like a finger pointing toward God.

He set the brake for a second time and found a place to climb the wall again. Here it was overgrown with weeds and brambles, but there was a lower section where he could just manage to get to the top. Not as flat, this one, he discovered, as he nearly pitched headfirst into the pasture.

Precariously balanced at best, he slowly drew out the glasses and lifted them to his eyes. Nothing in the fields.

But on the far side of the wall, not fifty feet from where he was, he could just see a bicycle tucked under the brambles and all but out of sight.

He walked toward it, sending the crows flying.

Hamish said, "Who hid it here? Yon constable before he went down to the wood?

Or his assailant, making certain no one found him quickly?"

It was a good question, and without a good answer.

Rutledge lifted the bicycle, brushed off the earth and dried leaves, and walked it back to the place where he had come over the wall. It took some effort on his part to get it into the rear of the motorcar, and by the time he had finished, the storm, hovering in the low gray clouds all day, broke in earnest.

He made a point to stow the bicycle behind Hensley's house in the bare back garden, covering it with a tarpaulin he found in the tiny shed where picks, shovels, and spades were kept.

There must have been a dozen people who saw him bring it with him, he thought, but until gossip had spread that word, he wasn't going to make an issue of his find. He wanted no questions about where and how he'd come up with it.

After washing his hands and cleaning his boots, he crossed the street to Emma Mason's grandmother's house and knocked.

This time an elderly woman came to the door. She was tall and handsome, but when he spoke to her, introducing himself, she leaned forward as if uncertain what he'd said.

He repeated his name and asked if he could come inside. She invited him into the house rather reluctantly.

The parlor was feminine, with lacy curtains, crocheted antimacassars on the arms and backs of the chairs, and a long lacy cloth over the table by the piano. On it were photographs, and one was of a young girl holding a black and white kitten and smiling up at the camera. She was quite pretty even at the age of around ten, with good cheekbones and a high forehead, framed in hair that appeared to be dark and thick and curling.

Mrs. Ellison offered him a chair and sat down herself. In the flat tones of the near deaf, she asked him his business.

"I'm looking into the . . . accident that befell Constable Hensley in Frith's Wood," he said, pitching his voice so that she could hear him.

"I'm not deaf, young man," she retorted, and he smiled.

"Apparently not."

"I do have trouble sometimes with what the words are. Putting them together to make sense."

"Do you know Constable Hensley well?"

"I'm his neighbor across the street. I don't invite him to my house to dine."

"Is he a good policeman?"

"How should I know?" Her lips tightened, as if to hold back what else she might have said.

"He investigated the disappearance of your granddaughter. And couldn't find her," he reminded her gently.

"It's always been in my mind that she went to look for her mother. My daughter. When her husband died — Emma's father — she wanted no more to do with the child. I think it was too painful a reminder of happiness lost. I don't know what became of her, to be truthful. She never wrote to me in all these years. Not even to ask how young Emma fared." Her face crumpled, but she recovered and said in a reasonably steady voice, "Beatrice was pretty too, and it was her downfall. Sad, isn't it, how blood can tell."

When he asked to see Emma's room, Mrs. Ellison raised her eyebrows in disapproval. "This has nothing to do with Constable Hensley's unfortunate accident!"

"She's not here," he prompted her. "I shan't be intruding. But it might help me to see what interested her."

"Even that Inspector Abbot, from

Letherington, respected her privacy," Mrs. Ellison retorted. "I can't think what good it would do you. Unless it's voyeurism."

Stung, he said with some harshness, "You can't be the judge of what's important in a police matter. I can go to Northampton and ask for a warrant to search. It would be far less pleasant than five minutes in her room."

"Very well." She rose, led him to the stairs, and climbed ahead of him, her back stiff with protest.

The girl's room was on the front of the house, and when he went to the windows, he could see that one of them, the one nearest the dressing table, looked directly into Hensley's bedroom across the lane.

II

The walls of Emma Mason's room had been painted a pale yellow, with cream curtains at the window and a patterned cream coverlet on the bed. The skirts of the dressing table were a yellow and cream print, matching the cushions on both chairs. The carpet was floral, with splashes of cream and ivory and yellow mixed with a pale green. The effect was like sunlight pouring in, on such a gray day, even though the lamps hadn't been lit.

"Her granny treated her well enough," Hamish commented as Rutledge looked about him. "It wasna' unhappiness at home that made her leave."

To Rutledge's eyes nothing appeared to have changed since Emma Mason's disappearance. The room was clean, fresh, ready for its owner to step back into it again, as if these three blank years hadn't existed. The delicate scent of lavender filled the air, and Hamish said, "It lacks only flowers."

It was true. Something in keeping with the pretty surroundings. Daffodils in a slender glass vase, violets in something silver, roses in a cream pitcher. Rutledge could imagine it.

But there was nothing personal in the room, no dolls long since outgrown, only a few well-read books on the shelf by the bed, and a single photograph of Mrs. Ellison as a younger woman, placed by a ticking china clock on the bedside table.

A shrine? Or was this simply the way a grieving grandmother preferred to remember her grandchild?

He walked over to the wardrobe and was on the point of opening it when Mrs. Ellison said sharply, "Only her clothing is in there. Dresses and coats and shoes. A hat or two. You needn't pry into what she wore, surely."

He had seen what he had come to see.

On the way down the stairs, he asked, "I understand Emma had been interested in practicing with a bow, when she was younger."

They had reached the foot of the stairs by the time she answered, and she made a point not to invite him back into the parlor. "Emma went through a stage where she admired that young woman who was in the Robin Hood tales. I can't think what her name was."

"Maid Marian?"

She frowned. "My memory isn't what it once was. It hasn't been since — since she left me. At any rate, she read every book I could find for her about that forest —"

"Sherwood."

"Yes. Thank you. She begged me to take her there. But it isn't a great forest any longer, is it? I did ask the rector, and he said it would have been disappointing."

"Frith's Wood," Hamish said. "She would ha' seen it as filled wi' bandits and heroes."

It might have seemed an exciting, enchanting forest to a girl with an imagination that ran to old tales of adventure and damsels in distress.

"Can you tell me where her bow and arrows are now?"

"Good Lord, how should I know! It wasn't I who gave them to her, and I disapproved of them from the start."

"Then who did?"

"She never told me. I only discovered them by chance, and after that they were never left lying about."

"Do you remember the coloring of the feathers at the end of the shaft?"

Mrs. Ellison stared at him. "You must be mad! Of course not. I'm not always certain what day of the week it is, young man. Dr.

Middleton tells me it will get worse, this forgetfulness. Worry, he says, that's what does it. But what do I need to remember, anyway? Losing my daughter and then my granddaughter? Hardly events one wishes to take into the shadows with one."

He thanked her then, and left.

But he had the strongest feeling that she was watching him from behind the parlor curtains as he crossed the street and opened the door of Hensley's house. She was right that he had no authority to poke about in an old mystery.

The problem was, it seemed to intrude of its own accord into the inquiry into Hensley's wounding. And he'd learned, long since, not to ignore distractions until he was sure that they had no bearing on the main issue.

His next step must be going to Letherington to speak to Inspector Cain about Hensley and about the Mason girl. His excuse was the recovery of the bicycle. If he needed one.

There was a man sitting in the constable's office, and Rutledge stopped in the doorway, wary and on his guard.

But the visitor came forward, his hand out, and said, "Inspector Cain. You must be the man they were sending from London.

You got here sooner than I'd expected."

Hensley's superior officer.

Hamish said sourly, "He doesna' know the Chief Superintendent well."

Had Old Bowels's need for haste been intended to shut Cain out of the inquiry?

The Inspector was young, with fair hair and a ruddy complexion, and his carriage was military.

"In France, were you?" Rutledge added, after introducing himself.

"Yes, worst luck. Took a bullet in my hip. The doctors patched me up, but if you want to know tomorrow's weather, come and ask me."

Rutledge lit the lamp, and they sat down, Cain choosing Hensley's side of the table desk as if by right.

"Chief Inspector Kelmore sent word to me that you were here, but I had to wait for transportation from Letherington. Not much for bicycles yet, you know. And the carriage I generally use was busy elsewhere." He grinned. "My wife had errands to run. We're expecting our firstborn in three months. It's costing me more to set up the nursery than it will to send him to Eton."

"Congratulations," Rutledge said. "Yes, I visited Hensley in hospital. He's still in a great deal of pain, but the surgery appears to have been successful."

"Yes, well, he's a tough old bird. I never understood why he came here from London. I'd have preferred to be working in a city, myself, given half a chance."

"Much trouble in Letherington or Dudlington?"

"Not to speak of. This is cattle country, you know. Anyone who wakes up for milking at four in the morning isn't good for mischief by eight at night."

"I've hardly seen a man, much less a cow."

"They're in the barns in this weather. Most of them will bear calves in late winter. Lose a cow, and you lose the calf as well."

"Makes sense. Did you see Constable Hensley in Letherington on Friday last?"

"Everyone maintains he was on his way there, but if he was, he never reached us. None of my people at the station saw him, and he wasn't at his usual haunts. I've asked around. The fact of the matter is, I'd taken a bit of leave for personal business, because it was a quiet week. Or so we thought."

"Which would lead us to believe that there wasn't any pressing reason for him to speak with you. Nothing, for instance, so urgent that someone would go to any lengths to stop him."

"I can't imagine that's the case. Here, in Dudlington? It's probably the quietest of the three villages. And if there *was* an urgent problem, I'd have got wind of it by now."

"Since the attack occurred in broad daylight, we can't make a case for mistaken identity. Any idea who might have set out to kill Hensley?"

"God, no. I'm glad to see you feel it was attempted murder, by the way. In the first place, it doesn't make sense that someone would choose that benighted wood to play at archery. And in the second, Hensley's too big a man not to be heard as he came through the trees and into range. Finally, no one's stepped forward bow in hand with an apology. I've only been here two years — mustered out in late '17. Still, I can't think why anyone would wish him harm. I've had no complaints against him from the local people. That's generally the precursor to any trouble."

"What do you know about Emma Mason's disappearance?"

"I wasn't here, of course, when it happened. Pretty girl like that, though, might easily have her head turned by talk of better prospects than she could hope for here. Her mother ran off, I'm told. That's probably what put the notion into *her* head. No trace was ever found of her, and that's bothersome. But I would think that if she didn't want to be found, she would make sure she couldn't be. Grace Letteridge always believed she'd come back one day, weeping and repentant. If not pregnant."

"I haven't met Miss Letteridge."

"She's probably seen you, all the same. She lives at the corner of the main street and this lane. The thatched house, with the courtyard in front, and a garden."

"Did she know Emma well?"

"I don't know. The fact is, she doesn't talk about Emma at all. And the general impression is that Emma disappointed her. Well, of course, so much was expected of the child. Mary Ellison is a Harkness on her mother's side. And the Harkness family owned all the land here for miles around. It was the Harknesses who didn't care to see the muddy little village of Dudlington at their gates. And in 1817 they tore it down and rebuilt it here, out of sight — and presumably out of smell. That's why Dudlington is all of the same period, it started from scratch. The church is said to be a simplified design of Wren's. At least the spire is. And then in 1824, the Harkness manor house burned to the ground in a great conflagration, killing three people. Some said it was fired in revenge for moving everyone into the new village. But I expect, like many great houses of its day, it was likely to burn without any help. Gives me the willies to see my wife walking about with a candle. But there's no hope of electrical power in these scattered villages. There's no money for starters."

"How have you learned so much about the history of this place?" Rutledge asked, curious.

"I married into the history, old man. My wife's family has lived in Letherington for at least five generations. My mother-in-law reminds me of that daily. Another reason I pine for Canterbury." He shrugged. "I met my wife there, in fact, and never dreamed she would expect to live in a house across the road from her mother, after we'd married."

"Any suggestions about Hensley's past or present that might lead me in the right direction?"

"To be truthful, I can't imagine who would have the gall to shoot Hensley. You might ask yourself if it was something to do with his cases in London. I've learned that he was involved with a number of inquiries there. One into a German waiter who was a spy. Or said to be a spy. I doubt that he was. But in 1914 people could find spies under their beds. And there was another case, I don't remember the ins and outs of it. But a man named Barstow, in the City, claimed he was burned out by his rivals. Everyone agreed it was a case of arson — what it took some time to determine was exactly who had set the fire. Barstow was looking to rebuild, and he had a taste for revenge. He'd burned his own place of business, and blamed it on his enemies. And they actually went to trial for it."

"I remember hearing about Barstow. Hensley was involved with that?"

"Possibly involved in it, more to the point. It was rumored that Hensley took bribes to look the other way. Bribes he was supposed to share with his superior. But he stoutly denied any such thing and was rewarded with Dudlington, a quiet backwater. Markham, the old constable, had just retired and gone to live with his daughter in Sussex."

And Hensley's superior at the time was

then Chief Inspector Bowles.

Hamish was reminding Rutledge what Hensley had said in the hospital ward.

"Was it Old Bowels who sent you?"

And Bowles had been furiously angry about the attack on Hensley.

It wouldn't do to bring his name back to the attention of either the police or the newspapers, if there was any hint of scandal attached to his departure.

"What became of the file on Emma Mason?"

"Damned if I know. There's a good bit in my office, but not the whole of it. My predecessor in Letherington wasn't what you might call compelled to put every detail down on paper. I'd have thought Hensley kept some records of his own interviews."

Cain got stiffly to his feet. "I don't know much more about Dudlington's skeletons than you do. I relied on Hensley's experience when there were problems. I have a good constable in Fairfield and an even better sergeant in Letherington now, who see me through. Any help you can give me here will be appreciated. Come back in five years' time, and if I'm still here — God forfend! — I'll know my turf like the back of my hand."

"Where is your carriage?" Rutledge

asked him at the door. "I didn't see it as I came in."

Cain grinned. "My constable's at The Oaks. He's very good at gossip. I depend on him to tell me what's being whispered in the dark corners of the bar."

And he was off, favoring his left leg as he walked through the rain toward Holly Street.

Rutledge saw him out of sight, and then climbed the stairs to the bedroom.

The cartridge casing was still there, where Rutledge had left it.

Rutledge made a point to search out the house belonging to Grace Letteridge.

It was one of the few buildings in the village that boasted a thatched roof. Thatching had always reminded Rutledge of a woman wearing a marvelous hat and feeling slightly self-conscious about it. In the case of this particular house, the comparison was apt. It was set farther back from the lane and stood out from its neighbors in the fineness of its stonework. Someone had built a low wall around the front, creating a courtyard of sorts where roses, cut back for the winter and mounded over, like tiny graves, marched across the brown grass.

He ducked his head under the low thatched roof that covered the porch, and knocked at the door.

It was opened by a woman in her late twenties, her hair a dull gold and her eyes a very pretty amber in a very plain face.

"Miss Letteridge?"

"And you're the man from London. How is Constable Hensley?" There was a derisive note in her voice as she asked.

"He's expected to live," Rutledge answered, and waited for her response.

Miss Letteridge led him into the small parlor before answering. "I'm sorry to hear it. I never liked him, and I shan't be two-faced about it."

"That's rather coldhearted."

"Sit down. I won't offer you tea, because I don't care for it myself and don't keep it in the house. I do have some sherry . . ." Her words trailed off, indicating that she would prefer not to offer him that either.

"Why don't you like Constable Hensley?" he asked again. The room was well furnished, with a number of watercolors on the pale blue walls that caught his attention. They had been done with great skill.

It clearly irritated Miss Letteridge that he appeared not to be giving her his full attention.

"For the same reason I don't particularly care for any policeman," she answered tartly. "They look after their own, don't they? Hensley was sent here under a cloud, and we weren't told of it. He wouldn't get into trouble here, would he? After all, we're very peaceable in Dudlington, and he only had to walk the streets and mind his own business until he could collect his pension. That was the theory, anyway."

"How did you know he was under a cloud when he came here?" Rutledge asked, intrigued.

"Why else would a London police constable be sent to an out-of-the-way village where nothing ever happens? Where he wouldn't attract attention? I'm not a fool, Inspector, I know something about the world outside Northamptonshire. I worked in London during the first two years of the war. There weren't enough able-bodied men to do half of what was needed. Women were pressed into service at every turn, and a police constable worth his salt would have risen quickly through the ranks as men enlisted. Instead his superiors banished him."

"That may well be the case. But so far I haven't heard that it affected the performance of his duties."

"No, I doubt if it affected his duties. You're right. But once a murderer, always a murderer."

Rutledge stared at her. "Do you know for a fact that Constable Hensley murdered someone in London and got away with it?" Even Sergeant Gibson hadn't told him that. Nor had Cain.

"He condoned arson. And a man was caught in that fire, so badly burned that even his wife couldn't identify him. I went to London myself and read accounts in the newspapers. They weren't very helpful, so I talked to his widow. She's bitter because the police swept it all under the rug. He didn't die straightaway, you know. Harold Edgerton. He lingered for nearly a month, but in the end the doctors couldn't stop the infections that overwhelmed him. By that time, there were rumors that he'd started the fire himself. All he'd done was to go back to his desk that evening to retrieve some papers."

"Constable Hensley knew all this?"

"Why else were they in such haste to get him out of London?"

"And what you're trying to say, then, is that you believe he killed Emma Mason."

It was her turn to stare at him.

"You already know about her!"

"I only know that her name comes up when people talk about Constable Hensley."

"As God is my witness, he killed her and buried her in Frith's Wood. I can't prove it, mind you, but there's no other explanation for her disappearance."

"Did you shoot him down with that arrow, out of revenge? One of Emma Mason's arrows, perhaps, as a sort of poetic justice?"

"Was it one of Emma's? How fitting! I gave that archery set to her, you know. For her birthday. But I wouldn't have missed my aim, Inspector. If I'd held that bow, Constable Hensley would have died where he stood."

12

The vehemence in Grace Letteridge's voice was chilling, and Rutledge, listening to her, realized that she could indeed have killed.

The question was, why?

Hamish said, "She was plain — and the other lass was pretty."

Rutledge asked, "Where is her archery set now?"

"Truthfully? I have no idea what became of it. Even if I did, I'd be mad to tell you, wouldn't I?"

"What was Emma Mason to you, that you'd have killed for her?"

She looked at him pityingly. "What was Emma to me? A mirror of myself. Mother-less. Her grandmother living in a world of pretense and denial. Only in my case, it was my father who couldn't cope with the realities of life. My mother died in child-birth, and my father felt that God had cheated him. And so he drank himself into an early grave — the only reason he lived until I was twenty was an iron constitution that refused to give up as easily as he had.

Mrs. Ellison, on the other hand, saw in Emma a second chance. The perfect child who would make up for the loss of her daughter, one who wouldn't fail her the way Beatrice had."

"You're very frank about your own life."

"I've had to be. I grew up very quickly. It wasn't pleasant, but I refused to let it break me the way it had my father." She met his glance with her chin lifted, defiant.

Hamish said, "It didna' break her, but the hurt went deep."

"I was going to say," Rutledge commented, "that you're very frank. But was Emma as frank? Or did you read into her circumstances more than was there?"

"I didn't read anything. I didn't need to. Beatrice was amazingly pretty, and people made much of her, the way they do. She was talented as well — a wonderful pianist and a very accomplished watercolorist. She painted these —" Grace Letteridge gestured to the watercolors on the wall. "You've noticed them, I saw your eyes on them. She gave them to me, before she left Dudlington the first time. She didn't want her mother to have them, because her mother was against Beatrice going to London to study art. She saw it as a waste. Women got married and had babies. That was their duty and their purpose. Accomplishments were fine, as long as they enhanced the bride price, so to speak. But a woman most certainly didn't pursue a career among *artists*. Prostitution was only one step away, in Mrs. Ellison's view."

"But Beatrice Ellison married."

"Yes, of course she did, but she made a poor choice. He wasn't very good to her, and in the end, he left her with a child, no money, and no prospects. She had to swallow her pride and bring Emma here to live with her grandmother. I can understand why she didn't want to stay in Dudlington herself, but she knew what her mother was like, and I consider it very selfish of her to abandon the child like that." She got up, restless, and went to the window to look out at the street. "She wouldn't talk to me when she came home. She was unhappy and unsettled. It was a difficult time. But Emma grew up to be prettier than her mother, and that was the trouble."

"Trouble in what sense?"

"Everyone made over Beatrice," she said, turning from the window. "But Emma had inherited her father's charm, and there was something about her that attracted the wrong kind of attention. It wasn't just old women cooing over her, it was men old enough to be her father or her grandfather watching her on the street, or stopping her to make comments. 'That's a pretty dress, young lady.' Or 'I like that hair ribbon. Did you know it was the color of your eyes?' It made Emma uncomfortable, long before she was old enough to understand why."

"Did you tell her grandmother what you'd observed?"

She laughed harshly. "She told me I was jealous of the attention being paid to Emma. And my father punished me for bearing tales. I was sent to bed without my dinner for a week. People see what they want to see — or expect to see. So I took it on myself to be Emma's protector, and I was hardly more than a child myself. It wasn't a task I felt I could do, but I didn't have anywhere else to turn."

"And Emma accepted this — protection?"

She shrugged. "She appeared to be grateful for it. Or so she said. We more or less looked after each other."

"How old are you?" Rutledge asked bluntly.

Grace Letteridge bristled. "It's none of your business."

But he thought he'd been wrong in his earlier estimate of her age. Young herself,

147

vulnerable, and perhaps reading more into what she saw around her than was true, she might have made up the notion that Emma needed protection. It might, indeed, have been her own loneliness that made her seek out the younger child, and cling to her. Anything but coming home to a drunken father filled with his own misery.

"Why are you so certain that Constable Hensley killed Emma Mason?" he asked.

"He would stop and talk to her, tell her about London, and plays and concerts — which he'd probably never attended in his life — or describe an evening at the opera, watching the King and Queen step into the royal box, and how the Prince of Wales had spoken to him one morning as he rode his horse into the park. It was pathetic, an attempt to hold her attention, and he would lie in wait for her, ready with a new tale to spin, making London seem glorious, and she knew — *she knew!* — her mother lived there somewhere. I listened to her concocting schemes to go there as soon as the war ended, and find her mother and live in this fairy-tale world. He had no idea what harm he was doing, and it's possible he wouldn't have cared."

"More a reason for you to kill him, than

for him to kill Emma."

"Ah, but what you don't know is that Emma fell in love! And that put a spoke in Constable Hensley's wheel. I believe he killed her in a jealous rage."

Try as he would, Grace Letteridge refused to tell him who it was that Emma had thought she was in love with. "It doesn't matter. He's dead, anyway. In the war."

But Rutledge could tell it did matter, a very great deal.

As he left, Hamish was pointing out that very likely Grace Letteridge had been in love with this man herself. It might explain why she went to London — leaving Emma to her own devices — and why she came home.

"I canna' believe her father would let her go sae easily. Unless he was dead in 1914."

In 1914, Grace Letteridge couldn't have been more than nineteen. Which would make her four and twenty now. And Emma would have been a very impressionable fourteen.

Rutledge walked to the churchyard, feeling the cold wind across his face as he reached the gate, and went inside to search the gravestones for Grace Letteridge's father.

It was a wild-goose chase, trying to find one man amongst so many gravestones, most of them green with moss and over-grown with lichen. But a 1914 grave would still be raw enough.

What he found was unexpected. The young men of the village had not been brought home from France, but stones had been set in a garden for them, and the lonely rows of names struck him as sad and forgotten.

The cold wind had brought more rain in its wake. He stood there, looking at the line of empty graves, and felt a sadness that went deeper than his compassion for their deaths. It was what all of them, the living and the dead, had lost in four years of suffering.

Hamish was silent, for he too was only a marker in a lonely churchyard, his last resting place a muddy hole in France with none of the trappings of home to see him into a peaceful rest.

"There are poppies," Hamish said finally. "They'll grow again."

Rutledge could see the poppies on the shell casings, and hear again the roar of a revolver shot over the sound of his heavy motor and the calls of the crows as they flew up, startled. The flight of the bullet, close enough for its breath to touch his face and its whine to be heard over all the other sounds, brought back more than the war, it brought back his willingness to die for what he'd done.

But not like this, not shot by someone who hid in the shadows, with no reality and no right to be his executioner.

It had all begun at Maryanne Browning's house in London.

And it was time he went back to the beginning and found out what had gone wrong on the eve of a new year.

He could hear someone shouting and looked up, distracted from his thoughts.

Hamish said, "Yon rector."

It was indeed Mr. Towson calling from the porch of his house, his voice thin in the rain and wind.

"You'll take your death standing there, young man. Come and have a cup of tea before I freeze to death just watching you."

13

Rutledge splashed across the churchyard, found the gate in the wall that led to the rectory, and reached the porch like a wet dog, wondering what the rector would think if he shook himself violently. Not so much to rid himself of the water, but to rid himself of the mood that had swept over him.

Towson reached for his hat and coat, tut-tutting over their condition.

"I watched you for a good quarter hour, out there. Paying respect is one thing, foolishness another. I can't think you knew any of our dead."

Rutledge followed him from the hall into the parlor, gloomy in the light of a single lamp.

"I was looking for the grave of a Mr. Letteridge. Grace Letteridge's father."

"Ah. Well, it's nearer the rectory than the memorial garden you were standing by." He spread Rutledge's coat across the back of a chair and stooped to put a match to the fire already laid on the hearth. "Sit down, do. Why did you want to find him? Clifford Letteridge has been dead for five years, I should think. Yes, it must be going on five."

"I called on his daughter an hour or so ago. I was curious about him after our conversation."

"I'm not surprised. She's bitter, is young Grace, and I can't say that I blame her. She's had a sad life, and yet no thanks to her father, she's become a very fine young woman. Or could be, if she'd let go some of the anger inside her."

"She told me he drank himself into oblivion."

"His heart was dead long before he died, and that's the truth. He put food on the table, clothes on her back, kept a roof over her head, and sent her to church of a Sunday with strict regularity, and called that fatherhood."

"I wonder that she didn't marry, if only to leave such a cold and empty life."

Towson smiled. "I'm no fool. You're here to pry the secrets of other people out of me. Sit there and warm yourself, and I'll bring in a tray of tea."

He left the room, effectively cutting the conversation short.

Rutledge looked at the dark paneling on

the wall and somber drapes at the window, then turned his attention to the portrait of an elderly man — a cleric, if he was any judge — hanging over the hearth. A grim face, with no humor in it or even kindness. Who did it remind him of?

Hamish said, "The minister who railed against my Fiona."

Yes, of course, that pitiless man in Scotland who would willingly have hounded a defenseless young woman to her death. And it had been a close-run thing. She had loved Hamish, and it had nearly been her undoing.

The similarity was not so much in their features, but in the unbending view both churchmen must have held of human frailty. Impatient to cast the first stone.

Towson came in, bearing a tray. "Lucky for you the kettle was on the boil," he said. "This should put some heart into you."

"Who is the man in the portrait?"

"One of my predecessors. He comes with the house, so to speak. I expect no one else wanted him. I've often wondered if he roams the rectory at night, unwilling to lie quiet in his grave."

Rutledge laughed. "What would you say to him if you met him in the passage outside your door?"

"I doubt we'd have much in common beyond 'How do you do, sir.' "

Rutledge offered to pour the tea, aware of the gnarled hands handling the pot, but Towson said, "I consider it a point of independence not to need help. At least until I've spilled scalding hot tea on one of my guests."

"You aren't going to tell me about the man in Grace Letteridge's life." It was a statement, not a question.

"If she wants you to know, she'll tell you. You must understand it could have no possible bearing on Constable Hensley's assailant."

"No, but I wonder if it had some bearing on Miss Letteridge going to London in 1914, leaving young Emma Mason to fend for herself. And whether this man's death in the war brought Miss Letteridge home again, shortly before Emma disappeared."

"You're an imaginative sort, aren't you?"

"Then why does Emma Mason's name crop up so often in connection with Constable Hensley?"

"Yes, well, I expect every man wants to appear brave and worldly and exciting in the eyes of impressionable young women. When Hensley first came to Dudlington, he kept his head down, as a newcomer should. After all, he was the outsider, and he had to earn our respect, constable or not. But it wasn't long before he was bragging to anyone who would listen about his experiences in London. I can understand that Emma might be curious about the sort of life her mother lived, and so she encouraged him more than was proper. Mrs. Ellison would never have painted London in such a glowing light. She's convinced that London is little short of Satan's second address."

"I'm told it went beyond mere bragging, that he used his experiences to impress a young and vulnerable girl. What if she believed his stories, and ran away to London on the basis of them? Leaving Hensley to take the blame for her disappearance."

"To find her mother? It could have happened that way, yes. Still, I gave Emma credit for more sense."

"The fact is, she's missing. Surely if she went to London to find her mother, Mrs. Ellison would have been told she was there and safe. Or Mrs. Mason herself would have sent Emma home again, with orders to stay here."

Towson stared at him briefly over the rim of his cup. "Are you trying to tell me that after only a few days here, you believe that Emma is dead, and that Constable Hensley is being blamed for her death? That that was why he was shot?"

"I'm saying that whatever became of Emma — whether she died here in Dudlington or something appalling happened to her on her way to London — on her own she might never have considered doing anything so rash as running away."

"Yes, well, that's one way to look at it." Towson sighed. "I'm a trained priest, I know the shortcomings of human nature as well as most. It's just that I don't want to think of the child as dead. I'm sorry. I'd like to believe that her mother came back, and so one day might Emma."

"With or without a child?"

Towson stared. "You are a very hard man, in your own fashion. That was a cruel thing to say."

Rutledge, leaving the rectory with a borrowed umbrella in his hand, asked the Reverend Towson if there were other strangers in the village, either as visitors or on business.

Towson, shivering in the cold air after the warmth of his parlor, answered, "I've not heard of anyone. And as a rule, in time I hear most gossip. Are you suggesting now that it could be something in Constable Hensley's past that caught up with him? Rather than trouble over Emma Mason?"

Rutledge fell back on the tried-and-true formula of an inquiry. "Early days, yet, to be sure of anything. I'm keeping an open mind."

Towson said doubtfully, "Yes, I see."

But Rutledge tilted his umbrella against the downpour and began picking his way over the flagstones that made up the path to the rectory gate, unwilling to be drawn into any explanation for his personal interest in strangers.

When he reached the constable's house again and climbed the stairs, intent on changing out of his wet clothing, the shell casing was gone.

He left early the next morning, as soon as it was light and the rain had become a raw drizzle.

Hamish was in a worse mood than the weather warranted and kept up a running argument about what Rutledge was intending to do.

It was a long drive back to London, and he was, in fact, absent without leave from his duties.

But Hensley was safe in hospital, and his

wounding could wait for twenty-four hours.

"Aye, but no' if he's released, and you havena' taken anyone into custody."

"Hensley is as safe as houses. For now. On the other hand, someone was there in Dudlington, to leave and retrieve that cartridge case. He's playing with us. When he's bored with that, or satisfied that he's put the fear of God into us, he'll decide whether we're to live or die. It's a matter of time. Do you want to take that risk?"

He hadn't realized that he'd used the plural *we*.

Hamish said, "I willna' die twice. Until I'm ready."

"No. But it's rather like crossing No Man's Land again. You don't know where or when death is coming. And there's no way to stop this fool, unless we look into the shadows for him."

Outside London there was a brief smattering of sleet before the temperature climbed again and the sun bravely tried to find a way through what was left of the clouds.

Rutledge stopped at his flat long enough to look through the post lying on his parlor carpet and then put in a call to Maryanne Browning.

She was at home and surprised to hear from him.

"Ian, how are you? Frances had said you were in the north on a case."

"I am, or should be. Other business brought me back to London. Can you give me Mrs. Channing's direction? I'd like to contact her."

"What on earth for? Don't tell me you believe she could help you with your inquiries?"

He laughed. "Hardly that, Maryanne. Where can I find her?"

"Well, she's on the telephone," she answered doubtfully, and gave him Mrs. Channing's number.

"I don't want to ring her up, I want to know where she lives."

"Oh, why didn't you say so?" She rummaged in some papers, their rustle coming through clearly to him, and he could picture her sitting in that tiny closet, looking for her address book. Finally she gave him what he needed, and he rang off.

Mrs. Channing lived in Chelsea, in a small house near the hospital. He'd interviewed witnesses in Chelsea any number of times, but now he felt a sense of unease as he reached her door.

It was intensified by stiff resistance from

Hamish, who clearly wished to be else-where.

"I didna' care for this woman then, and I do na' care for her now."

She answered his knock herself and said without any inflection of pleasure or sur-prise, "Mr. Rutledge. Or should I address you as Inspector? This isn't a social occa-sion, I take it." Her voice was as he re-membered, low pitched and compelling.

"I want to talk to you, if I may. About the séance," he told her baldly, and she stepped aside to invite him into the house.

He wasn't sure what he had expected to find here. It would have been easier if the furnishings had been exotic, with gypsy flair or an aura of the Arabian Nights, to dismiss her as a fraud. A woman who used her parlor tricks to gain entrance to society homes. Instead he'd walked into the sort of house any relatively well-to-do widow might own, for there were no men's coats on the rack in the entrance hall, no hats on the hooks, and no sign of a man's taste in the small drawing room decorated in pale shades of lavender and rose. She herself was dressed in black, with a white lace collar, an ordinary woman on the surface.

But what lay below that surface?

She sat down opposite him and waited.

He suddenly found it awkward to begin. Mrs. Channing's face showed only polite interest, her hands folded in her lap, her serenity unruffled by the brief, uncomfortable silence.

"She kens why you're here," Hamish warned silently.

Finally she said, "It was something about the séance, Inspector?"

"I left early the evening you entertained Mrs. Browning's guests. As you may recall. And I found something unexpected on the step outside her door."

He reached into his pocket and took out the first of the machine-gun cartridge casings, which he'd retrieved from his desk at the flat.

She leaned forward to see it more clearly but made no effort to take it and examine it closely. "It's a cartridge case, of course. I have no idea what kind."

"It's from a Maxim machine gun."

"Indeed," she commented, sitting back in her chair. "Why have you brought this to me? Did you think it was mine?"

"Or meant for you. Anyone who knew the guest list might have assumed that a woman alone wouldn't choose to stay as late as a couple. But I received an unexpected call from the Yard, and so I was the first of the guests to go down the front steps."

She smiled. "My dear Inspector, I'd never have given it a thought, even if I'd seen it. And if Dr. Gavin had left before you did, I don't believe he'd have paid it any attention either. Commander Farnum on the other hand was in the Royal Navy. He'd have recognized it, no doubt, and even wondered how it had got there, but he wouldn't have picked it up and kept it."

"Yes, I've considered that."

Mrs. Channing studied his face for a moment. "But you were in the trenches, I'm told. This would have taken you back, I think, to the killing. And you'd have wondered why the war had intruded again on a peaceful London."

It was so close to the mark, he was silent.

"Have there been others?"

Rutledge was on the verge of denying it, and then answered truthfully. If this woman had had anything to do with the cartridges, she already knew the answer. And if she hadn't, telling her would do no harm.

"There've been three others."

Hamish was clamoring for his attention, warning him to walk carefully.

"Yes, that's when you realized that the

163

first one was indeed intended for you. But why have you come here, if you knew the answer to that? Why would you think I might recognize them?"

"A policeman always makes certain his information is correct. You were the only person at Maryanne's party I didn't know."

"I see." She digested that.

"You hold séances for the amusement of your friends. What would you do, if you raised the dead during one of them?"

"I'd be stunned, Inspector. It isn't my intention and I have no — talent in that direction, thank God! What I do have is a rather good instinct for what people find entertaining. As soon as one of Maryanne's guests thought that the King's spaniel was her own beloved dog, I made certain not to tread in that direction. We had a rather interesting discussion instead on whether or not Charles II had climbed that oak tree, or if it were merely a legend. After that we had a few words with Lord Nelson, to amuse Commander Farnum. You had nothing to fear, you know."

"What makes you believe I was fearful?"

"It was there in the strain of your voice, and in your eyes. I had no intention of exposing your secrets. I'd have avoided them. But you couldn't believe that, of course.

Whether that was a policeman's natural distrust of everyone or your own vulnerability, I couldn't say. I should think it was the latter."

"My secrets?" He made it a question. Hamish was loud in his ears.

"Ah, we come at last to the real reason why you're here today. I saw you once before New Year's Eve, if that's what's worrying you. But I'd never have said so, unless you spoke of it first. I was in a casualty station in France, well behind the lines, but still close enough to receive the worst cases. You'd come to ask about a young soldier, and when the doctor told you he was dying in spite of all we could do, you sat there with him until the end. I never forgot that."

He didn't have to ask who the man was. He remembered him vividly. Sergeant Williams, who should have died on the battlefield but somehow held on long enough to be sent back. Machine-gun fire had struck him in both legs. Rutledge had had to write a letter to his parents that night. *Your son was a good and brave soldier. It was an honor to serve with him, and you can be proud of his courage under fire and the care he showed to his men . . .*

It hadn't begun to say what Rutledge

knew about Williams — little things, like how fond he was of sweets, and how he shouted at his wounded, telling them they weren't to die on his watch, by God, and how he hated the machine gunners —

Coming back to the present, Rutledge asked, "And was that the only time you saw me?" For it hadn't been many months before he'd been brought in to the same station suffering from shell shock and claustrophobia, barely alive because Hamish's body had given him a tiny pocket of air to breathe long enough to be dug out of the shell hole in time and carried half-conscious back to the doctors. They had patched him up and sent him forward again, after a few hours' rest and a shot of whiskey.

"It was." She didn't add that it wasn't the last time she'd had news of him.

"You'd make a good policeman," he said, trying to divert the conversation.

She laughed, a throaty laugh that was warm and filled with humor. "Surely policemen aren't the only ones who understand human nature. A good clergyman must, and a good doctor as well. Why shouldn't a mere woman have the same gift?"

He smiled in response. "I never thought

of you as a 'mere woman.' But you use your gifts in unexpected ways."

"Your intuition brought you here. My intuition can take me places as well."

"Then tell me, if you will, where these shell casings are coming from. Why I've found them wherever I go." It was a challenge.

After a moment, she said, "May I see it again?" And this time she took the casing and held it for a moment without looking at it. Finally, she examined the design.

"Were the others the same? Just poppies in rows, perhaps a reminder of the dead in France?"

"No. Look just there. See that face, or skull, just visible? It grows more noticeable in each of the others. And the last one had no pattern at all."

Turning the case, she found the skull and nodded. "Perhaps whoever is doing this only had three that were engraved."

He had considered that possibility.

"If I were to tell you what I think, you must realize it's nothing more than an educated guess."

"I'll accept that."

"Someone would like to see you suffer as he's suffered. You're to feel hunted, persecuted. Afraid. The suggestion is that you belong among the war dead, not here in London, alive —"

Mrs. Channing broke off as she saw the expression on his face.

"You've already thought about that, haven't you?"

"Many times," he managed to say. But he had answered her with the unvarnished truth as well as his interpretation of the designs on the cases.

"You must ask yourself whether whoever is doing this chose you — that is to say, Ian Rutledge — or if you are, so to speak, a surrogate for others. As opposed to a purely random target."

He was beginning to feel claustrophobic in this handsome, feminine room. Hamish, in the back of his mind, was keeping up a barrage of furious comment. And the woman before him was too aware of what he was thinking. What he was feeling.

Rutledge got to his feet. "I must go, I've a long drive ahead of me."

"Yes." She made no attempt to persuade him to stay. Instead she followed him to the door, handing him his hat and coat.

"You've been very helpful," he told her, trying to make amends for his rudeness. "Thank you."

"I've only confused you more, Inspector," she answered ruefully. "I'm sorry."

She closed the door before he was halfway down the walk.

He searched the motorcar carefully as he got in, expecting to find another casing there. If he could be followed to Hertford and Northamptonshire, he could be followed back to London.

But there was nothing on the seats or on the floor.

For some reason that was not reassuring.

It wasn't until much later that he realized he'd left the original cartridge case behind.

Rutledge drove to within a mile of the Yard, left the motorcar behind a hotel, and stood on a street corner within sight of the main entrance of the Yard. He waited there for half an hour, watching for Sergeant Gibson to leave at the end of the day.

Gibson was surprised to see him and said bluntly, "You're supposed to be in the North. Sir."

"I know. I need information."

"About Constable Hensley?"

"Exactly."

"I don't know more than I told you. He was posted to the North without fanfare."

"Something to do with the Barstow inquiry."

"Talk in the canteen was that he'd

stepped on the wrong toes and was being exiled. Out of sight, out of mind, so to speak."

"I've heard that there was a fire at Barstow's place of business, and that someone died, a clerk who had come back to the office unexpectedly."

"He was badly burned, I remember that. And died months afterward."

"Will you find out what you can about the man, the fire, and Constable Hensley's role in the inquiry?"

Gibson gave him a sharp glance. "The minute I start to ask questions, word will fly to the Chief Super's ear."

St. Margaret's Church was just visible from where Rutledge was standing. It was where he'd last seen Jean, going in with her bridesmaids a few days before her wedding to the diplomat. He wondered if he would feel the same sense of loss today, if she walked up to the church door. The same grief.

He wanted to be gone from here. "If all else fails, there are newspaper files. Don't call me. Send the packet by post."

"Do you know what you're doing, sir?" Gibson asked, his eyes still on Rutledge's face.

"In my view, that arrow couldn't have

been an accident. If it isn't Dudlington that's behind the intent to kill Hensley, then London must have caught up with him. If anyone gives you trouble over this, tell them we have to eliminate other possibilities."

"I'll be sure to do that, sir. In the fervent hope it'll do some good."

With that, Gibson pulled his collar up and walked off.

It was a long and cold drive back to Northamptonshire. The rain caught up with him again thirty miles outside London, as if it had been lying in wait.

He regretted going to speak to Meredith Channing. It had achieved nothing, and he felt he'd betrayed more than he'd learned.

It had been unsettling to hear that she'd seen him in France. It was what he'd considered from the beginning, and he hadn't been pleased to confirm it.

For the next thirty miles, he debated her role in what had happened. He couldn't picture her shooting at him from behind a hedgerow.

"It was a dead soldier," Hamish reminded him. "So the lad said."

"Dead soldiers don't lie in wait with a real revolver. Whatever Tommy Crowell saw, it wasn't a corpse."

But then what had it been?

"It doesna' signify," Hamish told him. "You have a duty to yon constable."

"It won't help Hensley if I'm dead before he is," Rutledge retorted.

He stopped in Northampton. Matron was not pleased to see him, but late as it was, he received permission to step into the ward and have a look at Hensley.

"But you're not to wake him, do you hear? He's still in a great deal of pain, and we've just given him something to ease it so that he can sleep."

"I won't speak to him," Rutledge promised.

When he walked quietly down the row of beds, he was accompanied by a cacophony of snores. He couldn't help but wonder how anyone could sleep through the noise.

He reached Hensley's bed and went to stand beside the man stretched out there, half on his back, half on his side. Lines of pain marked his face, visible even in the dim light of the single lamp on the ward sister's table, and Hensley was not snoring. The sleep was deeper, drugged. One hand was curled into a fist, as if it had been clenched as Hensley drifted into unconsciousness.

After a moment, Rutledge turned and walked back the way he'd come.

The sister at the table said quietly, "You look very tired, Inspector. I hope you don't have far to go tonight."

"Thank you, no." She wasn't the plump nurse who had been angry with him on his first visit. A much younger woman, with kind eyes and a pleasant smile. A face it would be nice to wake up to, in the morning, if you were ill or in pain.

And even as he thought it, he realized how tired he actually was.

By the time he reached Hensley's house in Dudlington, closer to dawn than to midnight, he felt bone weary. Still, he walked through the rooms, torch in hand, and searched them carefully.

In one corner of his mind, he'd half expected to find the shell casing that he'd left in Chelsea sitting somewhere here, waiting for him.

14

The cold rain had given way to colder sunshine, and Rutledge felt the stiffness in his body that came from heavy sleep in a room without a fire.

Hamish, apparently already awake, said sourly, "The Oaks would be mair comfortable."

"That's very likely." Rutledge swung his feet out of bed and looked at the clock. He'd missed his breakfast. Mrs. Melford would be furious with him for missing his meals yesterday as well.

Just then he heard her calling to him from the foot of his stairs, and remembered that there was no key to the house door.

"Inspector! Your eggs are growing cold, and I shan't keep them warm more than five minutes longer."

The outer door slammed, and Rutledge went to fetch his shaving gear.

In the event, he was a good seven minutes late, and Mrs. Melford glared at him as he came into her dining room. But she brought his breakfast, and he found he was hungry.

"Any news of the constable?" she asked, as if assuming his absence had been spent in Northampton.

"Resting."

She went to fetch a rack of toast and set it before him with a pot of marmalade.

"Are you any closer to finding whoever it was shot him?"

"Not yet."

"Yes, well, we'd all expected the Yard to be more efficient."

"The Yard," he answered her shortly, "works with information. Apparently in Dudlington, there's none to be had."

She disappeared again and came back with warmed milk. He found himself thinking how different mornings had been in Westmorland, where the kitchen had seemed an oasis of warmth and brightness. Had it been love he'd felt there, three weeks ago — or only his loneliness responding to something rare: unforced companionship? He'd probably never know the answer to that now. And he must learn not to wish for more than a brief friendship. The letter from Elizabeth Fraser had been clear. *Don't come back —*

Hamish was restless, urging him to finish

his meal and leave the past where it could do no harm. "Ye canna' marry anyone. It's no wise."

Mrs. Melford was saying, "Everyone in Dudlington has been wondering why it was you interviewed Grace Letteridge."

He came back to the present with a jolt. "Do you suspect her of complicity in Hensley's attack?" he countered.

Her mouth tightened. "Really, Inspector!"

"Miss Letteridge had spent some time in London. In the early years of the war. I spoke to her about that."

Disappointed, she said, "She'd been a good friend to Emma. We were wondering if that had anything to do with your visit. So soon after you'd spoken with Mrs. Ellison."

"You knew Emma Mason, then?"

"Everyone did, Inspector. She was a bright, pretty, sweet-natured girl."

"What does Dudlington think happened to her?"

"She's buried somewhere in Frith's Wood. That's what they say. Although the wood was searched and there was no over-turned ground or other evidence of digging. Still, whoever it was could have waited until after the search to put her into the ground," she added ghoulishly.

He thought about the empty rooms in Hensley's house, and how easy it would be to leave a body there until it could be moved.

Hamish reminded him of the unlocked door.

That's true. But no one appears to go beyond the parlor. More to the point, Hensley is Caesar's wife — a policeman and above suspicion, he answered silently. And then aloud he asked, "I'd have thought her grandmother would have contacted Emma's mother, to ask if Emma was there."

"Poor woman, she doesn't know where her daughter is. She won't admit that, you know, but Miss Arundel, our postmistress, says that letters have come back marked *Unknown.* For years now."

"Which means Emma could indeed be in London with her mother. And Mrs. Mason doesn't intend to send her back to Dudlington."

Mrs. Melford frowned. "I suppose that's true." But her tone of voice indicated that she was far from believing it was.

He finished his tea and rose to leave. "Thank you for waiting for me this morning. It won't happen again."

Without acknowledging his apology, she

turned and went back to her kitchen. He found his account on the table by the stairs and paid it.

Rutledge walked down Church Street to the far end. Beyond the rectory stood the barn from which Ted Baylor had heard his dog barking.

Baylor was a younger man than Rutledge had expected. Dressed in muddy boots, dark corduroy trousers, and a heavy coat that emphasized the width of his shoulders, he stopped stock-still as the man from London came down the stone-flagged passage between the milking stalls where cows were lined up head-in, their rumps steaming in the cold air.

"Mr. Baylor? Good morning," Rutledge said. "I've been told it was your dog that alerted you to trouble in Frith's Wood the day that Constable Hensley was shot."

Baylor regarded him warily. "It was."

"Had you noticed anything else unusual that day? Crows taking flight across the field, for example, or other signs that there might be something going on?"

"Never saw the crows," he answered.

"Perhaps the dog had, and that's what started the barking."

"Pity you can't ask *him*," Baylor retorted.

"Does he bark at the wood from time to time? Scenting rabbits —"

"Not much of anything lives in Frith's Wood."

"What about your wife — or children?"

"I have no wife — nor any children. My half brother lives with me. And he doesn't tend the cattle."

"I'd like to ask him, all the same."

Baylor shrugged. "He won't see you. Now I have work to do."

"Not just yet," Rutledge replied briskly. "What did you see when you went into the wood?"

"I saw nothing but trees, and I didn't much like that. I was about to leave when the dog started rooting around, and it was then I saw a foot showing from behind a bush. Went around to the other side of the bush, and there was the constable, facedown in the leaves, white as a sheet, and cold into the bargain."

"Had he been moved, do you think? From where he'd been shot?"

"I didn't notice. But there were scuff marks, as if he'd dragged himself a bit."

Signs lost, Rutledge thought to himself, when the men came in to rescue Hensley. "Did you point these marks out to anyone else?"

"No, why should I have done? He'd lain there for two hours or more, it was natural he'd tried to help himself."

"You work with cattle. Could you have lifted Hensley and carried him some distance?"

"Look here! I never touched him."

"I'm sure you didn't. My question was, could you have carried him to safety, out of the woods, if you'd had to?"

"I very much doubt it. Not with that arrow in his back. It was obscene, him lying there, cold as a fish, and an arrow jutting from him, for all the world as if Red Indians had been at him. I'd not have touched him, without the doctor asking me to try. Besides, once I'd told the doctor to come right away, I fetched a hurdle from the barn and took it back with me. And some others heard me shouting and came to help."

He slapped the flank of a cow, moving her over a little, and added, "Bad enough when Dr. Middleton had us hold Hensley firmly while he broke the shaft well above the wound. You'd have thought he'd done it all his life, he was so clever at it. Hensley never moved." His voice was admiring. "Not something you see every day. Not even in the war."

"How do you explain someone using a bow and arrow in Frith's Wood?"

"I don't. That wood is not like any other I've ever seen. If I were a drinking man, I'd swear the place is full of God knows what, and Hensley was a fool to tempt whatever it is lives in there."

"Was he looking for Emma Mason's grave?"

A change in expression crossed Baylor's face. "The whispers say she's buried in there. I was in France, I don't know the truth of it. But in my view, there's no one who'd have gone in there to dig a grave, in the first place. There's no telling what might have come to light."

"Hensley went there. At least once."

"The constable comes from London. What does he know about Frith's Wood? I saw you going in there, walking about. What did *you* think of it?"

Hamish said, "It's a challenge."

Rutledge was on the point of quoting Hamlet, that there were more things in between heaven and earth than were dreamt of in most philosophies. Instead he replied, "I don't know that I'd like living so near to it. As you do."

"The cows won't go near it, even when they're in the pastures closest to it. Not for

181

shade in summer or protection from the weather when it rains. But I'm safe enough here." He turned and looked in the direction of his house, even though he couldn't see it from inside the barn.

"Why do you think the dog barked?"

"He heard the constable groaning, very likely. He's trained to work the animals, he'd have paid heed to it."

Rutledge thanked him and left.

Hamish said, "A stiff man. And honest enough. But with something worrying him, all the same."

"The half brother, perhaps," Rutledge answered.

He stopped at the kitchen door and knocked, but no one came to the door or to any of the windows overlooking the back garden and the sheds.

He made himself a note to ask about the elusive half brother. If Mrs. Melford wouldn't tell him, Dr. Middleton might.

Walking back to Holly Street, Rutledge decided to stop in the shops on Whitby Lane and found himself in the greengrocer's, stepping over a basket of apples from the south. He remembered the wizened, sour ones that were good only for jelly in the Lake District, where the growing season was so much shorter.

The sign over the door had read FREEBOLD AND SON, and Rutledge nodded to the man standing behind the cabbages. "Mr. Freebold? Or son?"

"Son. My father and grandfather, God rest them, have gone on to their just rewards," he responded affably. "How may I serve you, sir?"

Turning his back on the two or three women in the shop, Rutledge introduced himself and said, "I'm interested in Frith's Wood. Everyone tells me it isn't a safe place to go. And yet Constable Hensley appears to have gone there, of his own free will. I'm trying to find someone in Dudlington who might have seen him walk that way."

"I've not heard of anyone," Freebold answered, glancing over Rutledge's shoulder at the women in his shop. Apparently they had shaken their heads, for Freebold turned back to Rutledge and said, "Someone did say early on that he was seen leaving for Letherington that day."

"On his bicycle?"

"Yes, he was a great one for the bicycle." Freebold patted his own girth and added, "My days on two wheels are long vanished, right enough."

Behind him, Rutledge could hear one of the women titter.

"Then what became of the bicycle, do you think? I'm told no one found it there in the wood."

"Which isn't to say he didn't come home and go out again. He wasn't what you'd call overworked here in Dudlington. He'd take an hour or so and pay a visit to The Three Horses in Letherington, if he found that Inspector Cain wasn't about. He was something fond of The Three Horses."

"Why not stop at The Oaks?"

"I expect Constable Hensley and Frank Keating didn't see eye to eye," Freebold answered with some reluctance. "You'd best ask Keating about that."

Rutledge thanked him and left.

Half an hour later, he was walking into The Three Horses, in Letherington. It was a sizeable village, with two churches to Dudlington's one, and three pubs. The Three Horses was the oldest, with a smoky interior and old oak walls set with horse-racing memorabilia.

The owner, it transpired, had once been a jockey.

"Rode three winners," he said to Rutledge, pride in his eyes. "Derby winners at that! Josh Morgan is the name." He was a small, wiry man with a large head and lively gray eyes.

Rutledge asked for a pint and, when it was brought, engaged Morgan in conversation about his winners and then asked, "I understand Constable Hensley came here when he was in Letherington."

"Oh, yes, we were blessed often enough with his company. A quiet man, except when he got to talking about London. Then he could go on for an hour without repeating himself!"

"Much of a ladies' man?"

"He would chat up whoever was in the saloon, but it was more in aid of his own view of himself. He never gave them — or me — any trouble, I will say that for Constable Hensley."

"You've heard about the arrow in his back?"

"Inspector Cain was telling us what happened. I'm glad to hear the constable survived. Nasty piece of business! But then I'm told Frith's Wood isn't a place to meddle with. I've never been there, you understand. I'm not what you might call superstitious, except perhaps on race day, but I believe in leaving well enough alone."

"Had he been in Letherington that day? I hear he sometimes stops in at The Three

Horses when he knows Inspector Cain isn't likely to find him taking his time getting back to Dudlington."

"He didn't show himself here," Morgan answered, shaking his head. "And that would be unlike him. Always one for the road, he'd say. Not a drinking man, mind you," he added hastily. "But he'd have a pint, sometimes two, before heading back. Ale was his choice. The darker the better. And he could carry what he drank. No harm done."

"What did he talk about, as a rule?"

"Racing. He was a football man as well, and he hated Manchester with a passion. Nearly came to blows over that one once, when we had a Manchester man in the bar. Lorry driver, he was. Big as a house." Morgan grinned. "I was on my knees praying there'd be no brawl. They could have wrecked half the bar, between them. But Constable Hensley said he must get home to the missus, and he left. I offered Manchester a drink on the house, to see him on his way. Just to prevent the two from meeting on the road somewhere."

"I didn't think Hensley was married," Rutledge commented. The house in Dudlington was empty. Was there a wife hidden away somewhere else?

Morgan laughed again. "There's a woman who nags him if he's late for his dinner. He always said it was as good as being married, but without the fuss."

Barbara Melford, then. She would be furious to learn she was being described as Hensley's "missus."

"Do you think Hensley was afraid of someone? Or worried about being followed?"

"He never said as much to me. Of course it's possible. He was a policeman, wasn't he? They're after telling everyone what to do, if we get out of line. Hensley was no exception. It wouldn't endear him to everyone."

No one else at the pub was helpful, although they appeared to be concerned about Hensley's condition and wished him well. A far cry from the attitude just a few miles away in Dudlington.

On his way back to the motorcar, Rutledge heard Hamish say, as clearly as if he had followed at Rutledge's heels, "The bicycle was hidden in the field, but he didna' ride it this far."

"Which means," Rutledge answered, "he either changed his mind about coming to Letherington, or was waylaid before he could get here."

"It's verra' likely," Hamish said, "that he lied about where he was going."

"And someone caught him in the wood."

"He willna' tell ye that."

A motorcycle roared past as Rutledge cranked his engine into life. He watched it out of sight, then said thoughtfully, "That's an easy way to get about. If I had distance to cover."

"Aye, but where do you hide it? It's no' like a bicycle, shoved into the weeds."

But Rutledge was searching his memory for the sound of a motorcycle near Beachy Head, or on the road to Hertford. And drew a blank.

"Aye, but if yon laddy, Tommy Crowell, was right, the shooter is dead," Hamish told him, his voice a taunt.

15

Once again his luncheon was waiting for him on the sideboard in the dining room, covered by a serviette embroidered with Mrs. Melford's initials. Sandwiches, with ham and a very good cheese. There were pickles in a dish, and sliced apples, looking very much like those he'd seen that morning at the greengrocer's.

Rutledge sat down in the silence of the house, wondering if Mrs. Melford was at home and avoiding him, or if she had gone out.

He was halfway through his second sandwich when there was a knock at the house door. Rutledge hesitated, unwilling to answer it if Barbara Melford was not at home. Then it opened, and a male voice called, "Barbara, are you in there?"

The man came into the hall and then as far as the dining room, on his way to the kitchen. And almost fell over his own feet when he saw Rutledge.

It was Ted Baylor, his boots cleaned and his trousers changed, his hair freshly brushed.

"Good afternoon," Rutledge said, concealing a smile. Baylor was completely disconcerted, uncertain at first what to say, like a suitor stumbling over his rival.

"I didn't know you were invited to lunch here," he finally blurted out.

Hamish said, "Yon's a verra' possessive man!"

Choosing his words carefully, Rutledge answered, "Mrs. Melford was kind enough to offer to prepare my meals. I'm staying in Hensley's house, and his kitchen leaves much to be desired."

"Is she here, then?" Baylor looked around the room, as if half expecting her to be hiding behind the furniture.

"I haven't seen her. If you'd care to wait —"

For an instant he stood there, debating his choices.

"The hell with it, then," Baylor said finally, and turned on his heel.

The front door slammed. Hamish commented dryly, "He willna' screw his courage up to come again."

Rutledge answered, "You may be right. I don't think I'll tell her she missed Baylor."

He finished his sandwich and the apples, then took the empty plates and his cup into the kitchen.

It was his turn to stop on the threshold in surprise.

Mrs. Melford was sitting at her own kitchen table, her face in her hands, crying.

"I'm sorry," he began, uncertain now what to do with the dishes.

She looked up at him. "Why couldn't you stay in the dining room, where you belonged?" Her voice was bitter and accusing, as if he'd come into the kitchen on purpose, with malicious intent to embarrass her.

"I thought you'd gone out." He set the dishes by the sink and turned to go. "Is there anything I can do?" he asked, concerned for her.

"No! Yes! You can go away and leave me alone."

"When you've assured me that you're all right."

She took a deep breath and found a tea towel to wipe away her tears. "It's nothing. Or at least nothing you can repair. Worst luck."

"You ken, she heard the man's voice. But you were there, in the way, and he wouldna' go on to the kitchen."

Rutledge disagreed. There was more to her distress than a missed rendezvous. She could have come through from the kitchen and taken Baylor into the parlor, out of earshot.

He felt helpless, uncertain whether it was best to leave her to cry or to try to comfort her. Because there was anger mixed with her tears, he decided he ought to go.

After a brief hesitation, he walked to the door and reached out to push it open.

She said, at his back, "Sometimes I don't understand how a man can tell you he loves you more than life itself — and then can walk away, leaving you to believe he's a liar."

Without turning, he stood there facing the door and said, "Had he made promises?"

"He wrote to me during the war. He said if he lived, he wanted to marry me. I'd lost my husband only a year after our wedding, in 1912. Ted and I had known each other since we were children, and I cared for him. I told him I'd be here waiting when he came home. And he was one of the fortunate ones, he survived. The day he came back to Dudlington, I was twenty again, as excited as a girl. You can't imagine how I felt. He went past the house, without a glance, I saw him. And he shut himself up in that farm of his and never said a word to me. Then or later. I could hardly knock at his door and ask him *why*. I had my pride."

"Why did he come here today? After all this time?"

"God knows. I don't. Oh, we've met before — this village is too small to avoid running into each other at St. Luke's or in the shops. We nod without speaking. I have my *pride*," she repeated, through clenched teeth. "I won't let him see that it matters. And it's too late to make amends. What I might have felt for him is *gone*." Her voice broke again on the last word.

Rutledge stood there, waiting. But she'd said all she needed to say. He pushed open the door and left her in the kitchen.

When he came to the house for his evening meal, he expected to find the door locked. But it was open, and his food was ready for him on the sideboard. Mrs. Melford didn't put in an appearance then or at breakfast.

The post brought Rutledge a package the next morning. The handwriting was unfamiliar but graceful.

Inspector Ian Rutledge. Dudlington, Northants.

There was no return address.

He opened the small box and inside, folded in a sheet of paper, was the cartridge case he'd inadvertently left at Mrs. Channing's.

The sheet of paper was a note.

I asked Miss Rutledge for your present direction, and she has found it for me. You had forgotten to take this with you when you left, and I dislike having it in my house. I don't know why, it's merely a metal casing. But the more I look at it the more uncomfortable I feel. There's something evil about it, in a way. I'd have liked to bury it in the dustbin and be rid of it. However, it isn't mine to dispose of, and so I return it.

He could hear her low, pleasant voice in the words as he read them, and for a moment he could see her sitting at the little walnut desk in her drawing room, writing the letter. It was such a vital image that he was surprised.

He laid the letter aside and looked again at the case.

Once more he asked himself if the shot on the road to Hertford had been meant to kill him. Or only to frighten him?

Hamish said, "If it was to kill, why leave the three casings in the hedgerow?"

194

Because, Rutledge thought, he came prepared. For either eventuality. Which said that he hadn't really cared how it had turned out. He had just folded the letter and put the shell case in his pocket when there was a timid knock at the door, and a young woman stood on the threshold, poised to back away. He put her age down as sixteen.

"Come in," Rutledge said, giving her his name and moving around the desk to the far side, to leave the room to her.

She stepped shyly into the office, looking around as she introduced herself as Martha Simpson.

He thought, She's never been in Hensley's house before. "Please." He pointed to the chair across from the desk.

"I'm so sorry to disturb you. But I've overheard my mother tell a friend that you'd been asking questions about Emma . . ."

What had the rector said about gossip?

"Yes, that's true. Did you know her?"

She glanced at the other chair as if uncertain whether she ought to sit or remain standing. "I went to school with her. We weren't the best of friends — her grandmother didn't approve of me."

"Why on earth would you believe that?" he asked, trying to put her at her ease.

"You seem perfectly respectable to me."

She laughed. "I'm the baker's daughter, you see. Not grand enough for Mrs. Ellison. But I rather liked Emma, and I've been very worried about her. I wondered if you'd had news of her. I couldn't ask her grandmother directly, I was always afraid I'd be told to mind my own business."

"Sadly, no, I haven't anything new to tell you. I asked questions for the simple reason that Constable Hensley had put down very little about her disappearance in his files. It seemed strange, given the fact that it was possible that murder had been done."

Martha winced at the word. "I'd not like to think of anything awful happening to her." She appeared to have conquered her initial shyness and finally sat down in the chair across from him. "She was talented, like her mother," she went on earnestly. "I've seen some of the watercolors belonging to Grace Letteridge. Emma could draw nearly as well. She did a portrait of me, once, in pastels. I still have it, it's framed in my room."

"Was Emma a good student?"

"She was very bright, yes. I rather admired that. I'm hopeless at mathematics, and she often helped me when I couldn't see how to do a problem. We sometimes studied together at Grace's house, after tea. I looked forward to it. She never made me feel young and useless."

And then with an unexpected maturity that came welling up as her confidence increased, she added, "I'd always believed that Emma went to find her mother, in spite of all the rumors to the contrary. Dudlington is a backwater, with nothing to offer a girl like Emma. There isn't an unmarried man here that her grandmother would have considered worthy of her. She wrote to her mother, from time to time, you know. And the letters were returned unopened. But we always suspected, Grace and I, that her mother felt Emma was far too young to come to London then. She needed to finish her schooling and grow up. That's understandable, since Mrs. Mason had brought her here for that purpose in the first place."

"You saw these returned letters? Do you by any chance know Mrs. Mason's direction?"

"No, Mrs. Ellison always burned them, angry with her daughter for treating Emma so shabbily. My mother often said it was shameful the way Beatrice Mason ignored her own flesh and blood. She'd known Beatrice, and she said she'd never expected her to turn out to be such a snob." She smiled deprecatingly, in defense of her mother. "But then you must have seen Mrs. Mason's exhibitions in London. She must be quite famous by now."

He not only hadn't seen them, he had never heard of an artist by that name. But then Beatrice Mason was rather staid for a painter hoping to take London by storm. Frances would know who she was . . . or who she pretended to be.

But Hamish was taking a different tack. "If she wasna' sae successful as that, mayhap she didna' care for her mither or the daughter to know the truth."

"I understand Miss Letteridge spent nearly two years in London at the start of the war. Did she look up Emma's mother while she was there?"

Martha Simpson had risen. "I've asked her that. She said she saw no point in it, since Mrs. Mason had never shown any desire to hear from Emma."

He wondered if Grace Letteridge had lied for Emma's sake.

Standing now, he asked casually, as if it wasn't important, "I'd have thought, at seventeen, Emma might have given her heart to someone here and lost interest in London altogether. It happens."

She bit her lip, as if misleading him came hard to her. "I don't know anything about that, Inspector." The denial had come too quickly. She added, "Emma never confided in me."

"But you knew her. You might have — er, guessed where her affections lay."

Martha shook her head vehemently. "No. There was no one she cared for. She went to London. I'll always believe that."

He pressed her. "If she's not with her mother, and not with a man she fell in love with, then what is the alternative?"

"She was too young to marry without her grandmother's permission. And she wouldn't have gone away with anyone, no matter how she felt about him — she'd been brought up to respect her grandmother. Emma wouldn't have caused her such shame."

He could imagine how the wives of the baker and the greengrocer and the butcher would have relished that sort of scandal, and taken pleasure in rubbing Mrs. Ellison's nose in her disgrace. He had to agree with Martha there.

"It's possible that Emma hoped her mother would give her the necessary permission."

"No. Somehow I can't believe — she'd

have come back if that were true." She was agitated, as if he'd accused Emma of being immoral. After a moment, she added, "I've made a mistake in coming here. I'd hoped for news. Constable Hensley wouldn't answer me either. It's frustrating when everyone believes you're too young to know the truth! But please don't tell my parents I was foolish enough to come here alone. They'll be angry with me. I'm sorry —" And she was out the door, without looking back.

He called to her, but it was too late.

Restless, he went for a walk to clear his head. He went as far as The Oaks, and then turned right, cutting across the wide sweep of fields that ran down to the little stream, where trees marked its winding path through the pastures behind Dudlington. The wind caught up with him as soon as he was out of the shelter of the village, and he could feel the cold penetrating his coat and touching his skin with icy fingers. No wonder the village turned its back on the fields, however picturesque they might seem — they faced west, and the prevailing winds met no resistance on this open land until it reached the stone and mortar of man's huddled world.

He turned and looked back. The sky was

a leaden bowl overhead, and the fields were a withered brown. Dudlington looked small and insignificant from here. Constable would have found very little of interest to paint on these highlands, even if the cattle in the barns were put out to graze.

From here he thought he could see the backs of brown sheep in the pastures across the main road. They were the color of dark rich gravy, and their winter coats were thick and heavy.

The fell sheep in Westmorland had been white under their blanket of snow. He wondered what they'd make of these tamer surroundings, protected and cosseted by Lake District standards. It was, he thought, a measure of the will to survive, that living things learned to cope. Then why had Ted Baylor chosen today, of all days, to try to mend Barbara Melford's broken heart? What had changed in his circumstances, or hers? Or had he come for an entirely different reason? Love? Or an attempt to survive? Baylor had been the first to find Constable Hensley lying there cold enough to be counted as dead.

Suddenly, without warning, Rutledge felt vulnerable, as if standing here he made a perfect target for anyone hunting him.

There was nothing to explain the sensation. Only a sixth sense honed in war. The small windows of the houses he could see from here were blank, closed against the wind. And from the long barns that held cattle, well out of the village itself, it was a very difficult shot. Even if someone lay concealed behind the sheep, it would take a rifle to hit him at that distance.

Still, he stood there, searching the land all around him, turning slowly.

It was empty, he would have sworn it was empty. But so was the headland in Kent and the Upper Pasture in Hertford.

Something caught his eye as he looked at the taller building sitting at the crossroads. He could have sworn he saw someone at a window of the inn, a slight movement.

Hamish said, "Ye're imagining trouble where there's none."

"You'll be as dead as I am, if I'm wrong," Rutledge answered tersely, the wind snatching the words out of his mouth.

"Aye. I'm no' ready to die. You willna' fail me a second time."

But Rutledge was already walking briskly toward The Oaks, his mind busy, his eyes no longer scanning the fields that seemed to stretch empty and forever around him.

He didn't care to be stalked. It was something that gnawed at the back of one's thoughts, always there.

Will it be here? Or will it be not at all?

And he found himself clenching his teeth with the sense of walking once more into heavy fire, as he'd done so many countless times in France.

I was in the war, he told himself. *And whoever it is hasn't counted on that.*

If the Germans couldn't kill him, by God, it wasn't going to be some coward lurking —

He stopped short.

Hamish said, "The dead soldier."

Dead, but without a gravestone in the churchyard.

"Yes," Rutledge said slowly, already moving again. "Only he wasn't dead after all. He'd disguised himself. Somehow. But Tommy Crowell wouldn't have known that. He'd have walked up to whatever it was he saw, to satisfy his curiosity. And the hunter, not wanting to risk shooting the boy, had frightened him instead."

"It wouldna' hae taken much to frighten him," Hamish answered. "The lad wouldna' understand."

"And if someone had heard him talking about a dead soldier lying in Mrs.

Massingham's grounds, he'd have been laughed at, made fun of."

He was halfway to The Oaks now, his strides long and angry.

Someone came out of the inn, walked over to a motorcar, and drove away, disappearing up the main road to the north.

By the time Rutledge reached the entrance of The Oaks, he was out of breath. He'd run the last hundred yards, swearing to himself as he went.

"Keating?" he called, striding into the bar.

There was no one there, and he crossed to the door of the saloon and stepped in.

The fire hadn't been lit, and the dark-paneled room was cold, shadowed. For an instant he thought he saw someone by the window and realized that it was a long portrait of a man in riding dress, standing in a leafy glade, his face turned toward a distant view that only he could see.

Shutting the door again, Rutledge went down the passage to the kitchen and startled Hillary Timmons into dropping a spoon she was drying.

"Oh, you did give me a start, sir!" she exclaimed, her hands going to her breast, as if afraid he was about to attack her.

He realized his anger and frustration

must be visible in his face. Striving to control both, he said, "I'm sorry, Miss Timmons. I was looking for Mr. Keating."

"I can't think where he might be," she answered, still tense. "But we're closed, sir. He may've stepped out for a bit."

"There was a motorcar just leaving. Do you know who the person was, driving?"

"I don't know, sir! I wasn't serving in the bar today. We'd only a handful of people there, and Mr. Keating said he'd see to them himself."

"Damn!"

She jumped again, and he apologized.

"Tell Keating I'm looking for him. I'll expect him to come to Hensley's house, as soon as he returns."

"He — he doesn't take lightly to orders, sir."

"Well, then, you can tell him that if he doesn't come to me, I'll come after him and drag him there myself."

And with that Rutledge turned on his heel, left the door to the kitchen swinging wildly, and walked out of the inn.

By the time he'd reached the house where he was staying, some of his anger had cooled.

But he felt that he was on the track of answers now.

16

Certain that Keating wouldn't be on his heels, Rutledge went into the bakery to find the postmistress.

A warm wave of yeast and cinnamon and rising bread greeted him as he stepped inside the door. The trays of baked goods displayed in a counter were already well picked over, as if the baker's shop had done a brisk business in scones and poppy seed cakes and dinner rolls.

There was a woman behind the counter who was so much like Martha Simpson that he assumed she was the girl's mother. Her face was pink with the warmth of the shop, and her apron was dusty with flour. He nodded to her and walked on to the tiny cage in one corner that served as the post office. Mrs. Arundel, a rangy woman of about thirty, was sitting on her stool, counting coins into a tin. She looked up as Rutledge came up to the cage, and smiled at him.

"Inspector Rutledge," she acknowledged. "What can I do for you?" She had tucked the coins out of sight and was reaching for a large book of stamps, as if prepared to send a letter for him. "You found your little box from London, did you? I asked Ben Lassiter to drop it by Constable Hensley's house on his way home."

"Yes, thank you. I wonder," he began, lowering his voice as Mrs. Simpson listened unashamedly to the conversation, "if you can recall sending letters to London for Emma Mason or her grandmother. I'm trying to locate Emma's mother."

"Indeed." She peered at him. "I do remember the letters going out with the post. But they were returned, for want of a proper address."

"How often did you see these letters?"

"Oh, not often — I expect one or two a year at most. It was sad, you know. Emma would come in with them, such hope in her face. And I took it personally when the letters came back, as if I were responsible for misdirecting them." She shook her head. "Very sad."

"How long have you been postmistress here?"

"Since August 1914, when my husband went to Northampton to enlist. He didn't come home, though he'd promised he

207

would if I let him go."

"I'm sorry."

"It was a waste," she said, "such a waste. We lost ten young men from Dudlington. And they're our dead. We've got seven more trying to cope with severe wounds. Another shot himself rather than live with both legs gone." She cleared her throat, as if the memories were too fresh. "Yes, well, letters to and from Beatrice Mason. I remember her, you know. Such a pretty girl, and so talented. I wished her well when she went off to London, and I always believed that Mrs. Ellison was too hard on her. Giving her an ultimatum, so to speak. Go and I shan't take you back. That's what Beatrice told my older sister. It's a choice, she said. I must make a choice. I can't imagine a mother being so harsh to her only child! But it's brought bitter fruit in its wake, hasn't it?"

"Why was Mrs. Ellison so adamant about Beatrice leaving? Was it money?"

"No, Mrs. Ellison is a stickler for the proprieties, I think, and the idea of her daughter hobnobbing with bohemian artists and naked models was more than she could bear. Nice girls didn't concern themselves with all that."

Mrs. Simpson spoke, breaking into the

conversation. "Beatrice was like her father. He would have taken her to London himself, if he'd been alive. To show her what sort of life she could expect there and prove to her that it wasn't the lovely adventure she'd dreamed it would be. Her mother just put her foot down, and for Beatrice, that was nothing short of the red flag in front of the bull."

Rutledge turned so that he could see both women. "What was Mason like, the man Beatrice married? Did Mrs. Ellison approve of him?"

"I doubt she ever met him," Mrs. Simpson commented. "He was dead by the time Emma was three or four. That's when Beatrice brought her home to be cared for by her grandmother. I don't think he had any desire to come to Dudlington, to tell you the truth. Beatrice had probably told him what a witch her mother was."

"What did he do for a living? Do you know?"

"Another artist, very likely," Mrs. Arundel said. "I never heard, other than that he was poor as a church mouse and left poor Beatrice nothing with which to feed herself or the baby."

"Mrs. Ellison told you that?"

"Lord, no!" Mrs. Simpson laughed. "We

got it from the woman that did for her sometimes, Betsy Timmons. I wouldn't put it past her to listen at keyholes —"

The shop door opened, and a woman came in with two small children. Mrs. Simpson turned away to greet her.

Mrs. Arundel said, in a voice that wouldn't carry, "I was told that Mr. Mason came from a very good family that had cut him off, much as Mrs. Ellison had cut Beatrice off. While he was alive, selling his work, they lived rather well. But after he died, there was no one to bring in such grand sums of money."

"Who told you that?"

"I believe it was Grace Letteridge. Who got it from Emma, most likely."

Hamish said, sourly, "Aye, the granny's fairy tale. To save her daughter's good name."

It would, Rutledge thought, be just like Mrs. Ellison to put as good a face on her family's trials as she could.

The door opened again, and a man stepped in, breathless and anxious, his eyes sweeping the shop and lighting on Rutledge.

"I'm looking for Inspector Rutledge."

"I'm Rutledge. What's happened?"

"Dr. Middleton sent me to find you. The

rector's had a terrible fall. He — Dr. Middleton — says it would be best if you come at once."

With a nod to the postmistress, Rutledge was out the door on the messenger's heels.

"What's happened to Mr. Towson?"

"He was in the attic, searching for something. He shouldn't have gone up there by himself. The stairs are small. He missed his step and fell hard on his hip. Dr. Middleton thinks it's broken."

"Who are you?" Rutledge asked as they hurried down Whitby Lane and turned into Church Street. "I don't believe we've met."

"My name is Ben Staley. Farmer. It was my wagon that carried Constable Hensley to Northampton."

At the rectory there were four or five men milling about in the parlor, their muddy boots tracking up the wood floors. Rutledge recognized Ted Baylor among them and asked, "Where's Middleton?"

Baylor jerked his head toward the stairs, and Rutledge went up them fast.

The passage that led to the bedchambers was dark, the doors shut.

Hamish was saying, "Which one?"

But farther along the passage to his left,

Rutledge could see light pouring from an open door, and he turned in that direction.

It was, as he thought, the door to the narrow, uncarpeted stairs leading up to the attics. Lying sprawled across the landing between the two flights was the rector, his face twisted in pain. Dr. Middleton was busy examining him with some care, trying to determine the extent of his injuries without doing further damage.

Hamish said, "It's a wonder he's no' dead."

Middleton looked up as Rutledge arrived, and said in a low voice, "I sent for you because there's something of a mystery about his fall. Here, take this."

He passed a bottle of laudanum to Rutledge and added, "I don't want to give him anything until I know whether the hip is broken, bruised, or dislocated."

His hands went on gently exploring the rector's body.

Rutledge took the bottle. "Shall I fetch a glass and a little water?"

"No, stay here and fend off the men below. I don't want them upsetting him."

The rector seemed half-conscious, his eyes sometimes rolling back in his head.

"Who found him?"

"It was Hillary Timmons. She comes to

212

clean for him in the afternoon, while the pub is closed. She heard something, thought it was an animal in pain, and went to look. When she found the rector, she was terrified out of her wits and went screaming next door to Ted Baylor. Fortunately he was in his barn, and he came at once for me. It was Hillary who told everyone else. I sent her home with Bob Johnson, with a powder to calm her."

He had spoken to Hillary Timmons at The Oaks. "I saw her not half an hour ago. How long has Towson been lying here?"

"No way of telling, except that the bruises are already showing up on his arms and his cheek, there. He might have been here for an hour or more."

The doctor rocked back on his heels, sighing. "Well, I don't think that hip's broken, thank God. Just badly bruised. With his rheumatism, using crutches would be difficult. But look at his arm. See the knot just there? It could mean a fracture. Time will tell."

"How are we going to move him from here, without hurting him appallingly?"

"That's where the laudanum comes in. Baylor was all for a stiff whiskey, but that's the worst possible solution to shock. We'll ease him a little and then find something to use to shift him to a bed."

"You said there was something wrong with the way he'd fallen?"

"Not so much that. He was awake for a few minutes, when I got here. He said he'd been in the attic searching for something, he couldn't recall what, and someone came to the stairs and called him to come quickly, there'd been an accident. Old fool turned, hurried down the steps, and missed his footing."

"Who was it?"

"That's the problem, Rutledge. There was no one here when Hillary came to clean. You'd have thought, with all the noise of the fall, whoever had been standing in the passage there, calling up for him to come at once, would have looked to see if Towson was alive or dead."

When Towson was quieter and in less discomfort, the men in the hall below took a leaf from the long dining room table — fit for a clergyman's large family — and brought it to the attic stairs. Middleton sent Rutledge through the bedchambers to collect blankets to pad it. Then between them, they lifted the rector onto the improvised stretcher and carried him to his own bed.

He lay there, white as his shirt, groaning in pain. Middleton sent the men about their business, with instructions to put the table back together before they left, and drew a chair up to the bedside.

After a moment he said to Rutledge, "That arm's fractured. Now I can feel the bones scraping together. But it isn't compound, and I can brace it. That knot on his head" — he parted the white hair to point out a large lump — "may mean he's concussed, worst luck. I'll have to ask someone to sit with him. And I'm still worried about that hip. It will keep him in bed for a bit. Why it didn't break is a mystery. Unless that arm took the brunt of his fall."

"Very likely," Rutledge agreed.

Hamish was busy asking who would want to kill the rector and supplying his own answers to the question. Rutledge ignored him until a word caught his attention.

"The attic windows. Ye ken, they look out toward yon wood."

"Can you spare me a moment?" Rutledge asked. "I'd like to have a look at those stairs again."

"First help me get him out of those trousers, while we can. It will take the two of us."

They removed the rector's black shoes and stockings, and then gently persuaded his trousers to peel away without lifting his body more than was necessary.

Middleton got him under the blankets, wrapped him well against shock, and then began to unbutton Towson's shirt.

Rutledge was surprised at how light the man was. Towson had seemed very vibrant and active, despite his rheumatism.

"Aye, and the fall should ha' kilt him," Hamish reminded Rutledge again.

Free at length to go back to the stairs, Rutledge examined them. The edges of the risers were worn, and the steps were steep, narrow, and not well lighted. It would be easy for a man to come down too quickly and fall.

He went on to the top of the steps and saw that the attic was fairly empty, some luggage, a trunk, and a few oddments of furniture hardly filling the vast space. Two rooms had been built in here for servants, one to the east and one to the west. They had windows, as did the central room. Rutledge pushed aside the iron bedsteads under the casements and stood there, looking out.

To the west he could see the long sweep of pasture, the line of the stream, and in the far, far distance, the tower of another church, barely visible.

"The next village," Hamish pointed out.

The east window looked out on the barns at the Baylor farm. He could see them clearly, and the kitchen door, the windows on this side of the house, and the chimney.

But from the central room the windows, a pair of them, looked out toward Frith's Wood. Only the treetops were visible, and the bend of the main road as it turned toward Letherington. And he could see the fields beyond the wood, rolling down to it.

If there was movement in the wood — a man in a dark coat, for instance — he thought perhaps he could follow it to some extent. It would have to be tested, to be sure, but it was certainly a possibility.

Hamish made the connection nearly as quickly as he had.

"If yon wood is sae clearly visible from here, I expect it can be seen from the house next door. Did you see that yon upper floor is a bit higher still?"

Rutledge went back to the east servant's room and looked again. Hamish had been right. The Baylor house, while not precisely turned toward the wood, must have windows that looked out on it, just as the rectory did.

It was an interesting point. But whether it would prove useful was another matter.

The question now was who had come to the stairs and called to the rector?

Rutledge sat with Towson for another hour, spelling Dr. Middleton, who had gone to his surgery for splints.

The rector did wake up for a brief period, amazed to find himself in his bed and hurting all through his body, as he put it.

Rutledge said, "Don't you recall falling down the attic stairs?"

Towson frowned. "Was I in the attic? I seldom go there."

"Today you were. And someone called to you, telling you that you were needed directly."

Towson lifted his good hand to his forehead, as if to find the memory there somewhere, within reach.

But whatever he had told Middleton in the first few moments after the doctor had arrived, he had no recollection of it now.

17

After Dr. Middleton had found someone to sit with Towson — Grace Letteridge, as it happened — Rutledge was free to return to Hensley's house, and he walked into the parlor office feeling depressed.

Hamish said, "You ken, it's likely he'll remember when he's slept."

But Dr. Middleton had not been very sanguine.

"Well, who knows? It was a shock, that fall, and he lay there afterward, unable to call for help. It would have been trying for a younger man."

"Still, he told you when you got there what had happened."

"Yes, well, I was salvation arriving on a white steed. Hillary is a sweet girl, but she's not reliable in an emergency. I was, and he must have held on, hoping for someone sensible enough to talk to. Then he could let it go."

Middleton had offered Rutledge a sherry, dug out of Towson's private store in the study, before he left the rectory.

"God knows I need it, and you might as well have the benefit of it too."

Rutledge didn't argue. And it was good sherry, at that.

"Why should someone call to him, tell him to make haste — and then walk away when he fell? It makes no sense," Middleton asked, sitting down in the best chair and stretching his feet out before him. "Unless of course he'd had some sort of seizure and only imagined he'd been called. That's possible too, you know."

But Rutledge, striding up Church Street, couldn't afford to ignore the alternatives. No policeman would.

Rutledge, taking the chair behind Hensley's desk, found himself thinking aloud out of long habit. "Two incidents of this magnitude in one village in a matter of a single week. The question is, Are they connected? Or only a coincidence?"

Hamish said, "Mysel', I'd ask why sae close together."

And that was a point to be considered. Why had this quiet little village suddenly erupted into violence?

Unless Hensley had found something in that bloody wood. But if he had, he'd held his tongue even in hospital. Why? Had it been self-incriminating? That was possible.

But even if the rector had fallen through his own carelessness, Hensley hadn't shot that arrow into his own back. Which still brought in a third party into the picture.

If Keating had come to the house in his absence, Rutledge found no sign of it. He debated going back to the inn, but it would be a wild-goose chase. Keating was no Josh Morgan, of The Three Horses, glad to stand and gossip with his custom. Short of searching the building, there would be no way of flushing him out if he didn't want to be found.

Had Keating played any role in what was happening in Dudlington? He appeared to hold himself aloof from the other inhabitants, except for Hillary Timmons's services as a barmaid and cleaning woman. And there he'd chosen well — Miss Timmons was a mouse terrified of lions, and he could probably count on her to keep her mouth shut.

What were the man's secrets? Most people had one or two.

Hamish said, "Aye, and you've kept yours. But would ye keep it here, where there's no' sae much else to do but gossip?"

There had been a few times dealing with

perceptive people when he'd feared his would slip out. They had stood on the brink of discovery, and yet he'd managed somehow to forestall them. Set apart from the village as he was, the owner of The Oaks just might succeed as well.

Hamish warned, "You mustna' have anything to do with yon woman in London. She worked wi' casualties in France. She'd ha' seen and heard more than most."

And Mrs. Channing had remembered him very clearly.

He couldn't picture her hiding in hedgerows to shoot at him.

"It needna' be her, but someone she put up to it," Hamish reminded him.

Circle upon circles.

As for Keating, it would probably prove to be more useful to confront him while he was working in the pub, with his patrons looking on. He wouldn't find it as easy to walk away then.

For the present — for the present, it might be useful to speak to Hensley again. He ought to be out of the woods, and therefore awake for longer periods.

Traffic was heavier than he'd expected on the road south to Northampton, and Rutledge found himself walking into the hospital just as dinner was being served.

He thought of his own on the sideboard at Mrs. Melford's.

He was once more cornered by the plump sister, who disapproved of interrupting a patient's meal, and he said, "Shall I have Chief Inspector Kelmore to speak to Matron?"

It was a threat that worked. He went down the line of beds, some of them empty now, others filled with what appeared to be new cases. Hensley was sitting awkwardly propped against half a dozen pillows, and he was trying to feed himself with his left hand. From the state of the towel under his chin, it wasn't going well.

He looked up at Rutledge, a sour expression passing across his face. It had more color now, but there were still lines of pain around his mouth.

"What is it now? Sir?" he asked.

Rutledge took the man's knife and fork and cut up his meat into manageable bits, then drew up a chair.

"There are more questions than answers in Dudlington. Inspector Cain can't help me, and the man you replaced, Constable Markham, has retired to Sussex. It's your turn."

"What questions?" Hensley asked warily, trying to appear unconcerned and failing.

Rutledge found himself thinking that a man in bed, with his dinner down his front, has no dignity. He said, "Mr. Towson, the rector, fell down his attic stairs today. Someone had come to the door and called to him to come at once — and then went away. He couldn't have missed the sound of Towson tumbling down the steps or crying out in pain. Yet he went away."

"Towson's *dead?*" Hensley demanded, appalled. His fork had stopped halfway to his lips. "Good God!"

Rutledge left it. Instead he said, "I think it's time you told me what took you to Frith's Wood, the day you were shot."

"As God's my witness, I didn't go there. I was on the road on my way to Letherington, and that's the last I remember." The words had become rote now.

"That you were on the road is true enough — I've found your bicycle where you left it, behind the pasture wall."

"I didn't leave it anywhere. Whoever shot me and dragged me to the wood, he put it there."

"Hensley. You were lucky to live. Towson was lucky to survive his fall. How many more people are going to be hurt, so that you can deny being in Frith's Wood? I looked for myself. From the attic windows at the rectory, there's the best view of the wood, short of climbing the church steeple."

"Towson survived?" Hensley was quick, his mind already leaping ahead. "Why are you here, then? Why not ask *him* who it was called to him on the steps?"

"If you weren't tied to this bed," Rutledge retorted shortly, "I'd have suspected you."

"Me?"

"Only someone in that attic could have seen you walk of your own accord into that blasted wood."

Hensley stared at him, a stubborn set to his chin. "Well, they'd be lying. I never went there."

Changing direction, Rutledge asked, "Tell me about the fire at Barstow's offices in the City."

Hensley nearly choked on his tea.

"What's that in aid of? You can ask Old Bowels, I had nothing to do with Barstow."

"There's someone who tells a different story. That you looked the other way the night of the fire."

"Then they'd be a liar!" He swore, nearly upsetting his tray. *"Sister!"* he shouted.

But she was busy at the other end of

the ward and didn't turn.

"Tell me what became of Emma Mason. And why you watched her with your field glasses while she was in her bedroom."

His fingers kneaded the piece of bread in his hand. "You can't prove it," Hensley told him belligerently.

"She was what, seventeen, at the time."

"She was no innocent lily, I can tell you that," Hensley snapped, glaring at Rutledge now. "Half the village thinks her a saint. The others won't open their mouths because Mrs. Ellison rules the roost. But just ask Constable Markham, he'll tell you he saw our pure Miss Emma rolling in the grass behind the church with Miss Letteridge's fiancé. And she wasn't seventeen then."

It was Rutledge's turn to stare at Hensley.

Hamish said, "He's telling the truth."

It was all too apparent that Hamish was right. Hensley's eyes were blazing with fury, and there was no uneasy prevarication in the words he'd spat at the man from London.

"It does you no good to blacken her character."

"Blacken it? Hardly that. Reveal it, more like."

"Was she promiscuous?"

"She wasn't having any of me or anyone else. But there was no doubt that Constable Markham was right. It explained why Miss Letteridge left for London, just afterward."

"And the man? Who is he?"

"That's not your business. Besides, he's buried in the churchyard. That's why Miss Letteridge came back."

On their way out of Northampton on the road north, Hamish said, "I willna' believe she murdered the girl."

Rutledge, avoiding a milk wagon and gearing up to pass a lorry, said, "Grace Letteridge? At least it gives her a motive."

"Then why did she no' rid herself of the girl before leaving for London?"

Hamish was right, he thought. Jealousy was a hot-blooded crime, impetuous and filled with anger.

"Her hands may have been tied then. She might have been afraid to touch Emma, for fear the man would guess she'd been responsible, and reject her a second time. But when he was killed, she was free to come home and balance the scales. Anger and blame are a part of grieving."

Hamish wasn't convinced. "Ye ken, she

could ha' traveled to London to make it right wi' him before he went to France."

And she'd gone as soon as her father died. Her father might not have approved of her following any man on such a slim hope.

But then there would have been no need to kill Emma.

Unless of course Grace Letteridge had waited in London until the man got leave, only to discover he was marking time until Emma was of age and free to marry where she pleased. It would have been an appalling blow, especially if he'd died soon after their meeting, leaving her with an empty future.

If either case was true, then Grace Letteridge, for all her dramatic pronouncement, had no reason for taking a bow and arrow to shoot Hensley. She knew the truth.

"Or was covering up her own crime," Rutledge said aloud as the busy city road became industrial and then open countryside. "Especially if he was pressing too hard on her heels by searching the wood. Why wouldn't he admit to that?"

He knew, better than most, how jealousy could eat at the soul. He'd seen it in more than one murder inquiry, and he'd felt it himself when Jean walked away from him to marry a diplomat on his way to take up a station in Canada. She had vanished from his life as surely as if she'd evaporated into thin air.

"She wouldna' stoop to murder," Hamish said again in defense of Grace Letteridge. "She'd ha' walked away and no' looked back."

And Hensley appeared to have had problems of his own with jealousy of Emma Mason's alleged attentions to another man.

Rutledge stopped at The Oaks as he came to the fork that led to Dudlington. The inn was dark, and there were no motorcars in front of it. He went to the door, intending to knock, and then thought better of it.

Keating could look out any window to see who was at his door. And when he recognized Rutledge standing there, he wouldn't bother to come down.

Rutledge wasn't about to give him that satisfaction.

He didn't sleep well that night, and by the time the clock had struck two from the church tower, he got up and went to the window.

Dudlington lay quiet in a shower of moonlight that touched the cold roofs with silvered shadow. The streets were empty, and the houses were dark.

But even as he watched, a light appeared in Emma Mason's bedchamber, and he reached without thinking for the field glasses.

The room seemed to bloom before his eyes, and he could see someone's shadow cast by lamplight against the far wall. It was hard to tell who who had walked into the room. The lamp was nearer the door than the windows, and only the shadow was visible from where Rutledge stood.

"The grandmother," Hamish said.

"She doesn't hear well. It could be anyone slipping into the house after finding the door unlocked."

The lamp burned for a quarter of an hour, and then went out. Rutledge was on the stairs in almost the same instant, going down them fast on his way to Hensley's office. There he had a clear view of anyone who might come out the Ellison door. But though he watched for nearly ten minutes, the door remained tight shut.

Hamish said quietly, "There's the kitchen door."

"I'm not going to be caught by the neighbors prowling in a woman's back garden at this hour. And if he slipped out through the rear of the house, he's had a long head start."

He waited another ten, and then quietly went out Hensley's front door and crossed the street.

Turning the knob as silently as possible, he gave the door a little push.

It opened easily into the dark and empty hall.

Early the next morning, he crossed the street and tapped lightly on Mrs. Ellison's door, then knocked more firmly.

She came to answer it after several minutes. Dressed, her hair neatly brushed and in place.

"I thought I'd heard someone." She was abrupt, unwelcoming.

"I'm sorry to disturb you," he said, ignoring her coldness. "I saw a light in your house when I came in last night. I felt I ought to see for myself that all was well."

"Thank you." She was about to shut her door in his face.

"You do know that the rector fell yesterday."

Her eyebrows went up. "No. I hadn't heard."

"He was fortunate. He broke his arm,"

he told her, watching her face. "It could just as well have been his back."

"Indeed."

Her refusal to be dependent on anyone or anything was evident.

He made one more attempt. "Do you lock your door at night?"

"I don't need to lock it. For my sins, I live just across from the police. Good morning, Inspector."

And this time she was successful in shutting him out.

After breakfast, he went to see Dr. Middleton, to ask how the rector was faring. Middleton was just finishing his own breakfast, the smell of burned toast heavy in the room.

"Very upset with himself for being so foolish. Sit down, there's tea in the pot."

"Thank you, no. What took him up to the attic in the first place?"

"There was something about hunting for gloves — he wasn't very clear on that, but Hillary discovered woolen ones he'd apparently washed himself and set out to dry. He must have grown impatient and gone in search of a second pair." Middleton reached for the pot of marmalade and spread it thinly across a slice of scraped toast. "I told him he was growing as dotty as Mary Ellison, and he didn't find it very amusing."

"I don't recall a pair of gloves on the landing."

"Nor did I. I asked him what had become of them, and he thought he'd been distracted from his errand. But he can't think why. His best guess is the teakettle whistling, though for the life of me, I can't believe he'd hear it all the way from the kitchen. He's a logical sort of man, and these ambiguities are worrying him more than they should."

"Are you sure he was coherent when he said something about a summons?"

"Oh, yes, there was no doubt of that. When I reached him, he was dazed and fretting. He began by apologizing for taking me away from the other sufferer, or words to that effect, and wanting to know if all was well now. I asked him what he was going on about, and he said I'd sent for him. Well, I hadn't done anything of the sort, so I questioned him — concerned about the knot on his head and whether there was concussion — about who'd brought this summons and where he was to go. He said he hadn't seen the messenger, and I should know the answer to where he was needed better than he. I told him it was nothing to be agitated over, and he was to stop thinking about it, that he hadn't failed in his duty. He closed his eyes and let me get on with my examination. I can't be sure he was altogether conscious after that. I had to move him more than I liked, to see what the damage amounted to. And he'd held on far too long already."

"He was lucky," Rutledge said, meaning it.

"He should have broken his neck, or at the very least, his back. It was nothing short of a miracle. Tough old bird, as I've said before, and not about to give up. Hillary told me this morning that he was begging to be out of bed, even though I'd expressly forbidden it. If he's dizzy, he doesn't need to go over on his head a second time."

Rutledge left it for a moment, and then said, "I saw a light on in Emma Mason's bedroom, last night. In the middle of the night. I went this morning to see if Mrs. Ellison was all right. She bit off my head."

"She can't sleep, and I shouldn't be surprised if she walks about the house at night and broods. She won't let me give her anything to help her sleep. She doesn't want to spend her days befuddled."

"That may be. She's also slightly deaf, and yet she doesn't lock her door. I tested it myself."

Middleton chuckled. "Just as well she didn't catch you doing it. Policeman or not, you'd have been up on a charge before you knew what had happened to you."

"I was talking with Hensley yesterday — he's improving," he added hastily, as Middleton was about to interrupt. "But it will be another week before they allow him to leave. Meanwhile, there's another matter I want to bring up."

Middleton was suddenly wary. "A doctor, like a priest, can't go about talking about his patients."

"It's not a medical question, actually. What do you know about Keating, up at The Oaks?"

"Never been ill, to my knowledge. Beyond that, I can't tell you much."

"He's an independent devil."

"You aren't the first to notice that. He came here out of the blue early in 1911, so I'm told. He bought The Oaks and stayed to himself. The mothers of Dudlington watched him like a hawk — as it happened, he had no interest in their daughters, either to seduce them or marry them." He chuckled again. "He's not from around here, and that was one strike against him. Another was his reluctance to talk about himself. And finally no one knew his aunt or his third cousin or his great-grandfather. The men who frequent The Oaks were happy enough to have a local pub and didn't concern themselves with gossip. And after a time it died down. He's accepted as an anomaly, and ignored."

"Which is apparently the way he wants it."

"Nothing wrong with that, is there? Why the interest? Did he have a grudge against Hensley?"

"Possibly. He was ferocious in his defense of Emma Mason's good name and reputation."

"And a good many people would like to think that Hensley knows more about her disappearance than he's willing to say. Yes, I see where you're going."

"What I'd like to know is how Keating came to know Emma well enough to defend her."

"You may have it backward, you know — it could be Keating has something against Hensley, and Emma's just the smokescreen to conceal that."

Hamish said, "Aye, if yon constable recognized him."

Almost as if Middleton had overheard the voice in Rutledge's head, he added, "Wasn't Hensley a policeman in London, before he came here?"

18

Rutledge walked up the hill from Holly Street to The Oaks, and this time found Keating in the bar serving a late breakfast to two travelers driving to Lincoln. He listened to the conversation for some time, the man and the woman chatting with Keating about an inn they'd stopped in the night before in Colchester. Finally, their meal finished, they went up to their rooms to finish packing, and Rutledge followed Keating through the door into the kitchen.

Keating had done the cooking himself. Hillary Timmons was still watching over the rector, and Keating had shown himself to be competent in the kitchen. The clutter of pans and dishes on the worktable and the spills on the stove indicated haste, but the remnants of toast, poached eggs, a side dish of bacon, and a plate of sausages were cooked well. He took off his apron and turned to face Rutledge.

"I have to be there when they come down to pay their reckoning. What do you want?"

"How long have you known Constable Hensley?" he asked abruptly.

"Since he came here three years ago. Why?"

"There's reason to think you knew him in London."

"Has he told you as much?"

"Someone else suggested it."

"Well, 'someone' is wrong."

"There was a motorcar here yesterday morning. It left quickly, running up the road to the north. Who was driving?"

"How the hell should I know? A man came in to ask directions, and then walked out. I'd never seen him before, and I don't expect to see him again."

"What sort of directions?"

"He asked if he was on the right road for Stamford. I told him he could reach it from here, but it was more direct if he took the turning at Letherington and got himself over on the main road."

Keating had met Rutledge's eyes as he spoke, and there was no way Rutledge could call him on his answer. Not yet.

And Hamish was hammering at the back of his mind.

"You've let your imagination run away with ye."

He remembered his certainty just before

he'd seen the motorcar that someone had been standing in an upstairs window watching him. But that certainty had begun to fade. And he felt suddenly angry with himself.

The cartridge casings had got to him after all.

After Keating had carried the luggage of his guests out to their motorcar, and seen them off, he came back to the kitchen where Rutledge was still standing by the cluttered table.

"Not satisfied, are you?" he asked. "Look, I've kept myself to myself, ever since I came here. I have no truck with Dudlington, and Dudlington has none with me. I prefer it that way."

"Hillary Timmons works for you. She's from the village."

"So she is. She needed the work, and I gave it to her, on the condition that what happens here stays here. And I made it clear that if I learned she'd been gossiping about me or my patrons, she was out on her ear. She makes good money. She's not likely to go against me."

"She cleans for the rector as well, when she's not here. And perhaps for others."

"She's got a father who can't work. And there're three younger ones at home. She's the only income they've got."

"Not much of a life for her, is it?"

"I pay her a fair wage. That's all I'm responsible for. I can't save the world."

"No. Why do you like your privacy so much? Dudlington's small enough, you might have done better if you'd tried to fit in."

"I'm not interested in fitting in. Or doing better. My life satisfies me the way it is. And I'll thank you to keep out of it."

As Rutledge was walking back to Hensley's house, Hamish said, "Ye're no closer to finding who shot the constable than you were when you came here. It's been time wasted."

Rutledge swore. It was true, he'd found himself caught up in his own troubles and intrigued by the disappearance of Emma Mason, rather than looking strictly into the attack on Hensley. And yet he could see that the constable, Frith's Wood, and the girl's fate must somehow be tangled together. Find the answer to one, and the others might fall tidily into place.

Hamish said, "Aye, but yon constable's an outsider. He wouldna' ha' felt the same about a Saxon wood. Wouldna' have feared it."

"Yet he knew, very well, that the villagers avoided it. And I don't think Hensley would have set foot in it either, if he hadn't had a damned good reason. That reason has to be something to do with Emma Mason. It fits too well. But it was personal, not a part of his duty. Otherwise there'd have been a file. And it's not likely that we'll have the truth out of him anytime soon."

"Why was he shot and left? It would ha' been easy to finish him, if that was the intent."

Rutledge had reached the house and was stepping in the door. He said aloud, "I think we may find it was a warning."

"What was a warning?" Inspector Cain stood up from the chair behind Hensley's desk. "Don't tell me you've started talking to yourself! A bad sign, man!"

Rutledge could feel his face warming uncomfortably. "Bad habit indeed. What brings you here?"

"I found this last night, when I was going through some of my predecessor's files. I thought you might be interested."

He held out a folder, and Rutledge opened it as they sat down.

It was a query sent to Inspector Abbot about a missing woman. Her name was

Beatrice Ellison Mason, and the letter had come from London.

Rutledge could see, reading the first sheet of paper, that a Mrs. Greer had let a room to Beatrice Mason for several years and was now asking the Northamptonshire police to find her and inform her that she was in arrears for six months' rent. The period in question was March to late August 1904, and the letter was dated July 1906.

It ended, *"For I am a poor woman and in need of that money for a new roof. I'd be obliged if you would tell Mrs. Mason I can wait no longer."*

"Mrs. Greer ought to have spoken to a solicitor, but it appears she couldn't afford one," Cain said. "That's why she wrote to Abbot."

"This letter may also explain why Mrs. Mason brought Emma to Mrs. Ellison for safekeeping. When her husband died, she must have been destitute. So much for the famous artist living in Paris."

"Yes, well, that's another interesting bit. Read on."

Rutledge turned the page. Abbot, Cain's predecessor, had noted in an awkward scrawl, *Spoke to Mrs. Ellison. She says her daughter is studying on the Continent, and she herself will see to this outstanding debt with an apology for the oversight.*

Cain, watching him, said, "Which she apparently did. Pay the debt, I mean. There's no other correspondence on the subject. And by the time Emma went missing, the local police, Abbot in particular, had either forgotten this file or felt that it had no bearing on the girl's whereabouts. After all, her mother hadn't lived at that address since 1904. Ancient history, in fact."

"Still, he should have looked into it."

Cain was defensive. "He may have asked Mrs. Ellison about it, of course. As I've told you, his strong suit wasn't keeping records. But stepping into his shoes, I've discovered how good Abbot was at dealing with people."

It could be said of many policemen in villages and small towns, and was probably the secret of their success as an unarmed force. The opposite side of the coin was that some of them grew set in their ways and bloody-minded.

Rutledge mended his fences. "I'm sure you're right." But he made a mental note to have a word with Mrs. Ellison.

"I don't know what bearing this has on anything. But it rather puts paid to the idea that Emma is alive and well, living with her mother in London, doesn't it?" Cain prepared to stand up, gathering his bad leg under him. "I'd not like to think that my constable had anything to do with her disappearance."

"What's become of your sergeant and the motorcar?"

"He's gone round to speak to the rector. I'm not sure I like the sound of that fall. My sergeant says Towson is crippled up with rheumatism and oughtn't to be clambering about in attics or cellars either, for that matter. Mrs. Melford brought me a cup of tea, that's how I learned the news."

"He was lucky," Rutledge said, repeating his earlier words to Dr. Middleton. "The question is, was the fall an accident or not?"

"Good God!" Cain said, staring. "You're not telling me we're about to have a rash of unexplained attacks on people."

"Hardly a rash of them. Yet. Time will tell. But I might add that the attics of the rectory look out on Frith's Wood. It's one of the few places that do, short of climbing the church tower."

"You *can* climb that tower, you know," Cain informed him. "There's a rickety stair up to the bell, above the clock face. I haven't the foggiest notion what can be seen from there, but at a guess, it would be the best viewpoint of any."

"How did you come to know that?" Unspoken between them was the reference to Cain's war injury.

But Cain grinned. "Two boys went up there on a lark when the Armistice was declared in 1918. They rang the bells, and half Dudlington believed we'd been attacked by Germans, or worse. My sergeant told me about it. Hensley summoned him to come and read them the riot act."

Rutledge laughed. But he made a second mental note to look at that stair for himself.

When Cain had gone, Rutledge collected his torch and Hensley's field glasses, then walked to St. Luke's. The door was unlocked. A heavy, twisted ring of iron, reminiscent of the Sanctuary Rings of the medieval period, when clinging to one protected a man from arrest, was newer than the church, as if added to give the building a feeling of age.

He stood there for a moment, looking up at the soaring spire. There were several square stages forming the sturdy footing of the tower, each level diminishing in size as it rose upward to the housing of the bell. The spire itself, reaching upward from there in a graceful inverted cone, had tiny windows counter set on opposite sides, two facing north and south, two facing east and west.

Hamish said, "I wouldna' care to climb that high."

"Then stay here."

The tower door led to another one carved of heavy dark wood, and beyond that lay the sanctuary. The nave was high-ceilinged but flat. Someone had painted trompe l'oeil ovals there, three of them, in Renaissance style, with scenes of angels and saints floating on clouds. And in the center panel, Christ was seated in glory, one hand reaching high into the painted sky. The aisle columns were Doric with carved capitals, and they appeared to up-hold, without effort, this deceptively vast expanse above them.

The pulpit was tall and heavily carved. Rutledge thought it might have come from an earlier building that had been replaced.

There were long windows, some with simple stained glass, and a brass rail around the communion table. The chancel was rather plain, with an old painted wood crucifix behind the altar.

No tombs here, the church wasn't old enough for Crusader knights and Elizabethan ladies. There were only a few monuments.

He did find a nice memorial tablet to a man who had served in the Sudan with Gordon. His name — it was Harkness — rank, dates, and his regimental insignia had been inlaid in the stone in brass. Rutledge wondered if he'd been the last of the family's male line, leaving to a distant cousin, Mary Ellison, pride in continuing the female line.

He returned to the tower room and saw the narrow stairs to one side that disappeared through a square hole in the ceiling. The steps were stone for the first flight, in keeping with the construction of the church, but as he started to climb, he could see very quickly that the next flight was wood, without backs to the risers. Not a very pleasant prospect.

He reached the next stage of the tower and could just see the bell rope disappearing into the darkness high above his head. He looked down past his feet, where it hung like a mesmerized snake suspended in midair with nowhere to go. Only, he thought, there was no visible head or tail. He grasped the sides of the narrow stairs firmly and went up another flight, hand over hand to steady himself. And he refrained from looking down, for the stairs were fixed to the outside walls and a well of darkness was opening up in the empty center. Overhead, shining his torch straight up, he could see the great bronze bell.

Another flight, and the space was filled with the mouth of the bell, the clapper swaying lightly in the movement of cold air through the shuttered openings on four sides.

"Yon draft must come from the Cairngorms," Hamish said, startling Rutledge.

His foot missed the next step and he swore as his body began to swing out over the bottomless space yawning beside him. But his handhold on the rough side rails was strong enough to pull him back again to safety. There was a distinctly hollow pit in the middle of his stomach until he felt his dangling foot settle once more on the solid strip of wood.

A dozen more steps, and he was at the head of the bell, where massive beams held it in place at the top of the tower.

The clock was hung on the outer side of the window arch facing toward the village.

And over his head, a single ladder disappeared into the spire. Shining his light up into the darkness, he could see the wooden skeleton of the tower, the framework on which it had been built, like an octagon that narrowed more with each foot of height. How old was that ladder? It might still hold a boy's weight, but what about a man's?

Rutledge thought, I don't need to climb farther —

But he knew he did. Coming down was something else, and he wasn't prepared to think about that yet.

The ladder was steadier than he'd expected, and with a sigh of relief, he started up it.

When he came to the first window, he realized that it looked toward the village, while its brother on the far side overlooked the fields.

But the next pair of windows, facing north and south, gave him a bird's-eye view of Frith's Wood, and he could see more detail from here than he'd anticipated. With his arms wrapped tightly about the side rails of the ladder, he brought up the field glasses. Through them, he could have roughly followed movement across the breadth of the wood, and even down into the thickets of undergrowth. Especially at this time of year, when the trees were bare and even the briars and weeds mere stalks and thorny strands. It was interesting to see just how closely he could bring it in. Far better than from the rectory attic, surely.

Who would have the courage to come here, just on the off chance of seeing where Hensley had gone?

Letting the glasses hang from their leather strap around his neck, he began to back down the ladder. It was just light enough to see where he was going without the aid of his torch, but the tolerances were much tighter at this height, and he was beginning to feel the pressure of claustrophobia sealing him in. A nail sticking out farther than most of its neighbors plucked at his coat, yanking at him. It was easy enough to free himself, but the sense of losing his balance was strong.

Taking a deep breath to steady himself, he went down the ladder another few rungs.

God, but it was dangerous! And just behind him, making it impossible to look down, was Hamish —

He continued his descent and finally arrived at the lower pair of windows. He stopped for a moment to look at the village, a toy city for a child. Like seeing it from an airplane, he thought, picking out the narrow canyons that were the streets, and the chimney pots of houses he recognized.

The nearer ones showed him their back gardens, where sheds held tools and other gear, and lines for drying clothes ran helter-skelter across the space available, to give them as much length as possible.

A child's bicycle lay against the back steps in one, and in another a man was just visible bringing up a giant cabbage from the coal cellar where it had been stored. A wagon moved into view, leaving one of the shops. The rectory's slate roof was mossy, and he could see into the rector's bedroom, glimpsing the foot of the bed and the edge of a door through the open drapes.

He was staring at the Baylor house, beyond the rectory, when he saw that someone was at a window on the top floor, apparently staring directly back at him.

It was a shock, because inside this tight cocoon of wood, he'd felt invisible. The question was, could the figure at the window actually see him, or was he only gazing out at the church?

Rutledge brought up the field glasses, but it was impossible to pick out details through the windowpane. A dark, irregular shape, but certainly human. He'd have missed it altogether if the figure hadn't moved and drawn his attention. And yet he seemed to feel the intensity of the watcher's scrutiny.

Curiosity, or something more sinister?

On the other side of the coin, the sun had just come out from behind the clouds, reaching through the narrow opening beside him and touching the ladder on which he stood, highlighting his right shoulder. He was pinned there, vulnerable, with the long descent blocked by Hamish just below him. Caught like a bird in a sack.

But that was nonsense. Any threat to him would come from outside Dudlington, not from a house whose owner he knew.

He tried to shake off the sense of urgency pressing him now and concentrated instead on the placement of each foot, feeling his way downward. There was a sense of relief when he finally reached the mouth of the bell and the real stairs. However rudimentary they had seemed before, they felt sturdier and safer than that abominable ladder. He reached out to touch the bell for a moment, his hand against the icy cold metal. And from this angle, he noticed for the first time the mechanism that connected the bell to the clock.

"Hark!" Hamish warned, from somewhere below him, and he saw the gears begin to move.

The clock was about to strike, and he was standing there beside the bell.

Wasting no time, he went as fast as he dared down the next set of stairs, reached the last flight, the one of stone, and was halfway down it when the great bronze tongue over his head tolled the hour, the wash of sound enveloping him.

On solid ground at last, he went straight to the sanctuary and found a pane of clear glass facing the direction of the Baylor house.

But if there had been someone in the upstairs window, he was gone now. All Rutledge could see was the movement of clouds reflected in the dark glass, like the shadow of leaves stirring in the wind. He was beginning to think he'd let his imagination run away with him up in that spire.

Hamish taunted, "Aye, you've lost your nerve. It wasna' a stalker standing there, only a man looking out his ain window."

"To hell with my nerve. What I want to know now is whether someone's accustomed to standing there. And did he see what happened in Frith's Wood last Friday, or at any other time? If there was someone looking at me through the spire's opening, had he seen anyone else up there in the past few weeks."

"There's verra' little warmth at the top of yon house in winter," Hamish countered derisively. "And only two people, ye ken, with no' much time to stand about watching ithers. It's no' likely they'll ha' seen anything. Unless they were verra' lucky."

"Then it's time to find out how good their luck is."

19

When Rutledge used the brass knocker on the door, there was no answer. He walked around the side of the house to the kitchen garden.

The door there was ajar, and he stepped in, calling, "Baylor? Are you there?"

He could hear voices somewhere inside, and he walked down the passage to the kitchen. It was empty too. Although it was tidy, the room was masculine in tone — shades rather than curtains at the windows, and an oil cloth covering the table. The only feminine concession was a frilled but worn cushion on one of the chairs, as if this was where a woman had once sat.

The door on the far side led to the rest of the house, and he walked quietly down a second passage. He'd just reached a room with an open door when Baylor came out and nearly collided with him.

"What the hell!" he exclaimed, startled to find someone in his house.

"I've knocked on the front door and called from the kitchen — perhaps it's time to think of answering. You must have heard me."

"Damn you, you've no right to come in like this." Baylor was furious, his face red.

"I came to ask if I could look out your upper windows toward Frith's Wood. Surely there's no harm in that. It's probably the best observation post in Dudlington."

"What are you saying, that someone here used it to watch the wood? You must be mad. We had nothing to do with Hensley's attack that day. Except to save his life."

"Don't deliberately misunderstand me, Baylor. I simply want to stand at the window to judge how much of the wood is visible from there."

Hamish said quietly, "There's someone in yon room. And you must pass it to reach the stairs —"

Rutledge could feel the presence in the room, silent and apprehensive.

"Look, I'll just go up the back stairs to the attic, if you'll lead the way. I needn't disturb the rest of the household."

Torn, Baylor considered the alternatives. "Oh, very well. This way."

He brushed past Rutledge with the intention of irritating him and walked back toward the kitchen. Through another door were the back stairs, narrow, curving, and with short treads. Baylor went up them with accustomed ease, but Rutledge had to duck through the door and keep a hand on the wall as he climbed.

They came out on the floor above, and then walked a short distance to a second flight of steps going up to the next floor.

It wasn't an attic as Rutledge had thought, but another passage with small rooms intended for children or servants. The doors were shut, giving a claustrophobic air to the corridor, making it appear to be narrower than the one below. The carpet running down the center was worn with use but sound.

It would, Hamish was pointing out, muffle footsteps.

Baylor opened the door into a bright corner room, with square windows and an iron bedstead against one wall, a washstand nearest the door, and a tall chest of drawers to Rutledge's left. The room seemed unused, empty of personal touches or the ordinary signs of someone's presence. There was a desk between the north windows, and he went to it to lean his hands on the wooden top so that he could look out.

He could see the wood quite well, but not into it as clearly as he had from the church spire.

"It would be helpful if I could send someone into the wood and then stand here to observe his progress," Rutledge said. "A test of sorts. Would you be agreeable to walking there for ten minutes or so?"

"I don't set foot in the wood if I can help it. Find yourself another ferret."

Without haste, Rutledge turned to the west window, where he could look toward the church, and found himself facing the narrow east opening where he'd stood on the ladder not twenty minutes before. A pale light came through from the opposite side of the spire, illuminating the interior, and he thought, *Someone could have seen me, it's not impossible.*

"Do you have a woman who cleans for you?" he asked aloud, turning to Baylor. "Or perhaps your brother comes up here from time to time, to look out at the fields. It's really quite a fine vantage point."

"Nobody uses this floor. We haven't since we were children, and my parents were still alive."

"Can you be sure of that?"

"I told you. We don't use this floor."

But Rutledge was nearly sure someone had, at least for a short time, not more than half an hour ago. There was the partial print of a hand in the dust collecting on the windowsill beside him.

As they came down the stairs and into the kitchen, the kettle was just on the boil.

Baylor said, "I won't offer you a cup of tea."

It was a clear message to leave.

"Thank you for your willingness to help." Rutledge went out the door and heard it shut behind him, almost on his heels.

He retraced his steps as far as the rectory, and an exhausted Hillary Timmons opened the door at his knock. She stood aside, almost wary of him, and he remembered his outburst of anger in the kitchen of The Oaks.

"How is the rector?" he asked after greeting her.

"Tiresome." She smiled a little to take the sting out of the word. "He doesn't feel like doing much of anything, and that drags at his patience."

"Perhaps a visitor will help."

"Oh, if you would, please. I need to see to his dinner, and there's been no time."

He went up the stairs to the first floor and down the passage to the rector's bedroom. Towson greeted him with undisguised relief. "Thank God you're here," he said. "I need so many things, and young Hillary is hopeless."

"What would you like?" Rutledge inquired, setting his hat to one side and tossing his coat over a chair.

"Tsk! There's a coat-tree in the hall, didn't she point it out?"

"It doesn't matter. What can I find for you?"

"There are three books by the desk in my study. Paper, pens, and something to write on. Ink. My blotter —" He went on urgently, as if afraid Rutledge would desert him before he'd finished his requests.

"I'm surprised Hillary couldn't have helped you earlier," Rutledge said. "It doesn't seem all that complicated."

"She doesn't like touching anything in my study. She never even ventures in there to dust it. You'd think she was afraid of it, as if God lived there, to help me with my sermons."

Rutledge laughed. "Very well, I'll do my best."

He went to the study, a small room overlooking the church, and began to search for the items Towson had listed.

The books were easy enough to find on the shelf by the rector's desk, and the writing materials lay next to the blotter. Rutledge was just looking around the room to find some means of carrying the lot back up the stairs, when he noticed a framed photograph on the small table by the only upholstered chair in the room. A lamp stood on the table as well, next to a book filled with strips of paper to mark various chapters. He crossed the room to look at the photograph, and then was distracted by the book.

It was leather bound, an album of sorts, with cuttings pasted to the pages. He could see the curled edges sticking out.

Rutledge reached to open it, and Hamish said, "I wouldna' pry —"

He ignored the voice.

The cuttings had come from various newspapers, with the name of the paper and the date written in ink on each of them.

Most of them were obituaries. In the front was Mrs. Towson's, short but flowery, identifying her as the beloved wife of our dear rector. Others were of local men killed in the war, each one pasted carefully in the center of a sheet of black paper, as if honoring them. He ran his eye down one or two, thinking as he did that each of these young men hadn't had time to live very far beyond boyhood. The war had given them their only reality; their rank and dates and the battle in which they'd fallen stood out starkly as their only achievement.

Son of . . . Young men who hadn't married, hadn't had families of their own, had left no mark in the world, and no posterity.

How many of them had he seen go into battle and fall? How many had he tried to remember as individuals, repeating their names to himself as he stood in the trenches during the dark nights of winter and the short ones of summer. MacKay, Sutherland, Gordon, Campbell, Scott, MacIver, MacInnes, MacTaggert, Chisholm, Kerr, Fraser —

He found himself reminded of Elizabeth Fraser, seeing her against the snow light, her hair so fair, like a crown, her body long and slim. The memory was slipping away from him now, and it hurt him to think that he was beginning to forget.

He made himself return to the album, scanning the names and ages and battles.

And then one name in particular caught his eye.

Robert Baylor, age twenty, son of the late Robert and Ellen Baylor of Dudlington Farm, survived by his brothers

Theodore and Joel, and his fiancée, Grace Letteridge.

He closed the album carefully so as not to lose any of the markers.

Hamish said, "It wasna' well done, looking without permission."

"But now I know," he answered. One more of the dead on the Somme. A young man who was engaged to marry one woman — but who had been seen by Constable Markham rolling in the grass near the church with Emma Mason.

Rutledge brought the books and writing materials to the rector, and set them on the bed where he could reach them. "I couldn't find anything to write on."

"That small flat handkerchief box over there will work nicely," Towson told him, pointing to it. "I shan't do it any harm."

Rutledge brought it to him and set that within reach also.

"How can you write?"

"I'm accustomed to using either hand. When the rheumatism is worse, I switch. My mother was told when I was a child that I was contrary, using my left hand more than my right. My schoolmaster forced me to use my right, and it took me nearly thirty years to forgive him." He added ruefully, "Now I'm grateful."

"Who will deliver your sermon on Sunday?"

"I shall, of course. Propped in the pulpit like a log. There's nothing wrong with my voice, and as soon as the tenderness in my leg and back has passed, I'm allowed to be up and about."

Rutledge grinned at him. "You must be careful on the pulpit steps."

"I always am, with my robes trailing about my ankles."

"I was just across the way, speaking to Ted Baylor. His windows look out on Frith's Wood, perhaps a better view than yours."

"Baylor told me once that the servants when he was a child hated that view and would refuse to sleep in that room, for fear of seeing something unspeakable in the night."

"What became of the servants?"

"Off to the war, of course, or to the cities, to work in the factories. There were only the three boys, after their parents died, and I expect they fared well enough. The house stood empty for two years, you know. Half of Dudlington helped care for the livestock. It muddled social standings when you were ankle-deep in muck, cleaning out the barns."

"And all three of them survived the war? That's astonishing."

But Hamish was chiding him for misleading the rector.

"Ted did, although he was wounded twice. Robert was killed. Joel came back with strange notions about what had been done to the common soldier. He's not quite right in his head, I'm told. Ted takes care of him, but there's no one to take care of Ted. Life's not always fair."

"What do you mean, not quite right in his head?"

"I can't say with any certainty. Can you pass me that glass of water? Thank you. Joel never comes to church services, and he never sets foot out of the house, as far as I know. I doubt anyone has seen him at all. We leave him in peace, hoping one day he may heal."

Rutledge stood to go as he heard Hillary Timmons coming up the stairs.

She thanked him for spelling her and added, "I've found you a nice bit of ham for your dinner, Rector."

"You feed me better than I feed myself, my dear."

She blushed. "Mr. Keating says I'm a terrible cook. But I've noticed the inn guests never complain."

265

"What did Mr. Keating do, before he bought The Oaks?" Rutledge asked her.

"I don't know," she told him simply. "He never talks about himself. If I didn't know better, I'd say he had no other life before The Oaks. But he must've. There's a wicked scar —"

She clapped a hand over her mouth, suddenly frightened.

"I won't tell him," Rutledge assured her. "It's all right."

But she hurried from the room, looking as if she was on the verge of tears.

"What was that in aid of?" Towson asked, worried for her.

"She's been warned not to talk about Keating. It's worth her job."

"Then you shouldn't have pressed her," Towson told him roundly. "She needs the work, to help her family. That's why I pay her to clean for me. As do several others. She's vulnerable."

"There's no harm done," Rutledge answered him. "I shan't say anything about it, and neither will you."

But when he left, he noticed that the rector didn't ask him to come to visit again.

On the way back to Hensley's house, he thought about what he'd learned that day.

It was still a jumble of impressions and facts, and he wasn't sure where they were leading. But he had come to rely on intuition over the years and never discounted the smallest bit of information. It sometimes loomed large in the end, once he'd pried open the secrets locked in a silent village.

Hamish said, "Ye're wasting time climbing the kirk tower. It willna' tell you who hated yon constable."

"Grace Letteridge for one. Possibly Keating. There may be others keeping their heads down. Even Ted Baylor, who had the best view of Frith's Wood and may have seen his chance. Though what he has against Hensley I don't know yet. Unless it has to do with his dead brother and Emma Mason."

Rutledge listened to his footsteps echoing against the stone walls of Whitby Lane, keeping pace with his thoughts.

Were the small windows of Dudlington meant to keep the cold out or to conceal what was inside?

He realized, glancing up, that there was a motorcar just by the door of Hensley's house, and he stopped, trying to place it.

But it wasn't one he could recall seeing at The Oaks.

He walked through the door, but there was no one in the parlor. He went through to the sitting room beyond it, and stopped stock-still on the threshold, unable to believe his eyes.

In the chair on the far side of the room, half-hidden in the shadows, was Meredith Channing.

20

Mrs. Channing spoke first.

"Yes, well, I thought I ought to come."

It was as if she had answered the thought in his head.

Hamish, unsettled and pressing, hissed, "Send her away."

"There have been no more casings," he said baldly. "I think it's finished."

"No. Not finished. Waiting." She began to remove her gloves.

"How could you possibly know that?"

"It doesn't matter how. You're being lulled into dropping your guard. Forgetting to look before you find yourself in a position where you can't fight back. Where you're a perfect target and helpless."

Rutledge saw himself in the spire, pinned there in the wooden octagon of boards, unable to protect himself. His skin crawled.

"You understand, I see." She dropped her gloves into her handbag.

"Why should it matter to you one way or another?"

She smiled. "How like a man! You're a

friend of Maryanne's — I've met your sister. And a few of your other friends. How could I turn away?"

"It was a long distance to drive, just to deliver a warning. You might have written instead."

"Oh, do stop being suspicious and sit down!" She had lost patience with him. "I'm here. What I want to know is, what can I do?"

He stood there for a moment longer, then realized how foolish he looked, like a defiant child. Crossing the room, he sat down in the chair on the other side of the oval table at her elbow.

Glancing around, she said, "These are spartan quarters! Waiting for you, I looked in the kitchen, hoping for a little tea to warm me. There's none in the tea tin, and none on the shelves."

"It's Constable Hensley's house," he said. "I'm using it while he's in hospital."

"I've a very nice room at The Oaks. I'm surprised you aren't staying there."

He smiled grimly. "Then you haven't met the owner. He'll have nothing to do with a policeman under his roof."

"Have you asked yourself why?"

"He's something of a curmudgeon, I'm told."

"I found him very polite. Although he may not go on being polite, if he discovers I'm here to see you."

"How did you find me?"

"I sent you the small package, if you remember."

He felt like a student being put in his place by his teacher. "Yes, of course. Sorry. I've got other things on my mind."

"I can see that." She rose to go, and he stood as well. "I'll find out if the inn can run to a cup of tea." For a moment she regarded him intently. "If there's anything I can do, please ask. I'll only stay on for a day or two. But I was worried, you see. And you did come to me first."

With that she walked out of the room, and he let her go.

Hamish said, "She's an outsider. She's no' afraid of the wood."

It was a change of mood that surprised Rutledge. But he answered slowly, considering the matter, "Yes, it's true."

He crossed the street to Mrs. Ellison's house and knocked loudly. She answered the door and for a moment was clearly considering shutting it in his face. But he said, "It's about your daughter."

She allowed him to come in, then, to

stand like a tradesman in the entry.

"What do you want with my daughter?"

"Inspector Cain discovered a letter in his predecessor's files. It was from a Mrs. Greer, of London, asking to be paid for six months' lodging at her house. Your daughter had left without settling her account."

She replied curtly, "To my shame. But I will say on her behalf that she'd lost her husband, she had had to give up her child, and she went to France to heal. I haven't told anyone, it's too embarrassing. I hope you'll respect my request to keep the matter between us."

"What's become of Beatrice Ellison Mason, Mrs. Ellison. You must know."

She looked away from him. "She's dead. I never told Emma that. She preferred to think her mother was in London, painting. She went to Paris, you see, married a Belgian there, and she was in Liège when the Germans bombarded the city. She must have been one of the casualties, because I haven't had any news of her since July of 1914."

"She wrote to you?" he asked with surprise.

She turned away from him, scorn on her face now. "No. I had other means of learning her whereabouts. Someone I went to school with was living in Paris, and she sent me news when she could. That's how I knew of my daughter's second marriage. I would think that other children had come then, and Beatrice must have felt awkward telling her new husband about Emma."

"Why should he care, if he loved her?"

"Beatrice often made rather free with the truth. And Mason isn't the most romantic name for an artist. She called herself Harkness, I understand. It has a finer ring to it, I expect."

"Is she telling the truth?" Hamish asked.

Rutledge thought she was. There was conviction in her voice, and he could see that she was tense with feeling, her hands clenched together until the knuckles showed white.

"Why did you let your granddaughter write to a London address that didn't exist? That must have been a cruel disappointment when the letters were returned unopened."

"You aren't a mother, Inspector," she snapped at him. "How can you be the judge of what's best for a young, easily impressed child who thought Maid Marian was a heroine and who wanted to spread her own wings?"

"The truth from the beginning might have been easier. There's still the chance that she went to London in search of her mother. And London is no place for a young girl alone. Anything could have happened to her there. Doesn't that frighten you?"

"She would never have done such a foolish thing. You didn't know her."

"Then perhaps she went there looking for a young man who had marched off to war."

If he had struck her, she wouldn't have looked any more shocked and angry. *"How dare you!"*

"You were young once —"

"My granddaughter was a God-fearing young lady. I saw to that. Get out of my house!"

He left then, aware that he had upset her and that any other questions would have been useless.

Mrs. Ellison had barricaded herself in a comfortable, private world of her own, secure from hurt. Struggling to ignore the loss of her only child and her only grandchild. Refusing to understand that she might have driven both of them away with her strong sense of propriety and family duty. Artists came to a no-good end, and it

274

could be argued that Beatrice had chosen her own fate. But that young girl's bedroom was still waiting for young Emma, regardless of the fact that she might have grown into an entirely different person if she was still alive. Harder, perhaps, disillusioned, certainly, and possibly no longer innocent.

After the door had closed, he wished he'd asked her for the name of her school friend in Paris.

As he walked through Dudlington, trying to clear up the mounting pile of evidence that went nowhere, contradicting itself at every turn, Rutledge saw Grace Letteridge coming out of the butcher's shop.

She hesitated when she looked up and found he was striding toward her, then straightened her shoulders and stood there waiting for him.

As if I were the guillotine, he thought, and Hamish added, "She doesna' want to talk about the past."

When he came up to her, she said, "I'd like to hear that Constable Hensley has died of infection."

He made himself smile. "It wouldn't help, would it? He's not the source of your anger."

"What do you mean?"

"It's cold, and the street isn't the proper place to talk about private matters. Will you come to the police station, or shall I accompany you to your house? Either way, there's no tea to be found in either of them."

She laughed ruefully. "I do have tea. Come on, then, and I'll make us both a cup."

They walked back to her house in silence. She'd refused to let him carry her purchases, and he didn't press.

She took his hat and coat and pointed him toward the parlor. He stood there, studying the watercolors done by Beatrice Mason. They were good, he couldn't fault them technically. But he wondered if she would have made the essential leap to London tastes, a quality that would have made her first-rate. As Catherine Tarrant and others had done in oils. It would depend, he decided, on her dedication and how quickly her skill matured.

"She had a husband and a child," Hamish reminded him. "They would ha' dragged her down."

What if her dreams had faded, and she realized that a little talent could be more heartbreaking than none? It might explain her decision to marry her first husband and then her second. Security, while she played at being an artist. Security while she went to parties or showed her portfolios, and talked about her work. Hardly the glory she might have hoped for, but talented wives were given a very different reception from young women struggling alone in rooming houses with no entree into society.

He turned as Grace Letteridge came back with a tray of tea things. "You'll have to make do without cakes or sandwiches. But at least it's warm."

Rutledge took the cup she handed him, adding sugar and milk from the tray.

"You like her work, I think?" Grace said, glancing up at the paintings.

"She has a wonderful sense of light," he told her.

"Yes, that's what struck me. Harder to achieve in watercolors, I should think, than in oils."

She took a chair on the far side of the room and said, "All right, what is it? You're bursting to ask questions, aren't you?"

"I've been trying to piece together some of the things I've learned as I asked questions about Hensley and Emma Mason —

and lately, asking questions about her mother as well. Is Beatrice Ellison Mason living comfortably in Liège, do you think? Or did she die in the German attack in 1914?"

"Liège? I'd never heard that Beatrice had moved to Liège. Why are you asking me? You know we never kept in touch, or I'd have known where to search for Emma. What does Mary Ellison have to say about that?"

"She believes her daughter went to Paris, married there, and shortly afterward, moved to Belgium."

"Well, then, what's the matter with that?"

"I think Mrs. Ellison has been covering up the truth, that Beatrice was dead." It was what he himself had begun to accept. "Did Emma ever suspect that?"

"Of course not. She believed her mother was living in London. It's what the whole world — well, what the Dudlington world believed, anyway." She set her teacup down and considered the policeman in her parlor. "Are you suggesting that Beatrice killed herself? That she couldn't face living without her husband, and after seeing to Emma's future, she did something awful?"

Mary Ellison would never admit that her

daughter was a suicide — it was not something that happened in respectable families, and her pride would prefer that people believed any plausible tale rather than stumble on the truth.

"My friend in Paris writes . . ."

"It needna' be suicide," Hamish said. "There's prostitution."

Social suicide, by anyone's standards.

"Perhaps that's why Mrs. Ellison paid the debt at the rooming house, when Mrs. Greer wrote to demand her money. It could have been quiet blackmail."

"What debt?" Grace Letteridge asked him. "And who was blackmailing whom?"

He'd answered Hamish aloud. Cursing himself, he said, "No one. I was just speculating on something that Inspector Cain discovered in the records Inspector Abbot had left. An address for Beatrice Mason in 1904. But it was useless by the time Mrs. Ellison learned of it two years later." He quickly shifted the subject. "Do you remember Abbot?"

"Of course. We saw him about as often as we see Inspector Cain. He would pay brief visits to Dudlington from time to time, looking in on the shopkeepers and the rector and the doctor. Keeping his ear to the ground, he'd called it."

"What sort of policeman was he?"

"He was disastrous when it came to something serious like Emma's disappearance. He couldn't fathom why she'd left a loving and comfortable home to run off to London. He was close to retirement, old-fashioned in his thinking about women, and unwilling to believe that a Harkness could do anything approaching the scandalous. He left most of the questioning to Constable Hensley. Mrs. Ellison was distraught, and it didn't help when Inspector Abbot badgered her, practically tearing poor Emma's room apart in an effort to learn how she'd hoped to make her way to London. The fact is, no one came forward and admitted to helping Emma leave, and in the end the inquest returned a verdict of foul play by person or persons unknown. That upset Mrs. Ellison even more, and I lost my temper with Constable Hensley, calling him incompetent and stupid. And that's when I began to suspect him. I couldn't believe a London-trained policeman was so inept. He had to be covering up something, and the only thing that made sense was his part in Emma's murder."

"Murder is hardly more socially acceptable than suicide."

"Yes, well, even the fact that Mary Ellison is related to the Harkness family isn't much comfort to her now." The words were bitter, spoken with anger.

"I'm told that someone saw Emma somewhere behind the church one day, rolling in the grass, as he put it, with a young man."

She stared at him. "So that's —" And then she broke off.

"That's what?" Rutledge asked when she failed to go on.

Grace Letteridge shook her head vehemently, but her mouth had tightened.

"Who was the young man?" he persisted.

But she was already collecting the tea things and carrying them out to the kitchen, effectively closing the subject.

He followed her through the house.

"I even know the name," he told her as she set the tray on the kitchen table, her back to him. "It was Robert Baylor —"

She whirled so quickly he wasn't prepared, couldn't even defend himself. Her right hand slapped him so hard across the face that he saw pinpoints of light dancing in front of his eyes.

"Don't ever say his name to me, do you hear? Don't you ever *dare!*"

And before he could prevent it, she was

out of the room and going up the stairs where he couldn't follow her.

Rutledge stood there in the kitchen, his face stinging and his own anger mounting.

"You shouldna' ha' pressed her sae hard. No' if the young man was hers."

"If it was Robert Baylor who seduced Emma Mason, why does she feel so strongly that it was Hensley who killed the girl?"

But then there was no proof that Emma had been seduced. She could just as easily have fought Baylor off. Especially if the attack had been a trial balloon, as it were. A test to see whether this very pretty girl was willing or not. Hensley, on the other hand, hearing about what appeared to be a successful seduction, might well have tried his own luck, and when Emma threatened to tell her grandmother, rid himself of the girl and the problem.

Then why had Hensley even brought up what Constable Markham thought he'd seen?

Because, Rutledge realized, Robert Baylor was safely dead in France and couldn't deny it. And Hensley had quietly managed to shift suspicion to Grace Letteridge.

Hensley was clever. He'd escaped one

black mark against his name in London. He couldn't have risked a second one here, particularly not laying hands on a young girl whose grandmother was connected to the Harkness family.

Was that a strong enough motive for the first murder? Emma's?

Bowles had given the constable a second chance, allowing him to redeem himself in the backwaters of Northamptonshire. But even Bowles would quickly wash his hands of Hensley if there was a raging scandal of that nature. Chief Superintendent Bowles valued his title and his position more than he valued a subordinate.

Rutledge had the feeling that the disconnected bits and pieces were beginning to make more sense.

But what about the second attempt at murder? Hensley's own?

Rutledge had made an enemy of Grace Letteridge, bringing up Robert Baylor's name. And if she'd shot Hensley in revenge for what she believed he'd done to Emma, Rutledge realized he'd better be watching his own back.

Then where exactly did the relationship between Robert Baylor and Grace Letteridge fit into this picture?

21

In late afternoon, Rutledge walked to The Oaks and received a chilly reception from Keating.

"When am I to have my barmaid back again?"

"It won't be long. Towson is showing improvement."

"What brings you to my door? I've nothing more to say to you."

"I've come to speak to one of your guests. Mrs. Channing. Is there a parlor where we can speak privately?"

"You're not to upset her," Keating told him belligerently. "Not under my roof."

Surprised by such unexpected protectiveness, Rutledge said, "I've come to ask a favor of her. Not badger her."

Hamish said, "She has befuddled him."

Keating went away to speak to her and after several minutes returned to conduct Rutledge to a small but pretty sitting room done up in cream and gold, as if Keating had followed the existing color scheme when he repainted the room for his use.

Meredith Channing was there, standing.

"Is anything wrong?" she asked anxiously, trying to convey her concern without giving the listening Keating anything to whisper about over the bar.

"I need someone I can trust to help me test a theory."

"Ah." She nodded to Keating, thanking him and dismissing him at the same time.

The innkeeper left the room reluctantly, and Rutledge wouldn't have put it past him to listen outside the door.

"I didn't know I was someone you trusted," she told Rutledge with a wry smile. "You continue to surprise me."

He had the grace to flush and said, answering her smile, "It's your eyesight and your honesty I want to put to the test."

"Then tell me what you need."

"Will you come with me first, to pay a visit to the rector, Mr. Towson? He's taken a nasty fall, and I think you might cheer him a little."

He inclined his head toward the door, and she glanced at it, recognizing his suspicion.

"Of course. Let me fetch my coat, Inspector, and I'll come directly."

He waited in the entrance hall, and after a time she came dressed in a warm coat of deep burgundy and a very attractive hat. He thought of his sister Frances, who enjoyed hats and wore them with grace and style.

She walked with him down the hill to Whitby Lane and then to Church Street. When they were out of earshot of the inn, she said, "Do you really wish me to visit the rector? I can't quite believe you've got the time to take up good works."

"As a matter of fact, you'll spend a few minutes with him, and afterward I want to take you to a window in his attic. I'd like you to wait there until I've walked to Frith's Wood, and then mark my progress. After that, depending on what you've got to tell me, I'll take you to stand at another post."

"Why me?"

"Because as far as I can tell, God help me, you haven't got any connection to anyone here, and you have no reason to lie about what you see. I need that objectivity."

She laughed. "Ian — I may call you Ian, I think, if I'm pressed into service by the Yard — what is it I'm supposed to see?"

"Wait a bit, until I've shown you the setting. Then it should be very clear."

They walked on in silence. Her stride

matched his; this was a woman who was independent and self-assured — and more than a little unsettling.

When they turned into Church Street, she said, "Oh, what an interesting church!"

"As a reward for good behavior, I'll show you the ceiling before I take you back to the inn. Which reminds me, do you think Keating is trustworthy? You're the only guest now. And his barmaid is currently nursing the rector."

"Oh, I think I'm quite safe. My virtue as well as my life. What is Keating's history? One seldom meets an innkeeper who is surly to his guests, as if he would prefer it if they never came at all."

"I don't know, frankly. He appears to like The Oaks because it isn't in the center of Dudlington, as most pubs and inns generally are. He isn't watched, I expect — not a part of the rampant gossip that keeps the village on its toes."

"Yes, that could be. The bar isn't rowdy at night, I can tell you that. Oh, people laugh and they play at darts and there's even a chessboard in one corner, if anyone is interested. I peeked in there this afternoon when he'd gone to Letherington to buy my dinner."

"You'd make a good policeman," he told

her, opening the gate to the rectory walk. "Watch the flagstones."

But she'd turned to look beyond at the encroaching fields. "It's so barren, so empty."

"There are fruit trees here and there. In fact I think that's a pear in the corner of the wall. It might be pretty here in the spring — or pastoral in summer, when the cattle and sheep are out there grazing."

"Yes, I'm sure. But just now, I feel — I don't know — the word that comes to me is naked."

"A target," Hamish said, and Rutledge shivered.

She turned back, and he followed her up the walk.

He went to the rector's room first and told him that there was an attractive visitor downstairs.

"Who is it?" He raised himself on his pillows, drawing his dressing gown across his nightclothes.

"You don't know her. But I think you'll enjoy her company."

Towson, his spirits lifting, said, "Have I shaved properly? And my hairbrush, it's there on the top of the tall dresser."

When Towson was satisfied, he said, "Is Hillary still in the kitchen? I might ask her to bring us tea." His expression was longing, and Rutledge laughed.

"I'll see to it."

When he returned with Mrs. Channing, Rutledge watched in amusement as the rector's eyes widened.

"I'm so sorry to meet you under such unhappy circumstances," she said warmly, walking to the bed to take his hand. The Queen herself couldn't have done it more graciously, moving down long rows of wounded in a hospital ward.

Rutledge, standing in the door, saw Towson rise to the occasion and, even in his dressing gown, put on his churchman's face, finding the right words to welcome his guest.

Leaving them to get acquainted, he went down to the kitchen and asked Hillary Timmons to prepare tea.

By the time Rutledge came back with the tray, Mrs. Channing and the rector were gossiping like old friends. He found himself pouring the cups and passing them, listening to a conversation about the works of Dickens.

He had already told Mrs. Channing what he wanted of her, and now he explained what he needed to Towson. He borrowed Mrs. Channing for a few minutes to show her the way to the attics and warn her to beware on the stairs.

And then he left, going out the door to the back garden, letting himself out of the back gate, and walking openly up the sloping pastures toward Frith's Wood.

It took him no more than fifteen minutes to reach the wood and step into the outriders of trees. They seemed to close in after him, and he was in the heart of the wood, walking without haste first one way and then the other.

Hamish, unhappy with the exercise, made no bones about it, telling Rutledge roundly that he was asking for trouble.

"Nothing is going to happen," he said, his voice steady.

But he felt again that sense of being watched, and of something unpleasant surrounding him.

He moved on, in a half circle, then began to make his way to the fringe of the wood, before walking briskly back to the rectory.

Only once did he let himself glance at the windows of the Baylor house, but he could see no one there.

He found a very distressed Meredith Channing waiting for him by the stairs as he came through from the kitchen.

"You hadn't told me about the wood —

not the truth!" she exclaimed, her hands clasped together in front of her.

"It's an old wood, surrounded by legend —"

"It's a cold and brooding place. And I thought I saw a shadow following you, looming there among the trees. I couldn't call out a warning — you couldn't have heard me if I had. But it was all I could do to stay by the window and watch."

"What kind of shadow?"

"I don't know, a darkness, something. I was too far away to tell."

He wondered for a moment if she'd made it up.

"You could see me moving through the copse then. Could you tell who it was, walking there? Or see what I was doing?"

"I could only be sure a man was there, in among the trees. Because I knew it was you, I could identify you, yes. If it had been a stranger, I couldn't have sworn to what he looked like. And there were times when you were concealed behind a knot of branches or thick patches of undergrowth. It really depended on the line of sight through the trunks and brush."

"You've just met the rector. Could you have identified Towson if he'd been out there?"

"I think I probably could have. Unless he was heavily bundled up in a coat and scarf. Then I'd have been less sure."

"Tell me about the shadow. Who was it?"

"It wasn't — you'll think me mad — it wasn't really human. It was something shapeless, hovering near you."

Someone heavily disguised, like the soldier in Mrs. Massingham's pasture? Hamish had felt it too, that sense of danger.

"Was it something I could have turned around and touched? Or a sixth sense, created out of what you felt about that wood?"

Meredith Channing shook her head. "Don't ask me to answer that. I don't know. But I can tell you this much. I had the strongest feeling while I was watching that if you went into that wood after dark, you might not come out alive."

They thanked the rector and said goodbye, walking out into the golden light of an approaching sunset. It gave the cold and empty fields a glowing warmth, and set shadows by the stream, while the church spire seemed to be on fire.

"Come into the church," Rutledge said.

"It may be too dark, but I'd promised to take you there."

Mrs. Channing was still distressed by her experience in the attics and her first thought was to refuse. He could see it in her face. But then she went with him to the tower door.

In the sanctuary there was still an afterglow, spilling through the stained glass and giving to the painted ceiling just the right blend of light and shadow to make it seem real, rising high above their heads into a blue sky with cushions of clouds that seemed solid enough for saints and angels to float on.

"How lovely!" she exclaimed, walking farther into the church and turning a little for the best view. "And how unexpected out here in the middle of nowhere."

"It's a trick of the eye," Rutledge told her. "Move this way and look again."

"Good heavens. That's quite amazing, isn't it? And very suitable here."

"Yes." He let her walk around on her own, her head tilted, the light sometimes touching her hair or her face or the burgundy of her coat.

"I imagine it wouldn't be easy to do this on a flat surface over your head, and know as you worked that it would have dimensions. When was it done?"

"Sometime in the early nineteenth century, when the village was moved here and rebuilt."

"Well, it was a gifted hand, I should think." She took one final look, and then went back to him, where he was waiting by the sanctuary door.

They stepped through it and shut it and were crossing the flagged floor to the main door, when there was a sound well above their heads.

As if something — or someone — had accidentally touched the clapper of the bell. The echoing note seemed to be caught somewhere above them, a resonance that had nowhere to go.

Rutledge looked up at once, to see if the bell rope had moved. It was stirring a little, but whether from being touched or from the wind through the shuttered windows by the clock face, he couldn't be sure.

He was strongly tempted to go up the stone steps to the wooden ones, and see for himself, but there was Mrs. Channing to consider as well.

She must have read something in his face, for she said, "Don't —"

"I think there's someone above us," he told her quietly. "I want to see who it is.

Open the tower door and go back to the inn. I'll be all right here. He can't stay up there forever."

"No, if I leave he'll see me. He'll know you're waiting and be ready. No!"

It was true.

He debated for only a moment longer and then said, "Stay here."

He went up the stone steps swiftly and as quietly as he could, though his footsteps seemed too loud, filling the tower room with their noisy progress.

He came through into the level where the wooden flights began and looked up into the darkness of the tower. A single rotted leaf drifted down from above, brushing his shoulder.

The shutters cast slanted bars of light across the face of the bell, but below and above, there was gloom. And as he watched, the bars of light began to fade, and the gathering dusk left the tower completely dark.

There had been no one on the stairs when he had begun to climb. And no one beside the bell. He'd have wagered his life on it.

Whoever it was had climbed well up into the spire and was hidden there in the shadows that were growing deeper by the minute. And he himself had no torch with him.

Rutledge stopped.

There were better ways to catch whoever it was.

He made his way back down again, making no attempt to conceal his movements this time.

Mrs. Channing was standing there, face upturned, a pale blur in the dimness. "Ian?"

"Let's be off," he said, and opened the tower door for her.

In silence, they went down the walk to Church Street and then turned into Whitby Lane.

"Go to Hensley's house and wait for me there," he said to her. "I want to make my way back to the church."

"I'd rather you didn't —"

"Yes, but there isn't much choice. Go on, before I lose him."

She did as she was told, walking briskly up the lane without looking back. A sharp wind swirled a dust devil at her feet as Rutledge retraced his steps to the end of the street. There was a house on the corner, but no lamplight shone out its windows. He flattened himself against the outside wall and moved on to the next house, which faced Church Street.

He stopped there, his view toward the church open.

The houses fronting the street were quiet, and no one was about except for a large dog sniffing at the gutters. There was an empty motorcar standing in front of one door, and a lorry by another. He could hear the sound of hammering from that house, as if a tradesman was finishing work on a door or other wooden surface. The banging was rhythmic and steady, and then silence fell. From somewhere he could hear a child's voice, raised in a question, and another dog barked at the first, warning it to mind where it stopped.

Rutledge waited a quarter of an hour. And then the church door opened and someone came out, shutting it quickly behind him. He studied the night, looking for movement, and then began to walk around the church on the side away from the rectory.

Rutledge broke into a sprint, going after the dark shape.

He was fast, and he was determined, but by the time he reached the church, it was too dark to see where the figure had gone — out into the open fields, or north toward Frith's Wood, or whether it had simply disappeared into a back garden where it was to all intents and purposes invisible.

Rutledge searched for a good half hour but came up with nothing.

As he walked back toward Hensley's house, he said, "It wasn't a dead soldier this time. It was a living human being."

"With no guid reason to climb yon tower. Unless he'd followed you from the wood."

"Did he know the church tower could be climbed, before I went up it?" he asked, thinking it through. "Did he step inside the church while I was in the spire, unable to see him? I was so busy searching for the best view, I could have missed the sound of the church door opening."

Hamish didn't answer him.

"And where has he vanished to now?" Rutledge went on. But he'd seen the houses from the spire, each with its back garden and a few with a narrow alley that led to a street. There were a hundred places where someone could hide, without drawing attention to himself. He had the advantage, squatting in the dark, leaning into the shadow of a chimney, flattened into a doorway. It was a cat-and-mouse game that Rutledge was not likely to win.

That thought made him swear.

His footsteps echoed, the lane was quiet,

the shops dark. Everyone had gone home. Soon Mrs. Melford would be setting her table in the dining room, expecting him to come. And Mrs. Channing was waiting for him as well.

There was a lorry coming up behind him, he could hear the changing of the gears as the corner was turned, and the sound of the motor gaining speed to take the slight rise in the lane.

At first he didn't make the connection. He assumed that the workmen had finished for the day and were leaving Dudlington. Or heading to The Oaks for a pint before going back to their place of business.

The odd thing was, they'd forgotten to turn on the lorry's headlamps.

The heavy vehicle was almost on his heels when he realized it wasn't workmen behind the wheel. Not at that speed — not without lights.

Hamish was shouting something, and Rutledge made a wild dive for the small rose garden in front of Grace Letteridge's house.

The wing of the lorry struck his leg and clawed at his shoe. He landed hard among the stubby rose canes, one of them stabbing into his shoulder, and his arm hurt as it took his full weight. Then he rolled.

A long, high-pitched screech of metal on stone filled the air, and the lorry's wing scraped heavily against the wall, knocking it inward on top of Rutledge before veering away. The heavy stones rained down on Rutledge's ankles and shins, even as he tried to see who was behind the wheel.

From down the lane there was shouting, two men racing toward the lorry, ordering it to stop. And doors were flung open on either side of the lane, light spilling out onto the cobblestones, silhouetting people attracted by the noise. He heard a woman's voice crying out, and then the lorry was gone, taking the turn into Holly Street with squealing tires before disappearing up toward The Oaks and the open road.

Rutledge was beginning to feel the battering he'd taken, his ankle throbbing, his arm going numb under him, and something gouging at his stomach, as though trying to tear through his shirt into his flesh.

He lay there for an instant, trying to collect himself, and then Grace Letteridge was standing above him.

"Look what you've done!" she was exclaiming. "My roses —"

"The lorry —" he said.

But she was too angry to listen. "It wouldn't have happened if you hadn't been here, poking about! It's your fault."

The two workmen went thundering by, their breathing loud and one of them swearing, the same words spilling out over and over again, threatening what he would do when he caught the thief.

Rutledge got slowly to his feet, nearly as angry as Grace Letteridge was. Taking her by the shoulders, he shook her lightly, and said, "Shut up and listen to me. Did you see who was at the wheel?"

Shocked into silence, she glared at him. Finally his words seemed to sink in and she retorted, "No, why should I have? Look at my poor wall — look what you've done to my roses."

"The wall can be repaired, the roses put back in the ground." He turned to the faces staring at him from windows and doorways. "Did any of you get a good look at the person driving?"

There were head shakes, denial, and one man said, "There wasn't time."

Dr. Middleton was hurrying through the garden gate, staring around at the damage. "My good God!" he said, looking Rutledge up and down. "Are you in one piece, man?"

"Barely." Rutledge looked at the torn cloth of his trousers, and he had a feeling the dark lines marking his leg were blood from a cut.

"Here, Grace, we need your house until I find out what's broken," Middleton ordered.

"I don't want him in the house," she cried. "I've enough work to do here."

A voice called from up the lane. "Here, Doctor. Bring him in here."

Rutledge swung around to see Mrs. Channing standing beside Mrs. Melford, outside Hensley's house.

"Can you make it that far?" Middleton asked him.

"Don't worry, I'll get there." He turned his back on Grace Letteridge and walked stiffly, limping a little, out of the garden and toward the two women.

He could feel her staring at his back, her anger still palpable.

22

Both Mrs. Channing and Mrs. Melford followed him into Hensley's office, with Dr. Middleton at their heels.

Mrs. Channing disappeared toward the back of the house, and Mrs. Melford pushed a chair forward for Rutledge to sit in.

He sat, grateful to be off his feet.

Someone came to the door to hand Dr. Middleton the shoe that Rutledge had lost by the wall. He glimpsed an unshaven face, and then it was gone.

The doctor took the other chair from behind the desk and propped Rutledge's right leg across it.

"These trousers won't be mended," he said, and searched in his bag for his scissors, cutting the cloth to peel it back from the wounds.

There was a darkening bruise near his thigh, and the back of his leg was bloody, a long cut running down the calf. Middleton looked up as Mrs. Channing came in.

She said to him, "There's water on to

boil. Fortunately the fire hadn't gone out."

She took in the damage to Rutledge's ankle, already turning red over the strengthening blue of a bruise, and said, "You were lucky, you know."

"Stupid," he answered, "is more to the point."

Middleton straightened, turning Rutledge's face toward him. "You've scraped your cheekbone on something. Where else?"

Mrs. Melford followed Mrs. Channing back to the kitchen as Rutledge opened his shirt. The canes of the rosebushes had left their mark on his shoulder and across one arm, on his stomach, and along his side. Their thorns had torn at his hands. Dr. Middleton went for the water himself, came back to bathe Rutledge's wounds and sprinkle an antiseptic powder on them, then cleaned the gash on his calf.

"You're going to be sore tomorrow," the doctor warned him. "Who was that fool driving, I'd like to know. He ought to be shot."

"A good question. There's a clean shirt in my luggage in Hensley's room and another pair of trousers." He looked ruefully at the earth caked on his coat, and all but filling one of his shoes.

The doctor finished his work. "That's

three," he said tightly. "Hensley. Towson. You. I'd like to know what's going on here."

"Damned if I know." Rutledge's cheekbone had begun to throb. He put up a hand to touch it, realized the hand was filthy, and let it drop again.

"Who's the lady with Mrs. Melford? A friend of hers?"

"No. She's from London." He flexed his arm and shoulder, then bent his knee a time or two. He wouldn't be climbing back up the spire ladder anytime soon.

"I don't understand. *Was* it an accident? You'd have thought the driver might have stopped, if it were!"

"It was intentional. Someone had taken a lorry standing outside one of the houses on Church Street."

"That would be the Lawrences'." Middleton nodded. "They had worm, and much of the wood has to be replaced. I say my prayers every night that there's none to be found in my house. Insidious little beasts!" He paused. "I hesitate to ask, but you don't believe it was anyone at the Lawrences', do you? I can't for the life of me —"

"No." Rutledge bent to drag his stocking back over a rapidly swelling ankle just as the door opened, and the two workmen, clad in overalls, stepped inside.

"The lorry was just at the top of the rise, where Holly Street runs up to The Oaks," the older of them said. "Door open, no one inside."

Rutledge saw Middleton's look. Whoever it was could have slipped back into Dudlington, or was long since gone up or down the main road.

"Who's to pay for the damage, then?" the second of the men demanded. "It'ull cost a pretty penny to set things right."

"Submit your charges, and I'll look into it," Rutledge said. "Did you see anyone prowling about outside the Lawrence house while you were clearing away half an hour ago?"

"Their little dog was shut in a bedroom. He barked madly for a few minutes. We thought it might be a passing cat. Ill-tempered little beast, that dog. Working around him will cost the Lawrences, I can tell you. Too bad he didn't sink his teeth in whoever it was stole the lorry."

"I'll bring you a list of damages tomorrow," his companion promised Rutledge. "We're late as it is." He considered Rutledge's injuries. "Nasty piece of work, the bastard. What did he want to go and do that for?"

With that pronouncement, he turned on his heel and ushered the other man out.

Rutledge had buttoned his shirt and was gingerly shoving his foot into a scraped and flattened shoe.

Mrs. Channing came in at that moment. "Mrs. Melford has gone to fetch your dinner. She doesn't feel you ought to be walking about just yet. I'll see myself to the inn, and we can talk more tomorrow."

"Stay —" he began.

But she shook her head. "You've had enough on your plate, Inspector."

"You shouldn't walk up that road in the dark. They've just found the lorry abandoned there."

Grace Letteridge stuck her head in the door, half expecting to be turned away. Her anger had faded, and she waited for Rutledge to acknowledge her.

"I'm sorry for yelling at you," she said contritely, then looked from Rutledge to Mrs. Channing. "I realized afterward that you had nowhere else to go to get out of that fool's way. What on earth was he trying to do?"

He made no effort to introduce the two women. "Someone stole the lorry and lost control of it as they sped away."

"Yes, well, I'd like to know who it was.

I'll make him pay for the damages."

"You're in line behind the workmen who lost the lorry."

"Is he seriously injured?" Grace Letteridge turned to ask Dr. Middleton.

"He'll live," the doctor said. "You were rude, Grace. I'm not best pleased with you, just now."

"Yes, it was ill done," she admitted. "Mr. Rutledge."

And she was gone, shutting the door behind her.

"Thank you, Doctor," Rutledge said, getting to his feet and testing the bad ankle. "I can manage now, I think."

"If you need anything to ease the pain, send for me." The doctor gathered up his things and closed his bag. "Stay off that ankle, if you don't want it twice its size tomorrow. A cold bath wouldn't hurt."

He nodded to Mrs. Channing and left.

"He's a good man," she said, staring after him.

"Yes." He had drawn on his coat. "I don't like the idea of you staying at The Oaks."

"I'm safe enough there — you aren't intending to walk me home, are you?"

"Of course."

He took several steps while Hamish

badgered him, and said, "It doesn't hurt, however bad it might appear to be."

"You're a liar, Inspector. Well. There's more hot water on the stove. You must soak that ankle for a bit, when you come back. Then use only cold water."

She collected her own coat and said as she returned, "You could have been seriously injured. Who was it? Did it have anything to do with those wretched casings?"

"Probably." He held the door for her, and she stepped out into the street.

"Why should someone want to kill you? What have you done, to earn such hatred?"

"I don't know that he's ready to kill just yet. He's trying to frighten me. You called it waiting."

"Was it the person in the church tower?"

"Very likely."

"Then perhaps you're wrong about the casings. It could be that you've come too close to the truth here in Dudlington."

He could feel the ankle stiffening in the cold night air. "I don't know that I've reached that stage yet."

"Yet you wonder if it could be Keating who drove at you."

"I don't wonder so much as leave the possibilities open."

She took his arm to steady herself over

the cobblestones, or so she said, but he rather thought it was to help him manage them. They walked in silence the rest of the way.

Finally he said as they came to the door of the inn, "How do you live with what you feel — or know — or glimpse?"

"Very uneasily. How do you live with what you suspect, when you're halfway through solving a terrible crime? How do you even conceal what you feel?"

He thought about Westmorland then, and the doubts he'd felt there. And in so many other investigations.

"I decided to become a policeman to speak for the dead. They have no one else, you see. Somewhere there's always proof of what happened, some piece of evidence that will obtain a conviction. It's important for the guilty to be brought to justice, I think. Without justice, there's chaos."

"That sounds very like revenge, Inspector."

"No. I leave it to the court to judge. If I'm wrong, I expect the court to discover that during the trial."

Hamish said, "Nell Shaw."

And he could see her again, rough and awkward and bent on bringing him around to seeing evidence as she did. Evidence to refute her husband's guilt.

"Your cases stay with you," Meredith Channing remarked, as if she'd followed the direction of his thoughts.

He came quickly back to the present and remembered the woman he was speaking to.

In the dark, as they approached the lights of The Oaks, he glimpsed her face. It was withdrawn, looking inward. How much did she really know about what was happening to him?

Was she an enemy? Or a friend?

Rutledge left Mrs. Channing at the door of the inn.

As she went up the stairs, lighted by a faceted chandelier overhead, he could hear voices from the bar. They were talking about the accident with the stolen lorry. He listened for a moment, curious to see how it would be viewed.

Someone was saying, "— better if we were rid of him. I've heard it said he's not interested in what happened to the constable, it's an excuse to pry into other matters."

"What other matters?" a second voice asked. "There're no secrets here."

"I for one," a third voice broke in, "would like to know the truth about that brother of Baylor's. They say he's scarred, afraid to show his face on the street."

"That's ridiculous," the second voice retorted.

"Well, then, have you seen him yet?" someone else asked.

"No, but —"

"Yes, well, if you ask me, he's dying. Gas in the lungs, my wife heard in the greengrocer's."

"Ted won't talk about it."

"No. He's lost one brother, he doesn't want to lose the other."

"Of the two," the first voice put in, "I'd take Robbie over Joel any day. Robbie was a good man."

There was general agreement, and then the sound of chairs scraping on the floor.

People were leaving. Rutledge turned to go as well, before anyone found him there, eavesdropping.

Just as he reached for the handle to the door, he happened to glance back at the staircase.

At the top of it, barely visible in her burgundy coat, stood Mrs. Channing, her face a pale oval as she looked down the stairs straight at him.

He left, without acknowledging her presence there.

Rutledge found his dinner waiting on the table in Hensley's bare dining room.

It was still warm, and he sat down gingerly to eat.

His ankle ached like the very devil, and he realized he shouldn't have walked to the inn and back in the night air. But Mrs. Channing had said something about hot water on the stove.

Finishing his meal, he carried the dishes into the kitchen and turned up the lamp.

The teakettle was where Mrs. Channing had told him it was, and a hand over the spout told him that the contents hadn't cooled yet.

He poured water into a basin from under the sink, and sat down to take off his shoes. The stocking on his right foot was hard to remove, and he looked at the discolored ankle with distaste.

Lowering his foot into the water, he felt the warmth rise up his leg, and the gash on his calf began to sting. Ignoring it, he leaned his head back in the chair. Before long he could feel himself slipping into sleep.

It had been a long day, he thought. And it hadn't ended well.

Hamish said, "Listen!"

And he lifted his head.

There was a sound from the dining room.

He called, "Mrs. Melford? The dishes are here in the kitchen."

She didn't answer or come through.

After a moment, he got awkwardly to his feet, and leaving wet tracks behind him, he hobbled into the dining room.

No one was there.

Imagination, he thought. Or the brink of dreaming.

But Hamish wasn't satisfied, and Rutledge looked around a second time.

It was then he saw what was lying in the seat of his chair.

A shell casing.

Picking it up, he examined it. No carvings. Just a reminder that he was vulnerable, and might well have been run down by the lorry if he hadn't been agile enough to leap over the wall into Grace Letteridge's garden. An admission of responsibility.

He searched the house, but he knew it was useless.

Whoever it was had come and gone without being seen.

Rutledge slept poorly that night. For one thing his ankle throbbed, giving him no peace. For another, with the doors unlocked, there was no safety from intruders, and the smallest noise brought him up from restless sleep.

What did his stalker have to do with Constable Hensley? It was something Rutledge found difficult to believe — that Hensley's wounding had been a ruse to draw him north.

On the other hand, Dudlington offered its own peculiar opportunities for drawing him out into the open. And any killer worth his salt watched for his opportunity.

The question was, why should he, Rutledge, be stalked in the first place?

Was it Yard business? Then why the cartridge casings from a machine gun used in France? If it was something that had happened in the trenches, then why leave it this long, when the war had ended fourteen months before?

"He was in hospital."

Hamish's voice seemed loud in the bedroom, and Rutledge came awake with a start.

It made sense.

The more he thought about it, the more he believed it could be true.

But there were thousands of men suffering from war wounds, scattered all over the country. Trying to track down one man among them was hopeless.

Hamish said, "There's yon farmer's brother."

Rutledge considered Joel Baylor.

But they had never served together. The name was unfamiliar, and God knew, he'd learned the name of every man he'd sent into battle. He would have remembered.

Revenge was personal as a rule. Otherwise it was pointless.

He thought about what Mrs. Channing had said about revenge. And that brought him back again to Nell Shaw.

There was a very good chance that someone who had been sent to the gallows had left behind a family member with vengeance in his or her heart. Who was trying to say to him that the war might have delayed retribution but hadn't blunted the desire for it.

And since Rutledge hadn't died in France, he was fair game now.

"That sounds very like revenge, Inspector."

He could hear that warm, melodious voice speaking to him in the dark.

What had Meredith Channing to do with his past? She'd been in France, she said, and he believed her. She had seen him there, and he believed that as well.

But it was when they were brought together at Maryanne Browning's party that he had come within her reach once more.

She couldn't have followed him — fired at him — tried to run him down with the stolen lorry.

But she could very well have an accomplice, a son or nephew or even a paid assassin, to do what she physically couldn't.

It would explain, quite tidily, why she had learned his address, and why she had followed him here to Dudlington. To watch him die.

But was that true? Or only his feverish imagination searching for a real face in place of the nebulous one that seemed never to be quite mortal.

Hamish said, "Watch your back."

The night seemed to brighten suddenly, as a lamp was lit in the window across from his.

It took him longer to get out of his bed and to the window than he'd expected, and the floor was cold under his feet.

There was someone in Emma Mason's bedroom again, and although he watched for a good half hour, he couldn't tell who it was.

He was tempted to walk into the Ellison house to see for himself. But there was something else he could do.

Shoving his feet into his shoes and wrapping his coat around him with the belt, he walked down the stairs to the door and out into the street.

He found himself a vantage point from which he could see, just, the window in Emma's room and the rest of the darkened house.

When the light went out at last, he waited patiently.

The window on the stairs was lit for an instant, and then the light strengthened again in another pair of windows. After a minute or so, it was turned out.

Mrs. Ellison had been in her granddaughter's room and finally had found her way back to her own bed.

He hadn't been alone in his sleeplessness.

Loss, Rutledge thought, took many forms. And this was one of them.

23

Meredith Channing had also found it difficult to sleep.

When the scraping screech of metal had brought her to the door of the constable's house, she had stood there transfixed.

Rutledge was lying in the lee of a destroyed wall, one arm thrown out to brace himself, the other one pinned under him.

And then doors were flung open on all sides as the lorry roared on up the lane, and a young woman had come rushing out of a house to scream at the fallen man.

It was like seeing something in a dream, she thought, only the sounds were real, the shouts and the cries and that unbearable scraping of metal against stone.

The doctor had come running then, though she hadn't known who he was, taking charge and silencing the angry woman while Rutledge had struggled to one knee, then dragged himself to his feet.

She'd come to her senses at that stage, knowing what she must do.

And so she had called out to the doctor,

and the woman in the house but one had stood there with her, saying something about dinner and what on earth had been in that driver's mind, to do such damage and then flee.

When Rutledge reached the house, she had looked at the scrape on his cheekbone and the bleeding wound in his leg, his hands scratched and filthy from the soft earth in the garden.

Lockjaw, the woman called Mrs. Melford was saying, and she herself had hurried to the kitchen to heat water and find strong soap. After all, she'd been trained, she knew what to do in emergencies. More to the point, it kept her hands busy.

And all the while her heart had been thudding in her chest, like a drum.

It had been a near thing, she thought. Too near.

It wasn't until later, when she was walking through the winter darkness with her arm touching his, that she realized she had stopped thinking about him as a policeman.

It didn't do to know people, she thought. It was better to hold them at arm's length, and then it was easier, much easier, to stand aside and let them die.

She had learned that in the war.

Rutledge woke with a start and groped for his watch, lying on the bedside table. It was late, already half past seven. He groaned. How many hours had he slept? At most two or three. He felt as if his eyes had never closed.

He put his foot gingerly over the side of the bed and was relieved to feel less pain than he had during the night.

Hamish, his voice muted this morning, said, "Aye, but it's no' verra' handsome."

True, the swelling was still noticeable, the discoloration was worthy of an artist's palette. But he could stand with his full weight on it, after he had laced his shoes. The rest of his bruises were complaining, but not as vociferously. Stiffness plagued him, though, for a good ten minutes before he'd worked it out.

He shaved with haste and presented himself to Mrs. Melford, only two minutes late for his breakfast. He had to smile at her examination of the way he walked.

"Aye, she has a cane in yon umbrella stand."

And so she did. But she said nothing about it and disappeared into the kitchen as he sat down to eat.

When she brought in his tea, she finally

said, "I'm still shocked by what I saw last night. It was some time before I could sleep."

"Accidents do happen," he told her. "The driver couldn't have been familiar with the weight of a lorry."

"Inspector, you needn't try to put a better face on it. Everyone in Dudlington is talking about your narrow escape." She looked down at him in the chair at the head of her table. "That's three — Hensley, the rector, and now you. What's wrong here? What kind of monster are we harboring!"

Hamish clicked his tongue at the turn gossip had taken.

"I don't think —" Rutledge began.

But she shook her head. "I'd wondered why Scotland Yard sent an inspector all the way to Dudlington just because a constable had been injured. I couldn't see why Northampton shouldn't look into it. But you know something, don't you? That's really why you're here — there's something else that you're keeping from us. I might as well tell you what people are whispering."

She wouldn't listen when he tried to convince her there was no conspiracy to keep the truth from Dudlington. She simply walked away, saying she was tired of lies.

Trying to shrug off the depression settling over him, Rutledge finished his breakfast and was just stepping into the street when the postmistress came out of Hensley's house.

"There's a letter for you, Inspector. From the Yard. I thought it best to bring it to you straightaway."

"Thank you."

She smiled, one professional to another, and went hurrying back to her little cage in the corner of the shop.

"It'ull feed the gossip frenzy," Hamish told him. "A letter from London."

"Yes."

In fact, the letter had come from Sergeant Gibson.

"I'm writing this at home," it began. *"I dare not leave it lying about at the Yard."*

Rutledge sat down at the desk in the little office and looked through the two pages of Gibson's scrawl, hoping to find something of interest.

What the sergeant had written, distilled into its essence, was that the search for evidence against Hensley was hopeless. The sprawling black lines went on.

The file is straightforward. The fire, the blame settling on Mr. Barstow's competitor, and the charges brought against the man. But they never went to trial, those charges. Howard Edgerton's death was put down to infection. It's what took him off, true enough. I tried to look up his widow, but it appears she went to live with her family in Devon. The competitor, a Mr. Worrels, lost his business when the whispers had done their work. The file is presently listed as "Unsolved." I did discover the name of the man said to have set the fire. Barstow didn't do it himself, you understand. He hired a J. Sandridge, who was never caught. He'd been employed by Mr. Worrels and held a grudge over a promotion that never came his way —

Rutledge stopped reading.

Sandridge. Where had he heard that name?

Hamish said, "He doesna' live here."

But Rutledge had a good memory for names. It had served him well in the war.

He got up and went searching through the files in Hensley's box.

Sandridge — someone had written a letter inquiring for him. It was from a Miss Gregory asking if there was another address for him.

Coincidence? Or was there a connection?

Dudlington was too small to hold so many coincidences.

Rutledge went back to Gibson's letter, but there was nothing else of interest, except the last line.

I'd take it as a favor, if you burned this after reading it.

After committing the details to memory, he did as he'd been asked.

Although his foot was complaining stridently, Rutledge drove to Northampton to see Hensley. But the man was feverish, his face flushed, his body racked by chills.

Hamish growled something about infection.

As Rutledge drew up a chair, Hensley said, "I'm ill. It's that damned sister, she's been neglecting me."

But the ward was filled with cases, and the nurses were trying to cope.

Matron had ordered Rutledge to stay out of their way. The wall of a building had collapsed on Mercer Street, and five of the workmen had been brought in for surgery, along with two civilians unlucky enough to be walking beneath it. Rutledge had seen their families waiting in the corridor, wives white-faced and anxious, children with large, frightened eyes, clinging to their mothers and aunts.

He said, "Constable. Why did Bowles send you to Dudlington? There must have been a good reason for the choice."

"There was a man retiring. Markham. I was given his place. What does it matter? I was just as glad to be away from London for a bit."

"For a bit?"

Hensley moved restlessly, then grimaced. "They lanced my back this morning. I could have told them their incisions weren't healing properly. They thought I was a complainer and ignored me."

"Why were you happy to leave London and move to the North?"

"I was tired of hunting German spies. Half of it was someone's warped imagination. The butcher is surly, he has an accent, he's given some woman a bad bit of beef. Or the waiter doesn't look English. The man bringing in the luggage at a hotel seems furtive, won't meet the eyes of patrons when he's spoken to. You'd think, listening, that half the population of Germany was sneaking about England, looking to stir up trouble."

The speech sounded — rehearsed. As if Hensley had told the story so many times he half believed it himself.

"It had nothing to do with Edgerton, then." It wasn't a question.

Hensley turned to look at Rutledge. "Don't put words in my mouth, damn you."

"But you know very well who Edgerton was. And how he died. Did you also know someone named Sandridge?"

Hensley said, "Look, I'm not well, I shouldn't be badgered like this." His voice was sour. And he had long since stopped using "sir" when he addressed his superior.

Although Hamish was accusing him of badgering as well, Rutledge persevered. "Tell me about Sandridge."

"A woman wrote to the police in Dudlington, in search of someone by that name. I thought she might be looking for a soldier in the war, someone who'd made promises he didn't keep. Or he'd been killed, and she hadn't been notified, not being a relative, so to speak. I told her to try another village by the name of Dudlington, in Rutland."

"Your reply wasn't in the file."

"It ought to have been. I put it there myself."

Rutledge wasn't sure whether to believe him or not.

"And that's merely a coincidence. The fact that the fire setter in the Barstow arson was also a Sandridge?"

"I never put that together with London. Why should I? It's not that rare a name, surely. Sir."

"There were rumors that you'd taken money to look the other way, when the fire occurred. And rumors now that you were responsible for Emma Mason's death. Where there's smoke . . ."

"I didn't do nothing of the sort. Here, I won't stand for this, I'm a sick man. *Sister!*"

A tall, thin woman with reddish hair came at his urgent call.

"What is it, Constable?" she asked, beginning to smooth the rumpled bed linens.

"I'm not well, Sister, I need to rest. I think my fever is worse."

She touched his forehead, then turned to Rutledge. "I think you should leave, sir, if you would. We mustn't distress him just now."

Rutledge stood to go. But looking down at Hensley's face, the eyes turned away, his skin taut and red, he said, "When you come back to Dudlington, will you be safe?"

The eyes swung back to Rutledge, something in them that reminded him of a cornered animal.

Rutledge felt a surge of guilt.

"I won't be coming back," Hensley said tensely. "I've been thinking. I could take an early pension and go abroad. They do say Spain is all right. One of the night sisters lived there for a time, with an elderly couple. I think I might like it."

"They speak Spanish there, you know. Not English."

And then Rutledge was walking down the ward, toward the door.

When he looked back, Hensley was slumped in his bed, exhausted.

The drive back to Dudlington ended in a sudden downpour, wind whipping the rain through the motorcar. One sleeve was wet nearly to the shoulder by the time Rutledge turned down to Holly Street and put his car beside the house. And Hamish, still irritated with him for his callousness in the hospital ward, made certain that Rutledge was aware of it.

Still, he wondered if Hensley had told the truth regarding a copy of his response to the letter about Sandridge being in the file. Had he even written it? Or let sleeping dogs lie.

Rutledge got out stiffly, his ankle cold and more painful than he was ready to admit.

The house was chilly and dark, unwelcoming. And he always felt a sense of unease when he came in.

But there was no reason to think anyone had been there, although he went into each room to give it a cursory glance.

Changing out of his wet clothes, he laid a fire on the hearth in the sitting room and sat down, leaning his head against the back of his chair.

Hamish said, "I wouldna' let down my guard sae far."

Rutledge said, his eyes closed, "I'm not asleep."

"The lassie. With the garden. She came to apologize. You gave her short shrift."

"So I did. I was nearly as angry with her as I was with the bastard in the lorry."

"It was just as well yon woman from London wasna' with you when the lorry came up the lane."

"I don't know that he'd have tried to run me down, with witnesses there."

"On the ither hand, he could ha' waited until she was no' in the way, before taking the lorry."

Rutledge rubbed his eyes with both

hands, then massaged his temples. "I would like very much to know why she told me there was a shadow at my back, in Frith's Wood. What she'd really seen there." Yet he'd felt eyes watching him, every time he'd been in that wood. "Why would she lie? She has nothing to do with this business in Dudlington."

"You havena' asked her about Emma Mason."

He heard someone at the door, and then Mrs. Melford called to him.

He got up to walk to the parlor, his stiffened ankle giving him some difficulty. He found Mrs. Melford standing there with a basket in one hand and a streaming umbrella in the other.

"You missed your luncheon," she said. "I thought you might like the sandwiches for your tea."

"Yes, thank you."

He took the tray from her and said, "Come in, if you will. You've lived here for many years. I'd like to ask you a few questions."

"About what?" she asked, still holding the umbrella.

"About Beatrice Ellison, and her daughter, Emma Mason."

She reluctantly furled her umbrella and

stood it by the door, which she then shut behind her.

"I don't know anything other than gossip. You must know that. I haven't been friendly with Mrs. Ellison since Beatrice left. I thought the least her mother could do was to let the girl study painting for a bit and see if she was enthusiastic about the discipline of learning it properly. That must be quite different from painting for one's own pleasure."

"How did Beatrice get on in London?"

"Splendidly, as far as we knew. One had only to ask Mrs. Ellison, to hear a glowing report."

"Who was her daughter's teacher. Do you know?"

"If I heard the name, I don't recall it. You don't question Mrs. Ellison, you see. She'll tell you what she feels is any of your business, and nothing more than that. But I gathered that she was happy for the world to know that Beatrice had prospered. Even if she'd been against the whole idea."

"And then Beatrice came home with her child."

"Yes, that was the first and only time she'd come back. There were a few people who were terribly catty about it, saying that Beatrice had grown too famous to bother with Dudlington anymore. And of course there were others who were saying she hadn't come back because she had nothing to show for her years in London but the little girl."

"And then Emma left. What was the gossip then?"

"Of course it was that she'd gone to London to find her mother. We were sure Mrs. Ellison would rush after her and bring her back. That is, if it were true that Beatrice was a failure. And then the whispers began that Constable Hensley had had something to do with Emma's disappearance."

"What sort of whispers?"

"That since he knew London, he'd helped Emma escape her grandmother's clutches. That somehow he was involved. I can't tell you when the suspicion arose that he'd had more to do with her disappearance than was proper. That he'd asked a price for helping, and when Emma got frightened, he did away with her, to keep her from telling her grandmother. Mrs. Ellison is related to the Harkness family. Every one is wary of that, even the constable. I don't precisely know what she could *do* — but I imagine if she were to ask for an investigation, someone would listen."

"Do you think Mrs. Ellison knows about such whispers?"

"And who do you think would be bold enough to tell her!"

It was a good point.

"Thank you, Mrs. Melford. You've been very helpful." He was beginning to take her measure, the briskness that concealed her fear of being hurt again, the kindness that had remembered his tea. And he rather liked her. He thought she deserved more happiness than had come her way.

She nodded and turned to go, then asked, "Who was the woman with you yesterday? A relation?"

The gossip mill . . . She hadn't brought the sandwiches out of kindness after all. Or at least not completely.

"We have mutual friends," he said lightly.

"She was so clever about how to prepare for the doctor," Mrs. Melford answered, and picked up her umbrella. "It surprised me."

When she'd gone, Rutledge went back to the fire and ate his meal to the accompaniment of Hamish's voice, still in a foul mood.

The rain faded in another hour, and Rutledge limped down to Grace

Letteridge's house, stopping for a moment to look at the scene of the collision between wall and lorry. It had indeed been a near thing, he thought.

And Hamish, who had been silent for a time, said, "No' death, perhaps, but verra' severe injury. You'd lie like yon constable in a ward, with the sisters ignoring you."

Rutledge went on up the walk.

Grace Letteridge answered his knock and couldn't stop her eyes from dropping down to his ankle.

"You're walking, I see." She opened the door wider and reminded him to wipe his feet on the mat.

"I am. Someone has been seeing to your roses. The wall will take more work, I'm afraid."

"Yes, well, I had hoped this rain would settle the canes into the ground again. I won't know until the spring if they've survived."

"I'll pay for the damage," he said. "It was your garden that saved me from more serious injuries."

"Too bad for my garden," she answered, and led him into the parlor. "Was that why you came, to offer to pay? Or was there something else on your mind?"

He had intended to ask her outright if

she recognized the name Sandridge, and then decided, as Hamish growled in the back of his mind, that he wasn't sure where Grace Letteridge's loyalties lay. Instead he had brought a rough map he'd made of the village and asked her to pencil in the names in the box representing each house.

"Why bring it to me? Mrs. Melford or anyone else could have done it for you."

"That's probably true. On the other hand, I'd rather not have the fact that I'm doing this bandied about the neighborhood."

She took the sheet of paper and unfolded it, frowning over it. "You draw surprisingly well."

"Is there some requirement for policemen to be poor at sketching a map?"

Ignoring him, she began to put in the names of each householder. He waited patiently, letting her work without interruption.

After ten minutes, she sat back, the tip of the pencil between her teeth as she regarded her handiwork. Nodding to herself, she passed the sheet back to Rutledge.

He scanned it, searching for one name. But it wasn't there.

He did see that where Hensley's house ought to be was the name of the greengrocer, Freebold.

"Doesn't Hensley own the house he lives

in?" he asked, pointing to it.

"Perhaps he does. Constable Markham paid to rent it. I don't know what arrangement there is with Constable Hensley. I really don't care to know."

So Hensley could pull up his roots with ease, and make Spain or another country his home. He could also disappear with ease, and no one would be worried about property left behind. Certainly the furnishings in the house, while adequate, were far from valued pieces.

An interesting point, Hamish agreed. "But look you, where is the money he took as a bribe? He canna' put it into a bank, and he canna' leave it lying about, where anyone stepping in the door can find it."

Put his hands on that money, Rutledge thought, and he might have some leverage with Hensley to pry out the truth.

"Aye, but it's no' a part of your duty."

Just how much did Bowles know? Or care?

Grace Letteridge was saying, "Inspector?"

He came back from his thoughts. "I'm sorry —"

"I can't believe it was an accident. What happened last night. But why should someone want to kill Constable Hensley, and then when you come here, want to kill you as well?"

It was an echo of what he'd heard Mrs. Melford say.

He answered, "I don't believe the attacks are related."

"What else could they be? In a village this size?"

But he couldn't tell her about the cartridge casings.

24

Meredith Channing was waiting for him when he came home. She had set her umbrella by the door, and it was dripping a puddle of water across the floorboards when he stepped over the threshold.

"Ah. You've been away most of the day. I wondered how you were managing."

"Well enough."

She nodded. "So I can see. Sit down. You look very tired. It can't be easy, concealing the pain for hours. Even from yourself."

"You must have been a terrifyingly good nurse, if you could read your patient's mind."

"Some of them couldn't speak, you know. After a while one got used to making a fairly good guess about their needs."

"Why did you come here?" He'd asked it before and couldn't stop himself from asking it again.

"I don't know, to tell you the truth. What I felt with that shell casing on the table in my house was not particularly pleasant. And so I sent it back to you. But

339

the darkness was still there, as if it had left a — shadow behind. I could see it there, feel it even in the night. If it disturbed *me* so intensely, I was concerned about how it must have troubled you."

"Did you know anyone by the name of Edgerton, in London?"

"Edgerton. Wasn't there a cricket player by that name, before the war?"

"A tennis player, I think," Rutledge said, watching her face, but she showed no reaction to his fabrication.

"Well, then. What about him?"

"He died of burns after a fire."

"How horrible!" She stared at him. "Was he a friend?"

"I never met him."

"Then why do you think I may've?" She frowned. "Are you feeling feverish?"

Hensley was feverish, and that was a cause for anxiety. "I'm trying to learn how a man named Edgerton tied into this business with the constable."

"Your tennis player?"

He smiled at her. "Indeed. Never mind. I expect he died while you were in France. There's no reason you should remember him."

"No. We were quite cut off from everything but the fighting. We seldom had time to think about anything else. Sorry."

"There's another name I'm curious about. Sandridge."

Either she was a very good liar or this name also failed to mean anything to her. Shaking her head, she said, "No. Not familiar at all."

So much for that, he thought. He couldn't fathom her. As well as he read most people, she was an enigma. Behind the charming facade, behind the gracious manner and the warm, mesmerizing voice, what was she?

"I thought perhaps we might call on the rector," she was saying. "If you are up to walking so far. He must be lonely."

He went with her, though his preference, if asked, was to stay by the fire and let the ache in his ankle fade a little.

They reached the rectory in time to see a woman coming down the walk, and Rutledge recognized her as the postmistress, Mrs. Arundel.

She nodded to him, tipping back her umbrella to say, "I'm glad to see you suffered no lasting harm. From the look of Grace Letteridge's garden wall, you ought to be on crutches."

They knocked on the front door, and Hillary Timmons answered it, looking harried. "Good day, sir. They've all come to bring himself something — a pot of jam, a treat from the bake shop, a little broth. I'm fair run off my feet, trying to keep up."

"We've brought nothing," Mrs. Channing said soothingly. "Why don't I sit with him for an hour or so, and allow you to rest."

Hillary Timmons teetered on the thin edge of duty, and then capitulated.

"Just an hour, if you wouldn't mind," she said.

"Then have yourself a nap, and I'll stay with Mr. Towson. I'm even capable of making him tea."

"He's had tea twice already. First with Mrs. Freebold, and then with Mrs. Arundel." She sighed. "I've never seen such a man for a little bite of something sweet, as he puts it."

"Yes, well, then, we shan't be having tea. Go on, I'll show myself up to his room." And with that, Mrs. Channing started up the stairs.

Rutledge was on the point of following her when she said, "No. You'll be bored to tears, Inspector. But you might see if you can find a Dickens novel in Mr. Towson's study. I'll read to him, if he cares for a little distraction."

Rutledge discovered *Bleak House* sandwiched between a book of sermons and one of O. A. Manning's volumes of poetry. He took the novel up to the rector's bedroom, where Towson and Mrs. Channing were deep in a conversation that stopped as he came down the passage.

"I'm well enough, Inspector," he answered Rutledge's greeting. "But I'm told you've had an accident of your own. A stolen lorry! Who'd have thought it here in Dudlington? I'm happy to see Dr. Middleton didn't clap you in your bed and leave you to die of boredom."

"With only a bruise here and there?" Rutledge responded lightly.

"What I can't understand for the life of me is why someone should steal the lorry in the first place, and then abandon it not a quarter of a mile away. Mrs. Freebold was telling me that there was a dark-haired man with thin lips and narrowed eyes driving it."

"He wore a hat," Rutledge said. "Pulled down low. I couldn't see more than that."

"Ah. Well, that explains why Mrs. Arundel heard he was a large man with an evil expression." He smiled.

"I doubt if anyone got a good look at him. He left the lorry where no one was likely to see him walk away. Either from windows at The Oaks or from the houses on Holly Street."

Mrs. Channing looked at Rutledge with a questioning glance. But the rector was in full cry, now.

"Are you trying to tell me he was someone here in Dudlington?"

"I don't know," Rutledge answered. "What do your callers have to say on that subject?"

"That he must have held a grudge against the firm doing the work at the Lawrence house. He must have had the fright of his life when he learned later that the man he nearly ran down in the lane was a policeman from Scotland Yard. Serves him right too."

Rutledge found Mrs. Arundel in her little cage at the rear of the baker's shop. She smiled at him and said, "Is there a letter you wish to mail to London, Inspector? I'll see that it goes first thing in the morning."

He showed her the map of Dudlington that Grace Letteridge had helped him fill out. "Is this a fairly accurate list of residents?" he asked.

She examined it carefully. "Yes. Yes, it is.

344

You're very thorough, Inspector."

"And there's no one else living in Dudlington besides the names given here?"

"Of course you haven't listed the children, or any of the servants. And Mrs. Wainwright is a widow, Mr. Neville has never married —"

"Thank you." He took back his list and folded it again.

He could feel Mrs. Simpson's eyes boring into the back of his head as she strained to hear the conversation.

He found Mrs. Melford at home, busy with a stew for his dinner, and he showed her the list as well.

"That's correct, Inspector," she told him, handing it back. "I wonder you need the names of everyone in Dudlington. Surely we aren't all under suspicion."

"Not at all," he assured her. "But it helps me form a better picture of the village."

She said, "Then if that's all, I must get back to my dinner. Your dinner."

And he left it at that.

Hamish said, "It didna' work, yon map."

"In a way it did." Rutledge sat at

Hensley's desk and ticked off the houses he already knew. "Ellison, there. Letteridge. Lawrence. Simpson. Freebold. Hensley here. The rectory. Baylor. And of course Keating at The Oaks. There's no Sandridge here. I hadn't expected it to be that easy."

He put the map away and stood looking round the room. "If I were hiding something, where would I choose? It has to be safe from prying eyes sitting here waiting for Hensley to come back to his office. Or even a determined search by someone intent on finding where Hensley kept files or money. Where?"

Still favoring his ankle, Rutledge began a thorough search, starting at the top of the house and working his way down. It was hampered by the dark day, when lamplight let shadows fall in corners and made it difficult to judge if a board was askew or only appeared that way in poor light.

Hamish reminded him that the house still belonged to the Freebolds, and it wasn't likely that Hensley would choose a secret place they might already know existed.

Room after room, Rutledge examined every possible place where something could be hidden. The bedrooms, the bath, the stairs, the sitting room and dining room, the kitchen, the cellar where the coal bin filled one corner and old bits and pieces filled another. Digging through that, he came across a sled, a broken drying rack for clothes, a chair with a missing leg, a box of dishes with chipped edges and only one cup, a stack of old newspapers for starting fires, a carton of tools, and a doorknob that had been tossed in by itself.

"Ye're wasting time," Hamish told him. "There's naething to be found."

But he refused to give up.

He came back to the lone doorknob and stared at it thoughtfully. It looked to be a more recent vintage than the rest of the bric-a-brac.

And then he began to pull the litter out of the corner, working fast and stacking each item in the center of the earthen floor.

When he'd pulled an old trunk filled with clothing half a century old out of his way, he could just feel, rather than see, the rough edges of a door.

There was a hole that looked more like a knot in the wood than an actual cavity, but he thrust the doorknob inside. There must have been a matching knob on the other side, because he was able, gently, to pull the door open just far enough to bring it the rest of the way with his fingers.

The knob on the far side had been nailed in place, giving it stability. And as the door opened to the point that he could see in, he realized this cabinet was shelved as if once used for jams or preserves.

It was empty now except for a dark leather satchel and a collection of papers.

He was just about to draw them out, when he heard a voice over his head.

Swearing, he left the door where it was and hurried up the stairs as fast as his complaining ankle permitted.

Mrs. Channing was standing in the parlor office, calling his name.

"I've forgotten you!" he said contritely. "I should have come back before this."

"No, I expected to make my own way to the inn. But what have you been doing? Is that a cobweb in your hair?"

He realized that there was even coal dust on one sleeve and a smudge across the back of his hand. "Searching," he said, telling the truth. "I'd hoped that Hensley kept his more important files somewhere less accessible than this room."

"And were you successful?" she asked, no inflection in her voice.

"I was debating whether to shift a large pile of coal when you called me away. As

348

far as I can tell, that's the only task I have left."

"Yes, well, I'll not keep you. But if I were you, I'd be careful, digging about in cellars with those cuts and scrapes on your hands. They're still open wounds, and easily infected."

"I hadn't thought of that. I'll just find my coat and see you to the inn."

"Nonsense. I'm perfectly capable of walking that far alone."

He waited until he was certain she was gone, sitting in the dark parlor for a quarter of an hour. Only then did he go back down the cellar stairs with his torch and look into the closet.

The satchel contained money, far less than he'd expected. And the papers were an odd assortment. One of them was a letter to the young woman who had been searching for the man, Sandridge.

It was straightforward, just as Hensley had told him, denying that there was anyone in Dudlington by that name, and suggesting that she had got the wrong Dudlington.

The only interesting thing about the reply was that it had been written on official stationery, giving it the stamp of authority.

The others were a collection of interviews in the days following the disappearance of Emma Mason.

Rutledge took them to his bedroom, and in the course of the evening, read through them.

The first documented Mrs. Ellison's frantic summons one morning, reporting her daughter gone in the night.

The constable's notes were brief.

"She was very upset. Called Miss Mason to her breakfast, and when there was no answer, went up to room to wake her granddaughter. She was not there, and no indication of hasty departure. No letter left behind. Grandmother then searched rest of house, no sign of Miss Mason. I immediately organized a search party, calling in every available man. Spoke to everyone in village, house by house. Covered fields two miles in every direction, also barns and sheds . . ."

The next five or six pages were questions put to various people who had had some contact with Emma that last day. One of them was Martha Simpson. She'd heard words between Emma and Miss Letteridge that morning, and it had had to do with London, she thought. Betsy Timmons, Hillary's older sister, had remembered

Emma crying in her room in the afternoon as she'd gone upstairs to begin her cleaning.

Hensley himself noted, "I saw Miss Emma at around six o'clock as she was leaving the baker's shop, and she was carrying a letter in her hand. When I spoke to her, she ignored me. I had the impression there was something on her mind." He had added, "Her lamp remained burning until late in the night. I can't say when it went out."

The next interview was with the rector. He said only that he'd seen Emma Mason at the church the day before her disappearance. He had found her sitting there in a pew — not Mrs. Ellison's, as he remembered — and she seemed to be crying. But when he approached her and asked if she was unhappy, she'd shaken her head and told him that she was praying for her grandmother. He hadn't known what to make of that, but it was clear that she didn't want to confide in him, and he had left her there.

There was an interview with Mrs. Lawrence. She had seen Emma as she was leaving the church, but Emma had turned away from her and instead walked out toward the fields. Mrs. Lawrence thought she might be meeting someone there, because Emma had seemed furtive.

The final report came from Mrs. Simpson. As she was looking out her window just at dusk, she had seen Emma arguing with a man, but she couldn't identify him in the poor light. The girl turned and walked into her grandmother's house, shutting the door "with some force." Mrs. Simpson was reluctant to describe the man, "for fear she might be mistaken," and Hensley reported that he hadn't pressed.

Rutledge couldn't be sure whether these were copies or the originals, which Hensley hadn't forwarded to Inspector Abbot in Letherington. Neither could he be sure whether the constable had kept them to use in his own investigation or was trying to conceal his own personal role in the girl's disappearance. Had he, for instance, been the man that Mrs. Simpson saw but couldn't name?

Mrs. Ellison was growing deaf — she might not have heard her granddaughter leave in the night. For that matter, she might not have heard someone come to the door and on some excuse lure the girl out of the house.

All in all, Rutledge hadn't found anything incriminating one way or the other.

Not sufficient money to prove that Hensley had taken a bribe in London, nor any proof that he'd had something to do with the girl's disappearance.

What was odd was that the letter regarding Sandridge and the interviews regarding Emma Mason had been stored here together.

As if there was some connection.

Setting the interviews aside, Rutledge considered what he'd read.

Who had the girl been speaking with when Mrs. Simpson saw her at dusk? Was it Hensley? If so, he'd adroitly covered his tracks by admitting to encountering her on the street. And Mrs. Simpson had seen Emma walk into her grandmother's house afterward. But whom had she met when she walked into the fields after leaving the church?

If the baker's wife had suspected it was Hensley on the street with Emma Mason at dusk, it would explain the rumors blaming the constable for her disappearance. A comment here, a remembered remark there, a lively imagination adding another bit of information, and before very long, suspicion would be rampant.

Hamish said, "Ye're forgetting yon woman with the rosebushes."

Grace Letteridge might easily have been the person to start a rumor about Hensley. For reasons of her own.

She'd quarreled with Emma. Was it an old jealousy between them rearing its head again? Over Robert Baylor?

He'd said once that jealousy was a crime of hot blood.

Something could easily have stirred it back to life again.

Emma Mason might not have walked out of her grandmother's house in the middle of the night to meet a man, but she could very well have come down to the door if a distressed Grace Letteridge had knocked.

It was an image he couldn't get out of his mind. Emma, her bedroom lamp burning late into the night, still awake. Grace Letteridge, watching from her own windows until Mrs. Ellison had gone to bed, then waiting for the older woman to fall asleep. The village quiet, only the sound of the church clock striking the hour. Grace standing in her doorway to be sure no one was watching, and then slipping across the street. Emma, answering her door, because Dudlington was a village where she knew everyone and feared no one. And Grace standing there, tears in her eyes, saying she couldn't sleep, that they had to make up their quarrel then and there. Then coaxing, urging Emma to come to her house, where they could talk without disturbing Mrs. Ellison. And Emma, vulnerable and easily led, following her across the street and into the house, the door shutting behind her . . .

He wondered if Hensley had been standing at his own darkened window, watching Emma in her room pacing the floor, his field glasses offering him a clear view of her face as she moved back and forth across his line of sight. And then, tired, he put up the glasses and went back to his bed, Emma's light still burning. Unaware that in five minutes — ten — Emma would be lured to her death.

If this was true — any of it — then why had Grace or anyone else shot Hensley with an arrow? Why stir up the past by reminding people of Emma and the suspicion that she was buried in Frith's Wood?

What had happened that had forced Grace Letteridge to act?

25

The rain had been swept away by first light, the wind heralding clearing and colder weather. Rutledge went down to the kitchen and blew the fire into life to heat his shaving water.

Hamish said, "The men shaved in the trenches in cold water."

"Yes, well, our gas masks had to fit smoothly. I'm not in France now."

"You havena' thought of Westmorland for some time." The voice in his head had a hard edge this morning, turning from one harrying to another.

But it was true, he hadn't.

"Hostages to fortune," he said aloud, taking the kettle upstairs with him.

He knew himself, he was the sort of man who would have been happier settled into a good marriage, with children coming in a few years. If the war had never happened, if he'd married Jean in 1914, he might already have a child of three clinging to his hands or asleep on his knee, and another due in the spring. A very different world, that.

Instead he'd gone to France, had fought in the trenches for four horrific years, and then come home damaged by what he'd seen and what he'd done. He shuddered to think how a child might view Hamish. Children were quick to grasp the subtleties of emotions around them, to see through evasions and quickly identify prevarication. He couldn't explain and he couldn't explain away — how do you tell a child that its father is haunted?

There must be a way — other men had done it.

But that was a lie. And he was beginning to understand that whatever he might have felt for Elizabeth Fraser if he'd been free of his guilt and shell shock, he had nothing to offer her now. She had been right to tell him not to come back to Westmorland, even if she didn't understand the reasons why he would accept her decision. He must quietly shut that door and never open it again.

He stood there, looking in the mirror, damning the war, damning the men who began it and the officers who plotted each battle.

As he began to shave, Rutledge remembered one of the charges leveled against the highest-ranking planners and tacticians

357

at General Headquarters, that they had lost touch with the reality of war on the battlefield and had ordered charge after charge into the teeth of the machine guns, as if they were facing an inferior enemy who would break at the sight of sheer numbers. Officers far from the carnage of No Man's Land, for whom casualties were regrettable numbers on a morning report, weren't faced with the bleeding bodies one stepped over in a broken retreat to the lines.

What had these men brought back from France? How had they slept at night with their blunders and stubbornness and their guilt?

"They didna' suffer any guilt," Hamish told him bitterly. "They didna' see what they had done."

What of the hundreds of faceless men on the streets looking for work, trying to pick up the threads of family life, hoping that the dying had made a better Britain, and finding they were lost in it. Faceless men . . . People stepped around them now, ignored the brave boy who'd marched away to glory and now begged on the street because a one-armed man couldn't work. He thought sometimes, in the dark corners of his mind, that the dead were the lucky ones. They hadn't been disillusioned.

He was still in a dark mood when he went to his breakfast. Mrs. Melford was in the kitchen, he could hear her moving about. How did she feel, cooking meals for strangers, to make ends meet in the aftermath of war?

That train of thought took him to Mrs. Ellison, who had lost her daughter and her granddaughter but had held on to her pride in her name.

Mrs. Melford brought his tea and said, "There was a fire this morning, did you know?"

"A fire?" he repeated, trying to bring his mind to bear on this news. "Where?"

"I was hoping you could tell me what had happened. Mrs. Simpson said something about the Baylor house." Barbara Melford had avoided using Ted Baylor's first name.

She didn't add that that was the one place she felt barred from going. Any word would have to come to her secondhand.

"I'll look into it," he said. "Was there much damage?"

"I don't know — Mrs. Simpson did say that no one was hurt."

"That's good news."

He finished his breakfast, paid his account, and walked down the lane in the cold sunshine. The heavy odor of charred wood reached him on the wind when he turned into Church Street, but when he came nearer, he couldn't see any signs of fire in the front of the house.

He knocked at the door, and an angry Ted Baylor answered it. "Another vulture come to gawk?" he asked.

"I'm a policeman," Rutledge responded.

"Well, I can tell you, it was nothing that would involve Scotland Yard. My brother had nightmares in his sleep and knocked over his lamp. It burned a good part of the table, the cloth over it, the carpet under it, and scorched the floor before I smelled smoke and smothered the flames."

"He'd fallen asleep with his lamp burning?"

"Is there a law forbidding it?"

Rutledge himself had slept with his lamp burning for the first weeks after he'd left the clinic, in a vain attempt to keep the nightmares away. Before he'd left for Warwickshire, he had slept sitting in his chair more often than lying in his bed.

"There's no law forbidding it. But I understand the need for it."

"I don't see how you could," Baylor said,

his anger draining and his face lined with exhaustion. "Unless you were in the war."

"I was on the Somme," Rutledge told him simply.

Baylor pulled the door closed behind him and stood on the step with Rutledge. "It's been hard, dealing with the screams. I don't sleep much myself. He's all right when he's awake. He's been to London, to the doctors. They haven't helped. Sometimes I find myself thinking he would have been better off dead."

"You don't mean that."

"I don't know whether I do or not. Joel has always been a trial." He looked out over the fields. "This land is in my blood, but not in his. He wasn't born here, he doesn't have the same feeling for it. Maybe you have to be bred to it. Robbie was. He reminded me of my grandfather, an easy understanding of what animals need. Even a stray cat would come to him for petting. And he was thrown away in the war, his life wasted. Joel is city bred, he likes the crowded streets, the smell of the river when there was fog coming in, the way the nights were never really dark. First time he heard an owl, he was petrified." A smile lingered at the corner of his mouth, but he was unaware of it. "I told him it was a demon, out in Frith's Wood, searching for the damned. The night it screeched outside his window on that tree over there, he climbed in bed with Robbie and pulled the sheet over his head. And the next morning my father took his strap to me for frightening my brother. Well, half brother. We weren't as kind to him then as we could have been. He was a fish out of water, and we should have made it a little easier than we did. I've tried to make it up to him."

He had been talking like a man deprived of human companionship, spilling out his frustration and his guilt and his strong sense of duty.

Hamish was saying, "And how did yon brother see it?"

Baylor said, as if answering him, "I expect he forgave us after a bit. But we didn't know what to make of him when he came to live with us after his grandmother died. She was always partial to him, probably because he had no one else. But we were jealous, Robbie and I, for no reason other than the fact that he was different from us. Rougher around the edges, arrogant sometimes, generally off-putting when we least expected it. A trial at school, as well — better at football than we ever were, faster in his reactions, stronger."

He shivered as he stood there in the cold wind in only his flannel shirt, and yet he seemed reluctant to return to the warmth of the house.

Rutledge could sense that Baylor was ridden with guilt yet again, for wishing that Joel had died in the fire in his room, his lungs filled with smoke. But the man had saved his brother, and there was nothing the law could do about wishes.

After a moment Baylor turned to him and said, as if the words were pulled from him, "How is she?"

He didn't pretend he didn't know.

"I should think she's wondering what went wrong. I found her crying, after you left that night."

Baylor swore with feeling.

"It's hopeless. But I won't shame Joel by telling her that. I shouldn't have told you as much as I have. Sometimes the words seem to spill out, and I can't stop them. It was wrong."

"Have you talked with the rector? He seems to be a man of great understanding."

"That's why I can't talk to him." He looked at Rutledge. "He'd understand too much. I just have to soldier on, and get through it."

"What happened to Joel in the war?" Rutledge felt himself tense, knowing what the answer would be. Shell shock. But Baylor surprised him.

"He was gassed. At Ypres. His lungs are rotted out. I listen to him at night and I curse them all, the generals and the Germans and the wind blowing his way that morning. He said it smelled of violets. Odd thing for a city man to tell you. But that's what he said."

"Yes, I've heard the same thing."

There was silence between them. The church clock struck the half hour. Finally Baylor took a deep breath and prepared to go back inside his house. "You have a gift for listening. If I didn't know better, I'd say you tricked me into talking. But there's been no one since Rob died, and it's been building up. I'd ask you to forget what you heard, if I didn't think it was impossible."

"Go back to your brother. I won't add to the gossip mill."

He left Baylor standing there and walked back the way he'd come. The odor of smoke was still strong. He'd made a promise to Baylor, but he knew Mrs. Melford was waiting for news.

By the time he reached the lane, he knew what he was going to say to her.

Mrs. Melford was standing at her front window, just behind the lace curtains. The sun touched them and gave them an opaque quality that would have concealed her, if she hadn't moved as he came toward her door.

She opened it and invited him in.

"A lamp fell over. No harm done, just a small fire quickly put out. I expect it was alarming at the time."

"Did you tell him I was worried?"

"Should I have?"

Mrs. Melford shook her head. "No, certainly not. The worst fire I can remember in Dudlington was in a cattle barn. I'm glad it was not that."

She stood there for a moment longer, as if hoping he would give her more details, a verbatim account of what had been said. Then she nodded, saying, "Good morning, Inspector."

Rutledge drove into Letherington to send a telegram to Gibson at the Yard.

Cain, crossing the street, saw him and came to speak to him. "News, then?"

"A request for information, that's all."

He finished his telegram and then turned back to Cain. "Do you know anyone by the name of Sandridge?"

"Sandridge?" He shook his head. "Means nothing to me. Any particular reason for asking?"

Rutledge said, "In Hensley's files there's a letter requesting information about the man. He kept it in his files. I wondered why. Sometimes the most obscure fact can turn out to be useful."

"True. How is Hensley, by the way?"

"Feverish. I couldn't be sure how much of it was pretense for my sake, and how much was real. Infection, he said."

"You've not made much progress," Cain commented.

"So far, the best evidence is that the attack had to do with Emma Mason's disappearance. But the village is silent about her. They think she's buried in that wood, and there's the end of it."

"Is she?"

"I don't believe she is. I've looked at the ground. Digging there would be a major venture. There're the roots for one thing, and a deep layer of leaf mold. Any disturbance would be obvious."

"You're thinking of a real burial. Put a body out there under a bed of leaves and let the animals dispose of it. Where you have cattle and sheep, there's feed. And if you have feed, there're bound to be mice, if not rats. And the wood is an ideal habitat for creatures that eat bones. Rats don't know about the Saxons."

"Then why didn't the first searchers find her?"

"Do you really think they made a careful search of the area? There's no certainty they looked beyond the surface. A clever man could have made the ground appear untouched."

"You're the devil's advocate."

"No. I'm simply offering possibilities."

Hamish was not impressed. "Ye ken, he's ambitious, with an eye for London."

Rutledge said, "Then bring me a dozen men who aren't superstitious, and let's begin quartering the wood."

"Where are you going to find them? Not in Letherington or even Fairfield. Ask Chief Inspector Kelmore in Northampton."

"Come with me now," Rutledge said, "and we'll make a beginning. There should be shovels and rakes in Hensley's shed."

Cain laughed. "Is this a challenge, old man?"

"Just an eagerness to test your theory before we inconvenience the Chief Inspector."

"Where is she buried — assuming she's dead — if she isn't in the wood?"

"Someone's cellar," Rutledge answered him, and turned to walk back to his motorcar.

Cain followed him. "Beneath the floor of a cattle barn is more likely. Considering the stench there, a decomposing body would hardly be noticed."

Rutledge drove back to Dudlington with his mind on more than the road.

As he made the turn by The Oaks, he saw Mrs. Channing standing in the drive, looking up at the sky.

Keating, beside her, was pointing out a flock of geese flying over. She looked absorbed in what he was saying, and Keating appeared to be enjoying himself as he talked about the birds.

She had a knack, Rutledge thought, of seeming all things to all people. He wondered if she gave a damn about birds, but her face showed only interest, as if she had spent her life studying the habits of wildfowl. His last glimpse of her as he drove down Holly Street was of the burgundy coat snapping around her ankles in the wind, and one hand holding hard to her hat.

She must have noticed his motorcar, because she appeared on his doorstep not a quarter of an hour later.

"Did you hear about the fire?" she asked him as she walked into Hensley's parlor.

He had taken the time to stop at the green-grocer's for a packet of tea, and the kettle was already heating. She could hear it whistle from the door.

"It was the latest gossip over my breakfast."

She followed him into the kitchen and watched as he searched for sugar and tinned milk, then took down the cups and saucers. "Did you see the geese fly over? They're such a pretty sight, calling encouragement to one another, changing places in the lead to keep from tiring. I'm impressed."

"You didn't come here to talk about birds," he said, waiting for the tea to steep. "But yes, I saw you."

She quoted,

There's a beauty in birds on the wing,
That stirs the heart and makes
    earthbound creatures
Long for flight, but the larks above
    the battlefield
Are silenced by the sounds of war.
I have watched birds out at sea,
Catching the wind,
And longed to follow them,
To some safe place far from here.

He stopped short. It was O. A. Manning's poem "Safe . . ."

"Yes, I thought you might know those lines," Mrs. Channing said comfortably, as if she had discovered a fellow enthusiast. "Mr. Towson is fond of the poems as well. We had an interesting conversation about them."

He had investigated the death of O. A. Manning, and it had left a deep scar on his soul. Had she known that too?

"You're a woman of many talents," he said neutrally.

She took her cup and sipped appreciatively. "There's nothing like a good cup of tea on a wretchedly cold day. Why are you so suspicious of me?"

"Am I?" he parried.

"You have been since the night we met. I've told you. I've no reason to wish you ill."

"I wish I could believe that. You have an uncanny ability to make people like you, but there's that undercurrent of knowledge that you shouldn't, by rights, have."

"Do you think I wouldn't have warned you, if I'd known about the lorry?"

"I wish you could tell me who it was who shot Constable Hensley with a bow and arrow in Frith's Wood."

She frowned. "Are you asking me to help you?"

"It was a rhetorical question. Nothing more."

"I can't call up visions at will, you know. If I could, I'd have done a great deal of good in this world by warning others of their imminent danger. But sometimes I find myself uncannily accurate, and that's frightening. I don't want to know the day of my death. Or your death. Or any other sad thing that's better off hidden from all of us."

"Could you put your hand on patients in the aid stations and know which would live and which would die?"

"I didn't need to. I could look at the doctors' faces and read the answer there. But yes, in time, you come to have a sixth sense about such things. I didn't like it, and I fought against it. I even tried to distance myself, not allowing my emotions to be touched. It didn't work."

Mrs. Channing finished her tea and set the cup aside. "Thank you, Inspector. That was very good. Do you wish me to go back to London, and leave you to it?"

She had a way of interjecting a complete change of thought into an apparently innocuous remark.

"I don't know," he answered her truthfully. "I wish I knew what it was you wanted."

She stood there, looking down at him. "If I hadn't — alarmed you with my pretense of a séance, you wouldn't have left Mrs.

Browning's party early. Someone else might have seen that shell casing, and thought nothing of it. Instead, you found it, and it has brought something frightening into being. I feel responsible, in a sense, you see."

"You're saying that whoever came out first — myself or Commander Farnum — whoever set up the casing would have decided that man was his victim?"

She didn't answer him.

"What if it was the doctor? He hadn't been in the war."

"Then it would have been someone else on another day."

It was a very interesting possibility.

But she didn't wait to discuss it. He got to his feet to help her into her coat, and with a smile she was gone.

The quiet room seemed to close in on him. He got up and walked to the door, looking at the lock that had no key.

He wasn't certain whether it was worse to think of himself as the target of someone with a grudge against him, or to see himself as a target of opportunity. A man with a grudge was at least comprehensible, could even be tracked down and stopped. Someone who had chosen him at random was like smoke in the dark, invisible until his victim stumbled into it.

26

It was late, and the afternoon light was waning when Rutledge found a rake and a pitchfork in the shed behind Hensley's house, just where he'd expected them to be. There was also a shaded lantern and a sturdy pair of boots.

The wind was still very cold, but dropped with sunset. By seven o'clock the shops were closed and the streets all but deserted. He put the spade and shovel into the motorcar, tested the shaded lantern in the kitchen, found his torch, and as soon as his dinner was over, he drove out of Dudlington.

He left the car very close to where he'd found Hensley's bicycle, then climbed the wall on the far side of the road and made his way across the fields toward Frith's Wood.

Hamish, a good covenanting Scot, kept up a grumbling monologue in Rutledge's head, reminding him that daring the devil in the dark of night in a haunted wood was little short of madness. "It isna' wise to open doors that have no business opening."

"I'm here to close one," he answered.

Somewhere a fox barked, twice. He walked on, grateful that there was no moon to pick him out, a lone figure on the brow of the rolling pastures.

When he reached the wood he stopped to take his bearings. He could see lighted windows here and there in the village, and even the weathercock on the top of the church spire reflected their glow.

There was no one in the pastures, no one following him from the road, no one ahead of him in the wood. All the same, for a moment he wished he could tell Hamish to set a watch, as he had done so many times in the trenches.

Three years, he thought. A long time for a body to lie among the trees, but there were a few bones that might survive even now, if he knew where to look for them.

He began by working through the brambles and vines, using his hands where he could, bringing up the rake or the pitchfork for areas he couldn't reach.

The shielded lantern was used sparingly, for as his eyes adjusted to the darkness, he could see more than he would have believed possible.

He thought, this is how an archaeologist

must feel, exploring one small square at a time, unveiling what lay below the surface — or didn't lie there — with great care.

Rotted trunks and fallen branches had turned into crumbled wood, and there was layer after layer of well-rotted leaves. The rake was deep into one corner when a skull came to light, small and with a pointed muzzle. A fox, he thought, crawling in here to die in peace. He buried it again and kept going. There was the scurry of mice in another place, and he overturned a nest of fur-lined leaves and four tiny white shivering bodies. Setting it back in place, he thought he heard something behind him, like the bones of dead fingers clacking together, but it was only the boughs and bare branches rubbing together in the wind.

He worked for more than an hour, then stopped to catch his breath. It was a hopeless task, he told himself. One man on his own . . . The wood *had* been searched, after all.

"By men who were afraid," Hamish retorted. "They wouldna' care to find the devil under a bush."

There was some truth in that.

The church clock had struck two in the morning, and he was tired. But he had begun to learn the way the ground under his feet was constructed. And where the brambles grew thickest, he could pass on, because they had been settled here far longer than three years, their canes deep in the leaf mold, and their bases thick as his wrist with old growth.

By three, he'd covered more of the wood than he'd expected, and he began to think, looking around him, that he might finish before the late dawn broke.

But by four, he had still had no luck, and this particular part of the wood had seen some wind damage in the past, for there were more downed trunks than elsewhere. He moved each one, shone his shielded torch along the length, sending beetles and spiders fleeing from his light, before letting it go again. Some broke apart in his hands, and others, wet with dew and slick with green moss, left an unpleasant miasma in the air and a slippery coating on his gloves.

He had worn heavy boots borrowed from Hensley and a pair of the man's corduroys hanging in the closet and two layers of sweaters over his shirt. Now he was sweating heavily, and his muscles were beginning to ache. His ankle had been ready to quit an hour ago.

"A wild-goose chase," Hamish said

dryly. "Better a feather bed."

Rutledge chuckled, just as his pitchfork bit into something with a very different feel.

Leaving the tool where it was, he knelt to clear away the earth from its prongs, smoothing and pushing gently by turns until he had found what he was after. He brought the lamp closer.

The pitchfork had buried itself between a jaw and a shoulder blade, in what had once been a human neck.

Rutledge rocked back on his heels.

Hamish said, "The Saxon massacre . . ."

But Rutledge didn't think it was. There was more definition in the bones than something from the Dark Ages.

Whether it was Emma Mason or not, he couldn't judge. But it was time to call in experts who could.

Covering his find carefully, so that it was neither visible nor vulnerable, he stood up and shouldered his implements.

Hamish said, "Will ye stop now?"

It was a good question.

He had another two hours until daylight, and it was possible that he would never have a better chance.

His muscles complained, his hands were

cold through his wet gloves, he was tired enough to sleep on the open ground, as he'd done more than once during the war.

Still, he went back to work, as methodically as before, and after another hour and three-quarters of digging, he hadn't made any other gruesome discoveries.

He could see an opalescent light on the horizon as he trudged back across the fields, toward his motorcar.

He and Hensley's tools were filthy from the digging, and he tried to clean his boots a little before stepping behind the wheel. The seat was cold and damp with the dew as he drove back to Dudlington and left the car in its accustomed place, and he could feel his fatigue as he stowed the tools where he'd found them.

A hot bath helped to wake him up and took away some of the strain on his body.

And as soon as he had eaten his breakfast, he drove south to Northampton, where he could find a telephone.

His call to the Yard was patched through to Chief Inspector Bowles, who gave him a lecture on the speedy resolution of his cases.

"We don't have the time for arcane wanderings in the past, Rutledge. Whether there were Saxons on the rampage in the time of Alfred has no bearing on who shot Constable Hensley."

"I understand, sir —"

"No, you don't. I've been summoned by my own superiors, and all I've got to report to them is silence. What has this skull got to do with Hensley, pray?"

Rutledge took a deep breath. "If the skull is that of a missing girl, it may begin to explain why he was attacked. To prove that it is the girl, I need someone from the Yard experienced in skeletons. Mainwairing, for one. Can you spare him for a day or two?"

Mainwaring was one of the most experienced men at the Yard. He had been trained as a doctor, but he had found the dead far more interesting than the living, and he had made a study of bones. He could tell, very quickly, whether a skeleton was that of a man or a woman, what age they'd reached at the time of their death, and oftentimes, what had killed them.

There was silence at the other end of the line. Then Bowles said, "You're sure this could be the missing girl? I don't want Mainwaring wasting his time on those damned Saxons."

"Three days, sir. One to take the train as far as Northampton, one in Dudlington, and another to return to London. I'll be waiting for him at The Red Lion in Northampton."

Bowles was still reluctant. "Do you think *Hensley* killed the blasted girl? Is that what you want to prove?" His voice conveyed his disbelief.

"If the girl is buried there, then his presence in the wood would have alarmed the killer. If I found her, there's no reason Hensley couldn't have done the same, given the right conditions."

"I see. Yes, well, that makes sense. You can't be sure on your own, about the skull?"

"We must think in terms of bringing the case to trial, sir. If I'm wrong about the body there in Frith's Wood, then I must look elsewhere for a reason behind the attack before we make fools of ourselves in court." He managed just the right cajoling tone to mask the threat in his words.

"Frith's Wood. That's a pagan name if I ever heard it. Not surprised something nasty happened there. Very well. Mainwaring will be on the next available train."

The connection was cut as Bowles put up the phone with a heavy hand.

Rutledge, standing in the small telephone closet at The Red Lion Hotel, swore softly to himself. If he was wrong about Emma Mason, Bowles would never let him forget it.

Out on a limb was the last place the superintendent wished to find himself. Even on behalf of one of his own.

Waiting for Mainwaring to come north, Rutledge went back to the hospital in the center of town.

Matron forbade him to speak to Hensley. "He has a high fever, and Dr. Williams has moved him into a private room."

"Then let me speak to Dr. Williams."

"He's left for the day. I suggest you come back tomorrow. There may be some improvement by then."

Rutledge, feeling the first stages of exhaustion, had taken a room at the hotel, and he slept for five hours, hardly aware of where he was. By ten o'clock that evening, Mainwaring had arrived.

He was nearly as tall as Rutledge, broad shouldered and fair. He was also filled with curiosity. Rutledge, walking with him back to The Red Lion, was peppered with questions about the skeleton.

"You'll see it for yourself tomorrow," he finally told his companion. "Is it true you're leaving the Yard to work for the British Museum?"

Mainwaring laughed. "I'm putting in for Chief Inspector. If it doesn't come through, I'll consider the Victoria and Albert. You've been in the Yard longer than I have. Why hasn't your promotion come through?"

"I'm not happy sitting at a desk, directing others," Rutledge told him. "I'm content dealing with cases firsthand."

"Yes, well, we all say that, don't we? Until we're given advancement. Is the dining room still open, do you think? I'm starved."

They left early for Dudlington, and Mainwairing, who hadn't been to the area, found the drive interesting. As The Oaks came in view at the top of the rise, he said, "I have a wager with George Reston that there's only one pub in the village."

"You'd win. How is George?"

"His shoulder is much better, but the leg's taking its own sweet time. Motorcar accidents are the very devil, and getting worse."

"I hope you brought your boots. We've a long walk ahead of us." Rutledge had reached Hensley's house and turned in.

"The door is always open. You won't need a key. A bed is a different story."

They walked into the house, and Mainwaring looked around with surprise. "These are your accommodations? I'd have thought you'd been put up at The Oaks."

"This is Constable Hensley's house. A woman next door prepares his meals for him. He offered to let me live here while he's in hospital."

"An arrow is a nasty piece of work. If they don't strike something vital straight-away, then you die of septicemia from the dirty point."

"Don't say that. Hensley's got a fever now."

They waited until well after dark, as Rutledge had done before, driving up the north road, then walking out through the fields.

Mainwaring said, "Is all this secrecy necessary?"

"Possibly. The girl's grandmother lives in Dudlington. As soon as someone sees us carrying tools toward the wood, the gossip will fly, and I don't want it to reach her before I do."

"No, I agree."

They walked in silence for a time, and as

the wood loomed dark in its fold of land, Mainwaring whistled. "The Haunted Wood."

"That's exactly what most of the people in this vicinity believe."

"Has it ever been cleared out?"

"Who knows? It may have been larger in the past, and whittled away until this was all that was left. Or it may be the same size it's always been." He shifted the pitchfork on his shoulder. "But when the village was moved here and rebuilt in the shadow of it, the houses turned their backs to it."

"Superstition is a powerful emotion. My family live near Avebury. My grandfather swore he saw lights moving among the stones on moonless nights —" He broke off. "Speaking of lights."

They could see what appeared to be a shaded lantern bobbing among the trees.

"Get down," Rutledge murmured, and they dropped to their haunches, their silhouettes blending into the ground.

For another quarter of an hour, they watched the light. Then it was doused, and whoever had walked there seemed to vanish.

Rutledge dropped his pitchfork.

"Stay here." He started running at an angle to the trees, keeping his profile low, intending to cut off whoever had been in the wood.

After several minutes he saw someone walking up the slope of the Dower Fields toward the village. Whoever it was, he was wearing a long coat that flapped around his ankles as he kept up a brisk pace. A hat, pulled low, changed the shape of the head. Rutledge thought perhaps whoever he was chasing was glad to be out of the wood and trying to reach the security of the village as quickly as possible.

The figure had reached the far side of the church when Rutledge ran hard toward the back garden of the rectory and used the shadows of its walls to hurry toward the churchyard.

He stumbled over a low tombstone, choked off a curse, and then ran on, trying to watch where he put his feet.

As he came around the far corner of the church, he nearly collided with the figure.

It let out a cry of alarm, recovered, and tried to turn back the way it had come, but Rutledge was on it, catching at the nearest shoulder with an iron grip.

A lantern fell to the ground, rolling under his feet.

The figure ducked, twisted, and almost broke his grip, but as it struggled the hat came off, and Rutledge pulled his quarry around for a good look at its face.

Only it wasn't a man. It was Mrs. Ellison.

27

Rutledge was shocked into speechlessness. Of all the people he had expected to find in Frith's Wood, Mary Ellison was the last. He released her at once.

She stood there, and he could feel her eyes glaring at him, but her voice was husky as she spoke.

"You aren't the only one to watch from windows," she said. "What have you found in the wood? Who was the man you brought back to Dudlington with you? Inspector Cain? Is my granddaughter there in the wood? *Tell me!*"

"I don't know —" he began, still at a loss for words. What could he say to her?

Hamish answered his thought. "Nothing. It's too soon."

Rutledge said aloud, "We've been searching quietly, so as not to cause you pain. Or give people a reason to gossip."

She was still breathing hard. "I saw you putting the implements into the car. I saw you leave. Where else would you be taking a rake or a pitchfork at that hour of the night but the wood? I couldn't sit there waiting." Her voice shook. *"I have a right to know what you've found, and why you brought that other man here!"*

"Mrs. Ellison, let me take you home."

She seemed to shrink into herself. "It can't be my granddaughter. I won't believe it. In that heathen, unblessed place? No, I refuse to believe it."

"What did you find, when you got to the wood?"

"Nothing." She was still breathing hard. "It was dark, and the lantern cast shadows everywhere. I couldn't stay any longer, that place terrifies me. Nothing in the world could ever have taken me there but Emma."

"Let me see you to your house. It's very cold, and you've had a shock."

She shook her head. "I know my way. Go back there and do whatever it is you have to do."

As his own breathing slowed, he watched her walk steadily down Church Street and turn into Whitby Lane, and then he went on across the fields again to find Mainwairing.

He wasn't where Rutledge had left him, and it was clear that his curiosity had got the better of him.

388

Rutledge went down to the wood. The leaf mat under his feet was silent, and he walked carefully, almost from memory. Mainwaring had his torch and the lamp, and he was on his own.

"There." It was Hamish speaking.

A flash of light caught his eye and he went in that direction. Mainwaring nearly jumped out of his skin when Rutledge spoke from behind him.

"Found any bones?"

"Blast you, Rutledge! Did you catch whoever it was you were chasing?"

"Yes. Let's get on with it. This way."

It took him a few minutes to find the bones again, and he gently pushed aside the covering he'd drawn back over them.

Mainwaring squatted at his heels. "Interesting."

"Saxon massacre victim?"

"Lord, no, not at all. Look at the condition. This wood isn't the Irish peat bogs, you know. The conditions here are deplorable. Here, let me get closer."

They exchanged places, and Rutledge held the lantern while Mainwaring worked.

It took some time to clear enough of the skeleton to make a judgment. The small bones were gone, carried off long since to feed whatever animal had discovered them.

But the skull was there, and the shoulders, part of the rib cage — and the pelvis.

Mainwaring whistled under his breath while he worked, as if to keep the spirits at bay. At one point, he said to Rutledge, "I can see why the locals don't like this place. I don't much care for it myself. When I walked under the branches of the first trees, I felt as if I'd stepped back in time to something ugly. Do you believe in ghosts, Ian?"

"I could be persuaded to here. What are those, the thigh bones?"

"Yes. Best indicator of height. But the feet are gone."

He continued to work, the lantern light shining on his face and on the bones that came to light under his careful prodding, his hands moving delicately as he cleared away rotting leaves and earth.

"That should do it," he said, getting stiffly to his feet. "You can have the local man — Inspector Cain, was it? — bring in people to finish the work. There's no point in keeping this business secret any longer."

"You're telling me, then, that we've found what we came here to find."

Rutledge felt depressed. It was a sad end for the pretty, lively girl he had pictured in his mind. Now the question was, who had brought her here and hidden her body?

And what was he going to tell Mary Ellison tomorrow morning?

This morning.

Mainwaring was cleaning his hands on his handkerchief. "You were right to send for me. It wouldn't have done to pursue this case under the impression it explained Hensley's unfortunate wounding. He couldn't have had anything to do with our bones."

Rutledge said, "I'm sorry?"

"I've just poked a hole in your favorite theory. This isn't your lost Emma Mason. This is a man's body. Probably closer to thirty-five than to forty. But he didn't bury himself. Which says he was murdered. I can't tell you how, there's nothing on the remaining bones to show us."

Inspector Cain came with his team of workmen and watched them scour the area around the site of the burial, looking for more evidence.

The people of Dudlington clustered close by the church, watching silently but unwilling to come any nearer.

Rutledge had knocked on Mary Ellison's door as soon as he'd reached Dudlington, fairly certain she hadn't gone to bed.

She answered the door fully dressed and stood there staring at him, waiting for the blow to fall.

He said, "We didn't find Emma. I don't know whether that's a comfort to you or not."

He thought for an instant she was going to fall, for she swayed and then caught the edge of the door's frame with her hand.

"I can't tell you whether it is or not. At my age, there's not much time left to hope."

The body was brought out of Frith's Wood in a blanket and carried to Letherington.

Speculation was rife. Mrs. Melford and Mrs. Arundel had found an opportunity to speak to Rutledge, and Mrs. Channing had come down to Hensley's parlor, her face filled with sadness.

"I think I'm going to return to London," she told Rutledge when there was a chance to speak to him privately. "I don't like this place. It seems so bleak this morning, with everyone unsettled by what's happening in the wood."

"I saw the rector go into Mrs. Ellison's house, hobbling on crutches. I would have taken my oath that I'd found her granddaughter. And I think she believed I had as well, although I didn't tell her what we'd discovered."

"Just as well. She's a strong woman, she'll manage. Still, it brought everything back to her, I'm sure."

"Yes."

"Who is the young man who was working with you?"

"He's from London."

Mainwaring had gone up to Hensley's bed and fallen asleep there, not stirring for several hours. Rutledge wished he could have done the same. Two nights without rest had left him groggy. And the ankle that had plagued him for several days had begun to ache again like the very devil from stumbling over the grave in the churchyard.

Hamish, withdrawn and silent, seemed tired as well.

Mrs. Channing, her mind elsewhere, said thoughtfully, "This exonerates Constable Hensley. The girl wasn't buried in the wood after all. Or so everyone is saying. But what happened to Emma Mason?"

"I don't know. I don't suppose anyone will."

"I don't think I'd be very good at police work. It's dreadful sometimes, isn't it?"

"Dreadful, yes."

"I took the liberty of making tea," she told him. "You'll find it on the dining room table."

"Thank you. I don't seem to have much appetite this morning." He walked into the dining room and poured himself a cup, adding sugar and a little milk.

She followed him there and stood in the middle of the room, as if uncertain what to do, go or stay. "Did you really want those bones to belong to the girl?"

He reached in his pocket for a telegram that Inspector Cain had handed him that morning, while waiting for his men to do their macabre work in the wood.

"I asked one of my best men in London to find what he could about Beatrice Ellison and her daughter, Emma Mason. He couldn't trace either of them. Mrs. Ellison believes her daughter died when the Germans marched through Belgium. It may be true. Even so, it doesn't explain what became of Emma."

She took the telegram and scanned it. "Yes, I see. This, then, was your last hope. The body in the wood."

"It may still be there, of course. But I have a feeling it isn't."

"I understand."

She went back to the office to fetch her

coat. "Was there a young man involved in the girl's disappearance, do you think? If she's married and living elsewhere, she'd be hard to find."

"There was a young man — he was set to marry someone else. Whether she got herself involved with him or not, I don't know. He died in the war. There's a memorial to him in the churchyard."

"Then she disappeared by her own choice. Perhaps because of that someone else. It would be hard to live in a village this small with the other woman, so to speak."

"For a time," he said, "I thought the other woman had killed her."

Her eyebrows went up. "It could still be true."

"I'd dig up that rose bed, if I thought it would do any good," he said, half to himself.

It was Hamish who answered him. "Or look beneath yon wall."

Grace Letteridge came to call shortly after Mrs. Channing had gone back to The Oaks.

She stepped briskly into the office and said, "I expect I owe Constable Hensley an apology. I always believed it was he who killed her. That he went to the wood time and again to see if anything had been disturbed. It made sense that he couldn't stay away, that he wasn't able to put it out of his mind. Out of guilt. But she's not there, after all."

Rutledge said, "Hensley isn't well. He may not live. Whoever shot him may be guilty of murder."

"I didn't do it, if that's what you're accusing me of."

"You told me once," Rutledge said, taking the chair behind the desk and leaning back in it, "that you would like to see him dead."

She made a gesture with her hand, as if brushing away his words. "I'm not a murderer. Although I do have a temper sometimes. I won't deny that."

"We're back where we began, then. Tell me, how old is your rose garden?"

"If you're asking me if Emma is buried there, you're a fool."

"We could dig it up and find out. Inspector Cain can bring his men back to do it, after they've finished in the wood."

She turned to go. "You'll have to get a warrant, first," she told him. "I won't let you touch it without one."

Rutledge was leafing through the file on Emma Mason when Mainwaring came in from conferring with the police in Letherington.

"I've talked to the local people — Cain, and his sergeant, and their coroner. Your body has probably been out there in the wood for some time. We aren't in agreement about how long, but if you want my best guess, it would be forty years."

"Forty —"

"Indeed. We've examined the bones in good light and in more detail, looked at the condition, and sifted through the soil around and under them. And this is what came out of the earth under them."

He held out a slim gold toothpick.

Rutledge took it, turning it in his fingers. It had been engraved: *Christmas 1881.*

"It doesn't prove he died then. He could have carried this for many years."

"And this."

It was a farthing, cleaned of its earth and corrosion. And it too bore the date 1881.

"Whoever went through his pockets missed both of them."

"How many memories go back that far, to 1881?"

"Cain has promised to go through his predecessors' files."

"Yes, that's the right place to start," Rutledge agreed. "Our bones must have come from one of the villages close by, if not Dudlington itself. Frith's Wood is too far off the main road, and half hidden to boot. It's not the most likely place for a stranger to conceal a body. For one thing, he wouldn't know of the stigma attached to the wood."

"The reverse could be said for the local people. They want no part of that wood, and I can't say I blame them. Cain had the devil of a time getting his work party together."

Hamish said, "I wouldna' wait for yon inspector to sift through files. There's no pressing need to hurry, by his lights."

It was true. But then Mrs. Arundel, the postmistress, could give him a list of the oldest inhabitants of Dudlington.

"I must say, Ian, that you do have the most interesting luck. I'm glad not to be in your shoes when Bowles hears of this." Mainwaring held out his hand. "Cain has found someone driving to Northampton, and I should just make my train. Good luck, old man. You're going to need it!"

Rutledge said, "Early days yet."

They shook hands, and Mainwaring took the stairs two at a time on his way to fetch his case.

When he came down again, Rutledge had already gone.

Mrs. Arundel, sitting behind her brass cage, considered Rutledge's question.

"The oldest residents . . . Well, Mrs. Lawrence on Church Street, for one. She lives with her grandson and his wife, Patricia. Mr. Cunningham, of course, but he's not very clear in his mind, most days."

It was the lorry belonging to workmen at the Lawrence house that had run him down. Mrs. Melford had informed him that they were turning one of the smaller bedrooms into a nursery.

"Yes, I think I know the house." He thanked the postmistress and left.

Patricia Lawrence answered Rutledge's knock. She was clearly pregnant, her maternity smock hardly concealing her condition. When he'd explained his business, she said doubtfully, "My husband's grandmother is a lovely old lady, but she can be quite dotty at times. I don't know if you'll have much luck."

The elder Mrs. Lawrence was reading in a small parlor on the first floor. Her glasses were perched on her nose, but her eyes were shut, and a soft whistle accompanied her breathing, just skirting a snore.

"Grandmama?" Mrs. Lawrence said, touching her shoulder lightly.

"Eh?" the old woman said, looking bemused. "I'm reading, can't you tell?"

"There's a policeman to see you, if you're up to speaking with him."

"Not that bold as brass constable, is it?"

"No, Grandmama. Inspector Rutledge is from Scotland Yard."

Watery blue eyes moved to Rutledge, standing just behind the younger woman, and she looked him up and down. "He's no policeman I know."

"I'm here for a short while, until the constable recovers from his surgery," Rutledge said, stepping forward. "I'm sorry to disturb your reading," he added, pulling up the chair nearest to hers. "But I'm told that if anyone knows the history of Dudlington, it's you."

Sarah Lawrence smiled, delighted. "On my good days, I can tell you what it was like to see the old Queen married. A pretty slip of a girl she was, then. Hardly came up to the Prince's shoulder, but running to plumpness, if you ask me. I never saw that wicked Scotsman she was so fond of, but even as a small girl, I was quite taken with her Prince. Pity he had to die, but there you are."

"Yes." He glanced up at Patricia Lawrence, indicating that he'd like to speak to her husband's grandmother alone.

She nodded and said, "I'll just fetch some tea. You'd like that, I think?"

Sarah Lawrence squinted her eyes to see the mantel clock. "Is it teatime already?"

"No, Grandmama, but we have a guest."

"Yes, indeed. Very well, young man, tell me why you've come. It isn't about the Queen, I'm sure. She's dead."

She was swathed in shawls, but her hair, pure white, was beautifully brushed, and her black dress was of good quality. Her grandson and his wife, Hamish noted, were taking good care of her.

"I remember my own granny," he added, "and how she ruled the house."

Rutledge said to Mrs. Lawrence as the sitting room door closed, "I'm looking for a man who went missing many years ago. Perhaps as early as 1881. Do you remember gossip about that?"

"What was his name?"

"Sadly we don't know it."

She stared at her lap, thinking. "In 1881, you say? That was the year we put in the pear tree, my husband and I. The one blown down in the storm of 1894. A pretty thing it was too, white clouds of blossoms covering every limb. I was that fond of the pear tree."

"What was happening in Dudlington that year?" he prodded gently.

"When the storm came?"

"When you put in the pear tree."

"Ah. I told you, that was 1881."

He tried another tack. "Who was the doctor in 1881, Mrs. Lawrence? Do you remember his name?"

"It was Blair. Dr. Blair. I never liked him. Thought he knew more about children than their mothers did."

"And who was the rector?"

"That would be Mr. Anderson, I think. Or, no, Mr. Anderson came in the next year. It was Mr. Fellowes."

He walked her through the village, asking about the postmaster, the greengrocer, and every other person he could think of, to jar her memories.

"Do you remember Mrs. Ellison's marriage? It must have been quite a social affair."

"Pooh! She wasn't married in St. Luke's, too small by her lights. Connected with the Harkness family, you know. Her aunt in Northampton arranged the wedding. There weren't that many invited from Dudlington, though her husband had family here at the time. They're gone, of course. That's why he sold the farm. Mr. Shepherd owns it now. He wanted cattle, not sheep. Said his name would become a byword, if he ran sheep. They lost their only son in the war. Sad."

"And who owned the baker's shop?"

"Simpson's father. He would let us have treats on our birthday."

"What do you remember about the Christmas of 1881?" he asked, guiding her slowly.

But she frowned. "Was that a special Christmas, do you think? I don't remember much good coming of it."

"Why?"

"There was a typhoid outbreak that autumn. And my best friend died of it. I wasn't intending to celebrate because of it. But Mr. Lawrence, my husband, told me we must think of the children. And the rector told me I mustn't forsake God."

He sat there for another ten minutes, priming the pump of her memory, to no avail. After all, it was many years ago, for a woman who must be well into her eighties.

But his questions had jarred some of the tangled threads in her mind, and as Patricia Lawrence brought in tea on a pretty painted tray, Sarah said, "Oh, do look, I'd forgot! The teapot! I broke the spout on mine, and Mr. Ellison found me a match for it in London. He was there a number of times in '82, and he said it might take my mind off Sally's death. My friend, you see."

"That was kind of him," Rutledge replied, taking his cup as the younger woman passed them around.

"Yes, he was a kind man. I never knew what he'd seen in Mary Clayton. Except that she was cousin to a Harkness and pretty as a picture."

She was off again on another line of thought, recalling that her own father had known old Mr. Harkness, "who died of a broken heart when the manor burned to the ground. He collected butterflies, you know. His niece kept some of the trays at her house. That's The Oaks, of course. It's seen a sad comedown since her day, let me tell you."

He finished his tea and rose to take his leave. Sarah Lawrence seemed disappointed, as if she had expected him to entertain her for another hour or so.

Rousing herself, she made an effort to hold his attention. "You were asking me about '81. Except for the typhoid, it wasn't an unusual year, you know. But '82, now, that was a year of tragedy. The rector's wife died, Gerald Baylor was nearly trampled to death by one of his bulls, and Mr. Ellison died in an accident in London. A runaway horse, that was. And him leaving behind that dear little girl. Beatrice was such a suitable name, you know. I can remember her christening as if it were yesterday."

Rutledge left soon afterward and found himself walking toward St. Luke's Church. It was a place of tranquillity, with no echoes of Constable Hensley, Emma Mason, or Mrs. Channing.

Inside it was chilly, the stone walls already letting go of what had briefly passed for the winter sun's warmth. He pulled up his coat collar as he chose a chair set near the pulpit, his mind working.

Hamish said, "It's nae use, it willna' all fit together."

"Somehow it does. In the end I'll see my way clear." His voice startled him, ringing hollowly through the empty church.

"You were sent here wi' only the ain duty."

"Murder is my duty."

"Aye, but no' a corpse long dead before you were born."

Rutledge didn't answer him.

Hamish persisted. "It willna' serve. There's nae proof. You canna' find it after a' this time."

"I must speak with the rector."

"He's no' the man to burden with such a tale."

It was true. The rector, for all his experience of the world, was also a little unworldly. He wouldn't believe what Rutledge had to tell him, and the gossip mill would soon have part of the story if not all of it.

"The doctor, then."

"Aye. The doctor."

After a time, Rutledge left the church and went to find Dr. Middleton.

Middleton would have none of it. "You're reaching for the moon, you know."

"I think what I just described to you is likely. Certainly it's possible."

"And how do you expect to prove it? Be reasonable, man, there's nothing to be gained by looking into it, and it could cause a great deal of pain if you're wrong."

There was that as well.

"You'll give me your word not to speak of any of this?" Rutledge asked.

Middleton smiled grimly. "I live here, you know. I'm not about to cut my throat to spite my face!"

Rutledge went back to Hensley's house and began to write his report.

An hour later, he finished it and set it

aside under a stack of papers on Hensley's desk.

Mrs. Channing tapped lightly at the door shortly afterward and said, "I've come to say good-bye. My bags are packed, and the car has been brought around."

"It isn't over yet," he told her.

"There's been nothing since the lorry ran you down. I think he's warned off after such a public display. Or tired of the game. I expect he wanted someone he could frighten badly. And if that's true, he chose the wrong man."

"You don't lie very well."

"I don't want to see you die," she said bluntly. "I've seen enough of death and destruction. I want to hold my séances and bring back dead kings and silly jesters and the ghost of Hamlet's father. There's no harm in that, and it makes people laugh. And it keeps my mind from dwelling on what it shouldn't be remembering. You were the soldier, Inspector, but I put soldiers back together. Or tried to help others do that. I don't know which is worse."

"I'm about to make an arrest. As soon as I do, I can leave Dudlington."

"I think you only want me here to keep an eye on me."

"It's partly true."

She was suddenly angry. "I'm going back to London. It's too late to change my mind."

"Then go."

Mrs. Channing said, in exasperation, "That's so like a man. All right, I'll call your bluff, Inspector. Good-bye."

She walked to the door and was on her way out when she stopped and turned.

"I think Frank Keating has been in prison. Don't ask me why. Perhaps the way he avoids people. If he's paid his price for whatever he did, it doesn't matter. But if you had sent him there — it might be worth looking into. Consider that bit of information my parting gift."

28

It was the middle of the night when Rutledge woke with a start. There was someone in the bedroom. Standing somewhere between the door and the window.

Half-asleep, his first thought was that it must be Hamish, coming out of the shadows of his mind, the voice at last assuming shape and depth and reality.

He lay where he was, fighting to hold his body quiet, keeping his breathing even.

A silhouette paused briefly against the pale light from the window, and then was gone. Rutledge had the distinct feeling that it had moved nearer to the bed.

He counted the seconds, waiting. *If it was Hamish —*

He didn't finish the thought.

He could hear the faint sound of breathing, but he couldn't see who was there, a shadow in among darker shadows. His heart began to pound.

Please, God, not Hamish — !

And then he was awake enough to realize his danger.

"I know you're there," he said softly into the blackness of the room. "Is that what you want? Or have you come to leave another shell casing by my pillow?"

There was silence.

"What do you want? What is it that makes you want to kill me?"

It was a challenge, thrown down deliberately.

But it brought him no response.

The lamp was on the table by his bed. It would take too long to light it. And he cursed himself for not bringing his torch upstairs with him. It was a blunder he wouldn't repeat.

"Did I send you to prison? Or does it have to do with the war?"

He'd lost track of where the breathing was coming from. And then the silhouette was passing the window again, on its way back to the door.

Rutledge had a split second to make his decision. Then he was out of the bed in one smooth motion, muscles tight as a spring as he launched himself at the figure.

But it eluded him, and he crashed into the tall dresser instead. Swearing as he hit his shoulder hard against the corner, he wheeled toward the door and felt cloth rip through his fingers, his hands coming up empty.

He went down the stairs as fast as was safe, plunging out the open door and into the empty street.

Whoever it was had gone, or had slipped into the shadow of a doorway, invisible in the night.

He went back inside, his bare feet cold from the cobblestones and the threshold.

"Was it you?" he asked Hamish. *"Tell me if it was you!"*

Hamish said, "He's still in the house. You were tricked."

Firmly shutting the door, Rutledge found his torch where he'd left it on Hensley's desk and began a search of the ground floor.

But as he walked into the kitchen he knew it was too late.

Behind him the outer door opened and closed so quietly he wasn't sure at first that he'd heard it. The intruder had doubled back and gone.

His presence had been a message. "I could easily have killed you as you slept."

So much for Meredith Channing's prediction that it was over.

Rutledge stood in the parlor that served as Hensley's police station and realized that without a key, he was at the mercy of someone intent on terrorizing him. It would be only a matter of time before the sport palled, and the decision was made to take this game to its logical conclusion.

And he had a feeling that he wouldn't see the blow coming.

Rutledge went to call on Grace Letteridge that morning, finding her brooding over her roses.

"I don't think this one will live," she told him as he came up the front walk. "The roots aren't stable." She rocked the offending canes back and forth. "I won't know for certain until spring, but the signs aren't good."

"Yes, well, that one left a thorn in my back, I'd swear to that."

She stood up and dusted her hands. "You're a liar."

"Probably. Come inside and let me ask you a few questions."

"Why should I do that? I'm not guilty of anything. And what's more, I don't know anyone who is."

"Still —"

She reluctantly preceded him into the parlor and sat down, prepared to block him at every turn. He could feel her resistance across the room.

"Tell me about Robbie Baylor — no,

412

don't fly off at me. This is more important than your pride."

Grace Letteridge glared at him. "That *is* my pride!"

"I know. It's why you went to London, to be rid of him and of Emma and of Dudlington."

"She was beautiful. He told me he couldn't help himself, that he hadn't meant to do more than take her in his arms, and the next thing he knew, he was pinning her down on the grass, kissing her. She clawed his face. And then he slapped hers."

"And so you left."

"He'd already decided to join the army. But every time I looked at Emma, she reminded me that he'd found her beautiful, and his pledge to me hadn't stopped him from — from whatever it was he intended to do. Emma wouldn't tell me her side of what had happened. I expect she was ashamed, that it had shocked and frightened her and made her feel as if she'd betrayed me. But for a very long time, I believed she must have encouraged him in some way. I preferred to blame her than blame him, even though I knew that was wrong. Constable Markham had taken pleasure in dropping hints, you see. And of course I'd seen the scratches on Rob's face. After nearly a week of wondering, I cornered him and forced him to tell me the truth."

"What brought you back to Dudlington?"

"When Rob was killed, they found a letter among his things. It was addressed to me, to be sent in the event of his death. He told me again what had happened, that he'd regretted it ever since, and that he didn't want to die with that on his conscience. That he had truly loved me — that he wanted *forgiveness*."

She bit back tears and looked away from him.

"What did you say to Emma when you came home?"

"I showed her his letter. I thought she had a right to know."

"All of it?"

"All that mattered. But our friendship was never the same. I hadn't trusted her, I deserted her when she needed me most, and I couldn't make amends."

"If you had your chance to live through that summer of 1914 again, would you have done the same thing — walk away?"

She turned back to face him. "Oh yes. I believed he loved me. But he couldn't have loved me as deeply as I thought he did, if he was attracted by Emma. And she was only fourteen then." She paused. "To try to kiss her was bad enough. To slap a child because she spurned him was a side of his nature I hadn't seen before. What hurt most of all was that I'd misjudged him so completely. I thought he was the best of that family, but he was just like his brothers, selfish to the core."

"The fact that Emma was Mrs. Ellison's granddaughter didn't stop Rob Baylor?"

Grace Letteridge laughed, but it was harsh and full of pain. "At the time, I don't believe he was thinking very clearly about anything, least of all the Harkness bloodline."

"Did Mrs. Ellison know that Emma had attracted such unwanted attention?"

"They quarreled about it sometimes. Mrs. Ellison was of the opinion that Emma encouraged men. That if she were truly a lady — and a Harkness — even the most hardened seducer would step aside, abashed." Her mouth twisted wryly. "That made Emma cry. She told me she wanted to go to London and find her mother. And I told her that she didn't even know where to begin to look. After all, her letters had come back, she couldn't be sure where her mother might have gone next. Bath —

Winchester — Oxford — Paris —"

"Do you think she heeded that? Or in desperation went anyway?"

"I thought she was dead. And that Constable Hensley had killed her. I always wondered, you see, what Robbie might have done if he'd gone too far. As it was, he'd slapped her and called her a tease. But she hadn't told her grandmother that part of it, she was too ashamed. Constable Hensley could have felt that he ought to be more successful than a farmer's son. And realized too late there was no turning back. Mrs. Ellison's name carries a good deal of weight in this part of the county. And she'd have gone after him tooth and nail, even if she thought Emma was to blame. He wasn't popular here, and everyone would have sided with Mary Ellison. Still, the skeleton you found in the wood wasn't Emma's, was it? So I was wrong, after all."

Hamish said, "You canna' be sae sure she's telling the truth."

"No, it wasn't Emma's body," he agreed, ignoring the voice. And after a moment, he added, "I find myself wondering if it was her grandfather's."

He held out the gold toothpick and watched her face.

Surprise gave way to a rapid shift in

416

emotions. Recognition. Understanding. Fear.

"It was the last Christmas present Beatrice ever gave him. Where did you find it? Surely not in the wood with the skeleton? *Dear God!*"

Rutledge said, "How did you know about the toothpick?"

"Beatrice told me about it. She chose it herself, a child of five, in Northampton. Her mother had taken her there to visit a cousin, and she saw it in a shop. I doubt if she knew at the time what it was, she just thought it was pretty, and the cousin let her buy it for her father. Mrs. Ellison wasn't pleased with the choice. But the cousin told her not to be silly, the child could do as she liked. And so it was engraved and wrapped in silver tissue and a green ribbon."

"And you're certain she gave this to her father?"

"Oh, yes, there's no doubt about it. She recalled it vividly and talked about it when she missed him, because she wished she'd found something more — I don't know — more respectable? A watch fob or shirt studs, even a chain for his keys. I expect Mrs. Ellison took mean-spirited pleasure in telling her that a toothpick, even a gold one, was hardly worthy of a Harkness. For whatever reason, Beatrice couldn't forget it." She reached out to touch the slender length of gold with the tip of a finger. "There couldn't be two such, could there?"

"What became of Ellison?"

"He died in London, struck by a runaway horse. It was sudden and dramatic — I remember my father saying that Mrs. Ellison screamed when she got the news. It was so out of character, everyone talked about it."

"Where is he buried?"

"You just told me he was the man in the wood."

"Yes, he probably is. But if he 'died' in London, there must have been an inquest, a funeral? His wife would have had to be present."

"Mrs. Ellison went to London to take care of the arrangements. She left Beatrice here with the rector's wife, because what could a child that young understand? He was buried there. She said she couldn't bear to bring him back to Dudlington, that she herself wished to be buried in London with him when the time came. My father remembered that too. He told me long afterward that he was shocked. But then it's what Mary Ellison wanted."

"And Beatrice never doubted that her father was buried in London."

"She even knew the name of the cemetery — Highgate. There was a great stone lion near the grave, and its name was Nero. Beatrice longed to go there and see it for herself. Surely, if she went to London — but that may explain why she was estranged from her mother. The grave wasn't there!"

"Would you be willing to swear under oath to what you've just told me?"

She clearly hadn't considered that. She glanced toward the window, as if she could see Mary Ellison from where she sat. "Must I? I can't — do you really believe that *Mary* —"

"If she told everyone that her husband was buried in London, then why is there a skeleton in the wood, with the toothpick that Beatrice had given her father? Do you believe Mrs. Ellison gave away the toothpick out of a callous disregard for her daughter's feelings?"

"I don't know. But why would Mary make up such a complicated story — the runaway horse, the cemetery lion. And how was he actually killed?"

"There's no way to be certain."

"Well, I'm glad that Beatrice isn't here. It would have broken her heart."

"I think Beatrice is dead as well. And Emma."

She stared at him, her hand to her mouth, her eyes wide. "No, please, I don't want to hear this."

"I can't prove it just yet," he said, "but I've got to try."

"But how — I can't see Mary Ellison, for God's sake, taking up a gun or a knife, or a flat iron to her own flesh and blood. She's not — it sickens me to even think such a thing."

Rutledge hesitated, and then told her: "It's often said that a woman's weapon is poison."

29

Grace Letteridge was still upset when he left her. Part of her had wanted to believe him, and another part of her refused to accept that it was possible. Rutledge said as he walked out the door, "You mustn't say anything. Not until I'm certain. And that may take me some time."

"But the constable — who shot him with a bow and arrow?"

"Do you have Emma's archery set? And if you don't, who very likely does? Mrs. Ellison is strong enough to bend a bow, I think, although she's probably not a very good marksman. But she only had to drive the point of that arrow into Constable Hensley's back deep enough to frighten him and keep him away from the wood. It's even possible she intended to retrieve the arrow, only it had struck bone. And everyone in Dudlington would have believed the Saxon dead had attacked him with a ghostly weapon. A perfect threat to keep people out of Frith's Wood, don't you think?"

"Why are you telling me this?" she asked, at the door. "I wish you'd never come here, not to Dudlington and not to my house."

"I had to trace that toothpick. I couldn't think of anyone else who knew the family as well as you did. Mrs. Ellison never let anyone get close to her. Perhaps because of her secrets, perhaps because of her nature. I can't be sure."

"Will you tell me *why*, when you know?"

"Yes. I'd like the answer to that myself."

Rutledge sat by the fire in Hensley's office, the toothpick in his hand.

If all the world thought Harry Ellison was dead and had been buried in London for all these years, no one would have set up a hue and cry over the fact that he had disappeared.

And it was in keeping with Mary Ellison's character that she would rather have her husband decently interred than for her to be gossiped about in Dudlington as a deserted wife.

Hamish said, "She went to the wood two nights ago."

"Yes, she wanted to be sure I hadn't found her husband. She let me believe it was Emma she thought I was searching for, which was clever of her. I believed her, even pitied her. What matters now is that all alone, in the dark of night, she'd ventured into Frith's Wood. She wasn't afraid of it because she hadn't been brought up in Dudlington and taught to fear it. That much she and Constable Hensley had in common. It's not surprising that she'd see the wood as a place to rid herself of her husband's body."

"Aye, but how did she lug him there?"

"I don't know. He may have been alive when he got there, but already feeling the poison. If she was capable of killing him, she could surely think of an excuse to lure him there to die."

There was a sound at the door, and he looked up, palming the toothpick so that it couldn't be seen.

Meredith Channing stood there, her face grim.

"I came back," she said simply. "I'm not the coward I'd hoped I was."

He laughed. "I'd take you to lunch in Letherington if I thought it wouldn't start the gossipmongers talking."

"I'm hungry. And not particularly worried about gossip. For that matter, you look as if you'd be better off out of Dudlington. What's happened?"

"If you wanted to kill your husband, how would you go about it?"

"I didn't kill him, if that's what your policeman's brain is telling you."

"No. I'm not accusing you. I'd like to know how you would go about such a thing, if it were in your mind."

She walked toward the window that gave onto the street, her back to him.

"Women don't care for bloody scenes. It's easier to use poison, if you aren't there to watch him die. I should think that would be the most difficult part. Watching." She turned back to him. "I don't like being drawn into your brutal world, Ian."

Had it been his brutal world that had decided Elizabeth Fraser not to welcome him back to Westmorland? He hadn't thought of that. But she'd had a taste of just how unspeakable murder could be. For the first time since he'd received her letter he could sympathize with what must have been a difficult choice for her, and in turn respect it.

Hamish said, "Aye, you wouldna' care to see her hurt."

And it was true. Taking a deep breath, as if a weight had been lifted from his shoulders, he brought his mind back to Meredith Channing.

"I'm sorry," he said as he shut the tooth-pick into a cabinet behind the desk and got to his feet. "I didn't intend to make you a part of it either. Lunch is still on offer. I'll just tell Mrs. Melford that I won't be in."

He left a note for her, when she didn't answer his knock, then brought around the motorcar for Mrs. Channing. As he held the door she stepped into the vehicle and found a scarf in her pocket to put around her hat.

When he turned the crank, he heard Hamish telling him he was unwise. But she was right, he needed to be away from Dudlington for a few hours. Yet he couldn't stop himself, as he got in behind the wheel, from looking up at the bedroom windows where Emma Mason had slept.

Luncheon was roast ham and potatoes, with boiled cabbage and a flan. It was the best the Unicorn Hotel could produce, but Mrs. Channing didn't complain. Instead she talked about her life in London, making it seem amusing and interesting. She'd been born in Somerset, she told him, and hadn't gone to the city until her marriage but learned to live there without too much homesickness for the West Country. She never spoke of her husband directly, as if talking about him was still painful.

Rutledge listened, interjecting comments now and then, but a good part of his mind was elsewhere. How does one prove that poison was used — and where were the bodies of Beatrice Ellison and her daughter, Emma Mason? Not in the wood, surely — he'd searched too carefully to have missed them.

But their murderer had learned, perhaps, from her first experience, not to rely on such a public place.

In the house, then — somewhere.

He came back to the present when Hamish whispered, " 'Ware!"

Mrs. Channing was sitting across the table from him, an amused look on her face.

"I'm sorry —" he began, embarrassed, and then realized it was the second time he'd apologized to her that day.

"Do you treat all your guests this way?" she demanded. "I've asked you at least twice if you'd pass the salt."

He had the grace to laugh as he handed the silver saltcellar to her. And then his hand stopped in midair.

It would be so simple to put something in the sugar bowl or saltcellar. So easy to abstain, one's self.

"What is it?" Mrs. Channing asked, watching his face.

As he gave her the saltcellar, he shook his head. "Remembering something, that's all."

But she was holding the saltcellar as if it might bite her, staring down at it with loathing before she set it aside unused. "Yes," she said slowly. "It would work, wouldn't it? Or the almond paste between the layers of a favorite cake. And then you could dispose of what was left without a worry. In the back garden under a pot of geraniums. Even burning it up in the stove, although the smell would be sickening."

A five-year-old child would never suspect that her mother had just killed her father. Death was loss, hard enough to understand.

Folding her napkin, Meredith Channing sat back in her chair, as if her appetite had fled.

"Small wonder you haven't married," she told him, then saw the look on his face and remembered what Maryanne Browning had confided to her about his engagement. "I'm so sorry! That was not called for. I was simply about to say that of all the men I've ever dined with, you're the first to put me off my food."

Her attempt at levity fell flat.

He thought, It's going to be impossible to prove. But if she shot Hensley, the killing hadn't ended.

The hotel receptionist came to his table and said quietly, "Inspector Rutledge?"

"Yes?"

"Inspector Cain has been looking for you and saw your motorcar in the hotel yard. There's been an urgent telephone call from Northampton. I'm to tell you that Constable Hensley is dying, and you're to come at once."

Mrs. Channing insisted on driving with him. "If you must stop in Dudlington before you go on to Northampton, you may be too late. There's nothing I can do, but I don't mind waiting until you know whether this is true or not."

"Why shouldn't it be true?" he asked, stepping into the motorcar beside her.

"Telephone messages can be contrived. As I remember, there are some very lonely stretches just south of Dudlington, open pasture rather than houses. A perfect place for an ambush."

If his nemesis could hide in the open land of Beachy Head, he could hide along the roadside as he did in Hertford, and wait for the motorcar to come by.

"No. That puts you at risk. If the shot kills me, I'll lose control of the wheel. You could die in the crash."

"I could have died nursing those poor soldiers with the Spanish influenza too. Or on the crossing between Dover and Calais. I could have been one of the nurses who went down with the *Britannic.* I'm not afraid. And someone else in the car with you might deter him. Who knows?"

She reached into the rear seat to lift up the woolen rug that he kept there, and Rutledge stopped breathing for a heartbeat as she seemed to have trouble retrieving it. Almost as if Hamish had held on to it, he thought. But she said nothing as she finally brought it between their seats and proceeded to spread it over her knees.

That, as he knew too well by now, was no proof that she hadn't sensed a presence there, just that she had chosen not to speak of it. For the moment.

They drove fast, trying to cover the miles as quickly as they could, but Rutledge kept his eye to the verges of the road, where Death could also be lurking.

Hamish, in the rear seat, was trying to tell him something, but Rutledge had no time to pay heed to the words that seemed to echo in his ear.

When they at last reached the busy outskirts of Northampton, where industry seemed to thrive, Rutledge felt himself relax for the first time. His neck and shoulders were stiff from tension. It eased as they made their way to the hospital.

"How is your ankle?" Mrs. Channing asked, when he got down and limped around to her side of the motorcar to open her door.

"Much better. Driving aggravates it a little. By the time I've walked a hundred paces, it will be all right."

And it was.

They found Matron in her office, and he asked to see Constable Hensley.

"There was a message to come at once," he said, dreading to hear the news that her patient had already died.

Matron nodded gravely. "His fever has risen — alarmingly last night, but it fell back a little this morning. Is this a relative?" She indicated Mrs. Channing.

"No," she said, holding out her hand. "My name is Meredith Channing. I was a nurse in the war. I was hoping you might let me sit somewhere quietly, while Mr. Rutledge speaks to the constable."

Matron, responding to that warm, compelling voice, said, "Yes, you'll find a small room down the passage and to your left, just across from the surgical theater. It's for the staff, and there's usually a fresh pot of tea on the hot plate. You'll find it quiet and comfortable, I'm sure."

"Thank you." Mrs. Channing turned and walked away, leaving Rutledge to follow Matron to the room where the doctors had isolated Hensley.

Hamish was saying, "There's no call to harass him. If he didna' kill the girl."

Rutledge answered silently, We'll see.

Indeed, the constable looked ill, his face flushed, his hands restless outside the sheet that covered him. His eyes were too bright, and as they focused on Rutledge, he said, "God, I'm afraid of dying."

Rutledge sat down by the bed, and said, "I don't know that you are dying."

Hensley shook his head from side to side in denial. "I can feel it, the fever, eating away at me. They've cleaned the wound twice, and it hasn't helped. They're afraid the infection's spread into my blood." He took a deep breath, trying to quell his distress. "I hope you've brought good news."

"Of a kind. While you've been away," Rutledge said, "we've had several new developments in Dudlington. We've found a body in Frith's Wood."

"I knew it!" the sick man said, rousing himself. "I knew that Letteridge bitch had killed her. Where in the wood did you find Emma? I'd searched until I was crazy with dread of that place, but I couldn't stay away."

It was the first time he'd admitted to going to the wood. Rutledge tried to describe where he had made his discovery.

Hensley said, "I'd looked there, more than once. But not as deep as you did."

"You didn't carry a pitchfork."

Hensley flinched. "Poor Emma. She ought not to have died like that!"

"Like what?"

"Alone in that blasted wood. She was afraid of it, you know. Her grandmother had told her tales about seeing lights there, in the winter."

He shivered and reached out to pull up the bedclothes. "I freeze and I burn. They've put a hot water bottle at my feet now. I was worried last night when they started going cold. It's the first sign of dying."

Rutledge said, "We found a body in the wood, but I didn't say that it was Emma's."

Hensley broke off plucking at the bedclothes, to stare at him. "Not Emma's? But I thought —" His eyes glittered in the light of the table lamp. He said wretchedly, "It's this fever, nothing makes sense."

"It was a man's body. I have several very good reasons to think it might be Harry Ellison's."

"Emma's grandfather? He's buried in London."

"I don't think he is. I'll have the Yard take a look tomorrow, but I don't expect them to find a grave."

"Grace Letteridge couldn't have killed *him*. She wasn't born when he died."

"I think Mary Ellison may have done it and buried him in the wood, then made up the story about the runaway horse in London."

"God help us!" He lay back in the bed with the back of his hand across his eyes.

Matron put her head in the door. "Please don't tire the patient, Inspector. He needs all his strength."

"Yes, thank you, Matron." When the door closed, Rutledge said, "Is Frank Keating actually a man by the name of Sandridge?"

Hensley took away his hand and looked at Rutledge. "On my word, he's not."

But if Hensley had been a cohort of

433

Sandridge's, he wasn't likely to admit the connection.

"What happened in London, Hensley? Did you look the other way when Barstow's place of business was set afire?"

Hensley moved restlessly. "You lied to me, you think I'm dying, that I ought to confess. What if it's a ruse, and I pull through this? I didn't kill Emma Mason, that much I'll tell you. But I won't speak of London." He turned his head aside. "You weren't there. And some people have a long memory. They'd know who talked."

He wouldn't change his mind, and finally Rutledge stood up to go.

He had just put his hand on the latch to open the door when Hensley said, "Here, you never told me. What's become of Emma, then?"

"We haven't found her yet. But I hope to, very soon."

Rutledge put in a call to the Yard to have someone look in Highgate cemetery for Harry Ellison's grave site.

"I'm told there's a great stone lion nearby, called Nero."

"I know the tomb you mean, sir," the constable on the other end answered him. "It shouldn't be hard to find out if there's an Ellison in the vicinity." He spelled the name again, to make sure he had it right. "Where can I ring you back, sir?"

"Inspector Cain, Letherington. He'll see I get the message."

"Thank you, sir, I'll make sure it's taken care of straightaway."

Before he left the hospital, Rutledge spoke to the doctor in charge of Hensley's care. The man looked drained, as if he hadn't slept in several days, but he sat down for five minutes to answer questions.

"If we can't stop the infection, he's a dead man," Dr. Williams told him bluntly. "But Constable Hensley's strong, he has a sound constitution. That may make all the difference. Everything that can be done has been done, but in medicine there are no certainties."

"Will you stay in touch?"

"Yes, that's why I asked Matron to put a call in to you today. He could be unconscious by tomorrow. If it was necessary to speak with him, time was of the essence. And we ought to ask, are there any relatives who should be notified?"

"He lived alone in Dudlington. I don't know what family he has. Sergeant Gibson or Chief Superintendent Bowles at the

Yard may be able to tell you."

"I've spoken with the Chief Superintendent. He's rung us several times, in fact. He seems most anxious for his man."

Hensley had made no mention of that.

"Yes," Rutledge answered dryly, "he does care about this one."

30

The drive back to Dudlington was silent for a time, the miles speeding away behind them. Hamish, for reasons of his own, was withdrawn. And Rutledge, watching for the ambush they might have escaped on the drive south, wasn't in the mood for conversation. Meredith Channing sat quietly beside him, but he saw, when he glanced her way once or twice, that she too was watchful, her eyes never leaving the roadsides. The early winter dusk, bleak and concealing, had enveloped them some miles outside the city of Northampton, and the headlamps threw long beams of light across the drab landscape. He didn't think they would have much warning, if someone was waiting for them in the night, but then a hidden sniper would have to be certain of his target. It would cut down on his accuracy.

Towns and villages appeared and vanished, their houses and churches and farms noticeably empty of life, here at the dinner hour. A cold wind whipped through the motorcar.

"Is he dying? This Constable Hensley

you went to see?" Mrs. Channing asked after a time, as if needing distraction from her watch.

"The doctors are fighting to save his life. They're afraid it may be blood poisoning now, not just an infection at the site of the surgery. They don't offer much hope, but they also tell me he's strong."

It was difficult to carry on a normal conversation in the motorcar. But she said, "What a shame! Mr. Keating, at The Oaks, told me what had happened to the constable."

"It's far more complicated than Keating realizes. I want Hensley alive to testify in two cases."

"Yes, well, if wishes were horses . . ."

They were silent again for several miles.

"I'll drop you at The Oaks. Keating may not be up. I'll be sure you're safely inside before I go on."

"Thank you."

They reached the turning to Dudlington sooner than they had expected. The inn was dark, and the head-lamps were the only illumination to guide Rutledge as the road began to curve and run down into the village.

He had just made the turn toward Holly Street and the circular drive that led to the front of The Oaks, when something caught his eye.

Hamish shouted, "There. Left!"

A succession of thoughts ran through Rutledge's mind . . .

Someone saying that cows were kept in the barns this time of year.

And his own voice making a remark about camouflage.

"Hold on!" He twisted the steering wheel hard, and the tires skidded before leaving the road. In the same moment he cut the headlamps.

Mrs. Channing cried out as the motorcar went careening out into the meadow, bouncing wildly over the uneven ground into darkness, swaying and lurching as it went.

Rutledge fought the wheel and brought the heavy vehicle under control, then to a wrenching halt.

He was out of his door almost before the recoil of the sudden stop had settled, racing back to the cow lying in the grass, for all the world chewing its cud.

She turned her head toward him as he got nearer, her white and black hide giving her the look of a harlequin, half invisible. He could just see the whites of her eyes.

He realized, in that moment, that she was real — and pegged to the ground so that she wouldn't wander off.

It hadn't been a trap, with a marksman under the hide, but a ruse, and he had fallen for it.

He swore and went to pull up the pegs. The cow scrambled to her feet and shook herself. Then she turned and began to amble away, as if she knew where to find her barn.

He caught the rope around her neck and soothed her.

Mrs. Channing, opening her door, called, "Inspector?"

Leading the cow with him, he went back to the car. "Are you all right?" he asked. "I'm sorry, there was no time to warn you."

"A few bruises, nothing serious. What's this?"

"I expect he felt I'd drive straight over it, thinking he was under the hide and preparing to fire. Thank God I didn't, I'd have killed Bessy here, and probably myself as well, when the motorcar turned over on me."

She reached out a gloved hand toward the cow, then thought better of it. "Poor thing, she's probably frightened to death."

"Here, let me walk you as far as the inn, then I'll take her home. Before she wanders out into the road and someone else does hit her."

"No, I'm all right. I'll see myself to the inn."

But he wouldn't let her. He walked her as far as the stairs and gave her his torch to find her way up them.

Satisfied that she was safe, he turned back to the motorcar, and then untied the cow from the frame.

At first the animal was determined to go her own path, but soon enough she stopped pulling against the rope and followed him meekly down Holly Street. Her hoofs clattered on the cobblestones, and she walked with that swaying motion that made cows seem so slow and bucolic. But he could still see the whites of her eyes, telling him that she was anxious.

He led her down Whitby Lane and then along Church Street, toward the Baylor house.

Leaving her in the yard, he went to bang on the door. In a few minutes, Ted Baylor flung open the door, his braces down and his hair awry, as if he'd been asleep in his chair. "What is it —" he began, and then over Rutledge's shoulder he saw the cow.

"My good God! What's she doing out there!"

"I'd like an answer to that myself. Is she yours?"

Baylor reached behind him for a coat, pulling it on as he closed the door. "Yes, I recognize her. How many others are missing?"

He hurried around the house toward the distant barns. Rutledge, still leading the cow, fell behind as he matched his pace to hers. But she began to trot as she crossed the yard. Baylor had the great door open, the dark interior yawning behind him, by the time Rutledge got there. He was lighting a lamp and then holding it high as he walked down the barn, looking at the rows of cattle drowsing on their beds of straw. Rutledge followed him. A miasma of fresh straw, steaming animals, and manure filled the air.

"Here," Baylor said, pointing to a half stall that was empty. "This appears to be the only one, thank God."

Rutledge brought the cow up and handed him the rope. "Do you lock the barn?" he asked.

"Why should we? The cows don't try to leave. Where the hell did you find her?"

"Near The Oaks. I almost ran her down."

"I don't believe you!"

"Why should I lie about it? Besides," he retorted, "I have a witness."

"It doesn't make any sense." Baylor was examining the cow, running his hand over her sides and flanks. "She's mine, all right. As far as I can tell, she's not hurt. I don't like the look of this. Who would want to harm one of my beasts?"

"Where was your brother tonight?"

"In his bed. Where I'd have been if I hadn't fallen asleep while reading."

"Can you be sure where he was? You weren't awake."

"Yes, by God." He stamped his feet, warming them. "He's not likely to be out in the damp night air. Not with his lungs."

"Then why didn't your dog bark, if a stranger meddled with the barn?" ·

Baylor said, "I was thinking of the cow — where is that bloody dog?"

The cow was settling in at last, going down to her knees and then her belly. With an almost human sigh, she lay there, quiet as a statue except for her regular breathing.

"We'd better have a look for him," Rutledge answered.

They searched the yard and Baylor went to the kitchen door to shout for the dog in the house. But it was nowhere to be found.

"Where did you say the cow was? By the road? We'd best look there for the dog as well."

Rutledge said, "She'd been pegged down by the road, but there couldn't have been a dog up there. I'd have seen it, even if it didn't bark. Would Bossy allow anyone to approach her and lead her away, without a fuss? If she didn't know him?"

"Depends on whether or not the man knows cattle, doesn't it?"

Baylor went to the barn again, made a swift search, and came back to the door where Rutledge was waiting.

"He doesn't wander off, that dog. I don't like this."

"Nor I." Rutledge stood there in the night air, thinking. "Can you whistle him up? Give him instructions to bring in the herd?"

"Oh, yes." Baylor gave the signal, a series of low- and high-pitched whistles. They would carry for some distance — had to carry, when herdsman and dog were separated.

When there was no response, he repeated it.

Hamish said, "Listen!"

There was a sound, muffled and far off, that could have been an animal in distress.

Baylor cocked his head. "On the other side of the rectory, I think." And he set off at a trot in that direction.

Rutledge followed the bobbing lantern, but when they reached the far side of the rectory, there was no sign of the dog.

"Whistle again."

Baylor did, and the muffled sounds were louder, a strange whine, hollow and well above their heads.

Baylor held up the lantern, looking around, scanning the roofline of the rectory.

Rutledge, more accustomed to tracing sounds, said, "The church. The tower room, I'd say."

As they reached the tower door, Rutledge put out his hand for the lantern. "Let me go in first." For all he knew, it was a trap.

He pulled the door open and stepped inside.

The dog had been tied to one of the handles of the sanctuary door and muzzled with a length of dark cloth. He growled at the sight of Rutledge, visible mainly as a hulking shadow in the doorway as the lantern cast his silhouette against the wall.

There was no one else in the tower entrance or on the stairs.

"Baylor?"

Ted Baylor came in and spoke to the dog, reducing it to whines and wriggles of ecstasy. He took away the muzzle, and the dog began to bark in short, staccato yelps. Baylor soothed him as he untied the rope.

"I'd have killed him, if he'd harmed the dog," he said through clenched teeth. "Tell me who?"

"I wish I knew." Rutledge had opened the sanctuary door and lifted the lantern high, but there were too many places to hide. "Bring the dog here."

"He can't go in there."

"Not in there. To the door."

But the dog sniffed briefly at the air of the nave, then turned back to Baylor.

"There's no one in the church," Baylor said.

"You're right, I think."

"What's all this in aid of?" Baylor asked, nodding toward the north and Frith's Wood. "Is it to do with the bones they've found? Were they the girl's? That's the whisper going about."

"I don't know. I can tell you the bones don't belong to Emma Mason. You can scotch that rumor, if you would. There's no point in upsetting her grandmother, if it can be helped."

"And who's to gossip to the grand-mother, I ask you!" Baylor said sourly. "She all but accused my brother Rob of attempted rape, a few years ago. There's no love lost there. But yes, I'd not want to learn bad news that way."

He turned to go, taking the dog with him. "What you've done. It's appreciated," he said over his shoulder, his voice gruff.

And he was gone into the night, his lantern bobbing as he crossed the churchyard, the dog's wagging tail flicking in and out of the yellow glow.

Rutledge walked back through the quiet streets to the motorcar, where it sat in the field. He was about to crank it when a thought struck him.

What if someone had meddled with it in his absence?

"First the kirk, and now the motorcar. Ye're edgy, man!"

Still, without his torch or a lamp, there was no way he could be sure that all was well.

In the end he walked to Hensley's house and went in, to find Frank Keating pacing the floor, waiting for him.

"Where the hell have you been?" Keating demanded. "I've been here for close on two hours."

"I had other business to see to." He fought to keep weariness out of his voice.

"The bones?"

"Yes. Apparently word of them is all over Dudlington."

"A man from Letherington came into

the bar tonight. I heard him tell his mates about digging in the wood, and finding bones. I shut the bar then, and came to look for you."

There was something in his eyes that Rutledge couldn't judge. Fear, he thought, and a resistance, almost as if he had come here against his better judgment.

"Was it the girl?" he asked, finally, when Rutledge stood there, silent. "For God's sake, tell me who it was you found? Bloody hell, man, tell me!"

"It wasn't Emma Mason. In fact, it wasn't a woman's body at all."

Keating seemed to collapse into himself with relief.

"That's all, then," he said, brushing past Rutledge on his way to the door.

Rutledge put out a hand to stop him. Keating jerked his arm clear. "Don't put your hands on me!"

"Why should you care whether the bones belonged to the girl or not?"

"I told you. I've seen her about the village. Too pretty for her own good, and all the men leering at her. I hear how they talk in the bar, mind you. Foul-mouthed bastards! Hensley worst of all. I threw him out, told him not to come to The Oaks again."

"Do you think what he said was

bragging, or the truth?"

"If it'ud been the truth, I'd have choked the life out of him."

Rutledge said again, "Why do you care about Emma Mason?"

"Why do you think? I lost my own daughter and I'll never have another. The hurt doesn't go away, no matter what you tell yourself. It's there day and night. I'd have killed any man who touched her. Why should I stand for such talk about another man's child, if I wouldn't have stood for it about my own?"

With that he was out the door, slamming it behind him.

Hamish said, "It may be that yon constable lied to keep you from speaking to him."

"That he wasn't Sandridge? I'd considered that. I wonder how much he was paid to set the fire — and if it was enough to make it possible for him to purchase The Oaks."

In the early-morning light Rutledge examined the motorcar carefully, but no one had touched it as far as he could tell.

He drove it without incident back to the house and put it away.

The time had come to speak to Mrs. Ellison.

He waited until it was nearly ten o'clock, and then walked across the street and knocked at her door.

It was some time before she answered. Her face was lined, and she looked as if she hadn't slept well.

"Come in, Inspector," she said, and this time led him to the parlor, indicating that he should sit down. "I've seen all the activity at your door. Something has happened, hasn't it? You've — found Emma."

Her voice almost broke on the last word.

He said gently, "We didn't find her in the wood, Mrs. Ellison. I told you the truth, earlier. I'm sorry if you were still worried."

She almost fell apart, then drew herself together again, and faced him with no sign of pain. It was an act of courage, and he had to admire it.

"Thank you." She stood, the lady of the manor dismissing the policeman. "I didn't like to ask, you know. I didn't wish to break down in front of someone."

He sat where he was. Reaching into his pocket, he held the toothpick out to her.

She looked at it, then lifted her eyes to his face. "Am I meant to know what that is?"

"It was, I understand, a gift from your daughter, Beatrice, to her father. Christmas

1881. The date is engraved on it."

"I can't imagine what you're talking about, Inspector. It's not the sort of thing a girl like Beatrice would give her father on any occasion." Her expression was slightly puzzled, and she raised her brows, as if seeking an explanation.

"There are those who tell me otherwise."

"Yes, I'm sure there must be people eager to tell you what they want you to believe. But that doesn't make it true, does it? Good day, Inspector."

She walked to the door and stood there, waiting for him to leave.

"You've never seen this object before in your life?"

"No. I can't speak any plainer than that."

Hamish said, as they reached the street again, "She willna' break. And ye have only the word of the lass with the roses."

Hearsay. Hardly evidence that would stand up in a courtroom against the patrician calm of a Mrs. Ellison. The jury might not like her, but they would believe her.

"There's the nonexistent grave in Highgate cemetery, in London."

"You canna' be sure it isna' there. If she planned so carefully, she wouldna' leave that to chance."

But it was hard to believe that Mrs. Ellison had gone to so much trouble and expense, to bury an empty casket.

He drove to Letherington, to see if there was any news. When he rang up the Yard, he found himself talking to Inspector Mickelson, his voice cold and distant over the line. Rutledge asked for Sergeant Gibson and was told he was out.

Rutledge rang off.

His second call was to Inspector Kelmore in Northampton, who, after speaking with several other people, informed Rutledge that they hadn't any information on a Harkness of the age he described.

"We'll need more details before we can pursue it. Although Sergeant Thompson tells me there was a Harkness who lived here at the turn of the century. She died in the same year as the Old Queen, he says. It was a sad story, which is why he remembers it. Her maid claimed she was poisoned, but no one believed her. She died soon after herself, and that was the end of it."

"Was she a wealthy woman, this Miss Harkness?"

He could hear Kelmore in the distance, repeating the question. Then he came back on the line. "Thompson says she'd been very wealthy at one time but outlived her money, except of course for the house. That went to a family connection, who sold it shortly afterward to pay for the funeral."

"How did the maid die?" Rutledge asked.

There was further consultation. "In a fall down the back stairs, Thompson thinks. But send us more information about the woman you're after, and we'll be happy to run her down."

Rutledge thanked him.

He thought very likely he'd found the right cousin after all.

From the hotel he went to see Inspector Cain and discovered that he too had been called away.

Reluctantly, Rutledge drove back to Dudlington, feeling as if his hands were tied.

What he needed was a warrant to search the Ellison house, but he was inclined to believe that Inspector Cain would refuse to ask for it on such slim evidence. After all, Mrs. Ellison had connections. And Cain was ambitious. Rutledge had learned to be wary of ambitious men.

31

Rutledge found Mrs. Channing sitting in the small parlor at The Oaks, writing a letter.

She looked up as he came in. "I never heard the end of the story about the cow."

"She'd been taken from one of the barns past the church. Her owner was glad to have her back unharmed."

"I'm sure he was . . ." She put her hand into the portable correspondence box she'd brought with her from her room and held out his torch. "Thank you."

"My pleasure."

After a moment he added, "I need a favor."

"What is it?"

"I'd like you to invite someone from Dudlington to have dinner with you in Letherington. Mrs. Ellison. I want her out of her house for several hours."

She was ahead of him. "You'd search without a warrant?"

He said, "You don't want the answer to that. It makes you an accessory."

She looked at him. "You're risking your reputation."

"Yes. I won't do any damage, I won't take away anything. What I want to see is what sort of flooring she has in her cellar. I could go in at night, when she's asleep, but there are times when she walks about the house. I shouldn't like to frighten her."

"What possible excuse could I have for asking a stranger to dine with me?"

"That you knew — or thought you knew — her family. Harkness is the name."

"I'd rather not, if you don't mind."

He was disappointed but said, "That's all right. I understand."

That night, when the street was dark and all the lights were out in most of the houses on Whitby Lane, Rutledge, dressed in a black sweater and black trousers, walked boldly to the door of the Ellison house and tried the lock.

It was open. He slipped into the entrance and listened.

From somewhere in the house he could hear snoring, a steady, rhythmic sound that indicated a deep sleep. Hard of hearing Mrs. Ellison might be, but sudden sounds in the night penetrated dreams.

He moved silently toward the kitchen,

finding his way with his torch, his fingers shielding most of the light.

The kitchen was tidy, a kettle ready for morning, a cup and saucer set out on the table next to the floral tea caddy and the sugar bowl.

Looking at the doors leading off the kitchen, he decided that one was a pantry, another the door to the back garden, and the third possibly the back stairs. He tried them each in turn and found a fourth door near the back entry.

That proved to be a rough staircase into the cellar.

He went down carefully, as Hamish warned him to be wary.

"This isna' the way to find an answer," the soft Scots voice whispered.

"Cain won't listen if there isn't a very good chance I'm right."

"Aye, but how will ye tell him ye're right?"

Rutledge ignored him. He'd reached the bottom of the stairs and cast his light about the cellar. It looked like a hundred others, the door to the yard slanting over the head of a short flight of stairs, a collection of scuttles and gardening implements scattered here and there, a barrow, and all the oddments of a house lived in for many years. A shelf held preserves and jams and tins of fruit, another held jam kettles and strainers, and other kitchenware not frequently used. A third held a collection of chipped dinner plates, bowls, cups and saucers in at least two patterns. Old boots stood in a box by the outer door, and on hooks above them, he saw a man's trousers, a worn coat, and an old hat. Three umbrellas lay on a ledge nearby. Overhead in the rafters were bunches of herbs set to dry. From the look of them, they hadn't been used in many years, for something had been at them. As he touched one of the bunches of lavender, it crumbled between his fingers.

The floor under his feet was earthen, packed hard over the decades, certainly not loose enough for a woman to dig graves in.

"A wild-goose chase," Hamish said, urging him to go.

Where else but the cellar could Mrs. Ellison have buried the bodies of two women?

"Mind, it's already been searched by the constable."

"No. According to his notes, Hensley took her word that she'd already searched the house. Who was going to call that into question? Why would anyone even consider the possibility that Mrs. Ellison had murdered her own grandchild? She took a calculated risk, and won."

What's more, the back garden was overlooked by the windows of her neighbors, and she would have drawn attention to herself if she'd gone out to dig in her flower beds late in the night.

His torch went methodically from left to right, floor to rafters, without a break in the walls or floor to indicate past activity of any sort.

Taking two steps across the floor, careful not to leave the marks of his shoes in the dust, he turned to throw his light behind the stairs, and there he saw a large wooden cupboard up against the wall, its double doors barred with a short length of plank nailed across them. In front of it was an old bull's-eye target of straw with a faded canvas covering. The kind that was used in practicing at the butts with a bow and arrow.

The light stopped there as Rutledge absorbed what he was looking at. He thought, measuring the cupboard with his eye, that he could easily fit any two women he'd met in Dudlington inside those doors, providing they weren't unusually tall or heavy.

He walked around the staircase and put his free hand on the wooden bar. It was solidly nailed in, and he would need a crowbar to pry it off.

"It's no' proof," Hamish was saying.

Rutledge leaned forward to sniff at the tiny crack where the doors on either side met.

A musty odor met his nostrils, leavened with herbs. Rosemary, he thought, for one. And thyme. What else? Lavender, yes, that was it.

A blanket chest? Or a coffin for Beatrice Ellison and Emma Mason?

He made his way back up the stairs, walking carefully on the outside of the treads to keep the creaking of old wood at a minimum. Once in the kitchen he shut the door behind him, and took out a handkerchief to wipe the soles of his feet, so as not to leave dusty tracks on the kitchen's floor.

He had reached the dining room on his way to the front door when he realized that the snoring had stopped.

He froze where he was, flicked off his torch, and listened.

At the top of the stairs a light bloomed and faded, as if someone had walked across the head of the stairs with a lamp in hand.

Rutledge stayed where he was, breathing as shallowly as he dared.

A door opened, shut.

He thought he could move then and was halfway through the parlor when a voice called.

"Who's there?"

He stopped again, hidden beside the tall case clock against the parlor wall. He wasn't sure whether she had actually heard him moving about or sensed his presence.

Hamish scolded, "If she comes down wi' the lamp, there's no hope. She'll see you! And it will no' look verra' good in London."

Rutledge thought, She'll hear him.

But after a moment the lamplight faded again, and there was silence in the house.

He stood there by the clock for a good half an hour, unwilling to move in the event she was waiting at the top of the steps where she could see the door.

After a while, satisfied that she had gone back to sleep again, he moved silently to the front door and opened it, stepped outside, and closed it.

For the first time he was able to take a deep breath. It seemed to seep into every corner of his body, reviving it.

Moving swiftly but quietly, he went down the steps and into the street. There was no one in sight. He scanned each direction, his eyes taking in the windows overlooking him as he listened for any sound or footsteps. But not even a dog had barked as he stood there.

He was halfway to the door of Hensley's house when something made him look up at the windows of Emma Mason's bedroom.

He remembered then what Mary Ellison had said when he caught her by the church two nights ago.

"You aren't the only one to watch from windows."

He could just barely see her there, in the darkened room, staring down at him, the white oval of her face set above the black of her dressing gown.

And he was speared by moonlight, in the unshadowed middle of the street, his torch in his hand, his face upturned toward her, and guilt probably written there in his expression of surprise.

For an instant their eyes held.

And then Rutledge strode briskly into Hensley's house and shut the door behind him.

32

He asked Inspector Cain for a search warrant.

And just as Rutledge had expected, he was met with a reluctance that bordered on intransigence.

"You said yourself she denied any knowledge of that toothpick. It's only Miss Letteridge's word against Mrs. Ellison's, and it could be said that Miss Letteridge was feeling vindictive, for reasons of her own."

"You'll find your evidence when you make the search."

"You can't be sure of it. Look, I must live here long after you've returned to London. If we're wrong, if your search turns up no evidence whatsoever that this woman is a murderess, then what? And I honestly find it hard to believe —"

"— that a Harkness could poison someone," Rutledge finished for him, interrupting. "Bloodlines don't prove with certainty that she's innocent."

"But can you be absolutely positive those bones are Ellison's remains? Not just someone walking on the road who fell ill, got to the wood, and died."

"And buried himself afterward?"

"Time covered his remains, not a human agency. You've got to admit that that's possible. Look, you came here to deal with the attack on Constable Hensley. There was nothing in your brief about Emma Mason. Nor her mother, nor her grandfather. Who shot Hensley?"

"Mrs. Ellison. She's admitted that her granddaughter was interested in bows and arrows. She had the means."

"I've met Mrs. Ellison socially. Frankly, I can't quite see her wandering in Frith's Wood with the intention of killing anyone. Besides, how could she have walked boldly toward the wood with a bow in her hand?"

"She could have left it there for use if Hensley got too close. And she felt the time had come."

"Premeditation."

"Yes."

"No one goes to that wood, Rutledge, if they can help it."

"Do you think Mrs. Ellison is superstitious?"

Cain shook his head. "We're not getting anywhere. Bring me proof, Rutledge, beyond hearsay and suspicion. I must have something I can actually hold in my hand, as it were."

Rutledge left, his anger barely controlled. But he knew that Cain was right.

He drove back to Dudlington with Hamish making his presence known through an undercurrent of disapproval.

"She kens what you know. You canna' change that. And if she's been sae clever all these years —"

"She's not likely to give herself away now."

He concentrated on the road, watching the fields speed by his motorcar, thinking about Dudlington, and how blind the village had been to what was happening. Cain couldn't overlook Mrs. Ellison's connection with a once-prominent family, and neither could Mrs. Ellison's neighbors.

He arrived to find chaos.

Smoke was billowing out the door of Hensley's house, a dark plume that was acrid and choking. He could hear the coughing as the men worked to smother the blaze with water and blankets and buckets of sand from somewhere.

Hamish was urgently reminding him of papers that were at risk in the cupboard behind Hensley's desk.

Rutledge plunged through the door to see what the damage was. The fire hadn't reached the office, but it appeared that a live coal from the hearth had exploded onto the carpet in the sitting room, and the flames had run up the sides of a chair before someone had stepped into the office and smelled smoke.

Or had the coal had help moving from hearth to carpet?

There was no time to wonder. Rutledge inserted himself into the chain as those pumping water from the sink passed buckets down the line and others clattered down the steps with more bedclothes and linens to help smother the blaze.

Rutledge saw Keating stop and pick up papers being trampled underfoot in the office and set them out of the way. They had fallen from the desk and had been scattered by the multitude of feet hurrying through.

The greengrocer was there, the baker and his helpers as well, and someone from one of the houses on the other side, as well as a half dozen men he didn't recognize.

The burning carpet was now a smoldering, blackened ruin, and half the chair was gone. The wood of the floor had been heavily scorched. Ten minutes more, he thought, and the drapes would have caught as well.

Men were moving outside into cleaner air, and water sloshed under their feet and was tracked through the office.

Keating was still there, rapidly sorting papers, as if looking for something. Rutledge had put away most of the concealed papers he'd discovered, and the rest were the routine reports Hensley hadn't got around to filing. He turned away as Keating stepped outside and, without waiting for thanks, walked on up the hill to The Oaks.

Someone brought a bucket of hot tea, sweet and leavened with milk, and it was poured into mugs. Sweaty faces, covered in grime, grinned in reaction and relief. One man even called to Rutledge to ask if he'd ever worked with a fire brigade before. Then Rutledge remembered that the house wasn't Hensley's, only let from the greengrocer. The willing hands had come to help one of their own.

Still, he thanked them, walking among them and talking with each man.

Ted Baylor was there, saying, gruffly, "It's the least I could do," as if his presence was repayment for the safe return of his cow.

The air was still heavy with smoke, and the house would have to air before he could sleep in it that night.

Looking up once, toward the house across the way, he could see Mrs. Ellison standing back from the window but watching what was going on.

"You aren't the only one to watch from windows," she'd said. But had she had anything to do with the fire?

He left the men to their tea and went across to knock at her door.

To his surprise she came to answer it.

"Did you see who went in, before the fire was discovered?" And then he added, "It's not my house, or Hensley's. It belongs to Freebold."

"Why should I help you?"

"Because you're a Harkness, and must set a good example."

Her eyes were cold as glass. "You have enemies," she said. "And I wish them well!"

With that she closed the door in his face.

Mrs. Channing had come down from The Oaks and was helping Dr. Middleton bandage hands and offer a soothing cream for singed faces. When she'd finished, she came to stand by Rutledge, out of reach of the lingering wisps of smoke still coming from the house.

"Was it an accident — set on purpose?" she asked in a low voice.

"I don't know. It wouldn't have done much harm, unless I'd been in bed and asleep."

It was then he remembered the figure in his room in the middle of the night.

How could a village this size turn a blind eye to a stranger coming and going, without gossip flying?

He looked at the men still standing about, talking. The excitement had died, and ordinary conversations had sprung up among them.

They wore heavy corduroy trousers, sturdy boots, a tweed jacket or one of heavy canvas, and hats that they pulled down over their faces to fight the harsh wind blowing across the fields.

Turn their backs, he thought, and they were more or less indistinguishable, save for variations in height and breadth from man to man.

As a rule, people here weren't likely to stand at their small windows with nothing to do but watch the passing scene. On the other hand, the inspector from London glimpsed knocking at a neighbor's door would command a second glance. The familiar sight of a stockman striding past, hunched against the cold, would not. He could come and go at will, without attracting attention.

Even Harry Ellison had kept a set of work clothes by the outside cellar door.

It was similar to ex-soldiers in the cities, all of them so much alike, so many of them out of work or trying to fit into a world that had changed while they were away, that people looked away from them. Invisible.

"A dead soldier . . ."

He'd seen them in Kent and again in Hertford, and never given them a thought. But here, it would have been different. Disguise meant to fit in, and not stand out.

It explained why his tormentor was never seen, his appearances were never marked. He was invisible because he was not out of the ordinary.

When people had finally gone about their business, Rutledge went inside and spent an hour wiping up the wet floor where the scorched remnants of carpet had been cleared away to the dustbin. Then he finished cutting out the worst of the charred horsehair in the side of the wing chair. It helped, a little, to disperse the heavy odor of fire.

Hamish noted, "A fine way to cover up the smell of death."

Rutledge wondered if Mrs. Ellison had thought of that.

Afterward he walked to the rectory and found Towson sitting at his study desk, trying to write with his left hand and very frustrated.

"Pshaw!" he said as Rutledge tapped lightly at the open door. "I shall have to deliver my sermons from memory. This scrawl is hardly legible."

"No one will mind. You should have half a hundred committed to memory by now."

Towson grinned as he set his pen in the dish. "One of the great things about age is that what happened twenty years ago is more easily recalled than what happened twenty days ago." His grin faded. "You smell strongly of smoke. Has there been another fire? Has someone been injured?"

"There was a small blaze at Constable Hensley's house. A spark from the fire fell on the carpet. No harm done, except to the carpet."

"Poor man, he's suffered enough. I shouldn't like to think of him coming home to more adversity. What can we do? I'm sure we can manage to find him a new carpet somehow."

"He's developed a fever. The hospital staff is worried about infection."

Towson clucked his tongue. "I ought to go to Northampton and spend some time with him. Do you think you could see your way to driving me there?"

"I think Mrs. Channing might be happy to drive you." Rutledge paused. "What do you remember about the day you fell down the stairs?"

"It's still a trifle hazy, I'm afraid. Bits and pieces are coming back to me. There was something about money — I was happy about it. But I can't think what it was!"

"Had you by any chance just spoken with Mrs. Ellison?"

He blinked. "Mary Ellison? I don't believe — Mary Ellison?" He leaned back in his chair, his face changing from uncertainty to a growing surprise. "Yes, by God, that's who it was! I *do* remember! She came down the passage calling to me, and I answered from the head of the attic stairs. She scolded me for taking such a risk and asked if I went up there often." Towson suddenly looked sheepish. "I'm afraid I was annoyed. Hillary Timmons and Dr. Middleton have lectured me on going up there, in fact just last week. I'm afraid I told Mrs. Ellison rather blithely that I went up several times a day to enjoy the view from the windows."

Hamish said, "It wasna' the answer she'd expected to hear."

"Why had she come? Surely not just to scold you?" Rutledge persisted.

"That was what astonished me, you know. She didn't generally call on me. But she said she was here to donate fifty pounds to the church fund. It was an unexpected gift, but one we need rather badly. When I started down the steps to thank her, she told me to go on and finish what I was doing — which was searching out a pair of gloves, though I hadn't said anything about that."

"She didn't speak of an emergency?"

"Not at all. It was afterward that someone shouted for me to come at once. I'm sure she'd been gone for, oh, a good five or six minutes. I'd been thinking how best to use the money, enjoying the prospect."

But she hadn't gone very far, Rutledge found himself thinking. She must have looked in the kitchen and the laundry to see if Hillary Timmons was in the house. "Have you seen her since?"

"Now that was the odd thing. She came just this morning to ask me about a pot of chutney she'd left on the table in the hall a day or so ago, not wanting to disturb me while I was convalescing. Sadly she never mentioned the donation to the church fund. I wish I'd remembered it and brought it to her attention."

"Chutney?" Rutledge asked, feeling his heart lurch.

"Hillary found it there on the hall table and set it in the pantry. She didn't know where it'd come from, but she thought I did. So when Mrs. Ellison asked me about her gift, I blurted out that it was delicious, and I thanked her profusely. I was too embarrassed to admit I had no idea what she was talking about."

"Towson —"

"She went on to say she wondered if it hadn't gone off. She even suggested bringing me another pot. White lies do have a way of coming back to haunt you. Well, in for a penny, in for a pound. How was I to tell her I'd never seen it, couldn't return it if my life depended on it? All I could do was assure her it was of excellent quality."

"And so you found it and tasted it as soon as she'd gone." It was the sort of thing he was sure the rector would do, to make good his white lie.

"Good heavens, no! I asked Hillary if she'd seen it, and she told me where she'd put it. I don't care for chutney, you see, and so I told the girl she could take it home to her family."

"Rector. Will you take me to Hillary Timmons's house? I want that pot of chutney."

"I'll ask her for it tomorrow, if you like. I wasn't aware that you were so fond of it."

"You must take me there now!" He was on his feet, standing in the doorway, urging the bewildered clergyman to follow him.

"But I don't understand, why shouldn't Hillary enjoy it? They're not very well off, you know. I don't particularly like taking it back, as if I'd found someone else to have it. You've only to speak to Mary Ellison. I'm sure she'd be happy to give you your own."

And he was just as certain that she would not. "All right, first we'll look to see if Hillary already has taken it. If she has, we'll go directly to her house." He was firm, but when Towson didn't move, he started down the passage to the kitchen. Reluctantly the rector limped after him.

"You must tell me — what's wrong?"

"I don't know. Where's the pantry?" Rutledge asked, opening the door to the kitchen. It was warm and cheerful, and he remembered standing in Mrs. Ellison's kitchen, feeling like an interloper in her private world.

Towson went to the pantry, running his finger along pots of jam and honey and preserved plums. A man with a taste for sweets . . .

"Ah, this must be it. Perhaps she forgot to take it. Or doesn't care for it after all." Relieved, he picked up a small jar with a square of white linen over it, tied around the mouth with a silver ribbon. "Hillary did mention the silver ribbon. She thought it quite elegant."

"I'll buy her the finest chutney in London and have it sent to her. But I must take this with me now."

"Very well." But Towson was still doubtful, his eyes on the pot. "I'd be happier if this didn't come to Mary Ellison's ears. I'm still hopeful of that fifty pounds."

The rector saw Rutledge to the door, looking out at the light drizzle that had begun to fall.

He said, "I'm grateful that you helped me piece together part of what had happened the day I fell. It was like a hole in my mind, the sort of thing that people must feel after a seizure or an apoplexy. It's rather frightening, you know."

"I'm sure it must be." In truth, there had been a time when Rutledge hadn't been able to remember the war ending. He hadn't expected to see it, in fact for the last two years of the fighting in his mind he had been prepared to die. Only he hadn't. The appalling realization that he had lived in spite of what he'd done in the trenches blotted out everything else. The guilt of surviving, when so many around him had died, was insupportable.

His men that day had been equally shocked at first, the silence overwhelming as the guns that had fired so frantically all morning stopped their battering. And then neither jubilation nor relief followed, just a numbness that gradually filled with the knowledge that now they could go home. Rutledge had given them their orders, as he himself had been ordered to do, saw to their safety — and after that there was nothing, a blank space of time. The next thing he was aware of, he was in a clinic in England, with no understanding of how he'd got there or why. He'd feared those missing weeks. Feared what he might have done. And not even the doctors could give them back to him. It had taken him more than a year to do that, and a night in Kent when it had all come rushing back.

Towson was saying, "I'm sure the rest will come. In time. If I don't press too hard."

"I shouldn't worry too much about it," Rutledge agreed.

"Middleton tells me I might actually have had a seizure . . ." There was anxiety in his voice now, put there by a callous murderer who had used this man's goodness to bring him down.

"No. You'll realize that when you remember."

Towson smiled. "Has anyone ever told you that you're a kind listener? You might have gone to the church, rather than the police, you know."

Not with the blackness in my own soul, Rutledge answered him silently. And then with a wave, he pulled his hat down against the rain.

Rutledge carried the chutney in the palm of his hand, close to his coat as he walked back to the constable's house.

He couldn't take the chutney to Inspector Cain. He didn't trust the man to have it analyzed properly. Particularly if Cain learned it had been made by Mrs. Ellison. A wild-goose chase, he would complain. Another attempt by an outsider to point a finger at a woman of impeccable reputation in an effort to solve a murder he'd not even been sent to Dudlington to investigate. Inspector Kelmore on the other hand had no ties to Dudlington. And his people were capable and trustworthy.

That was the best solution.

He went into the house, something gnawing at the edges of his mind.

Hamish was silent, no help at all.

After standing there for a moment, Rutledge turned back to the door and went out to the motorcar.

The drive to Northampton seemed to take longer than usual. Rutledge glanced from time to time at the pot of chutney in the seat next to him.

Was it only his imagination, or was it somehow sinister, malevolent?

Time and a good laboratory would tell him the answer to that.

Inspector Kelmore was out of his office when Rutledge got there, but Sergeant Thompson took the little pot with its silver ribbon and held it gingerly between his thumb and forefinger, as if expecting it to blow up in his face. "I'll take it down straightaway, sir." He sniffed the air. "Do I smell smoke, sir?"

"There was a fire in Dudlington. I helped to put it out."

"And what shall I tell Dr. Pell to be looking for?"

"I don't know. Arsenic? At a guess." He told the sergeant where the chutney had come from, who had given it to the rector, and why he'd brought it to Northampton, leaving out only his concerns about Inspector Cain.

"Someone gave this to the rector?" Thompson shook his head. "What's the world coming to, sir!"

"I'll be at the hospital, if you need me."

"Very good, sir. I hope you find the constable resting comfortably. The last bulletin we had was that his fever has risen. I don't think they believe he'll make it. Worst luck."

Rutledge found Matron in her office and sat down across from her desk, his mind shifting directions as he said, "How is Constable Hensley?"

"No better. A little worse perhaps. He's not always conscious, now."

Rutledge swore to himself. "It's important that he recover."

"We're doing all we can, I assure you, Inspector. But there is a limit to what medicine can do."

"He survived that arrow in his back — he survived the surgery to remove it. I should think he could survive a fever." But even as he said it, he knew that it was not true. A raging infection was generally fatal. "May I see him?"

"Yes, of course. Sister will show you to the room." She rang the little bell on her desk, and a young nurse stepped through the door.

Rutledge thanked Matron and followed the young woman down the passage. Hensley was in the same private room as before, and Rutledge wondered if Chief Superintendent Bowles had ordered it. People sometimes rambled in fevers, and words spoken could never be taken back.

The constable was lying under a sheet, half on his side, half on his back. He looked very ill indeed, his flushed cheeks sunken, his body somehow reduced in power and size.

Rutledge went up to the bed and touched the arm lying on top of the sheet.

It was searing to the touch, as if a fire burned beneath the skin, invisible to the naked eye.

Hensley stirred, opening his eyes to stare blankly around the room, then shutting them again.

Rutledge said quietly, "Constable. Inspector Rutledge here. Can you hear me?"

There was no reaction.

He called his name again, and this time Hensley opened bloodshot eyes, trying to focus them.

"Who is it?" His voice was husky, as if his throat was dry.

The young sister came forward and held a straw to his lips, telling him firmly to drink from the glass.

Rutledge could see him drink thirstily, and then pull back, as if the water didn't sit well on his stomach.

"Thank you, Sister," he said, dismissing her.

When she'd gone out of the room, it took Rutledge several minutes to bring the constable back to a level where his voice reached the man.

He tried to lift his head, and then turned a little. "Inspector Rutledge. Sir."

"Constable Hensley. Do you believe it could have been Mary Ellison who shot you?"

There was a slight motion of his head. Negative.

"It's possible she killed her husband, her daughter, and her granddaughter."

The pain-ridden eyes considered him. "I

481

won't be there to see her hang, then. I'd have liked that."

"I still haven't found this man Sandridge. But I came across your money. You weren't paid enough to take the blame for what happened to Edgerton. I think it's time you told the truth. You don't want to die with it on your conscience."

Hamish, in his mind, said, "You mustna' badger the man!"

But Rutledge responded, "Time is short."

Hensley was feebly shaking his head. "Old Bowels looks after his own."

"But if you die, and Sandridge is still out there, he might be persuaded to talk. Is that what you want? Bowles will blacken *your* name, to save himself."

"It wasn't a great deal of money. I didn't know then that Edgerton would die. I'd have asked for more."

"Did you give a share of it to Bowles? Is that why he closed his eyes to what you'd done and let Sandridge go free?"

"He set me to watch over Sandridge. And I did. He's a dead man, any way you look at it."

"He'll hang, you're right, if he's taken into custody. Do you want to hang with him?"

"I won't live to hang." He turned a little, those fever-bright eyes on Rutledge's face. "You don't give a damn about me. It's Bowles you want."

"Why did you agree to look the other way?"

"Barstow told me either I helped or he'd see I was blamed. I was afraid of him."

"I don't believe you. Not of a man like Barstow."

"You didn't know him. He wanted his revenge, and he was going to get it. And who'd take my word over his, anyway? There was a German waiter we'd brought in, Old Bowels and I. He wasn't a spy. But the newspapers got hold of the story, and German fever was high. We held on to him for a bit, a warning to others, so to speak. I don't know how Barstow found out. A lucky guess, maybe, or he had someone inside the Yard. He said if Sandridge was taken, he'd let it be known we'd made a mistake on the waiter."

He lay there, his arrogance gone.

"Did you share the money with Bowles?"

But Hensley had nothing more to say.

"Who is Sandridge? Is he in Dudlington? Or Letherington? Is it Keating?"

"You lied to me about Mrs. Ellison, didn't you?" he asked finally. "Why would she kill her own flesh and blood?"

"If I knew that, I'd be ready to leave Dudlington," Rutledge told him.

"No, you wouldn't. You want it all. Who killed Emma, where Sandridge is, and whether or not Bowles was involved."

"Emma deserves to be found. She deserves to have her killer tried and convicted. She was only seventeen, for God's sake!"

"I lie here, and sometimes I can't tell what's true and what I dream. I can see Emma's face sometimes, and she's pointing a finger at me. I don't know why. I did her no harm."

"Not for want of trying," Rutledge said.

"She was that pretty! You never saw her."

"You were twice her age, and instead of protecting her, you hounded her like all the rest."

"She's in the wood," Hensley said. "I'd stake my life on that." He gave a gasping cough that was intended to be a laugh. "I did stake my life on it, I suppose. But you'll find her in that wood, mark my words."

He began to cough and choke, and Rutledge wheeled to the door to find the young sister just outside.

Dr. Williams came then and gave Hensley something to make him quiet again. Rutledge stood by the bed, listening to the ragged breathing, and waited, but Hensley had gone where Rutledge couldn't follow.

33

It was some time before Sergeant Thompson brought Rutledge a report on the contents of the chutney.

"It's preliminary," he said. "I'm to tell you that, sir. But Dr. Pell says you should know. He thinks it's arsenic. You did say you were in a hurry for the answer."

"How much arsenic?"

"Enough to kill a man. Or a woman. A good spoonful of the chutney might do it."

His mind brought him an image of the rector spreading a lavish spoonful of jam on his bread, and he thought, *If Towson hadn't disliked chutney, he'd be dead by now. Or the Timmons girl and her family.*

"I'd like a search warrant to go into the house of the woman who made up this pot. I've a strong suspicion that there are two bodies in her cellar. The sooner we retrieve them, the better."

Thompson said, "What if you're wrong, sir?"

Hamish interjected, "Aye, what if?"

"I don't think I am. Will you ask Inspector Kelmore for the warrant, or shall I?"

"I'll see to it, sir." Thompson walked out of the small room Rutledge had been given while waiting for the test results.

It was late when the warrant was issued and Rutledge could leave.

It was nearly midnight when he reached Dudlington, and he was hungry, wishing now he'd stopped for his dinner on the road. In the dining room under a napkin, he found a plate of roast ham sandwiches. Mrs. Melford had been kind to leave them, he thought, and he went through to the kitchen to make himself a pot of tea.

He had poured it, sweetened it, and was looking for the tin of milk when he realized what Hamish had been telling him for the last ten minutes.

"Ye canna' be sure Mrs. Melford made them — or who filled the sugar bowl. You canna' be sure."

Rutledge set down the cup of tea and pushed away the sandwiches.

He had been in Northampton for most of the day. The house was open, and anyone could have left the plate of sandwiches or added something to his sugar bowl.

He sat there for a moment longer, and then went to bed hungry.

Rutledge woke to a hand on his shoulder, gently shaking him.

For an instant he thought it was Hamish, and a half-stifled cry was wrenched from him as he froze, trying to shrink inside himself and away from the prodding fingers. And even as he realized it wasn't Hamish, but a human agency, he was unprepared for the voice in his ear.

"Inspector Rutledge — Ian!"

It was Mrs. Channing's voice, low and strained.

He was fully awake by that time and answered her quietly, "What's happened?"

"I don't know. It's Frank Keating. He's been drinking all day. Since the fire. He closed the inn, and I tried to talk to him, but he'd have none of it. I went to bed and left him there in the bar, still drinking. I thought, he's had enough that he'll fall asleep in his chair, and won't wake up before late morning."

"Is he still there?" Rutledge asked, his mind beginning to work with some clarity.

"That's the trouble. I couldn't sleep, and I thought I might try a little hot milk. That was at two o'clock, and when I looked into the bar, he wasn't there. But the door was standing wide, cold air filling Reception. I think he's gone out."

It had taken determination for her to walk this far in the night, not knowing where Keating was or what had sent him to the bottle.

Rutledge said, "Yes, all right, wait for me in the office. I'll dress and come down to you."

She was gone in a whisper of clothing, her scent, like jasmine, lingering behind her. He remembered the perfume that Elizabeth Fraser had worn and how it had suited her. Lily of the valley, very English and subtle. Jasmine on the other hand possessed a heady sweetness.

Dressing swiftly, he went down to Hensley's office. The heavy odor of smoke still seemed to be caught in the very walls, acrid on the night air. Mrs. Channing was waiting there, her coat around her and her hands clasped together, as if she were cold.

"I thought about making us some tea," she said, "but the fire appears to have gone out."

"No, don't touch anything in the kitchen. Stay here," he told her, "while I search for Keating."

"Oh, no, I'm going with you." She

looked around her and added, "I've never liked coming into this house. There's something here — despair, fear. I don't know. It took all my courage to walk in here, into the darkness. To search the house for you. If I hadn't seen the motorcar outside, I don't know what I'd have done."

"You should have come sooner, if he's been drinking all day."

"Oh, yes," she said, mocking him. "And where were you?"

He didn't answer, saying instead, "I've brought my torch and Hensley's field glasses. If you're ready?"

She got up quickly, as if afraid he might change his mind. They walked in silence back to The Oaks.

Rutledge took her to her room. "Is there a key?"

She held it out to him. He went inside and made certain there was no one in the armoire or under the bed.

"Wait here, and keep the door locked. I'll call you if I want you to open it, I won't knock."

"Yes, all right, I'll brace a chair under the knob. Just to be safe!"

"Not a bad idea." He waited for the sound of the key turning in the lock before going back down the stairs and into the public bar.

It was empty, as she'd told him it was. Still, he cast his light about the room, behind the bar itself, in the corners. One table held a nearly empty bottle of whiskey and a glass that had left rings on the surface, as if at the end Keating had been careless pouring from the bottle.

From there he began a methodical search of the house, beginning with the public rooms, the small parlor where he'd talked with Mrs. Channing, the dining room with table linens set out for use, serviettes folded with almost razor-sharp edges.

The kitchen was surprisingly tidy, pots and pans set out on a side table, the worktable well scrubbed, and dishes stacked by size and ready to hand. The light moved on, and next to a cabinet he found a drawer upturned on the floor, its contents scattered, as if they'd been kicked about in a search for something.

Hamish said, "Cutlery."

Their blades flashed in the torchlight, their wood and bone handles worn with use.

Knives of every size and kind, blades sharp enough to cut through hide and muscle and even bone.

"Ye canna' tell what's missing."

"No. He must have pulled out the drawer in a fit of temper, letting the contents fall, and then he took what he wanted, and left the rest."

If it was Sandridge, and he'd thought that the dying Hensley might give him up, he might have decided to kill himself rather than go back to prison, this time to hang.

The question was, where would he do it?

Rutledge went up the stairs two at a time, ignoring a dart of pain in his ankle. There were three bedrooms on this floor, and Mrs. Channing's made the fourth. He searched the others, then went up another flight of stairs to what had been the servants' quarters. He had given that up and returned to the quarters behind the kitchen where staff took their meals. Beyond there were sitting rooms for female staff and male staff, as strictly separated as in a convent in the year when The Oaks had been built.

One of the sitting rooms had been converted into a bedroom. It was almost monastic, the iron bed brought down from the servants' floor, a stand beside it, two chairs, a table-desk, and a rag carpet over the floor. What had been a tall chest for the servants to keep their coats in had been converted into an armoire for Keating's clothes.

There were few enough of them, and only one good suit among them. Rutledge shut the armoire and turned to the table that served as a desk. On it were meticulously kept accounts, receipts for goods and spirits, and a box of menus and recipes for various dishes.

He'd already switched the beam of light in the direction of the stand by the bed, when he realized he'd seen his own handwriting —

Moving round the table, he looked again, and there it was, under the accounts, only an edge showing. He lifted the ledger and found one of the sheets he'd written in Hensley's office, laying out in detail his evidence against Mary Ellison. It was water stained, and there were sooty fingerprints across the top, as if someone had rescued it after yesterday's fire and only then noticed what had been written on it. A pair of uneven creases showed that it had been hastily folded and shoved into a pocket.

That was how it had got here. Before he could consider the implications of why, he heard a voice in Reception, shouting his name.

Moving swiftly, he reached Reception and shone his light straight into the frightened face of Grace Letteridge.

"Inspector?" she exclaimed, surprise in her voice. "I've looked everywhere for you! You must come at once, there's trouble!"

"How did you know to find me here?"

"I didn't. You weren't in Constable Hensley's house, and I was desperate, I came here for Frank Keating."

"Mrs. Channing is upstairs —"

"There's no time! It may already be too late. Someone has broken into Mary Ellison's house — the door is standing wide, and all the lamps are lit."

Hamish said, " 'Ware!"

For there was something in Grace Letteridge's voice, an undercurrent of excitement that didn't ring true.

He had no intention of leaving Meredith Channing alone in The Oaks.

Taking the stairs again, he went to her door and called out, "I can't find Keating. But he's armed and may be suicidal. Now there's trouble at Mrs. Ellison's house, and I must go. I don't think you should stay here alone."

"No!" There was the scrape of something heavy being shoved aside, and then the sound of the key being inserted into the lock. She opened the door, her voice breathless. "I think of myself as brave but not foolhardy."

She was at his heels on the stairs, and together they hurried after Grace Letteridge, down the walk and along the road into Holly Street.

Hamish was saying, "I wouldna' trust the lass. Nor the ither."

They reached the corner of Whitby Lane and looked up at the Ellison house.

Grace had been right, lamps were lit in every room.

Rutledge left the two women in the lee of the constable's doorway and went up the steps into the Ellison house.

The first thing he saw were splatters of blood on the walls of the entry, bright in the light of the lamp hanging there.

"Mrs. Ellison?" he shouted.

There was no reply.

"It's Inspector Rutledge. Can you come to the door? Are you all right?"

Silence greeted his words as they seemed to echo through the house.

"Keating?" he called. "Are you here? Don't do anything foolish, man, I may've been wrong in my conclusions. That report was only one of many possibilities."

He listened to the silence now. Sometimes it was possible to tell if a house was empty, just by the feel of it, as if the air itself had more room.

"If she's no' here, where did he tak' her?"

"Frith's Wood."

Rutledge ran down Whitby Street, along Church Street, and into the tower of St. Luke's.

With his torch in one hand, he climbed the stone steps to the first level and illuminated the bell rope.

Setting the torch on the wooden flooring, he reached for the rope and began to pull down with all his strength.

There was a disjointed *clang,* and then he found the right rhythm on the rope: a strong pull down, let the rope slide through one's fingers, and when it had reached its apogee, another strong pull down.

The bell in the tower began to toll, a cadence that echoed over his head and filled the tower with its resonance.

He pulled it five times, and then silenced it. And a second five times. And a third.

Then he left the tower, racing down the

uneven stone steps and out the door.

Men were beginning to gather, most in clothes pulled on hastily over their night-clothes, buttoning coats as they walked.

"Mrs. Ellison may be in Frith's Wood," he called to them, his voice carrying as it had on the battlefield, against the noise of the guns. "We need lamps, as many as you can bring, and *hurry!*"

They stood there for a moment, staring at him.

These were local men, who wouldn't venture into that wood in daylight, much less in the dark of night.

"I'm not asking you to go alone," he told them. "Take a partner, keep together. But I need you to search. There isn't time to send to Letherington. And there may be someone with her — someone armed."

But he thought they were more likely to find her body, her killer long away.

He went back to Hensley's house, intent on taking Grace Letteridge with him to the wood. If anything was amiss, he'd be able to put his hand on her.

She was there, shivering in the doorway, her gaze on the house across the way.

"Where's Mrs. Channing?"

"She went inside. There. She had a feeling someone must be hurt. She wanted to help."

"Damn the woman!"

Had she seen the blood in the front hall and jumped to conclusions, or had she gone down to the Ellison cellar to look for bodies?

He turned and went back to the Ellison door, calling, "Mrs. Channing?"

She answered him quietly, her voice carrying a warning that something was not right. "Ian? Could you come into the kitchen, please?"

34

Rutledge stood there in the doorway, considering his options. But there were none. The only other choice was the door from the back garden, but it would plunge him too quickly into the midst of whatever was wrong in the kitchen, with no time to judge the situation.

There was nothing else he could do but trust in Mrs. Channing's warning.

Hamish was hammering in the back of his mind, urging him not to trust anyone.

He stepped inside the house, walking steadily through the dining room and down the passage to the kitchen, making no effort to conceal his movements. And then he was opening the passage door and about to step into the kitchen itself.

Mrs. Channing stood there, her back against the cooker, her face turned toward the cellar stairs. She didn't look at him. Her attention was on something he couldn't see.

Rutledge swung slowly toward the cellar door and found himself staring at Frank

Keating, holding a kitchen knife at the throat of a white-faced Mary Ellison, her eyes large and desperate.

One of her hands was bleeding, as if she had tried to shield herself. Someone — Meredith Channing — had given her a tea towel to wrap around the wound. Blood was beginning to soak through.

There had been a woman in Belton, Kent, stabbed and held hostage in her own kitchen. But he'd been well prepared for that, the local inspector knowing the people involved, suggesting what to expect and how to approach the angry man inside. Useful tools indeed. Here he was on his own.

Frank Keating wasn't angry. There was a coldness about him that was far more dangerous. He reeked of alcohol, the kitchen awash in the smell of stale beer and too much whiskey. But if he had been drunk, he wasn't now.

"Keating. What is she to you? What does it matter what she's done?"

"Have you been down in that cellar, Rutledge?"

"Yes. I have." He kept his voice steady, his hands at his side. He could just see Mary Ellison's expression as he answered Keating, a bleakness that was there and quickly smoothed away.

"Then you know what's down there."

"I think I know. Yes."

"Don't ask me what this woman is to me. You wrote that you had no proof. I've found it for you."

"Keating — I have proof now. I went to Northampton to find it. You needn't have done this."

"Don't lie to me. What proof is there in Northampton? *They're in the cellar, not in Northampton!*" He moved the knife so that the sharp tip pricked at Mary Ellison's throat.

"Tell him. *Tell him what you did!*"

"Keating," Rutledge began. "I can't use a forced con—"

"*Tell him!*"

But Mary Ellison stood there, the knife at her throat, and said nothing.

"There are witnesses here, Rutledge. You and Mrs. Channing. Myself. And the proof is down *there*." He jerked his head toward the cellar. "If she won't speak, by God I'll see she dies anyway."

"You'll hang."

"What difference does it make to me? I'm a dead man already. *What difference can it possibly make to me!*"

The anguish in his voice was so overwhelming that Mrs. Channing took an inadvertent step forward, as if to offer comfort.

"Stay where you are!" he shouted, his grip on Mrs. Ellison's arm tightening. She flinched but didn't cry out.

Mrs. Channing stepped back. "I didn't intend —" Then she fell silent, looking at Rutledge for guidance.

"Why are you a dead man?" Rutledge was already asking. The distance between them was too great. By the time he reached Keating and struggled with him, the knife would have plunged into Mary Ellison's throat. He fell back on words instead, to talk Keating out of what he was intending to do.

The rector had called him a good listener. It would be words in this case that would make a difference. Must make a difference, as Hamish was busy reminding him. He had to choose them carefully.

Keating was shaking his head, unwilling to be lured into Rutledge's trap.

Mary Ellison spoke for the first time. "This man," she said, such loathing in her voice that even Keating appeared to feel it, "*this man* is under the delusion that he's my son-in-law. Mr. Mason, Emma's father."

Stunned silence followed her announcement. Mrs. Channing uttered a little sound, half pity, half surprise.

Hamish said, "It canna' be true. He died of a tumor."

But so much of what Mary Ellison had told everyone was a lie.

"Are you Frank K. Mason?" Rutledge asked the man with the knife.

He spoke the name with authority, as if he possessed the knowledge to support it.

"You've asked London about me, haven't you? Well, be damned to you! I served my sentence, I have a right to live as I please."

It was beginning to make sense. Rutledge glanced at Mrs. Channing, then said to Keating, "Can she leave? The less she knows the better."

"And have her go for help the instant she steps out that door? She came of her own free will, I didn't bring her here. But here she'll stay."

"Then let's move into the dining room where the women can sit down. Mrs. Ellison looks ready to collapse."

"Let her!" The two words were savage. And then he said, "I wasn't guilty. But I couldn't prove it. I'd been out looking for work, and a man promised me thirty pounds to help him break into a shop. I walked away. I had a family, I didn't want any part of it, money or no. But when he came to trial, he told the court I'd planned the crime and carried it out. That he'd been persuaded against his will to help me."

"Why should the jury have believed him?"

"I was a locksmith," he said, with simple pride. "And a good one. He'd never been caught before, that's the truth of it. He'd been too careful. And he spoke well, like a gentleman. They tell me he'd all but cried in the witness-box, out of shame for what he'd done. And those twelve bastards in the jury box believed him. He went free, I was taken up and sent to prison, leaving my family destitute. Beatrice would never have come home to Dudlington if I'd been there to feed her and the child."

A locksmith married to the daughter of a woman with Harkness blood in her veins. It must have been a great comedown for Mary Ellison to learn that the daughter who had gone to London with such high expectations had married a working-class man. No wonder she'd told the world that he was dead. No wonder she'd taken in

Emma, and then seen to it that the daughter who had disappointed her didn't go back to London and her disgraceful life. Or worse, bring her unemployed husband to live in Dudlington when he was released.

Rutledge said, "And you came here, after you'd served your sentence, to watch over Emma."

"I didn't know she was alive. Mrs. Ellison had written to me in prison, to say that Emma and Beatrice had died in a fire in London. One day I came here, just to walk in the churchyard and stand at their graves. But there weren't any. And when the rector saw me and came over to speak to me, I asked him if he knew where Emma Mason was buried, here or in London. He said I must be mistaken, she wasn't dead, she was living here with her grandmother. I nearly broke down, but when he asked my name, I said it was Frank Keating. The next day I took every penny I could scrape together and bought The Oaks. It was languishing, but I was good with my hands, I could fix it to suit me. I couldn't tell the girl she was mine. I'd have ruined her chances. But I could see her, speak to her from time to time. And I didn't think Mrs. Ellison would have any reason to recognize me, if I stayed out of the village as much as possible. I could still look out for Emma."

He turned to Mrs. Channing and then to Rutledge, his eyes pleading but his words harsh. "If you tell anyone — anyone! — I was her father, I'll kill you too!"

He had dropped his guard. Only for an instant, but it was enough.

Rutledge shouted a warning, far too late for Keating to recover.

Mrs. Ellison twisted herself out of his grip, dodged the knife, and with the full force of her body, pushed Frank Keating down the cellar stairs.

Rutledge heard himself swear. Shoving Mrs. Ellison to one side, he went leaping down the steps to bend over the injured man.

"Find Dr. Middleton!" he shouted at Meredith Channing. "Bring him here."

Keating lay at the foot of the stairs, bleeding from one ear, his body crumpled and one leg thrust out at an awkward angle.

He looked up at Rutledge, his eyes trying to focus. "Never mind me. Stop her!"

Rutledge dared not leave him. He knelt beside Keating and said, "Help is coming.

Don't move. Where can she go?"

Mrs. Channing came back shortly afterward with Dr. Middleton. "Grace Letteridge told me where to find him," she said. "Now go do your work and leave Mr. Keating to the doctor and to me."

When Rutledge came back up the stairs, he found Grace Letteridge in the Ellison kitchen. She was shaking, her arms wrapped around her body.

"I was certain he'd kill her," she said. "Not the other way round. I was in the passage just now, listening. I couldn't stay there on the street, not knowing what was happening."

"Which way did Mrs. Ellison go?"

"She ran straight into me, pushing me out of her way, and went out the door. Inspector — I think she's taken your motorcar. I heard the motor turn over."

He went outside and looked. Somehow Mary Ellison had managed to crank the car and back it out of the narrow space between houses.

"Where would she go?" he demanded, turning to Grace Letteridge.

"I don't know."

He remembered Mrs. Channing's motorcar at The Oaks, and started out at a dead run.

The motorcar had been moved to the side of the inn, out of the way of custom stopping there. He cranked it, stepped inside, and gunned the engine. It roared in his ears.

Had she gone north — or south? As he sat there, looking out across the fields, he could see lanterns bobbing in a line, the search party returning empty-handed from Frith's Wood.

She'd have avoided them, he thought, and turned south.

He followed suit, running fast, his headlamps piercing the darkness. It was some time before he caught up with his own motorcar.

He could see it in the distance, tail lamps small red dots just vanishing around a bend in the road.

If he could catch up with her here in these rolling, barren fields, it would be better than trying to stop her in a town, where she could lose him in a tangle of streets.

Where was she going? What earthly reason did she have for fleeing? She might have stayed and faced Keating down.

But then Keating had opened the cupboard in the cellar. There would be no facing that down.

Hamish said into the wind, "She doesna' want to die in Dudlington. Or on the hangman's rope."

Somewhere anonymous, where she wasn't a Harkness, wasn't guilty of murder. A nameless woman taken from a canal or a river, buried in a pauper's grave. The vanished Mary Ellison would be whispered about, speculation would be rife, but after a few months her name would pass into obscurity, untarnished.

The certainty grew as he followed her. Mary Ellison was choosing her own end.

Her husband had failed her somehow; and then her daughter, running away in defiance, had failed to reach the heights of fame through her art. Instead she'd married a man who was to become a common felon. Rutledge didn't know what Emma's sin had been, but he thought perhaps the fact that she was so beautiful had something to do with it. Mary Ellison had watched men making fools of themselves over the girl, and in the end, she had blamed Emma. No Harkness would wish to be a public spectacle. It was somehow — unsuitable.

Then without warning, his motorcar's headlamps swept the sky ahead of him, leaping upward and then dipping in a wild arc.

His first thought was that he hadn't anticipated her decision to crash the motorcar. They weren't seven miles from Dudlington, her body would still be taken back for burial —

And then the delayed echo of the shot reached him. Rutledge pressed down on the accelerator, sending Mrs. Channing's motorcar speeding around the bend, only his driving skill keeping the tires on the road.

It was nearly too late by the time he glimpsed the other car skewed across the roadway in front of him, directly in his path, seemingly unavoidable.

His hand went out for the brake, pulling hard on it, putting his vehicle into a gravel-spewing skid.

Hamish was shouting at him, and he was fighting the wheel, wondering if both of them were dead men.

When the motorcar rocked to a hard stop, he was no more than two feet from his own bonnet. And through the windscreen he could see the driver slumped over the wheel, her head cradled in her arms, as if she had decided to stop and rest.

He was out and running, without thinking. When he opened the driver's door, Mary Ellison fell into his arms. Catching her, he laid her gently on the grass at the verge, then went back to look for his rug to cover her.

In the dark there was no way of telling where she'd been hit. Blood seemed to be everywhere, and he wasn't sure whether she had struck her head against the windscreen or if the wheel had caught her across the chest. He brushed back her hair and found the thin line of a cut there, blood welling out of it and into her face. It wasn't deep enough, he thought, to account for a gunshot wound. There was a long gash on her chin, half hidden by the collar of her nightdress, and it was bleeding freely as well.

Working frantically, he could see her staring at him, her eyes wide in her face. "I don't want to lie in Dudlington. There's an unused grave in London," she managed to say.

"Be still, don't talk."

She made an effort to bring her hand to her chest. "It hurts."

And he realized that most of the blood came from there, not the cut on her forehead or the scrape on her chin. This time the shooter hadn't missed. Rutledge tried to stuff his handkerchief into the wound, binding it tight with the belt from her nightdress, but he wasn't a doctor, there was no way to save her.

"Not in Dudlington," she repeated, trying to catch his hand and make him promise.

"What had your husband done?" he asked. "Why did you kill him?"

"He'd developed a taste for gambling. He was on the verge of losing all we had."

"And Emma? What had she done, to deserve to die?"

"She found her mother, when she went looking for that cursed bow and quiver." The face that had showed no emotion until now began to crumple. "I couldn't let my granddaughter go back to London to live with a common criminal. Even if he was her father. And after — after she'd found Beatrice, there was no turning back. It broke my *heart*."

Her breathing changed, and he could feel her body struggling to draw in air, her lungs fighting the injury.

"If I tell you something, will you bury me in London?" she asked rapidly, trying to hold on to consciousness.

"I can't promise —"

"Then I'll take what I know with me." Her eyelids fluttered a little, and then, without warning, she was gone.

35

Rutledge laid her back on the grass, covering her with the rug from the car.

She had been, he thought, a woman of great pride, and with it a strong sense of what was due her name. She had been the last of the Harkness family, and she would kill rather than bring dishonor to it. A paradox . . .

There was no time to think about Mary Ellison. Not now. Hamish was shouting in his ear, and Rutledge got slowly to his feet, turning to look at the hillside behind him.

He hadn't expected to come face-to-face with this man. Not tonight, possibly not ever, unless a shot was fired point-blank at him. And in his concern for Mary Ellison, he had left himself vulnerable.

"She took the bullet meant for you," the man said. "I didn't intend to kill an innocent woman."

He looked haggard, as if he'd slept rough and only a stubborn determination had kept him going.

And the revolver was still in his hand.

Rutledge said nothing, standing there in full view, waiting. The wind whistled down the hill, blowing through his hair. He couldn't remember what had become of his hat. He thought it was probably still in the parlor on Hensley's coat-tree. It didn't matter. It wouldn't save his life. They'd learned that in the trenches, that helmets were necessary. He wasn't sure what had happened to his . . .

He fought to keep a grip on the present.

Hamish was there, in the forefront of his mind now. "I'm no' ready to die. And I willna' let you die."

"There's nothing I can do," Rutledge said in response. For this time had been bound to come since he'd stood on the steps outside Maryanne Browning's house in London. He had been lucky that it hadn't come sooner. That he'd finished his work. He felt suddenly tired, unwilling to fight.

"Ye didna' want to die in Scotland. Ye canna' die now."

He was aware of the man across the empty road from him, dressed in workmen's clothing, muddy corduroys, a flannel shirt, and a heavy coat. It looked like the remnants of a cast-off officer's coat. The stalker seemed to be considering him in turn, both of them taking the measure of an adversary.

"I don't know you," Rutledge said at last. "Or why you have cast such a long shadow over my life. If you're going to kill me, at least tell me why."

"It's the war's shadow, not mine." And then he added grudgingly, "I hadn't expected you to show so much courage."

"What happened to you in the war?"

"What happened to all of us? You were an officer, you should know. You bled us without mercy, you sat in safety well behind the lines, and sent us out to face the guns, day in and day out. For inches of land! What we lost in one attack, the next must win back again. For your own glory. For no reason other than ignorance and stupidity and *sheer, bloody waste!*"

"I was in the trenches myself."

"Don't lie to me. I swore I'd make someone pay for what they'd done to us. I swore that if I survived the fighting, I'd come home and kill as many officers as I could find."

"How did you know that I was to visit Mrs. Browning on New Year's Eve?"

"The cook told me. I'd met her in a shop where I swept the floors, and sometimes we'd talked about France. That day she said to the butcher her mistress had guests coming to dine, and I asked her who they were. Commander Farnum, she said, and Captain Rutledge, she said. Was the captain in France? I asked her, and she said, He was. Four years, mind you, and home without a scratch on him! I knew then you'd been far from the Front. Safe as houses somewhere in the rear. Not many of my mates saw the war's start and the war's end. They fed the machine guns instead. Have you seen what those guns do to a man? Have you ever walked into a field hospital and *looked!*"

How to answer him without being accused of another lie?

"What's your name?" Rutledge asked instead. He was drained, his mind refusing to work with any clarity.

"You never cared to know the names of the dead. Or the living for that matter. We were numbers on the chart table, without faces, pushed forward because it suited the French or the Americans or the War Ministry. And when those were slaughtered, you found more to send up the line. You found my brother and my cousin, and my neighbors, and my *son*."

He stopped and looked at the body of Mary Ellison. "I didn't mean to kill her, and that's the truth. I wanted to make you afraid, as afraid as I ever was. I wanted you to know what it was like to look death in the face, to know there was no way out without shaming yourself. I wanted you to remember what the guns did to people like us. I didn't intend to kill a woman. Why did you let her drive your bloody motorcar!" There was a mixture of shame and anger in his voice.

"She borrowed it without asking. Have you lived out here, in the middle of nowhere? Where did you sleep? How did you eat?"

"It's better than the trenches."

Perhaps it was, Rutledge thought. But it was no way for a soldier to live.

The man steadied the gun. "You can beg for your life."

"I never begged for my life from a German, and I'm damned if I'll beg it from an Englishman!" Rutledge said, anger rising in him.

The revolver fired, and he could hear the whine of the shot passing his ear.

"Beg!"

Rutledge stood where he was. "Her death was an accident," he said. "Let me help you. Before it's too late."

The next shot seemed to ruffle his hair,

and he flinched in spite of himself.

"Damn you, beg!"

Another shot went wild, the revolver wobbling as the man began to cry, the tears running down his face unheeded.

Then it steadied once more, the muzzle pointed straight at Rutledge.

Rutledge steeled himself. He couldn't be sure how many shots were left in the weapon. But he couldn't reach the man, and he knew that if he tried, the next shot wouldn't miss.

"Listen to me," Rutledge began. "My death won't bring your dead back. It won't even satisfy you. Even if you kill a dozen like me, it can't change what happened in France. Nothing can."

"I never intended to kill you," he said at last. "I just wanted to see the fear in your face and hear you beg to live."

"Not for you, not for anyone."

Hamish was as angry as he was, helpless in the confines of death.

The muzzle held steady, and it seemed that minutes ticked by. And then the man moved.

For an instant Rutledge thought he was going to kill himself. The revolver rose to his temple in one fluid action, but instead of pulling the trigger, he touched the barrel

to his forehead in a salute. It was gro-
tesque, a mockery of the acknowledgment
of enlisted man to officer. And yet it was
also an admission.

He turned away, striding up the rise and
into the dark night.

Rutledge searched for an hour or more.
But without a torch or a sense of which direction the man had taken, he couldn't
find his lair, the place where he'd gone to
ground.

Hamish said, "Tomorrow. When it's
light."

36

Rutledge moved his own motorcar to the side of the road and then lifted the body of Mary Ellison into Mrs. Channing's vehicle, his rug still wrapped around her. There was nowhere else to put her except in the rear seat — where Hamish sat.

Turning to drive back to Dudlington, he wondered if the stalker was watching him, and what was going through his mind.

Meredith Channing and Grace Letteridge sat waiting in the office that Hensley used for police business.

Their faces were drawn with anxiety and exhaustion, and he thought, as he stepped over the threshold, that they had already said to each other all that there was to say, and silence had long since fallen in the room.

Mrs. Channing started to her feet when she saw him, her gaze sweeping him and the blood still wet on his coat, his hands.

"What happened?" Her voice was tense. "Are you hurt?"

"She's in the motorcar. Mrs. Ellison.

There was an — accident — on the road. She's dead. I must take her home."

"I'll come with you," Mrs. Channing said, as if she had read more in his answer than he'd intended.

Grace Letteridge stood where she was, waiting for a chance to speak to him. She seemed to have aged since he'd seen her last, not an hour before.

"I told you once that I'd kill Constable Hensley, if I discovered he'd murdered Emma."

"I remember."

"He's dead," she said. "The message came half an hour ago." She lost her composure then, and her eyes filled with tears of guilt.

Rutledge found himself thinking, *Beware what you ask for.*

But he'd lost any chance now of finding out the truth about what role Bowles had played in the Barstow affair. He would have to face that later, when there was time to consider it. He thought about this house, and how empty it was, yet how much Hensley had wanted to come back to it. The constable hadn't expected his life to end this way.

Hamish said, "You werena' prepared, yoursel' . . ."

Grace Letteridge, struggling to keep her voice steady, was still speaking to him. He tried to listen. "I also asked the messenger to tell Inspector Cain about — about Mrs. Ellison as soon as possible. Was that proper? He should be here, very soon."

"Yes, thank you. I don't think I could have driven that far tonight. And Frank Keating?"

"He's badly injured, but he'll live. They're to take him to Letherington, to be cared for," Grace said. "I don't think I could have killed anyone, after all. And I felt so certain." She shook herself, trying to come to terms with an old anger.

"Will you send Dr. Middleton to Mrs. Ellison's house?" he asked her.

"Yes. After that I'm going home." She turned to Mrs. Channing. "I'll make tea, if you'd like a cup." She glanced toward the street and said, "I'll just wait until — until she's inside."

Mrs. Channing held the motorcar's door as Rutledge lifted Mrs. Ellison's body and carried it into the house. He went up the stairs and laid her gently on her bed. It was all he could do.

"What happened?" Mrs. Channing asked again, standing a little behind him. "Was that man waiting on the road, as we'd feared?"

He told her briefly.

"How will you explain this gunshot wound to Inspector Cain?"

"I don't know. Somehow. I can't even give him a description of the man. He was ordinary, no different from thousands of others who came back in 1918. I must have passed him in the street half a hundred times and never noticed him. But I'm almost certain now he's the one who brought my shoe back, after my encounter with the lorry. Daring me to recognize him."

"He'll come for you again. When you least expect it."

"I don't know. Possibly not. I think killing Mrs. Ellison instead has shaken him."

"Until he discovers she was a murderess and deserved to die." Changing the subject, she said, "I haven't looked in the cabinet in the cellar. I didn't want to see."

"No. It's best you didn't."

They went through the house, turning out the lamps that Frank Keating had lit during his search for his daughter's body. When Rutledge reached the kitchen again, he said, "I don't think I want to go down to the cellar myself. We'll leave it to Cain, when he comes. It's his case, after all. Mine is finished."

"You look terrible. And you ought to wash off her blood."

"Thank you. As soon as Cain arrives."

Dr. Middleton walked in just then, looking from Mrs. Channing to Rutledge. "Where is she?"

"Upstairs. In her room."

He nodded and left. In a few minutes he came back to the kitchen and sat down at the table, his shoulders hunched. "Keating made me look in the cabinet. I didn't touch them. I couldn't. After all these years, you'd think I had become inured to death." He ran a finger around his collar. "Where was she trying to go? It seemed so — futile, fleeing like that."

"She wanted to die where no one knew her. There's an unused plot in London, she asked me to bury her there."

"I'll do what I can. I don't think anyone would want her final resting place to be St. Luke's anyway. Best if it's all forgotten. Who shot her? That's a gunshot wound, you know. And you weren't armed."

"I heard the shot. I wasn't there to see it. No one from Dudlington. I'm certain of that. No one here could have caught up with us in time. Someone out after a fox, who knows?"

He could hear motorcars arriving outside. He said to Middleton, "I don't suppose you know a man named Sandridge."

Middleton raised his head to look at Rutledge. "There's not going to be more killing, is there?"

"Not if I can prevent it."

"Sandridge is Joel Baylor's mother's name. His father recognized him when they were married, but I don't know that it's official."

"The brother who was gassed." Rutledge turned to go. "I'll send in Cain. And then there's one more thing I must do."

In the event, it was nearly dawn by the time he had finished with Inspector Cain. After that he walked to the barn where the Baylor cattle were housed. As he expected, he found Ted Baylor mucking out.

The man turned to him. "Haven't you caused enough trouble? That was a wild-goose chase to Frith's Wood."

"I didn't know at the time that it wasn't a matter of life and death. You've lost nothing except perhaps a few hours' sleep."

Grunting, Baylor turned back to his work, raking the warm piles of manure out into the center of the barn. "What do you want?"

"To speak to your brother. Joel."

"It won't do you any good to see him."

"It might clear up many things. For instance, why he hid from Constable Hensley. Hensley had known from the start that he was here."

"I didn't know about Hensley." Baylor sighed. "Not until I heard them arguing one night soon after Joel had come home. After that, they avoided each other. Hensley swaggered on the streets, but he knew better than to show his face here. I don't think they trusted each other, to tell you the truth. I was always afraid it was Joel in Frith's Wood with that bow and arrow. We had them as children. He knew how to use a bow. Look, I didn't know about what Joel had done either. Not until much later. When he learned a man had been killed in that London fire, he joined the army. And he's paid for what he did. I don't think it will do any good to bring him to justice. He won't live to see the hangman, you know that."

"Still . . ."

Baylor said, "All right. I want to be there." He stood his rake against a barn pillar and dusted his hands. "He's still my brother. The only one left. Let's get it over with."

They walked in silence from the barn toward the house.

A few flakes of snow began to fall, desultorily at first, and then with gathering intent.

"It won't last. But it will be colder tomorrow. By March the daffodils will be in bloom. Hard to believe, isn't it?"

"Yes." And then, endeavoring to bring something good out of so much pain and grief, Rutledge said to his companion, "Barbara Melford deserved better of you. You ought to tell her why you haven't kept your promise."

"It's not your affair —" Baylor started to say, but Rutledge cut him off in midsentence.

"Good God, man, are you going to throw away your life and hers? She'll wait for you, if you explain about Joel. And who's to inherit when both your brothers are dead, and you're locked in your own bitterness, too stubborn to beg her forgiveness?"

"You don't know anything about it." But in the snow-filled darkness, Baylor's voice was less sure.

"No, I don't. That's true. Perhaps you don't care, after all."

"Don't care?" The words were wrenched from him. "Gentle God!"

"Then tell her. When Joel is dead, she'll believe you've spoken out of duty. And she'll refuse, from pride."

"I didn't want to drag her into the shambles Joel had made of things. I thought it best."

Rutledge held the door for Baylor and followed him into the house and up the stairs. "Rightly or wrongly your brother lived his life as he saw fit. In spite of that, you owe him the obligations of blood. That's admirable. But Barbara Melford shouldn't be expected to pay for his sins too."

Ahead of him there was a quiet "No. I'll see she doesn't."

Joel Baylor's windows overlooked the barns and Frith's Wood. He wasn't asleep. Instead he was sitting in a chair, struggling to breathe through burned lungs. The sound of his efforts filled the room. He had been a strong and handsome man at one time. Now his clothes hung on his thin frame, and his face was lined with suffering.

"Hensley is dead," Rutledge said as he walked in. "I've just been told."

"Did he talk before he died?" The question was guarded but resigned.

"No. He was loyal to the end."

"Is that the God's honest truth?"

"Did you shoot him with that bow and arrow?"

"I probably would have, if I could have walked as far as that wood. He made me feel like a prisoner in my own house."

"Perhaps you'd like to tell me now what happened in London. The only witness here is your own brother. My word against his."

"You aren't interested in what happened to Edgerton. You didn't know the man. It's evidence you want, against Chief Superintendent Bowles."

"If he was a party to that fire, even if he had no way of knowing what might happen, then something must be done. Edgerton had a family, they deserve an answer."

Joel Baylor turned his head to look out the window. "If I'd stayed here and helped run the farm, my life would have been very different. But I was greedy." His words were punctuated with short breaths, his back hunched with the effort. "I wasn't raised to farming, that's the trouble."

"You can make amends. Even now. If you tell me what happened."

He turned back to Rutledge. "I don't know," he said, and it was hard to judge whether he was lying or telling the truth. "I can't tell you what lay between Hensley and Bowles. It might have had nothing to do with the fire. I set it, Hensley looked the other way. Barstow swore the building would be empty. Still, a man died. I was paid for my silence and Hensley for his. That's all I was privy to. And it was bad enough. I never asked Hensley who else was involved. You should have."

But Hensley was dead.

Joel began to cough, choking on the fluids in his lungs. It was some time before he was able to catch his breath again. His brother had been right. The man wouldn't live to stand trial.

Hamish said, "He's no' going to help."

But Rutledge wasn't ready to give up. "If you change your mind, you have only to send me word. Not at the Yard. It's better to send a message to my flat."

Joel Baylor shook his head in denial. "Nothing more," he gasped.

Rutledge was halfway across the room, on his way to the door as Ted Baylor quietly urged him to leave his brother in peace. Then he stopped and swung around.

"Did Hensley ever tell you that the girl you'd known in London had written to ask what had become of you? A Miss Gregory, as I remember."

That roused Joel Baylor. "No. I thought — *no, damn him, he never said a word!*"

"So much for loyalty, then," Rutledge responded, and walked out of the room.

It was nearly seven when Rutledge and Mrs. Channing drove to the place where he'd left his motorcar.

Rutledge was surprised to find it still there. He looked at the blood on the driver's seat and remembered Mary Ellison collapsing in his arms as he'd opened his door. Her body had been heavy, without the strength to help him.

He thanked Mrs. Channing for the lift, and then walked up the hillside to begin his search again.

In the early-morning light he found what he was looking for.

Someone had dug a hiding place out of the earth, making himself a safe haven in this winter pasture where no one came in January. It was so well concealed that Rutledge could have stepped on it in the dark and still not seen it.

There was a covering built of old wood and straw and earth, shielded by long stalks of grass and even mossy sod. Rutledge lifted it, not sure what he expected to find.

Hamish said, "He's gone."

In a way Rutledge was glad. He'd expected to find the man dead of a self-inflicted wound.

Whoever he was, he must have been a sniper in the war. Or a gamekeeper before it. He knew how to use the land in his favor, how to make it conceal him and protect him. He could have lain in wait for machine gunners to show themselves. Or poachers, coming for the estate game under cover of darkness. He'd learned from the animals he was paid to protect how to disguise himself and how to live off the land. But who was he? Where had he come from? And where had he gone?

Hamish said, "The shop where he swept the floor."

"Perhaps," Rutledge answered, not sure he meant it. *Let sleeping dogs lie.*

And he wondered what Dr. Fleming, who had brought him out of the darkness, would have made of the man.

There was a square of paper in one wall of the trench, caught between the prongs of a split stick.

Rutledge reached down to pull it out.

It read simply *I was wrong.*

Hamish said, "It was a near run thing."

Rutledge slowly let the top fall back

into place over the hole.

When he reached the motorcar, he found Mrs. Channing still there, waiting. That morning, just before Hillary Timmons had come to shut up the inn for several weeks, she'd packed her belongings and set the cases in her car, ready to return to London. Nothing had actually been said between them about her departure. But Rutledge had glimpsed her luggage in the boot.

She looked up as he came down the slope of the land, her eyes searching his face.

"He was gone," he said.

"Yes. I'd hoped he was. Let there be an end."

He stood there by her car, listening to the motor ticking over under the bonnet. "I thought perhaps you were behind what was happening to me. You saw too much that first night . . ."

"I know what you thought." She hesitated and then said, "I wish now I'd done as you asked, and taken Mary Ellison to dinner. It might have turned out differently."

"No. It was bound to end the way it did."

"You can never be sure of that." She met

his glance then, holding it. "Don't marry that girl in Westmorland, Ian. She's been through enough. Neither of you would be happy for very long."

She put the motorcar in gear and left him standing there, staring after her.

Hamish, the first to recover, said, "Ye didna' tell her about Westmorland."

About the Author

CHARLES TODD is the author of seven Ian Rutledge mysteries — *A Cold Treachery, A Fearsome Doubt, Watchers of Time, Legacy of the Dead, Search the Dark, Wings of Fire,* and *A Test of Wills* — and one stand-alone novel, *The Murder Stone.* They are a mother-and-son writing team and live in Delaware and North Carolina, respectively.

The employees of Thorndike Press hope you have enjoyed this Large Print book. All our Thorndike and Wheeler Large Print titles are designed for easy reading, and all our books are made to last. Other Thorndike Press Large Print books are available at your library, through selected bookstores, or directly from us.

For information about titles, please call:

(800) 223-1244

or visit our Web site at:

www.gale.com/thorndike
www.gale.com/wheeler

To share your comments, please write:

Publisher
Thorndike Press
295 Kennedy Memorial Drive
Waterville, ME 04901

The employees of Thorndike Press hope you have enjoyed this Large Print book. All our Thorndike and Wheeler Large Print titles are designed for easy reading, and all our books are made to last. Other Thorndike Press Large Print books are available at your library, through selected bookstores, or directly from us.

For information about titles, please call:

(800) 223-1244

or visit our Web site at:

www.gale.com/thorndike
www.gale.com/wheeler

To share your comments, please write:

Publisher
Thorndike Press
295 Kennedy Memorial Drive
Waterville, ME 04901